WINNER of the Peters Book Award

WINNER of the CrimeFest Best Crime Novel for Children

'Captures the excitement of top-level riding – **I loved it**.'
Mary King MBE, Olympic Eventer

'**Brilliant** – a vast adventure.'
Katherine Rundell

'Everything to make children **sit up and listen** to their bedtime story.'
Telegraph

'**Utterly life-affirming.**'
Observer

'Lauren St John's compassionate views on nature and its wild creatures **will leave no reader untouched**.'
Virginia McKenna, Founder of the Born Free Foundation

'**Unforgettably exciting.**'
Piers Torday

'**Compelling and compassionate.**'
Books for Keeps

ALSO BY THE AUTHOR

The One Dollar Horse
Race the Wind
Fire Storm

The White Giraffe
Dolphin Song
The Last Leopard
The Elephant's Tale
Operation Rhino

Dead Man's Cove
Kidnap in the Caribbean
Kentucky Thriller
Rendezvous in Russia
The Secret of Supernatural Creek

The Snow Angel

Wave Riders

FINDING WONDER

LAUREN ST JOHN

Interior Illustrations by
MARIE-ALICE HAREL

faber

First published in 2023
by Faber & Faber Limited
The Bindery, 51 Hatton Garden
London, EC1N 8HN
faber.co.uk

Typeset in Garamond Premier
Printed by CPI Group (UK) Ltd, Croydon CR0 4YY

The right of Lauren St John and Marie-Alice Harel to be identified as author and
illustrator of this work respectively has been asserted in accordance
with Section 77 of the Copyright, Designs and Patents Act 1988

A CIP record for this book
is available from the British Library

ISBN 978-0-571-37616-2

Printed and bound in Great Britain, at the same stage in line with our continuing
commitment to ethical business practices, sustainability and the environment.
For further information, see faber.co.uk/environmental-policy

*For my father, who gave me my dream horse,
Morning Star,*

*For my mom, who showed me India, Greece and the
Seychelles,*

*And for my sister Lisa, who keeps me believing that, for
every question, nature has an answer . . .*

ROO'S JOURNEY

1. Tower Hamlets
2. Greenwich
3. Forest near Knepp Estate, Sussex
4. Ritz Hotel, Piccadilly
5. Starwood Farm, near Horsham, Sussex
6. Bantham Beach, Devon
7. Dartmoor (near Wistman's Woods)
8. Queen's Reach Racing Stable, Newbury
9. Castle in the Sky, Scottish Highlands
10. Leumadair Beach, Edinburgh
11. South Uist, Outer Hebrides

SCOTLAND

ENGLAND

WALES

N
E
S

Tell me, what is it that you plan to do with
Your one wild and precious life?

MARY OLIVER

FEARLESS FIRE

1.

LOTTERY

When death came to Roo Thorn's door, it found her dreaming.

She knew it was a dream because she was at a pop concert with a friend, two treats that never entered Roo's waking universe.

Her imaginary friend was yelling something and trying to tug her away, but Roo was having too much fun. She was mesmerised by the band's drummer; by his wild, flying hair and blur of arms and sticks. His cymbals flashed like flames.

The singer gave up trying to make herself heard and flounced off the stage. The guitarist and keyboard player followed. Beneath the dazzling lights, the drummer thrashed on. The bass thudded in Roo's chest like an extra heartbeat.

Now she really did want to escape but she was trapped. Hemmed in by the sweaty, dancing crowd, she began to panic. Where was her friend?

'POLICE! OPEN THE DOOR!' commanded a disembodied voice, shattering the dream like glass.

Roo struggled upright. Blue lights strobed her bedroom, uninterrupted by the frayed curtains. Somewhere in the night, a siren popped.

It didn't surprise her that the cops were parked outside. Grimsby Grove was that sort of street. If it wasn't a punch-up involving the boys at No. 8, it was the dodgy dealers at No. 33.

World-weary constables often knocked on the Thorns' door, asking if Roo or her father had witnessed some incident or another, but never before had they knocked after midnight.

She wondered if an ambulance crew had the wrong house. Unlike some of their neighbours, the elderly couple next door were the sweetest people anywhere, but Mr Badawi had kidney problems and emergency services had been called out twice in the past week.

The pounding started again.

'Dad!' shouted Roo. 'Dad, wake up, there's someone at the door!'

To a regular person, that much would have been deafeningly obvious, but when it came to her father, Roo had learned not to take anything for granted.

Scrambling out of bed, she tripped over a line of model horses, sending them flying. Over the years, Roo had been told by everyone except her dad that she'd grow out of them.

Sometimes she felt guilty that, aged eleven and a half, she still staged whole Olympic events over the furniture in the flat, leaping upturned chairs, the old coffee table, and the tatty arm of the sofa, with Fearless Fire – the chestnut with the white blaze – clutched in her right hand.

In those moments Fearless Fire was as real to her as the chestnut showjumper on the poster on her bedroom wall. Wonder Boy, owned by teenage star Rhianna Cooper, was Roo's dream horse.

'If I had a horse like Wonder Boy, I'd be the happiest person on earth,' she'd told her dad. 'He's perfect in every way. I hope Rhianna knows how lucky she is. Perfect talent, perfect home, *and* a perfect horse.'

'Ruby Roo, perfect plus perfect plus perfect doesn't always add up to happy or lucky,' her father had chided. 'Life is not arithmetic. It's messy and complicated. Joy comes in unexpected packages, and when you're least expecting her. Sometimes you find Joy in the last place you look.'

And then he was off again, reminiscing about the time he'd collided, quite literally, with Joy, Roo's mum, as he'd rounded a corner on a London street, him on shore leave from the navy, and her walking on air after graduating from the Royal College of Nursing.

Ironically, thinking about Joy tended to make Roo's dad sad. Very soon, he'd remember that he had to nip out on some urgent errand or job-seeking mission (usually involving the Hare & Tortoise pub) and be gone for hours and hours. A couple of times, he'd been gone all night.

'When I win the lottery, everything will be different,' he was always saying. 'We'll get our lives back on track again. I'll buy you your dream horse.'

When I win the lottery was the soundtrack to their days.

Flicking on lights and picking up speed in response to a fresh bout of hammering, Roo banged on her dad's bedroom door.

Silence. No surprise there.

She was about to barge in and shake him awake when the knocking started again.

'I'm coming, I'm coming,' Roo shouted to the invisible visitor, breaking into a trot along the passage, her mind already whirling with excuses.

I'm so sorry but my dad has a migraine/bad back/has flu. No, he can't be disturbed.

Out of habit, she did a sweep of the living room, scooping up a pizza box and a couple of cans and tossing them out of sight behind the sofa. For ages she'd prided herself on keeping a spotless home the way her mum had but, recently, she'd been letting things slide.

That's what grown-ups never understood. Kids got tired too.

Deep breath. Best smile.

Roo unlocked the door.

A policewoman, truncheon raised to rap once more, seemed startled to see a child. She blinked, peering past Roo in her too-small pyjamas.

'Where's Mum, sweetheart?'

The blue light of the squad car swirled like a lighthouse beam, warning of deadly currents and jagged rocks ahead.

Inside the vehicle, another officer was spelling out her address on his radio. 'Thirty-two *Grimsby* – Golf, Romeo, India, Mike, Sierra, Bravo, Yankee . . . *Grove* – Golf, Romeo, Oscar, Victor, Echo . . .'

The chill that rippled through Roo had nothing to do with the arctic wind or grubby January snow. It was as if she knew what was going to happen before it happened.

A gaunt young man scurried from the shadows. 'Apologies, Officer Pooran. I came as quickly as I could.'

It was Roo's new social worker. The one who didn't believe her father's excuses about her frequent absences from school. The one who kept trying to catch Roo out. Only now, his fox face looked pale and anxious.

'Ruby lost her mother a couple of years ago,' he told the policewoman. 'It was just the two of them, Roo and her dad.'

4

Was.

The past tense slammed into Roo's chest like a cannonball.

Before they could stop her, she took off running down the passage. Her dad's silent bedroom was empty, the bed neatly made.

His last words returned to her as clearly as if he were standing right in front of her. Still smiling.

Still breathing.

Ruby Roo, you go on to bed. I'm going to nip out to buy a lottery ticket. Back in five minutes. You never know, it might just be our lucky day.

2.

RED COAT

Was he coming or going?

Roo's eyes were dry, as they had been since Officer Pooran and Iain, the social worker, had sat her down and carefully explained, as if she were hard of hearing, that her father had dropped dead outside No. 16, exactly halfway between the Thorns' flat and the corner shop.

'The owners at No. 16 are away and the cousin who's housesitting didn't know where your dad lived,' the policewoman explained. 'She rang for an ambulance, and they called us. It was a couple of hours before a neighbour was able to point us in the direction of your flat. Dad had no ID on him, you see.'

'Was he coming or going?' Roo asked again.

'Excuse me?'

'Was he on his way to the corner shop or heading home? He only went out to get a lottery ticket. He thought it might be his lucky day.'

Roo felt as if a porcupine was lodged in her chest. It hurt too much to cry. '*Our* lucky day.'

Officer Pooran and Iain exchanged glances.

'Life can be cruel like that,' sympathised the policewoman. 'Sadly, the paramedics suspect that your dad may have had a microscopic heart muscle defect he didn't know about. Strikes without warning and can affect anyone at any age.

6

Twenty-three-year-old footballers even. It was a heart attack waiting to happen.'

A heart attack waiting to happen.

The words scrolled through Roo's brain on a loop. Ever since her mum had been struck dead cycling to work, Roo had lived in fear of another bad-news knock at the door. Now the worst had happened.

'Oh,' was all she could manage.

'Ruby, you've had a huge shock and must be exhausted,' said Iain, looking at the clock, now ticking towards 1.30 a.m. 'We need to get you to a safe space. Somewhere you can be with family or friends. It says on your file that your only next of kin is an aunt, your mum's sister. Are you happy for me to call her? Do the two of you get on?'

Roo had a vivid memory of a screaming match between her father and her aunt a year earlier. Six months after Roo's mum died, Joni Jackson had shown up unannounced to find Roo not at school and her dad asleep on the sofa in the middle of the day.

Her views on childcare had not gone down well.

'Don't you dare lecture me on responsible parenting when you've never had a child and don't know the first thing about raising one,' Roo's father had shouted. 'When did you last have a proper job? Go away and don't come back until you've taken a long hard look in the mirror. Anyway, Roo's very happy, aren't you, Roo?'

'Very,' Roo agreed defiantly. 'Dad's the best dad in the whole world.'

She'd watched through a slit in her bedroom curtains as Joni's orange VW camper, decorated with flowers, butterflies, and a grinning surfer cresting a wave, lurched away down the street. The Thorns hadn't seen her since.

Iain was waiting for Roo to respond. 'Your Aunt Joni, is she nice?' he pressed. 'Do you enjoy visiting her?'

Roo was not about to inform him that she was more familiar with the postcards her aunt had mailed from New Zealand, Greece, and the Himalayas than she was with Joni herself.

As to where her aunt lived now, Roo had no clue. A surfing grotto in Devon? A yurt in Pembrokeshire? A garret for starving artists in Paris?

What did Joni even do? That much had never been clear.

It didn't matter. Roo's choices were stark. Either her aunt took her in, or she'd be deposited in a care home, where she'd wait in vain for someone to adopt her.

'Joni's the best aunt in the world,' lied Roo.

***

'That's not my aunt.'

Roo's voice was husky with tiredness and despair. Unsurprisingly, Joni Jackson had proven tough to track down. She'd changed her number and moved several times. When her new contact details were finally unearthed, her phone was switched off, and had stayed that way for most of the day.

Consequently, it was after dark and nearly nineteen hours after the police knocked on the Thorns' door when headlights swung into the driveway of the foster home where Roo had spent the day.

Her aunt had told Rayleen, the social worker who'd taken over from Iain at the end of his shift, that she'd be arriving at 'eight on the dot' and here was a visitor, at eight on the dot.

Roo peered between the blinds. She'd been expecting the orange camper, not a Porsche SUV with blacked-out windows.

The driver's door opened. Elegant legs encased in knee-length black boots stepped into the mashed-up snow. A slender figure in a red coat and scarf, woolly hat pulled down low, strode briskly up the path.

'That's not my aunt,' Roo repeated, recoiling slightly. The Joni she remembered had been cuddle-shaped and wearing a tie-dye T-shirt and flares with leopard-print patches on the knees.

'What do you mean, that's not your aunt?'

Rayleen, a stolid person with a no-nonsense attitude, moved with speed to the hallway. There were raised voices outside as the social worker demanded photo ID.

Next, the stranger in the red coat burst into the room.

'Oh, Roo, what a thing to happen,' she cried. 'What a terrible, terrible thing. I'm so sorry.'

Before Roo could object, she was enveloped in scarlet cashmere and breathing in orange blossom perfume and hair that smelled of coconut. She'd been cold all day, but now a wave of heat flooded her veins.

'Madam, stop! We need to sort out this question of your identity,' railed Rayleen. 'Ruby, do you know this person? Is she your aunt?'

Roo tugged away awkwardly. This Joni dressed nothing like the old Joni, but the warmth of her, the concern in her hazel eyes, was the same.

She nodded, not trusting herself to speak.

Joni squared up to Rayleen. 'I'd appreciate it if we could get the formalities over as quickly as possible. I'd like to get Roo home.'

3.

FOREVER IS A LONG TIME

The drive 'home' passed in a tear-streaked blur of city lights. Roo couldn't take in anything Joni was saying. Something about a new partner, Gary; a new job at a spa in Chelsea; and a new apartment: Gary's.

'It'll be a squeeze, but we'll adapt. And Gary will adore you, you'll see. He's away on business. Back late tonight. You'll meet him in the morning. The main thing I want you to know is, I'm here for you and always will be. You can count on me.'

Roo didn't answer. She was tired to the bone. Words were just words. What grown-ups promised and what they did were two different things.

When I win the lottery...

She sank into a daze, stirring when Joni pulled into an underground car park. A spotless lift whisked them up to a penthouse overlooking the Thames.

The lift doors opened to a vision of white and chrome and acres of polished wooden floor. The bathrooms were so large and shiny that Roo was afraid to wash her hands.

Despite being four times the size of the Thorns' council flat, the penthouse had just two bedrooms, one of which was being used as Gary's study.

'He won't mind,' said Joni, pulling out a sofa bed and wrestling a duvet into a cover.

The room was so small that, once in bed, Roo was sandwiched between a printer and more electronics than an air traffic control tower. When Joni handed her a mug of malted milk, Roo's nervous hands tipped half of it on to a white rug.

'I'm sorry, I'm sorry,' Roo panicked, tears searing her eyes again.

But Joni could not have minded less. 'Roo, it's my fault for making it too hot,' she said with a smile. 'Don't give it another thought.'

Roo must have fallen into a coma sleep after that, because next, she was roused by hushed voices – her aunt's and a man's. Gary, she assumed.

'I didn't even know you had a niece,' he was saying. 'Poor kid. Tragic to be orphaned at such a young age.'

'Yes, it's utterly devastating. She's asleep in your study. It'll take a bit of juggling at first, but we'll find a way to make it work.'

''Course, 'course. No problem at all, babe. She's welcome. Only . . . uh, how long's she staying?'

'Roo's lost both her parents, Gary.' There was a sliver of steel in Joni's tone. 'I'm – we're – her family now. She's staying forever.'

There was a loaded silence.

'Forever is a long time, Joni.'

As their footsteps faded away, Roo clung to her namesake, a floppy-eared kangaroo, a long-ago gift from her mum.

Beneath her pillow was Fearless Fire. The other nine horses, a small bag of clothes, and a framed photo of her parents laughing in happier times were her only possessions.

The picture had been taken at her old riding school, a falling-down, held-together-with-love-and-string place in East London. When her mum was alive, Roo had had lessons there every school holiday from when she was five. These days, the only fences she soared over were in her imagination.

Usually, when Roo was unhappy or lonely, she pretended she was living Rhianna Cooper's perfect life. She imagined waking up in Rhianna's luxurious bedroom at Starwood Farm, putting on breeches and boots, and strolling down to the yard to groom and tack up Wonder Boy.

Now all she could think about was her father, snatched from her too soon, and about the virtual strangers who'd taken her in.

Forever is a long time, Joni.

Hot tears soaked Roo's pillow. If they didn't want her, she'd run away.

4·
SHORTCUT

Two weeks after moving into the penthouse, Roo looked up from the lunch table to find Gary regarding her as if she were a fly who'd landed in his soup.

To begin with, businessman Gary, smooth as silk in his suits and designer sweats, had been all polite concern and barely concealed pity for her.

After what she'd overheard, Roo didn't trust him, but, to his credit, he'd made an effort to be pleasant and charming. He was a clean freak, though, and prone to moany remarks such as, 'Roo, would you mind putting the lid back on the toothpaste – *if that's not too much to ask.*'

Numb with grief, Roo didn't have the energy to be upset by them. Besides, it was a relief to be in a pristine home that someone else had tidied.

Today, however, Gary's charm had taken a vacation. Tension swirled around the walnut dining table.

'They can't do that,' Gary ranted.

'They already have,' said Joni, buttering a roll for Roo. 'Don't stress about it. There are plenty of jobs in the world. I can turn my hand to anything.'

Roo could tell that by the way her aunt's knee jiggled beneath the table that she was more concerned than she was letting on.

Earlier, Roo had heard her aunt being sacked over the phone by the spa in Chelsea.

'I understand that your clients want massages, but my niece has lost her dad,' Joni had said to the caller, her words carrying through the thin wall of the bedroom. 'I refuse to palm her off on a childminder she doesn't know. For the time being, I need to be with her, taking care of her. If you can't understand that, then go ahead and fire me.'

Judging by the abrupt end to the conversation, her employer had done just that.

'You should sue,' Gary told Joni over lunch, stabbing a pickled onion with his fork and pointing it at her.

'I'm not going to sue,' Joni said tiredly.

'Well, you'll have to do *something*. There are bills to pay and now we have *three* mouths to feed.'

He glowered at Roo, who was wriggling in her chair while anxiously making patterns on the table with salt and pepper grains. 'Stop fidgeting,' he snapped.

Things moved fast after that.

Putting a protective arm around Roo, Joni pleaded with Gary to 'BE KIND.' Gary responded by being extremely UNKIND, demanding to know when he'd be getting his study back because he had a Very Important Conference coming up.

'We also have theatre tickets for *two*, not three. Kids were never part of the deal, Joni,' he snarled.

'They are now,' Joni replied calmly. 'Roo's my family.'

'Well, she's not mine. You can have me or the child, but not both. You choose.'

Roo burst into tears at that point because she couldn't believe

14

that she was about to be orphaned for the second time in a fortnight.

But her aunt only hugged her closer.

'I choose Roo,' she informed a slack-jawed Gary.

***

When Roo had pictured herself running away, she hadn't imagined she'd be running away *with* her aunt, whose confident hands now gripped the worn wheel of her orange camper.

The headlights cast a weak glow up a spookily dark country lane. A red-eyed creature skittered across the potholes and shot beneath a hedgerow.

They'd taken a shortcut.

'It's annoying that my phone battery died, but we'll be fine,' Joni had said cheerfully as they'd exited the motorway. 'I've been to the campsite so often I could find my way blindfolded. The sooner we get there, the sooner we'll get a bite to eat and some kip.'

The ease with which Joni had walked away from her life made Roo suspicious.

'How are you going to look after a child when you can't even look after yourself?' Gary had yelled as Joni wheeled a suitcase containing her clothes and Roo's meagre possessions out of his penthouse. 'Next to "irresponsible" in the dictionary, there's a photo of you.'

Joni never looked back. Out on the street, there'd been a spring in her step as she'd hailed a cab to drive them to the home of the friend who took care of her orange camper.

Roo was no mechanic, but even she knew that older vehicles struggled to start in winter. The ones on her street had coughed and wheezed in the cold, and sometimes only spluttered into action after much cursing, pushing, and battery jump-starting by several people.

Surprisingly, 'Betty', Joni's ancient camper, had roared to life with the perkiness of a squirrel chasing down a nut. Her interior smelled of mildew, but she was clean and well-stocked with camping gear and cans of beans and long-life cashew milk. It was almost as if she'd been kept ready for a quick getaway.

Had Gary been aware that Betty was stashed in Joni's friend's garage with a full tank of petrol and a month's worth of supplies? Somehow Roo doubted it. If he had, surely Betty would have been parked beside his Porsche in the underground car park.

The only explanation was that Betty had been Joni Jackson's secret.

What other secrets did her aunt have?

'Where should we head to, Roo?' Joni had asked as she'd climbed into the driver's seat a couple of hours earlier. At the time it was barely 6 p.m., but night had fallen hard.

She'd handed Roo an AA Road Atlas, as if they were heading to the beach on a summer's day, not fleeing London – that's what it felt like to Roo, fleeing – for parts unknown, on the bleakest winter evening in memory.

'How about we aim for the coast?' Joni persisted in the chirpy manner of a fitness instructor. 'When did you last see the sea, Roo?'

'Don't remember,' mumbled Roo, although of course she did. A day trip to the beach in Brighton was the last fun thing she'd done with her mum and dad. A month later her mother was gone, knocked from her bike by a garbage truck.

After that, the fun had gone AWOL from the Thorns' lives.

While her aunt had made a call, Roo had stared blankly at the book of maps. Ever since the police had come knocking, she'd felt lost in a labyrinth with no path out.

The way Roo saw it, her future had been stolen. The road ahead was treacherous. She couldn't go backwards in time, and she felt too broken-hearted to move on. She was stuck.

She'd returned to the present to find Joni lifting the road atlas from her unresisting hands.

'Tell you what, Roo, we'll draw up a proper plan tomorrow once we've had a good night's rest and a hearty breakfast,' said her aunt. 'We'll be spending tonight at Green Acres Holiday Park, the best campsite in West Sussex. You'll love it there. Their Ranch House Café will have a crackling fire and fab organic food.'

Starting the engine, she'd cranked up Betty's feeble heater.

'Joni, are you sure this is a good idea?' her friend had asked, shivering at the window. 'It's hardly the best time of year for a camping trip. I'm sorry I don't have room for you, but I can loan you cash for a hotel.'

'Thanks, Celia, but there's no need to waste money on a hotel when we have Betty,' Joni had replied airily, putting the camper into gear. 'Anyhow, you know me. Once I get the wind in my sails, I like to go, go, go.'

'Yeah, I do know you,' Celia had muttered in a way that didn't exactly fill Roo with confidence.

A memory came to Roo. Her mum shaking her head about Joni being a 'hippy and a rolling stone'.

The phrase had lodged in Roo's mind, aged seven, because Joni, who'd stopped by their flat for a coffee with a tattooed, Harley-Davidson-motorbike-riding boyfriend in tow, looked nothing like a stone. Her mum had explained that she meant Joni was a free spirit who came and went with the breeze.

'A "rolling stone that gathers no moss" is someone who moves too swiftly to be dragged down by bills and other responsibilities. My sister's a hard worker when she works, I'll grant her that, but she can't stick to anything.'

How long would Joni stick to being an aunt? That was the question weighing on Roo's mind.

Now, as Joni steered Betty along a country lane so narrow that frosty twigs scratched at her sides, Roo's gaze went to the rucksack at her feet. It bulged with the brown paper parcel that the concierge had handed Joni as they'd left Gary's apartment block.

'The man who delivered it was in a rush, but said to make certain you received it.' The concierge scowled. 'Like there was some doubt.'

The moment Roo saw the sender's address, Doukis & Jain Solicitors, Brick Lane, she'd guessed the parcel had something to do with her dad. Her heart had done an agonising flip.

Joni had avoided her eyes as she stuffed it into Roo's half-empty rucksack. 'Let's open this when we're settled for the night, shall we, Roo?'

Despite this unpromising start, her aunt had managed to make the first part of their journey to West Sussex enjoyable. She'd played music that lifted Roo's spirits so much that, for a while, she'd almost felt happy. Their unplanned adventure had started to feel like an actual adventure.

Roo had never been camping. Everest climbers and survival experts excepted, she'd never in her life heard of anyone actively choosing to go camping in winter. The idea was strangely thrilling.

As the miles passed and the 'Big Smoke', as her dad had called London, fell behind them, Roo breathed easier.

She wasn't sorry to be saying goodbye to Gary and his sterile penthouse. Nor did she miss the council flat she'd shared with her dad. Too many memories. Within days of her father's passing, a new family had moved into No. 32 Grimsby Grove, erasing the Thorns' life there as if it had never been.

For those reasons, Roo had been glad to leave town . . . right up until Joni took the shortcut. Twenty stressful minutes on, the music had stopped, and Roo's stomach was once again a knot of nerves.

At the wheel, Joni frowned in concentration. Roo had a horrible feeling they were lost, though her aunt had yet to admit it. She was quite sure they'd passed the same crooked tree three times.

To distract herself, she prodded the rucksack containing the brown paper parcel with her trainer. The package was soft and squishy. It didn't seem big enough to contain forty-four years of her dad's life.

A tear trickled down Roo's cheek. Before another could follow, her nostrils twitched. There was a faint whiff of burning.

An amber warning light flashed up on the dashboard.

'Ignore that,' said Joni, steering the camper along another rutted lane. 'Just Betty showing her age.'

As she spoke, the amber light turned red.

'Don't worry, Roo,' said Joni, sounding worried. 'She's probably low on oil or water. I'll stop and take a look. I'm pretty sure we're nearly at the campsite.'

She pulled in beside a field gate and turned off the engine, but it was already too late. Betty was coughing up smoke like a flu-stricken dragon.

In one fluid motion, Joni unclipped Roo's seat belt and grabbed a fleece. 'Roo, get out, quick, and take your jacket and rucksack with you!'

The instant she leapt into the biting cold, Roo knew they were in trouble. Beneath her flowery bonnet, Betty spat sparks.

Joni made no attempt to douse them with the mini fire extinguisher. Instead, she flung open the camper's rear doors and hauled out the suitcase and a large blue backpack.

'Joni, look!' cried Roo. 'Betty's leaking!'

Her aunt's horrified gaze followed Roo's to the oily puddle collecting beneath the camper's low-slung belly.

'She's going to blow,' Joni yelled incredulously. 'Betty's gonna blow. ROO, RUN! RUN FOR YOUR LIFE!'

5.
END OF THE WORLD

Roo had a worm's-eye view from a frozen field as Betty exploded into the night sky. A murder of crows flapped away in terror and a great stag reared from the undergrowth, nearly trampling Roo as it swerved into the darkness.

She sat up dizzily, spitting grit, grass, and chips of ice. Beyond the field gate, an inferno blazed merrily. A smaller bang tossed the suitcase into the air. The flames devoured the contents as they fell.

For the third time in fifteen days, Roo was homeless. As if that weren't bad enough, her clothes and model horses – all except Fearless Fire, who, along with the photo of her parents, was in her rucksack – had been reduced to ashes.

'Well, this is an unexpected turn of events,' mumbled Joni, making Roo jump. She hadn't realised that her aunt had also face-planted on the ground behind her.

Joni climbed stiffly to her feet. There was a smear of dirt on her cheek. She helped Roo up and checked her for bruises.

'I'm so sorry, Roo; Betty was mostly very reliable. My bad for taking the rough track. A rock must have pierced her vitals.'

They turned to survey the ruined camper. Her smouldering frame resembled a barbecued dinosaur.

To Roo's astonishment, Joni began to laugh.

'I suppose it's fitting that the old girl went the way she lived – with a bang and not a whimper. Oh, Roo, what a friend she's been and what sights we've seen . . . Venice! Paris, Marrakech, and Montenegro! Cornwall too. I've lost count of the mornings we watched the sunrise paint the waves gold for the surfers of Fistral Bay . . .'

Joni seemed lost in her own world, reliving a montage of memories that only she could see. Belatedly, she remembered the newly bereaved child in her care.

'Right, Roo, let's get our bearings. We need hot drinks and a warm shelter, and we need 'em fast.'

She plucked a torch from her big backpack. Its powerful beam chased back the night. They were in a long sloping field on the edge of a wood. If there was a farmhouse or village nearby, no hint of light betrayed it.

A smothering silence descended. It gave Roo goosebumps. It was as if the world had ended and they were the only survivors.

'Can we walk to the campsite, or will your friends come and fetch us?' she asked hopefully. Her stomach growled at the prospect of the Ranch House Café with its organic food and crackling fire.

Joni grimaced. 'Sorry, Roo, walking to Green Acres is out of the question and we won't be calling for help any time soon. My phone was in Betty. We'll hunker down for the night and get our bearings in the morning.'

The resigned manner with which Joni hoisted the backpack on to her shoulders filled Roo with dismay.

'But you said we were nearly there,' Roo accused her slightly hysterically. 'You told me you could find your way blindfolded.'

Her aunt didn't even have the grace to look embarrassed. 'Once, that was probably true, but I haven't been in years and never at night. Don't worry, Roo. I've done a wilderness survival course, and I did remember this . . .'

Joni grinned as she patted the blue backpack. 'We have everything we need to camp out right here.'

'Here?'

Roo stared at her in disbelief. 'But BBC Radio said there were red weather warnings. They said the temperature could fall to minus five.'

'That's why we can't hang about chatting. See that cloud moving to block out the moon? That's snow cloud.'

Joni's eyes sparkled with anticipation, as if she relished the challenge. 'We need to put up a shelter and get a fire going at record speed.'

6.

PINK SNOW

Slipping and sliding in her charity shop trainers, Roo followed the bobbing torch beam nearly the full length of the field. Her own rucksack, the one stuffed with the solicitors' brown parcel, bumped against her spine.

A helpless fury simmered in Roo's empty belly. Her hands were so cold it was painful. Icy water had seeped into her socks. She couldn't even cry because her eyeballs felt frozen.

She was going to die in this perishing place, she was sure of it.

Up ahead, the yellow beam lurched left as Joni decided on a spot beneath an elderly oak overhanging a low stone wall.

Glaring at her aunt's disappearing back, Roo squelched along in her footsteps until she reached the great tree. Its outspread arms creaked and groaned as though they might snap at any moment. Anywhere less suitable for a campsite was impossible for Roo to fathom.

'This'll do nicely,' said Joni, propping her backpack against the tree's elephant-hide trunk. 'The wall and that thicket of holly will shield us from the worst of the wind, and there's plenty of kindling for our fire. Roo, if you gather anything that looks as if it'll burn, I'll put up our tent. We'll be snug as bugs in no time.'

Roo didn't believe her but didn't bother saying so. She was saving her energy for when things got a whole lot worse.

Still, the fire wasn't going to make itself. She began

groping about in the prickly shadows, praying that none hid hibernating spiders.

When she next looked up, a campsite had mushroomed almost beneath her feet. Roo abandoned her quest for twigs and acorns. She watched with undisguised amazement as her aunt threw up a purple tent, pinned down guy ropes, and unfurled a sleeping bag – all with professional ease.

Incredibly, Joni seemed to be enjoying herself.

Out of the Tardis that was her backpack came a camping stove, packets of hot chocolate, noodles, dried soup, instant oats, two mugs, water-purifying tablets, a first aid kit, a penknife, a solar lantern, and a flask of water.

After stowing their supplies in the tent and vestibule, she switched on the lantern with a theatrical flourish. 'Ta-da!'

The glowing tent bathed the clearing in a soft purple light. Tree shadows danced in it. Snowflakes arrived tinted pink. Roo gasped with delight when a white-winged owl skimmed low over the field.

Their campsite felt enchanted.

More pink snow whirled in, carried on the quickening wind.

A wicked gust sent the pair scrambling for the tent. As Joni rushed to seal the flaps of the vestibule, shutting the snowstorm out, Roo stared around in wonder. From a barren wilderness, Joni had conjured a magical, lamplit den.

The only thing it lacked was a hot bath. When the ground beneath her feet began to wobble and sway, Roo sank dazedly on to the sleeping bag. In vain, she tried to remove her wet trainers with fingers that had lost all feeling. Her aunt had to take over.

It was only then that it seemed to hit Joni that her niece was dangerously cold.

'Roo, your socks! They're soaking. Your feet are pure ice. Lord, your jumper's drenched too.'

Hurriedly, Joni tugged off her own fleece. 'Here, have this. It would fit three of you but at least it's warm and dry. Better put on my socks as well. Might whiff a bit, but at least they're wool.'

'B-but w-what about you?' asked Roo, teeth chattering. 'H-how are we going to m-make a f-fire in the snow?'

'Forget the fire.' Joni unzipped the sleeping bag and scooped Roo into its silky folds. 'No chance of that with a near-blizzard settling in. Hot drinks are what's needed. My camping stove was made for conditions like these. It'd cook a casserole in a gale in Alaska. I'll get it going outside the tent and bring you soup in a jiffy. Which would you prefer – tomato or mushroom?'

She started rummaging around in her empty backpack. 'All I need to do is find the matches . . . I'm sure they're in here . . . They *have* to be.'

Joni tipped up the backpack and shook it. Dust, crumbs, and a safety pin cascaded out.

A goose-across-a-grave shudder rippled through Roo. 'M-maybe the matches were in B-B-Betty.'

Joni sat back on her heels. She looked a little broken. 'They must have gone up in flames, along with the space blanket – two bits of survival kit we could really do with now.'

The twinkle in Joni's eyes had been extinguished. The missing matches were a game changer. For the first time, it seemed to strike her that they were in a deadly dilemma – one from which they'd be lucky to emerge alive.

Roo was on the verge of a panic attack when her aunt snapped into action.

'Sorry, Roo, the hot drinks will have to wait till the morning. At first light, we'll flag down a passing car and beg to be taken to Green Acres or the nearest coffee shop. Until then, we need to do everything we can to preserve body heat. We won't both fit in the sleeping bag, but I'll lie down beside you if that's okay.'

Awkwardly, they squashed up together. Joni put her neck scarf over her head to stop the heat seeping out. She folded the bottom of the sleeping bag over her bare feet and squeezed nearer to Roo.

The tent was like an igloo. Despite the socks, fleece, and sleeping bag, Roo couldn't stop trembling. Neither could Joni, however much she tried to hide it. Her long-sleeved T-shirt and leggings were no defence against the sub-zero temperatures.

As the storm intensified, the roof of the tent dipped beneath the weight of the snow. The wind wailed and tore at the seams.

'Next time I'll buy a four-seasons tent, not a summer one,' Joni murmured drowsily. Her cheek, close to Roo's, was as chilly as marble. 'Whatever happens, Roo, we must not fall asleep.'

Roo yawned. 'But I want to sleep. I've n-never been so tired in my life. If we sleep, it'll be morning quicker and we can go get breakfast.'

'NO!' Joni shook her hard. 'Sleepiness can be a sign of hypothermia and hypothermia can kill.'

Something inside Roo snapped.

'So, we are going to die? I knew it. I just knew it. I should have let social services take me to a foster home. At least then I'd be safe and warm, not lost in the middle of nowhere, about to turn into an ice cube.'

She squirmed away from her aunt and sat shivering and hugging her knees on the lumpy groundsheet. 'Could my life get any worse? Oh, why did Dad have to go out to buy a stupid scratch card? If he hadn't, he'd still be here, and I wouldn't be hungry in a snowfield with irresponsible *you*.'

Joni's eyes glistened with hurt, but she said gently: 'Roo, I know you miss your parents terribly, and I can tell you from experience that you'll miss them forever. I miss my sister – your mum – every day too. I'm also very aware that I'll never replace her.'

'No, you won't,' declared Roo. 'Not ever.'

'Nor would I want to,' said her aunt. 'And I'm sorrier than you can possibly imagine that we're "hungry in a snowfield", as you put it. But, Roo, tell me this. In your old life, did you ever, even once, wish that you were someone else, living somewhere else? Maybe in a tree house in a cloud forest in Costa Rica? Maybe on a yacht on the Great Barrier Reef? Did you ever wish that you were someone who had adventures?'

A picture of Rhianna Cooper and Wonder Boy came into Roo's mind. If she had a pound for every hour she'd spent wishing she could swap lives with Rhianna, she'd be a millionaire.

Not that she was about to admit that to her aunt.

She said furiously: 'BUT I NEVER WISHED TO BE BLOWN HALFWAY TO MARS BY A CAMPER, OR BURIED ALIVE IN A SNOWDRIFT. I NEVER WISHED FOR *THIS* KIND OF ADVENTURE.'

'You didn't?' Joni's mouth curled up at one corner. 'Well, Roo, I've got news for you. Adventures don't come gift-wrapped, with a bow on top. More often than not, adventures are a surprise. And not always a fun one. Some adventures are downright unpleasant. One minute you're enjoying a picnic in a wildflower meadow, the next, you're escaping a volcano or a rampaging bear. One day, you're relaxing on a luxury cruise, the next, you're swimming with sharks or icebergs. That's the reality of adventures when they're not safely between the pages of a book.'

Absently, she prodded the sagging ceiling of the tent. A pile of snow slithered off.

'In my experience, most people are armchair adventurers at heart. They'd rather read about the exploits of spies, detectives, or jungle explorers from the comfort of their own sofa than dodge bullets or risk wrestling with an anaconda themselves. And who can blame them? I adore a good adventure story myself.'

'Me too,' agreed Roo, softening a little. 'And mysteries. I love mysteries.'

'When they're in books, right?'

'Yes, when they're in books.'

Joni gave a barely audible sigh. 'That's settled then. Soon as we're out of this mess, I'll rent us a cottage in a quaint, quiet village. I'll get a nice, normal job and enrol you in the local school. There we'll stay, safe and sound, until you go off to university or join a band or whatever. No more exploding campers or freezing nights under the stars. No more adventures. We'll read about them instead. You have my word.'

'Thanks, Joni.'

Roo suddenly felt quite crestfallen. She wondered if, after all, she was the kind of girl who'd rather experience pink snow and ghostly owls in real life, even if she had to freeze a little (or a lot) to do it.

In her dreams, she was always brave and daring. Fast and strong. But now that she was living an adventure for real, it turned out she was none of those things. Embarrassingly, she was a bit of a baby.

Joni was watching her with an unreadable expression. Roo returned to the sleeping bag, flopped down, and let her aunt tuck her in.

'In future, we'll be model citizens,' Joni promised. 'But given that we're trapped in a summer tent in a snowstorm, we should probably put our heads together and figure out how to survive till daylight . . . On the plus side, there are no bears in Sussex. Or wolves, for that matter.'

Roo couldn't help giggling. 'No volcanoes or sharks either.'

Joni laughed. 'Definitely no sharks. Not on land, anyway. Now what do we have that could help us? What aren't we seeing?'

Their gazes fell on the small rucksack, partially hidden by the supplies. It was plump with the solicitor's parcel. As her aunt reached for it, Roo caught sight of the time on Joni's Casio watch.

'Wait! It's eleven minutes past eleven. If Mum was here, she'd say: "Roo, it's 11:11, make a wish."'

Joni smiled. 'Then let's wish. And Roo?'

'Yes?'

'Make it a good one.'

7.

WISHES & HORSES

'Is this what you wished for – hot chocolate?' asked Roo, sipping hers from a rainbow mug. It blazed a sweet, fiery trail down her throat.

'Among other things,' her aunt answered vaguely. 'I wasn't sure how many wishes I was allowed under the 11:11 rules.'

'There are no rules. Have as many wishes as you like.'

Joni laughed. 'Miss Roo, I have a hunch that, once we escape from this frozen wasteland, you and I are going to have so much fun together.'

Tongue-tied with shyness, Roo pretended she had to rearrange her socks. A warm feeling spread through her, adding to the heat of the hot chocolate and Thai noodles they'd eaten before it. Between courses, she'd cleaned the rainbow mugs with snow.

Warmest of all was her father's coat. It wrapped around her twice. So ingrained in its red tartan lining was the smell of tobacco, aftershave, and a spill or two of lager that when Roo lifted it out of its brown wrapper, it had felt, for one time-stopped minute, as if her dad was in the tent with her.

In the right pocket of the coat, the solicitor had tucked a small envelope and Jim Thorn's will, rolled up and secured with a scarlet ribbon. In the left pocket were the remains of a packet of 'rollies' – the hand-rolled cigarettes Roo used to plead with him not to smoke.

Ironically, it was because of those 'rollies' that he'd also carried a cheap plastic lighter. That apple-green lighter had lit Joni's stove and allowed her to heat noodles and drinks when the snowstorm was at its most violent.

It had made the difference between life and death.

Fifteen days after he'd walked out of No. 32 Grimsby Grove and never returned, Jim Thorn had, inadvertently, saved his daughter and Joni.

Now it was after midnight. Roo was no longer tired, but she was anxious. Joni held the will in her hand.

They'd traded places. Joni was trying to raise her body temperature in the sleeping bag, wearing her fleece. Roo sat beside her, snug in wool socks and the navy-blue coat. Its storm hood was pulled up over her head, her hands stuffed in its soft suede pockets.

'Ready, Roo?'

'I guess.'

Freed from its scarlet ribbon, the will unfurled like a scroll. Joni scanned it and passed it over.

'In short, your father's left you everything. All his worldly possessions – that coat, basically – and all the money in his bank account.'

Roo was surprised. 'I didn't think he had any.'

'He doesn't. His account is £50.42 in the red.'

Tears sprang into Roo's eyes. 'How am I supposed to pay the bank £50.42? I don't have a penny.'

'Believe me, that bank is not going to miss fifty pounds,' said her aunt. Roo gave her a look, and Joni added hastily, 'Don't worry. I'll transfer some money to cover it.'

For Roo, the toughest part of the whole night was reading her dad's letter.

It was dated ten months earlier, almost as if he'd had a premonition that some twist of fate might leave his daughter alone in the world.

***

My dear Ruby Roo,

I expect Mr Doukis has explained to you that I've left you all my worldly goods, such as they are. If I get lucky with next week's gazillion-pound Big Jackpot lottery (ha ha!), you should have more than enough to go on an exotic holiday or buy your dream horse. If my bank account is empty, I'm sorry. I've wanted to be the best father ever to you, I truly have, but I'm painfully aware that I've often fallen short. When your mum passed, it devastated you and me both. Don't think I don't know that. I've been in awe of your courage ever since.

It's just that, for me, Joy was my joy. When she died, a light went out in my heart, and it's tougher than you'd think to find a replacement bulb. It's not like they stock them in Tesco.

For that reason, if I do happen to get lucky with one of my dream tickets, the cash comes with a condition. You're to enjoy it immediately.

Mr Doukis has strict instructions to hand over any money right away, not lock it in some trust fund till you're twenty-one. Don't save it for a rainy day, or for when you're over the hill like me. Grab life by the wings and fly, Ruby Roo. When you're young, time seems as infinite as the stars, stretching out like an endless summer. Looking back, I took time for granted. In clinging to the past and making fantastical plans for the future, I forgot to cherish what was in front of me: you.

So, Roo, do what I didn't. Live every minute. Follow the compass in your heart and you'll never stray too far off course.

Wherever possible, choose the path that leads to happiness. Always remember that you'll never have to do another thing to impress me and your mum. We were proud of you the day you were born. Everything else is just gravy.

Love,
Your dad xxx
P.S. If anything happens to me before you're eighteen, I've told Mr Doukis that your Aunt Joni is to adopt you. Never mind what I said about her. She's all right.

***

'Gee, thanks, Jim,' drawled Joni, breaking the tension and making Roo laugh when she might otherwise have burst out crying.

Joni sobered. 'Roo, I need to be honest with you. Losing Betty was a big blow. Life won't be easy for us at first. But we'll figure it out one day at a time. I'll wait tables if I have to. And if your dream is to have a horse of your own, I'll do everything in my power to make that happen.'

Roo's heart gave a hopeful skip. A horse of her own. It sounded too good to be true.

Then she remembered that it was her fault that Joni was homeless and unemployed. Choosing Roo had cost Joni her job and camper, as well as Gary and his luxury penthouse.

'Oh, please,' said her aunt, waving away Roo's apology. 'You've done me a favour. Can you believe I was planning to marry that beastly man? Never trust a person who'd make you choose between them and a child, Roo. Run a mile.'

She smiled. 'Tell me more about your dream horse.'

'My dream horse is Wonder Boy,' Roo said at once. 'I love everything about him, from the tips of his chestnut ears to the way he tucks his forelegs up when he jumps.'

'Who's Wonder Boy?'

'The perfect horse, that's who. He's a champion Dutch warmblood owned by Rhianna Cooper. She's only seventeen but she's aiming to be the youngest Olympic showjumper since Reed Kessler rode for the US team back in 2012. Sometimes I wish I had Rhianna's life.'

Roo took the little chestnut horse from her pocket. 'Fearless Fire looks a lot like Wonder Boy. That's why I keep him with me. He's my lucky charm. 'Least he was before tonight. Maybe he's lost his lucky spark.'

'Oh, I wouldn't be too sure,' said Joni. 'If it hadn't been for Fearless Fire, we really might have been blown halfway to Mars. Maybe he's your talisman – your secret power. Let's keep him with us always. See where he leads us.'

Roo decided she'd never met a grown-up quite like her aunt.

The pitter-patter of snow had stopped. Joni closed the vent

and turned off the lamp. They'd swapped places again. Roo was in the sleeping bag. The triangle of night sky was electric with stars.

The constellations blurred before Roo's tired eyes. She made a pillow of her floppy-eared kangaroo, which she'd found in her rucksack. 'D'you think it's safe to go to sleep now?'

'Thanks to your father's life-saving gifts, yes, it is. Remember, if you get scared in the night, I'll be here, watching over you.'

Joni closed the vent and turned off the lamp.

'Aunt Joni?'

'Just Joni, hon.'

'Sorry for what I said about you being irresponsible.'

'Don't be. I've had great fun being a rolling stone and a hippy and everything else I've been called over the years. But people change. *I* can change. Starting tomorrow, let's have a clean slate and a fresh start. Anything is possible if we stick together.'

'G'night, Joni,' whispered Roo, smiling into the darkness. Her mind was a kaleidoscope of images from the long day. It felt as if weeks, not mere hours, had passed since they'd marched out of Gary's penthouse.

As she wrestled with sleep, her father's words came to her on the wind, like a lullaby.

Ruby Roo, do what I didn't. Live every minute . . . Grab life by the wings and fly.

8.

TALISMAN

Roo woke up chilled to the marrow and aching all over, as if she'd slept on a bed of pine cones. Turned out she had. In the early hours, she'd rolled on to the groundsheet and spent the rest of the night on a kidney-crunching lump of them.

But she was alive. That was worth any number of bruises. So was her aunt, who lay snoring on her back, mouth open.

Roo was as parched as a desert explorer. The water bottle was empty. If she filled the rainbow mugs with snow, Joni could melt it on the WindBurner stove.

Quietly, she pulled on her damp trainers and scooted into the vestibule. She eased open the tent flaps. Her aunt didn't stir.

The field was a glistening white Christmas cake, decorated with holly and flitting robins and blackbirds. Beneath a tangerine sky, mist veiled the woods and surrounding fields.

Breathing in was a shock, like inhaling a waterfall, but Roo enjoyed the mint-fresh taste of the air. The world smelled new.

Aside from the robins and blackbirds, trying to outdo each other in some songbird pop contest, all was peaceful. There was no traffic noise. Not even a lone car. Their chances of rescue before breakfast seemed slim.

As Roo bent to fill the mugs with snow, Fearless Fire fell from the back pocket of her jeans. She picked him up. A 'talisman', her aunt had called him. Was it silly to imagine that a toy horse might have magic powers?

What nobody could deny was that, with Fearless Fire by their side, Roo and Joni had made it through the night without frostbite or worse.

She kissed him on his tiny white blaze.

It was then that she heard a distinct 'Hrrmph' and snort, followed by a rhythmic thud, thud, stamp.

A starburst of sunlight spiked through the mist. Dazzled, Roo shielded her eyes. Three ponies were leaning over a gate about a hundred metres away. They were watching her, ears pricked.

It had been so long since Roo had been close to any horse apart from the police Percherons – aloof and tall as trees – which patrolled her London neighbourhood that she ran headlong through the snow, slowing as she neared so she didn't alarm them.

The ponies craned over the gate, pleased to see a friend.

Roo put out a careful hand. Their manes and rugs were crusty with mud, but their muzzles were soft and kind.

She laughed as they nosed her dad's coat, searching for treats. 'Sorry, guys, I don't have anything for you. I'm hungry too.'

One of the ponies was more persistent than the rest. He shoved her and nipped off a button, determined to find a snack.

Roo was backing away when she recalled that her father had often carried mints. Sure enough, she found a new roll of Polos and a penny in a hidden pocket in the tartan lining of his coat.

She was trying to extract the mints when she found something else – a small shiny card.

Roo's world tilted on its axis.

Blood roared in her ears.

Was he coming or going? she'd asked the social worker and Officer Pooran.

Now she knew. Her dad had been on his way home *after* buying a lottery ticket.

The ponies were frantic to get at the treats. In a dream state, Roo shared them out.

Then she took the Big Jackpot scratch card from its hiding place.

Instantly, she was seized with the urge to destroy it. Her father had collapsed because he'd ventured out to buy this lottery ticket on a cruel winter's night. Had he stayed home, his weak heart might have continued to beat for months or even years. A cardiac specialist might have spotted the defect before it was too late. The fault could have been repaired.

Roo blamed the stupid Big Jackpot lottery for every horrible thing that had happened since her dad made the fateful decision to spend cash he didn't have on yet another scratch card.

Then again, if she ripped up one of his 'dream tickets' without knowing whether her dad had won a 'little something', it would be as if he'd died for nothing.

As she hesitated, the cheeky pony snatched the card.

'No!'

Roo nearly lost a hand trying to retrieve it.

Wiping pony slime off the foil that hid the secret numbers, she wondered if the card was ruined. Her dad had gone on and on about the time he'd tipped his coffee over a winning ticket and the mean old newsagent had refused to pay him a measly £10.

Roo fished the penny out of her pocket and scratched at the foil.

'Roo!'

Joni came tearing down the slope to the gate, skidding in the snow. 'Roo, thank heavens you're okay. When I woke up to find you gone, I panicked. I should have known that if there were ponies in the vicinity, you'd find them.'

She put a hand on Roo's sleeve. 'What is it? What's wrong? You're as grey as that pony. Are you ill? Roo, say something. You're scaring me.'

Roo held out the card. She was shivering uncontrollably.

'W-what does this mean?'

DIAL 0800 LUCKY DAY

A farm truck loaded with hay came roaring over the hill. The ponies dashed off to meet it.

'I think,' Joni said, 'that we're about to find out.'

9.

PIE IN THE SKY

'You've had a fortunate escape, my dears. Most fortunate,' said Farmer Bud Sweetwater as he surveyed Betty's blackened carcass. 'A miracle, one might say.'

Shyly, Roo showed him the lottery ticket. 'We're hoping we have some luck left over for this . . .'

The farmer was lost for words. He turned the scratch card over and over in his rough hands. Eventually, he got out: 'I think you'd better talk to my wife. Martha will know what to do.'

They rode to the farmhouse on the back of Bud's truck, squished between two smelly sheep, an exuberant Border collie, and a heap of hay bales. One of the ewes mistook Roo's hair for grass.

Roo was determined not to get too excited about her dad's dream ticket. In a lifetime of buying them, the most he'd ever won was £100.

But Martha Sweetwater took one look at the number on the scratch card and said: 'That's not a phone call you want to make on an empty stomach.'

Sending Roo and Joni off to shower, she cooked up a storm on her Aga.

That farmhouse breakfast was the finest Roo had ever eaten, and not just because she was ravenous. She and Joni had so many helpings of sunshine eggs, fried bread, vine tomatoes, and portobello mushrooms they could barely move.

It was mid-morning when Martha handed her phone to Joni. 'Bud and I will give you both some privacy while you make the call.'

'That's kind but unnecessary,' said Joni. '"DIAL 0800 LUCKY DAY" is the sort of nonsense they print on these scratch cards whether people have won £5 or £50 million.'

Martha didn't contradict her. She simply smiled and settled back into her chair. Her arms were folded, as if she were waiting for a theatre curtain to rise.

For Roo, the wait seemed interminable. After a brief conversation with a clerk, Joni was on hold to Pie in the Sky Entertainment Limited, the company who organised the lottery, for thirty-three nail-biting minutes, during which the same torturous tune played on speakerphone thirty-three times.

The clerk had refused to reveal a thing about the ticket until he'd done a dozen identity, credit, and fraud checks.

'I'm surprised he didn't ask how many dental fillings we've had,' Joni remarked sourly to Roo.

The longer it took, the more anxious Roo became. Could this particular ticket be sprinkled with stardust? The one and only time her father had won £100, the newsagent had simply taken his ticket and handed him the cash.

Once again, she felt the urge to destroy the ticket. If she ripped it up, it would lose its power to change her destiny.

But when another Pie in the Sky team member came on the line, Roo sat motionless as Joni answered more questions. The new person requested that Mr Doukis, the solicitor, email a copy of her dad's will.

By then it was time for Martha to feed four orphaned lambs.

She brought them into the kitchen and asked if Roo would mind taking care of them while she warmed up their milk.

At the height of the snowstorm, Roo had been convinced she was the unluckiest girl in the universe. Sitting beside the Aga, bottle-feeding the fluffiest, most angelic lambs imaginable, she felt, momentarily, like the luckiest.

'Who cares about Pie in the Sky when I've won the lamb lottery?' she said with a giggle as the four covered her face and arms with lamb nose-kisses in a plea for more milk.

Trying to confirm whether or not she'd won the human jackpot was a lot more tedious. Even Martha was losing interest by the time a Pie in the Sky executive came on the line and said: 'Are you sitting comfortably, Ms Thorn and Ms Jackson? Congratulations! You're millionaires. You've won a million pounds.'

Roo felt as if she were in one of those films where winning numbers slot into line on a Las Vegas machine and $100 bills start raining down.

She couldn't decide whether to weep for her dad, who, if life was remotely fair, would have lived to enjoy his winning ticket, or to jump around like a mad thing at the thought of his reaction.

Joni switched off her phone like she was shutting out the world. She said carefully: 'Roo, the Pie in the Sky man had to congratulate me too, because, legally, under-eighteens can't win the lottery and I'm your guardian. But, just so we're clear, it's not *our* jackpot, it's yours. *You've* won a million pounds.'

For Roo, it was only then that it sank in that life would never be the same again.

She, Joni, and Martha began screaming the place down. The Border collie barked like a maniac and Farmer Bud said at intervals: 'Well, I never. Well, I never!'

Then they all held hands (and paws) and danced around the kitchen.

10.

NIGHT FLIGHT

The week that followed was a whirlwind.

Within hours of dialling 0800 LUCKY DAY, Roo and Joni found themselves heading back to London – this time in a chauffeur-driven Bentley.

At Pie in the Sky headquarters, they had their photographs taken with an enormous £1,000,000 cheque. They wore posh outfits bought in haste from a nearby boutique and paid for using an advance from Mr Doukis, the solicitor.

Technically, it was Roo's dad who'd won the lottery, not his daughter, so the million pounds would be sent to the solicitor for safekeeping later in the week. After that, Roo would have access to the money whenever she pleased – within reason.

As Roo's guardian, it would be Joni's job to help her make wise choices with the cash. Joni would also get an allowance to help her take care of her niece.

'Once again, the Big Jackpot money is *your* money, not mine,' Joni told Roo as she beamed for the Pie in the Sky photographer. 'But, under lottery rules, you need to be accompanied by a responsible – err, semi-responsible – adult.'

They both had a laugh at that.

A public relations person in sequins and stilettos shimmied over to ask if they'd like to be interviewed for a 'rags to riches' story in the *Sun*, or would prefer to keep their win 'confidential'.

'Confidential!' cried Roo and Joni with such fervour that the PR lady spilled her champagne.

That evening, Pie in the Sky treated them to dinner at the Ritz Hotel, where they'd be spending the night.

The restaurant was so grand and the décor so lavish that Roo found it difficult to decide which sparkled more – the chandeliers, or the jewels of its glamorous diners. Sheikhs and minor royals rubbed shoulders with celebrities and businessmen in tuxedoes.

It was interesting, but overwhelming. Wriggling in her gold and red velvet chair, attempting to make sense of the menu, Roo felt all wrong.

'What's celeriac, wild mushroom, and Madeira?' she asked her aunt. 'Can I just have the wild mushrooms?'

'I think they're sort of mushed up together, honey. Maybe try the damson and pistachio. That'll be delicious. I'm still trying to wrap my brain around the ox cheek pithivier and ballotine of quail liver. I'm picturing *Swan Lake*, only with dancing livers. I'm more glad than ever that I'm a veg—'

She ducked behind her menu. 'Oh no!'

Roo glanced around in surprise. 'Who are you hiding from?'

Joni's voice was muffled. 'I'm not hiding.'

'Yes, you are.'

Her aunt stage-whispered: 'That waiter serving the next table – the one who looks like Brad Pitt if Brad were short and bald – he reminds me of a former suitor of mine.'

'Suitor? You mean, boyfriend?'

It was too late. Not Brad Pitt was on his way over and he was bristling.

'Joni? Joni Jackson, is that you under the table? Omigod, have you won the lottery?'

'Orville! What a delightful surprise I was just retrieving my napkin.' Flushed and dishevelled, Joni returned to her chair.

'How much have you won?' pressed Orville.

'Don't be daft, Orville. I haven't won a dollar. Whatever gave you such a silly notion?'

'Because this is the table that Pie in the Sky reserve for their lottery winners. If you're rolling in cash, Joni Jackson, you owe me a new guitar as well as five or ten thousand for emotional distress.'

Roo watched this exchange with fascination. 'What happened to the other guitar?'

'Who the heck are you?' Orville demanded rudely, noticing her for the first time.

Joni shot him a withering stare. 'This is Ruby, my niece, and I'll thank you to treat her with respect. Roo, meet Orville.'

'Your *niece*?' He stared pityingly at Roo. 'Girl, you have my sympathy. You've no idea who you're dealing with. Has Aunt Joni told you about the time she stole my guitar and used it for firewood?'

The restaurant manager materialised at Orville's side and breathed a fiery warning into his ear. The waiter quaked visibly in his patent leather shoes.

'But, sir—' he whined.

'*Now*, Orville.'

As Orville slunk back to the kitchen, Roo heard him vow: 'You haven't seen the last of me, Joni Jackson.'

The manager favoured his guests with a hundred-watt smile. 'On behalf of the Ritz, please accept my sincere apologies. I'll have our head waiter bring you more, err, ginger beer, with our compliments. Enjoy the rest of your evening.'

The second he was out of sight, Joni said: 'Roo, we need to get out of here.'

Roo wasn't sure whether to be embarrassed or relieved when her aunt pushed back her chair and grabbed Roo's hand. Heads turned as they sprinted from the Ritz, pausing only to plead with the Pie in the Sky chauffeur to drive them all the way to Green Acres.

As the Bentley sped past the glittering night-time windows of Piccadilly, Roo glanced back. Orville was jumping up and down on the red-carpeted steps of the Ritz, soundlessly shouting after them. Roo watched him shrink to a pinhead in the rear-view mirror.

What just happened? she wondered. Was this a foreshadowing of how life with her aunt was going to be? Would every twist and turn unlock an old secret? Would they constantly be running from Joni's past?

All the same, Roo was glad to be out of the stuffy dining room. A night flight in a Bentley was far more entertaining.

'This is a first,' the chauffeur was saying. 'I've driven plenty of folk from dodgy dwellings to the Ritz, but none of them ever asked me to take them from the Ritz to a campsite.'

He grinned. 'You're a couple of true originals.'

Only twenty-four hours had elapsed since they'd last fled London in darkness, and they were once again hungry and homeless. But, Roo thought incredulously, they were a million times richer.

'Apologies for that unfortunate encounter and the lack of Ritz dinner,' said her aunt as the glaring headlights and city din gave way to moonlit fields and swirling trees. 'Honestly, some people need to get a sense of humour.'

Roo was sceptical. 'Did you really steal Orville's guitar and use it for firewood?'

'Absolutely not! It wasn't my fault that he forgot it in my camper after we broke up. Nor am I to blame for the fact that his £20 car-boot-sale guitar was the only wood in miles when Betty broke down in the Tabernas Desert. That's in Spain, by the way. How else was I supposed to send up an emergency smoke signal?'

It made Roo laugh, picturing a Spanish roadside assistance crew showing up in the desert to find her aunt reclining on a beanbag (she'd seen a purple one in the old camper) beside a smoking guitar.

'You told me that Betty was mostly very reliable,' said Roo, tongue in cheek.

'She was. Mostly.'

***

It was after eight and blowing a wintry gale when the Bentley turned down the snow-lined lane to Green Acres Holiday Park.

Through Roo's tired eyes, the campsite had a ghost town vibe – more Grim Acres than Green. Trailing after her aunt along yet another icy path, the lottery win felt like a barely remembered dream.

Apart from their mouldy rucksacks, she and Joni had no luggage and only the crumpled dinner outfits they stood up in. They'd been planning to shop for clothes the next day in London.

49

However, the welcome they received when they pushed open the swing doors of the timber Ranch House Café banished all regrets from Roo's mind.

The promised fire blazed in the hearth. The room was full of cheer and laughter. A rosy-cheeked chef served them smoky bean chilli from a copper pot, with sour cream, cheese, chives, and crackers on the side.

On a scale of one to ten, Roo declared the meal an eleven.

Bellies full, the pair fell asleep in a cosy shepherd's hut, still giggling about their mad exit from the Ritz.

***

For the first few days at the campsite, Roo and Joni were so exhausted that all they did was sleep, eat, and read books. The well-stocked campsite shop also provided them with PJs, bamboo toothbrushes, fleeces, joggers, and warm socks.

On the third day, the shopkeeper came to tell Roo that the latest edition of *Your Horse* had arrived.

That afternoon, she and Joni retreated to their shepherd's hut to escape yet another bout of foul weather. Roo stretched out on the top bunk, absorbed in the magazine.

All of a sudden, she screamed.

Joni, who was sitting in a rocking chair, lost in a thriller, dropped her book in fright. 'What happened? Are you in pain?'

'No, just shock. Rhianna Cooper, she's . . . No, it can't be true. I don't believe it.'

'What can't you believe?' Joni stood up. 'Has there been an accident? Is Rhianna injured?'

'Worse,' said Roo. 'She's selling Wonder Boy.'

'The world's most perfect horse?' Her aunt leaned an elbow on Roo's bunk. 'Surely that's a good thing.'

'*A good thing?* It's heartbreaking. Rhianna and Wonder have grown up together. Smashed records together. They go together like . . . music. Like notes in a symphony.'

Joni smiled. 'How poetic, but, Roo, just think about what this means – not for Rhianna, but for you.'

'*Me?*'

'You've just won the lottery and, out of the blue, this horse you worship, from the tips of his chestnut ears to his white stockings, is for sale. Does it say anywhere in the article how much Rhianna wants for Wonder Boy?'

'Top showjumpers cost more than cars,' Roo told her. 'He'll be expensive.'

She speed-read the story to the end. '*TWO HUNDRED AND FIFTY THOUSAND*. I knew he'd be a lot, but not a new apartment amount. Not a quarter of a million.'

Without missing a beat, her aunt said: 'A quarter of a million? Roo, four days ago, you won a cool million. Now your dream horse is for sale. What are the chances of the stars aligning twice in one week? Feels like fate to me. Why don't we pay the Coopers a visit? Check out Wonder Boy in the flesh. See if he's worth it.'

'We can't,' said Roo, awestruck. '*Can we?*'

'I don't see why not. Your father made his wishes clear. His dream was to leave you enough money to buy your dream horse. The least I can do is help you achieve that.'

'It's probably too late,' said Roo, her mind filling with obstacles. 'Wonder Boy will have been snapped up by a top rider. And I'm nowhere near experienced enough to manage him. Showjumpers are superpowered.'

But even as she spoke, she found herself thinking: *What if . . . ? What if that superpowered showjumper belonged to me?*

'We won't know if he's still available unless we ask,' said her aunt. 'As for being superpowered, I guarantee he'll be a handful. But if you're desperate to have him, we can afford first-class coaching for both of you.'

The air in their shepherd's hut felt charged with possibility. Roo pictured herself bouncing out of bed in the morning and running down to the stables to groom and tack up *her* Wonder Boy. His talent would be her passport to the stars. With the help of first-class coaching, she'd have a shot at her dream – becoming a famous young showjumper like Rhianna.

Joni rang the number in the magazine right then and there.

Next thing Roo knew, they had an appointment at Starwood Farm at 11.15 a.m. on Monday, February first.

***

Three days later, they left the campsite for their date with destiny.

Behind the wheel of their hired Range Rover, Joni was snappily dressed in a navy blazer, crisp white shirt, and Ariat paddock boots.

A million pounds had appeared in their solicitor's bank account overnight, but, Joni told Roo, cash alone would not be enough.

'We need to look as if we know one end of a showjumper from another. If Wonder Boy were mine, I'd want to feel confident that whoever bought him would take extra-special care of him.'

Roo agreed. The stylish manager of the equestrian superstore they'd visited had advised her on riding clothes, boots, and accessories, and helped Joni with a range of impressive outfits.

Roo had hardly slept she was so excited.

Before the sun set, she might just be the owner of the world's most perfect horse.

WONDER BOY

11.

STARWOOD

Roo had watched the online tour of Starwood Farm, Rhianna Cooper's home, a dozen times, but nothing could prepare her for the sense of déjà vu that flooded through her when Joni braked in front of its high iron gates.

It was as though she'd been here before in another lifetime.

In the centre of the gates was an ornate gold star. Joni lowered her window and pressed the button on the entryphone.

There was a crackle of static. 'How can I help you?'

'Joni Jackson and Roo Thorn to see the Coopers.'

'Come on in.'

Roo squirmed with nerves, sweating in her new black riding tights and LeMieux sweatshirt. 'Stop! I've changed my mind. I can't do this.'

'Then let's not,' Joni said easily. If she was nervous too, it didn't show. She put the Range Rover into reverse. 'I'll call the Coopers later with an excuse.'

The iron gates, their spikes as sharp as spears, were rolling open.

'Wait, no.' Roo raked her fingers through her hair. What if she'd forgotten how to ride? It had been eight months since her last lesson. It was all happening too fast. She wasn't ready.

'What do you want to do?' asked her aunt.

'Oh, I don't know! Rhianna's hardly going to sell her grand champion horse to some clueless girl, is she? I feel a fraud.'

'But you're not. The horse is for sale, and you have the money to buy him. You have a right to inspect him. From what I've heard, good chemistry between horse and rider is vital. If you and Wonder Boy don't connect, you shouldn't part with a penny and Rhianna certainly shouldn't sell him to you.'

Joni put a reassuring hand over Roo's. 'But, since we're here, you might as well take the opportunity to meet your hero and her superstar horse. Isn't that what you've always wanted?'

Roo squashed down her fears. 'Okay, let's do it.'

The gates had shut again.

Joni leaned out of her window and pressed the buzzer once more. The gold star winked in the sunlight as the iron spikes glided back.

For better or worse, they were going in.

***

The Starwood Farm of Rhianna's Instagram page was a tranquil paradise where shiny, happy horses gazed serenely from immaculate stalls, and Rhianna's mum made lasagne and strawberry cheesecake from scratch in the Coopers' Tuscan-style mansion.

Today, it looked as if a travelling circus had rolled in.

The circular driveway, with its plunging horse fountain, was crammed with expensive cars and the vans of assorted tradesmen. Joni had difficulty finding a parking space. On the steps of the dusky pink mansion, Rhianna's mum, Rosslyn, was talking animatedly to a man with a roll of cable.

She gave them a friendly but distracted wave: 'Are you here for

Wonder? They're expecting you at the yard. Just follow the signs.'

'She didn't ask our names,' remarked Joni when they were out of earshot. 'Do you think that means there are other potential buyers here today?'

'There'll be a queue,' Roo told her, feeling more like an impostor than ever.

On the paved path, they met Rhianna's father coming the other way. He was on his phone. Roo recognised him because he was also his daughter's manager.

A smile spread across his tanned face. He ended his call at once.

'Ms Jackson and Ruby? Such a pleasure to meet you. I'm Lloyd Cooper, Rhianna's dad. Ruby, I gather you're a big fan of my daughter and Wonder. Let's hope they live up to your expectations. Come this way. I'll show you to the yard.'

The path was lined with emerald paddocks. Roo thrilled at the sight of three colts playing like kids in the winter sunshine.

'Where do you keep your other horses, Ms Jackson?' Lloyd Cooper asked.

'We're new to the area,' was Joni's smooth response. 'We're on a quest to find the ideal home.'

His stride checked. 'So you don't—'

This is it, thought Roo. *This is where we're evicted for being know-nothing chancers.*

Fortunately, Mr Cooper's phone trilled then, and kept him occupied until they reached the yard. Rhianna's burgundy-and-gold horse lorry was parked outside a five-barred gate.

As Roo stood admiring it, the side door opened, and Rhianna came bounding down the steps.

'Daddy, how long till the Wi-Fi's sorted? My website's crashed.'

Her father gave her an indulgent smile. 'Depends on when the technician finds the fault, Rhi. Could be hours. Or days.'

'You're joking, right? *Days?*'

She stopped, noticing the visitors. Remembering her manners, she put out her hand with a smile. 'Hi, I'm Rhianna.'

In her dreams, Roo had rehearsed meeting her hero a thousand times, but now that it was happening, her brain was a blank.

In person, the seventeen-year-old had clear golden skin and the grip of a girl who'd been riding highly strung horses since she was six. Her jacket was the lush burgundy of her lorry, with Starwood's gold star embroidered on the back. Her black riding tights were the same brand as Roo's.

'Snap,' cried Rhianna, pointing at them. They both laughed and Roo felt less shy.

'I'm Ruby,' she got out, 'but everyone calls me Roo, as in kangaroo.'

'I like it. Wanna see around our yard, Roo?'

A white van was backing out of a parking spot. Rhianna waved but didn't smile. 'That's our new farrier, Russ Wheeler. I don't like him as much as the one we had before, but Russ is the best and that's what counts.'

'Have fun in Paris, Russ!' called Lloyd Cooper, lifting a hand. 'Happy anniversary!'

The van braked beside him and Joni. A clean-cut man with close-cropped russet hair leaned out. 'Thanks, boss. Me and Violetta can't wait. I'm on my way to pick her up now. We're on the Eurostar train from St Pancras tonight.'

J'adore Paris,' said Joni. 'Where are you staying?'

'Let's leave them to it,' said Rhianna, unlatching the gate. 'Hey, how old are you, Roo? You look a little young to be taking on a horse like Wonder Boy.'

Roo's heart sank. Was she going to be turned away at the stable-yard gate just because she was only eleven and a half?

Rhianna grinned. 'Duh, what am I saying? When I started competing on Wonder, I was twelve, and he's a lot easier to manage now than he was then. If you're considering buying him, naturally, you'll want to ride him. He's over in Barn A. Come, I'll introduce you.'

12.

DREAM HORSE

On one hundred lonely days and nights, Roo had kept herself hopeful and cheerful by imagining herself at Starwood Farm, chilling with her hero and the horses.

Now, she was here, and everything about it was perfect.

Gone was the freezing sleet and snow of recent days. The temperature was springtime mild. Against the neon-blue sky, colours popped like candy.

The yard hummed with activity. Roo tried to take in everything at once. The turnout rugs hanging in the sunshine to dry. A groom washing a bay tethered to a post. A trophy room briefly glimpsed and full of treasures.

The girls crossed the courtyard to the main building.

Music spilled out of a state-of-the art gym. Rhianna stood among the smart bikes and workout benches and talked Roo through her two-hour daily routine.

'Just the usual cardio and stretching.' Rhianna gave a punchbag a playful right hook. 'I like to mix up boxing, weights, yoga, cycling, and skipping. I do a ton of skipping.'

'Great for the legs,' commented Roo, doing her best to act casual while turning fangirl somersaults on the inside.

'You bet,' said Rhianna. 'And most days I exercise eight horses, so that keeps me competition-fit as well.'

Any worries Roo might have had about her teen idol not

being as nice as she appeared on TV were banished by the effort Rhianna took to show Roo her world. Peculiarly, she seemed nervous. It was almost as if she was the one trying to impress Roo rather than the other way round.

They continued along a wooden walkway, hanging back when a man in a suit barrelled out of a grey door emblazoned with Starwood's gold star.

'That's Dale Dering's office,' explained Rhianna. 'Daddy calls it the "Nerve Centre". Our whole showjumping operation radiates out of it, with Dale in the middle, masterminding everything. You've heard of Dale, I'm sure. He's a legend in the equestrian world. He's been my coach from day one.'

It was all very interesting, but Roo was so eager to meet Wonder and the other horses that she was ready to burst. Even the smell of them sent her spirits soaring.

Between the 'Nerve Centre' and the stable blocks was an outdoor arena. Roo slowed to watch a dapple grey being lunged. Silver mane flying, it moved through its paces, urged on by a curly-haired blonde with a whip.

Rhianna came to stand beside Roo. 'That's River Spirit, a talented young eventer. Dale thinks she'll go far. We're big believers in lunging at Starwood. Develops the crucial topline muscles. Gets the horse working long and low.'

'It's the best,' agreed Roo, who'd never lunged a horse in her life.

But as she said it, it struck her that something was wrong with the scene. She just couldn't work out what.

Taking out her new phone – bought so she could record the day – Roo videoed the horse.

She was about to turn away when her eye was caught by a slight movement. A boyish figure in a black hoody and black jeans was leaning against the shadowed timber wall of Barn B, camouflaged by the dark wood.

Roo watched Hoody Boy, watching River Spirit.

'Who's that?' she began, but a gaggle of young Rhianna fans descended, drowning out the question. They'd done a jumping masterclass with her earlier in the day.

When Roo looked back, the mysterious figure – a teenager, judging by his wiry build – had gone.

'Is Starwood Farm always this hectic?' she asked when Rhianna was done signing autographs and dishing out training advice. Roo marvelled at her confidence and professionalism.

Rhianna laughed. 'Grand Central Station, you mean? Not usually. It's only that everything's happening at the same time. The Wi-Fi died yesterday just as the decorators arrived to renovate our house. We have so many painters, broadband fixers, farriers, grooms, and vets coming and going that it's hard to keep track of everyone. Dad's going mad with the expense. I keep telling him that it'll all be worth it when we win gold at the next Olympic Games.'

***

Wonder Boy's home was a red barn. Beneath its silver roof, it was airy and spacious, with curved wooden arches and roomy stalls. The aromatic perfume of hay, wood shavings, and horses – Roo's favourite – hung in the air.

'Wonder's stall is down the far end,' said Rhianna. 'Later, I'll introduce you to the other three horses in my team. We have high hopes for my new lead ride, Fleetfoot Amberwell. "Pudding" is his stable name. Ironic, obvs.'

Before Roo could find out more, the coconut clip-clop of hooves on concrete echoed across the barn. A familiar silhouette came striding in. He arched his neck and danced a little, framed against the light.

Roo had imagined this moment for so long that she found it hard to take in that it was real.

'There's Wonder now, with Eddie, his groom,' said Rhianna. 'Come say hi to him.'

Up close, Roo's dream horse exuded charisma and energy. His muscles rippled like living flames.

Roo reached up and rubbed his white blaze. To everyone's surprise, he gave a loud snorting sigh and relaxed.

'That's a good sign,' said Dale Dering, materialising out of nowhere and giving Roo a start. 'Wonder Boy doesn't warm to many people nowadays, but he's taken a shine to you.'

He shook Roo's hand, crushing her small one in his leathery palm.

'I'm Dale, Rhianna's coach. Good to meet you, Ruby. I hear you're a long-time fan of Wonder Boy. Clearly, you're an excellent judge of horses. Would you like to ride him?'

'More than anything!' Roo glanced at her hero. She felt slightly guilty about riding Rhianna's horse. '*If* Rhianna's all right with it.'

'I'm more than all right with it,' said Rhianna, smiling. 'Don't be nervous, Roo. Wonder likes to pretend he's a too-hot-to-handle racehorse, but he's a total softy.'

'He seems perfect to me. I love his navy brushing boots.'

Roo bent to touch the fleece-lined bands that protected his forelegs.

'There you are, Roo!' said Joni, hurrying into the barn through the field exit. 'I've been searching everywhere—'

She got no further because Wonder Boy squealed and reared, hooves slashing. Roo had to fling herself to one side to avoid being trampled.

Rhianna and the groom leapt to grab his bridle. His chestnut neck was streaked with sweat.

Roo was shaken. She'd never imagined there might be another side to Wonder.

Joni was distressed too. 'I'm so sorry. I must have startled him.'

'Yes, you did,' snapped Dale. 'Never move suddenly around horses.'

Roo noticed a look pass between him and Rhianna before the coach gave a thin smile. 'Forget it. Happens to the best of us.'

He offered his hand to Joni. 'You must be Ruby's aunt. A pleasure to meet you, Ms Jackson. Let me assure you that what you've just witnessed was completely out of character for Wonder Boy. An easier, kinder horse would be hard to find. He's as good as gold now, isn't he, Rhi?'

''Course he is,' answered Rhianna, but she seemed upset. 'Like I said, he's a sensitive soul. Here, Roo, take his reins. I'll give you a leg up.'

Roo took the reins with trepidation. She'd dreamed of riding Wonder for as long as she could remember, but that was before discovering he was part wild bronco.

Obediently, she bent a leg. Rhianna boosted her into the saddle with such vigour that Roo almost flew over the other side.

Joni watched anxiously. 'Are you sure it's safe for Roo to ride him?'

'We wouldn't take the risk if it wasn't,' was Dale's curt reply. 'That horse is worth a fortune.'

We know, thought Roo, annoyed. *We're the ones offering to pay a new-apartment amount of cash for him.*

Perhaps remembering that they were potential buyers, the coach added more graciously: 'Ms Jackson, Ruby, allow me to introduce you to Wonder's groom, Eddie. He'll accompany your niece to the arena. Ruby will have a wonderful ride. Wonder's an angel, usually. Meanwhile, I'll show you to the viewing bench.'

He turned to the groom. 'Eddie, before you bring Ruby to the arena, please fetch some gloves for her. Rhianna, for the photos I was thinking the mulberry boots might be better. There are some in my locker.'

With the adults gone, the girls were briefly alone.

High up on Wonder Boy, Roo focused on calming herself. If she was nervy, the horse might pick up on it.

It wasn't easy. She was so scared of riding terribly and letting everyone down that she half hoped an earthquake would erupt to save her from making a fool of herself.

Absorbed in her own thoughts, it took her a minute to realise that Rhianna, who was changing Wonder's brushing boots, was fighting back tears.

'If you love him, why are you selling him?' asked Roo before she could stop herself.

Rhianna's shoulders stiffened. 'You're too young to understand.'

'No, I'm not.' Roo was indignant. 'I'm nearly twelve.'

Rhianna smoothed down the Velcro straps on Wonder's mulberry boots and tossed the navy ones into his stall. There was something defiant in her stance.

'Because showjumping is a business, that's why. Love is not enough. Wonder's amazing, but he's not Olympic-level amazing.'

Had Roo been bigger, she'd have put her hands over Wonder's furry chestnut ears. How could Rhianna say such a thing in front of the horse who'd carried her so faithfully and brilliantly for so many years?

Roo's heart hurt for him. She was certain right down to her bones that, given a choice between Wonder Boy and a gold medal, she, Roo, would choose Wonder every time. But if Rhianna was distressed about the sale, it meant she hadn't taken the decision lightly.

Maybe it hadn't been her choice at all.

Rhianna's jacket pocket started ringing. She took out her phone. 'Rhianna speaking . . . Sure, no problem. Be right there.'

She was smiling again. 'Sorry, Roo, I've got to run. Catch you later. Have fun on Wonder. Keep in mind that he jumps miles higher than he needs to. It's my favourite thing about him. Riding him feels like flying.'

13.

BACKSTAGE PASS

Entering the arena on Starwood's star showjumper, Roo had visions of crashing to the ground in front of her aunt and Coach Dering, and dying of embarrassment.

But from Wonder Boy's very first stride, when he moved smoothly into a collected canter, he was the perfect gentleman. As she put him through his paces, Roo had the oddest sense that he was taking care of her.

The only time he forgot his manners was when he approached the low jump Dale had set up for Roo. Veering around that one, he raced instead at a Grand Prix–height oxer. It was as if he were saying, 'Don't waste my time with those stupid nursery school jumps. They bore me.'

To Roo, who'd never jumped anything higher than a bathtub, the fast-approaching oxer looked as insurmountable as a skyscraper. Irrationally, she wasn't afraid because she was so sure that he'd run out. The cobs at her old riding school had routinely refused jumps small enough to step over.

By the time she realised that Wonder meant business, it was too late to do anything other than give him his head. His speed and strength took her breath away.

At any stage of that five-star leap, she could have fallen. Somehow, she didn't. She flowed with him. Soared with him.

It did feel like flying, only better.

After Wonder had returned to earth, he slowed to a walk on his own. It was just as well because reaction had set in. Roo was as weak as a kitten. Meekly, he carried her back to the barn.

'So, Roo, is Wonder Boy everything you hoped he'd be?' asked Joni as they stood in the sunshine watching the groom hose down the chestnut at the wash station. Steam rose from Wonder's fiery coat. 'Would you like to buy him?'

'Yes, he is, and, yes, yes, yes!' Roo could not have been more elated if she'd won the Show Jumping World Cup.

'Magnificently ridden, Ruby,' enthused Lloyd Cooper, arriving as Eddie returned Wonder to his stall. 'I have great news. He's yours if you want him.'

Easy as that, thought Roo.

Too easy, said a voice at the back of her head.

Joni read her mind. She gave Rhianna's dad an appraising look. 'Why us?'

He was taken aback. 'What do you mean? I thought you were desperately keen to buy him.'

'We are keen. Surprised, is all. We thought you might prefer to sell him to another top rider.'

Mr Cooper spread his large, tanned hands. 'My daughter likes you. That's good enough for me. We can proceed directly to the Nerve Centre – err, to Dale's office – and you can sign the sale contract now.'

'Fantastic,' said Joni. She slung an arm around Roo's shoulders and Roo felt an almost imperceptible squeeze, like a signal.

'Mr Cooper, I'll need to make a few calls to arrange everything. I'll meet you at Coach Dering's office in about forty minutes.'

Mr Cooper beamed. 'Excellent . . . Ruby, dear, why don't you stay and help Eddie? Get to know the horse a bit. He'll be yours soon enough.'

*****

Eddie was a groom of few words, but he took a professional pride in his work. He showed Roo his daily eight-step routine and grunted approvingly as she completed each task.

The horse shone like burnished copper by the time Eddie slung a burgundy turnout rug over him. As Roo buckled the straps, the groom broke his near-silence.

'He's a good lad, Wonder Boy. Always tries his heart out. You'll get along fine. You seem kind.'

He gave the chestnut a parting pat. 'If you'll excuse me, I need to tend to the other horses. Latch the door securely when you leave.'

Roo was about to go when she spotted Wonder's navy brushing boots lying on the shavings. The groom had forgotten them. Picking them up, she was startled to see a long thorn threaded through the navy fabric of one of them.

If it had been there when Roo touched Wonder's foreleg, it would have stabbed him. That explained why he'd reacted so violently.

The thorn seemed to confirm what Roo had suspected at the time but been too timid to mention. That whatever the source of Wonder's pain or fright, it hadn't been her aunt's fault.

After all, why would a seasoned showjumper, bombproof after years of big band prize-giving ceremonies, roaring crowds, and flights to Europe, the US, and Asia, bc freaked out by a woman walking quickly?

Laying the brushing boots on a ledge, Roo ran a gentle hand down Wonder's left foreleg. He flinched but nothing worse.

When she examined the brushing boots further, the lethal-looking thorn was gone. It had fallen into the shavings. Now she'd never know what kind of shrub or bush it came from or where Wonder might have picked it up.

Perhaps it wasn't a thorn at all. Perhaps it was a splinter. But Eddie was too good and careful a groom to miss such a thing. And it couldn't have been Dale, who'd seemed taken off guard by Wonder's reaction.

Who, then . . . ?

Roo put the puzzle out of her head. Today was one of the best days of her life. She planned to enjoy every minute, not start inventing conspiracies where none existed.

Giving Wonder a last adoring cuddle, she let herself out of his stall, tossing the brushing boots into a bin marked 'Equine Laundry' as she went.

A happy thought struck her. As the soon-to-be owner of one of the farm's most illustrious champions, she temporarily had a right to go anywhere she pleased at Starwood Farm.

For a horse-mad girl, it was a backstage pass to the greatest show on earth.

14.

RIVER SPIRIT

First stop on Roo's backstage tour was Barn A's tack room. She sauntered in and had a mooch around. She was admiring the highly polished bridles and saddles when she heard voices. Suddenly worried that she might be scolded for poking about on her own, she darted behind a rack of coats.

From there, Roo had a gauzy view of Dale's broad back through the open tack room door. He'd halted to greet a woman with an American accent. Roo recognised the swirl of blonde curls, just visible over his shoulder, from the arena.

'Hey, Dale, mind if I have a word about River Spirit? I tried lunging her, but she's favouring her right foot. I'm concerned that she's lame.'

'Nonsense,' barked the coach. 'Nothing wrong with her foot. The farrier examined her first thing. Sound as a bell.'

'But—'

'Shelby, there's greatness in every sinew of River's body, but she has a lazy streak. If she can slack off work by pretending she's stiff or under the weather, she will. You need to show her who's boss.'

'Understood,' replied Shelby in the manner of someone who didn't understand in the least. 'One more thing, Dale. There's a man asking to see you. He and his son have been waiting for over an hour.'

'What man?'

'A scrap metal merchant. Why, there he is now.'

Sturdy boots crossed the concrete. Roo couldn't see the merchant, only his son slouching in the background, hands in his pockets.

To her surprise, it was Hoody Boy. He had the hood of his sweatshirt pulled so far over his head it rendered his face invisible.

His father's voice was gruff and gravelly: 'Mr Dale, do you remember me? I'm Vano. I came in December to take away the old lawnmower and muck spreader. You told me to come again today to collect some other bits and pieces.'

'I didn't say that. Shelby, do you recall me saying that?' The coach's tone was cold and impatient.

'No, but—'

'Mr Dale, sir, you told it to me on the phone,' said Vano.

'Are you calling me a liar? Show me the number.'

There was a pause as the man dug out his mobile.

Dale said triumphantly: 'That's not my number. It's the general contact for Starwood Farm. Someone else must have rung you. Sorry you've had a wasted journey. Feel free to have lunch at the riders' canteen before you go. Tell 'em Dale sent you. It's on me.'

The man didn't bother arguing. Roo glimpsed his overlong silver-streaked hair as he walked away. Hoody Boy followed reluctantly, twisting to look over his shoulder. The slit of his sweatshirt hood was all shadow, but there was menace in his lingering stance.

As their footsteps faded, Dale snapped, 'Keep an eye on them, will you, Shelby? I don't want those gypsies loitering around here. I don't trust them an inch.'

Roo was shocked. Her parents would never in their lives have spoken to or about anyone like that. Neither, she was sure, would Joni. Just the other day, her aunt had told Roo that if everyone treated everyone else with respect, half the world's problems would be solved at a stroke.

More importantly, she knew from an incident at the hospital where her mum worked that referring to Roma people as gypsies was offensive and wrong.

Before Roo could think what to do about it, Dale turned. For one nervous moment, Roo thought he was about to walk into the tack room. Mercifully, he carried on by.

She counted to twenty and went after him. If she got a minute alone with Rhianna, she'd try to pluck up the courage to mention the incident. Maybe Rhianna could have a word with her coach. Tell him it wasn't acceptable to treat people that way.

Hearing footsteps, Dale swung around.

Roo quailed beneath his dark, brooding stare. 'Uh, excuse me, Dale. Have you seen Rhianna?'

'She's busy. Can I help?'

Roo didn't want to say that Rhianna appeared to have forgotten her promise to introduce Roo to her team of showjumpers. She fumbled for an excuse. 'It's nothing important. Mind if I use the bathroom?'

'There's one in Barn B. Turn right out of the field exit.'

He smiled, but it didn't reach his eyes. 'Congratulations on buying Wonder, Ruby. You won't regret it.'

'Thanks,' said Roo, but she moved on swiftly. Dale Dering might be a massive deal in the horse world but, as a human, she was liking him less and less.

Wonder Boy's stall was the last on the left before the barn door. Roo stopped to look in on 'her' horse. He was snoozing in his box. She tiptoed away with a smile.

Outside, the blue day was being nibbled away by clouds. Roo was about to take the path to Barn B when she saw a woman in paint-splattered overalls emerge from a mobile bathroom unit parked beneath the trees. Roo's hands needed washing, so she headed over and climbed the steps.

'Oi! Where do you think you're going?'

A cross man was glaring up at her.

Like it wasn't obvious.

'Uh—'

He softened. 'Sorry, love, I didn't mean to scare you. Don't want anyone else blocking up the loo is all. It's out of order.'

'But I saw someone—'

'That's why I'm taping up the door. Everyone ignores my sign. Wretched unit sprang a leak and we're waiting for a replacement part. There's another bathroom inside Barn B.'

Barn B had a different atmosphere to Barn A. Without skylights, it was darker and cooler. Roo moved quietly down the line of horses. Breathing them in. Stroking velvet nostrils.

As her eyes adjusted to the light, she saw River Spirit's name on the door of the stall opposite. The grey was at the back of her box, shifting restlessly. Roo wondered if Shelby was correct. Maybe the mare did have a sore foot.

She peered over the door and got the fright of her life.

Hoody Boy was kneeling on the shavings beside River Spirit, shaking a small brown bottle.

Every equestrian crime in the book – doping, nobbling, poisoning – flashed through Roo's head.

'Help!' she yelled. 'Help!'

The teenager leapt to his feet. He pressed a finger to his lips.

Roo realised to her shame that she'd leapt to the worst conclusions based on the boy's menacing appearance. River Spirit, who was probably a better judge of character, seemed completely unconcerned.

A groom came running. 'What is it? What happened?'

Roo couldn't bear the thought of getting the boy into trouble. Rapidly, she moved to head off the girl. 'Sorry, I yelled. A horse tried to bite me. I got a fright.'

'Which one?'

'That one,' said Roo, gesturing at an innocent bay horse.

'How odd. Zac's normally so gentle.'

'It was probably my fault. It usually is . . . Umm, where do you keep Wonder Boy's feed? Any chance I can see it?'

'Sure thing. You're the girl who's thinking of buying him, aren't you? The feed room's through here.'

***

By the time Roo emerged from the feed room, River Spirit was gazing calmly out of her stall, ears pricked. Hoody Boy had gone. A nostril-tingling herbal aroma lingered. It made Roo's eyes water.

As she stroked the mare's fine-boned head, she noticed messy scraps of wood shavings on the concrete near her feet.

The scraps resolved themselves into words.

Roo's heart rate accelerated. Was it a threat? A 'tell anyone what you saw and you'll be sorry' kind of threat?

Or was it about something else entirely? Strange how the words were the exact opposite of the ones Dale had used not ten minutes earlier. Could it be a warning: 'Don't buy the horse or you'll regret it'?

But, no, Hoody Boy could hardly have known that Roo was buying Wonder when she'd only just found out herself.

Despite this, the same instinct that had led her to protect the boy earlier made her pick up a broom and sweep the shavings away.

'Mucking out already? That's impressive,' teased Joni, strolling into the barn. 'Roo, honey, I've spoken to our solicitor. We can buy Wonder if you're sure you want him.'

'I'm sure.'

But Roo didn't feel nearly as ecstatic as she'd done earlier. The conversations she'd overheard, the Hoody Boy encounter, and the threatening/warning message had left her uneasy and kind of queasy.

Joni paused. 'If you've changed your mind, it's no problem ...'

'It's not that. Wonder's everything I ever dreamed of. It's not him, it's—'

Roo's gaze went from the bay horse practising flying changes in the arena to the architect-designed offices and barns. Everything was perfect.

And yet ...

'It's Starwood, isn't it?' said her aunt, understanding. 'There's something unsettling about the place. I can't quite put a finger on it.'

'Me neither,' agreed Roo.

'Then we're on the same page. Let's take things step by step. We're a team, remember.'

They found Rhianna's dad in Dale's office looking dapper and chipper. He thrust the sale contract and a fountain pen at Joni.

'Cast your eye over that, Joni. I'll fire up my laptop. We can do an instant bank transfer. Wonder Boy will be yours by lunchtime.'

Joni set down the pen very deliberately.

'Lloyd, I'm sure you understand that we can't pay you a quarter of a million right this minute. I'd like our solicitor to look over the contract. We also have livery stables to arrange. A couple of days ought to be enough. We'll pay a £1,000 deposit now and the balance if the vet certifies Wonder as sound when we collect him on Wednesday.'

'I agree with my aunt,' said Roo, impressed by Joni's business savvy. The morning had been such a whirlwind, it was no bad thing to have forty-eight hours to think things over.

A muscle began to hop in Lloyd Cooper's square jaw. 'I'm afraid that simply won't do. I must insist that you pay the full amount today or we'll sell Wonder Boy to a buyer who will.'

Roo was startled. Rhianna's dad suddenly seemed very different to the genial man who'd effusively greeted them on arrival. Why the rush to get their cash? Did he not trust them? Or should they not trust him? He was behaving like the salesman who'd tried to pressure her dad into buying an old banger of a car.

Roo had ridden Wonder. She was confident he was fit. An

unsound horse could never have flown over the giant oxer with such power and joy. But that didn't mean he didn't have some underlying health issue.

'Would *Rhianna* buy a horse without having a vet inspect it first?' Roo asked innocently. Joni shot her an approving glance.

A flush crept up Mr Cooper's neck. 'I suppose she wouldn't.'

Joni gave him a winning smile. 'Lloyd, as you know better than anyone, horses are unpredictable creatures. Anything could happen between now and Wednesday. Wonder could suffer a bout of colic, for all we know. We'll pay the full amount when we collect him and not an hour before.'

As Lloyd Cooper opened his mouth to object, the grey door swung open. Roo tried not to scowl as Coach Dering swept in. The change in Mr Cooper's expression was quite dramatic.

'A pleasure doing business with you, Joni and Ruby,' he beamed. 'Wednesday it is.'

15.

CROSSROADS

'Well, whaddya think?' the estate agent asked eagerly. 'Is it a winner? It has everything on your wish list.'

He consulted his clipboard. 'Idyllic three-bedroom cottage near the South Downs in West Sussex, with a real fireplace and modern kitchen. Most importantly, it has two spacious stables and a paddock. Have I missed anything?'

'Everything's great,' Roo told him. 'The cottage is so pretty, and the stables are clean and roomy. The field is a good size too.'

'It ticks every box,' agreed Joni. 'It's quaint. It's quiet. It's everything we wanted. There's even a bonus vegetable garden.'

And yet...

She didn't say the last part aloud, but Roo could tell that she was thinking it. She was thinking something similar herself.

It was the fifth rental property they'd seen that morning, not counting the thirty-six they'd inspected and rejected online. To the estate agent's dismay, Roo and Joni had found something 'not quite right' with all of them.

The Tudor house had woodworm in the beams and rats the size of cats in the attic. The converted barn was draughty. The ultra-stylish house with the pool had a bat colony in the falling-down barn.

The stone house was haunted.

But Jasmine Cottage was very nearly perfect.

And yet ... Roo's heart wasn't in it. Neither was her aunt's. Roo thought she knew why.

Joni was a free spirit. Everything they were doing to fulfil Roo's dream tied her down to Roo, her new horse, and a rental cottage with a stable for Roo's horse. Once they had a place to live, her aunt would also be tied to Roo's new school, with rules and strict timetables.

Nowhere in that picture was there anything Joni might have chosen for herself less than a month ago.

If Roo became an albatross around her neck, dragging her down, Joni might get the itch to fly away again. How could Roo stop her?

Love was the glue that held people together, and she and her aunt didn't have that yet. They were still getting to know one another.

Roo wasn't sure what to do about it. They couldn't stay at Green Acres forever, and Wonder had to have a stable ...

The estate agent looked from Roo to Joni and his face fell. 'What is it this time?'

'The wallpaper,' they chimed together.

'What's wrong with it?'

'Nothing,' admitted Roo. 'It just doesn't feel like home.'

'What she said,' added Joni.

The estate agent was so fed up that he virtually frogmarched them out of the cottage. He left in such a hurry that his tyres left skid marks in the gravel.

'Poor man,' sympathised Joni as they set off to visit the next property on their list. 'He'll be gnashing his teeth and ranting about time-wasters all the way back to his office.'

'What are we going to do?' fretted Roo, staring out at the bleak February landscape. Even the birds seemed depressed. 'How will we ever find a home?'

'Home is where the heart is,' Joni said blithely. 'We'll know home when we find it.'

'Yeah, but will we find it before we have to collect Wonder from Starwood on Wednesday?' was Roo's glum response.

She'd woken that morning missing her mum and dad so much it hurt. Not even the prospect of owning her dream horse could lift her spirits. She'd started to feel guilty about it. Rhianna would have a stroke if she knew the truth about Roo and Joni's circumstances. A homeless orphan didn't deserve a wonder horse like Wonder.

But, as their rental Range Rover splashed through a puddle on the country lane, Roo remembered Rhianna telling her that showjumping was a business first. *Love is not enough.*

Suddenly, she felt a whole lot better. That's what she, a homeless orphan, could offer Wonder. She could offer love. Oceans of it.

A bright sign flashed by: EASY RIDER CUSTOM CAMPERS.

Through a gap in the hedgerow, Roo spotted a riot of colour. She knew now what she could do to brighten her aunt's day.

'Joni, slow down! Did you see that?'

'See what?'

'A whole field packed with Bettys. Can we stop and look?'

'No, we can't,' said her aunt, speeding up. 'We need to stay focused on finding a proper house with four walls – ideally, one with a stable attached. We'll need wheels too. This hire car has to be returned in the morning.'

'Then wouldn't a camper solve all our problems?' persisted Roo. 'We'd have wheels *and* a roof over our heads. We could park it at Green Acres and put Wonder in a nearby livery yard. Oh, can't we just look?'

They were approaching a crossroads.

'I suppose there's no harm in looking,' smiled Joni, making a U-turn. 'You know what they say about campers . . .'

'What's that?'

'Home is where you park it.'

16.

BLUEBIRD

After the Betty disaster, Roo had vowed that nothing would drag her inside another camper.

But five minutes at Easy Rider Custom Campers changed her mind. Moving along the rows of VWs and Ford transit vans, listening to Joni and the salesman compare notes on past travels to the Côte d'Azur and the Canadian Rockies, she found herself filled with the urge to go adventuring.

Each camper was unique and skilfully crafted to order. The colours were epic, too. There was a black one with a flame-spewing dragon on the side, and a burnt-orange one with a purple 'Prince' sofa.

'We get all sorts buying them,' said the salesman. 'Weekend adventurers, stressed-out executives, surfers, musicians, and full-time nomads. "Lifers", we call those.'

Some campers had extra features such as showers or bike racks. Others were kitted out with solar panels or pull-out kitchens for outdoor dining.

All were eye-wateringly expensive.

'If Betty hadn't been given to me by a suitor, no way would I have been able to afford a camper,' said Joni, shaking her head at a £90,000 price tag.

Roo raised an eyebrow. 'Another suitor?'

'That one hardly counts. We met on a tiger safari in Rajasthan in India. Two dates later, he turned up in a saffron robe and announced he was off to join a monastery. He tossed me the keys to his camper back in Yorkshire and told me that Betty was as difficult as I was. "You deserve each other," he screamed. "Namaste."'

She shrugged. 'Maybe we did.'

They'd reached the end of the line of campers.

'Anything grab you?' asked the salesman.

'Not today,' Joni said wistfully. 'Come, Roo, we need to go.'

Roo was looking the other way. 'What's the story with that camper over there? Why's she on her own in a field?'

The salesman pulled a face. 'Bluebird's a bit of a heartbreaker, to be honest. I spent months fitting her out for a special order. Worked myself to the bone, alongside some of our most skilled craftspeople, to make her gorgeous.

'The day before the buyers were due to hand over the cash, they changed their minds and bought a house. I was so gutted that I couldn't even bring myself to pump up Bluebird's tyres and move her to shelter when the snowstorm blew in. She's languished in that field all winter.'

Roo glanced at Joni. Her aunt's face was alive with curiosity. She'd be unable to resist taking a quick peek.

'Any chance we can take a look inside her?' Roo asked the salesman.

'What? Oh, you're serious. She might be a trifle dusty, but, sure. I'll fetch the keys.'

Beneath her crust of winter grease and grime, Bluebird was painted what the salesman described as 'Mediterranean blue'.

Roo immediately decided it was her very favourite colour.

Joni said it reminded her of lazy summers in Provence when the lavender fields were in bloom.

As soon as she stepped inside, Roo felt a flutter in her chest.

A little wooden table and two aqua-blue cushioned seats were set against a white timber wall. The table was laid with mats and spoons and a couple of cherry-red bowls.

There was something oddly familiar and inviting about the scene. It was almost as if Bluebird had been expecting them. Roo could visualise her and Joni eating pancakes at the table.

Across the aisle was a shiny compact kitchen. Spice racks, pots and pans, and a couple of plants in need of water were cleverly secured.

Roo loved the bookshelves and pretty blinds in the mini living area. Joni was besotted with the modern shower and toilet.

But it was the beds that sealed the deal for Roo. There were two, each dressed in a white duvet cover brightened by colourful rugs and cushions.

The double bed had a large window behind it. 'Imagine opening your eyes to a vista of snow-capped peaks or rolling waves . . .' mused Joni, lolling against the pillows. 'Wouldn't it be bliss?'

Roo was climbing the ladder to the sleeping nook above. She crawled in and lay watching a rabbit-shaped cloud float across the skylight. The mattress was marshmallow-soft.

On impulse, she took Fearless Fire from her pocket and set him on a tiny shelf. 'Can this be my bed?' she called down to her aunt.

Joni laughed. 'If we were buying Bluebird, then, yes, of course, but we're not.'

'But this feels like home.'

Joni clambered off the bed. 'Roo, I gave you my word that we'd settle down and find a normal, sensible house, and I intend to honour that. No more campers or adventures.'

'But that was before we met Bluebird,' cried Roo. 'Who'd want normal and sensible if they could have a Mediterranean-blue camper with a shower and a sleeping nook? Anyway, I've decided I quite like adventures.'

As soon as she'd crossed Bluebird's threshold, something had stirred in her – the call of the wild and the great unknown. The rush of hope and exhilaration she'd experienced when she'd stepped from their snow-battered tent to be greeted by a tangerine dawn and three ponies had stayed with her.

Her aunt was amused. 'Then you shall have adventures, Roo, but they'll be safely between the pages of books. As for Bluebird, I'm going to be responsible and say no. N. O. Let's go.'

Roo was so upset that she forgot she'd left Fearless Fire on the sleeping-nook shelf.

The salesman looked as crushed as Roo felt.

'That's a real pity, and I'm not just saying that because I'm trying to make a sale,' he told Joni. 'I could picture the three of you together. You, your niece, and Bluebird. You match.'

'We'll find a house that's a match for us too,' Joni replied, but she sounded wistful.

'JONI, COME QUICKLY!' called Roo from the front of the camper. 'You have to see this.'

Her aunt rushed to her side. Between Bluebird's bumper and the classic VW symbol was a pair of silver wings.

Joni touched them in wonder. '*Grab life by the wings and fly . . .*' she half-whispered.

'It's a sign.' Roo was filled with the feeling that Bluebird was the home they were meant to have. 'Imagine – if we buy Bluebird, we can grab life by the wings and go wherever the wind takes us. If Wonder doesn't like his new livery yard, we can just move him somewhere else. You're only saying no to the best camper ever because you're trying to do the right thing.'

'Yes, I am,' said her aunt. 'And you're not making it easy.'

'But what if this *is* the right thing?' cried Roo. 'Dad told me to follow the compass in my heart. My compass is telling me to buy Bluebird. Don't you see? This way, we can both have our dreams. "Anything's possible if we stick together." Isn't that what you're always saying to me?'

They shared a long look. Joni grinned. 'Well, if you're absolutely sure—'

'We've changed our minds,' Roo said excitedly to the salesman. 'We'll take her. We'll take Bluebird.'

'How soon can you get her cleaned and up and running?' asked Joni. 'Any chance you could deliver her to Green Acres Holiday Park tomorrow?'

The salesman was so delighted, he was gushing. 'I'll need to have her cleaned and serviced, but I could get her to you by 4 p.m., if that would suit?'

His office was a space-themed camper. From the padded rings of a Saturn cushion, Joni made one phone call to the solicitor to sort out the cash, and another to organise insurance. Next thing Roo knew, Bluebird, a VW California Grand 600, was theirs.

The salesman gave the registration papers to Joni and smilingly passed Bluebird's keys to Roo.

It was like being handed the keys to happiness.

'All we need to do now is find a stable for your new horse,' Joni told her.

'A new camper and a new horse in the same week!' exclaimed the salesman. 'What a dream. If you like horses, no doubt you'll have been glued to the news this morning. Beggars belief. Gone without a trace.'

'We haven't seen any news today . . .' said Joni, putting on her coat.

'Crikey, haven't you heard? Watch this . . .'

He flipped open his laptop and clicked play on a BBC link.

Aerial footage showed police spilling out of squad cars in near darkness. At first, Roo couldn't make sense of what she was seeing. A woman in a dressing gown was comforting a girl sobbing in pyjamas.

Then the drone camera rose over barns and a stable yard, where a man was trying to lead a frightened horse.

Roo gasped as she recognised Eddie the groom.

'That's Starwood Farm!' Joni said in disbelief.

On the screen, blue lights swirled. A police radio crackled.

In a flash, Roo was back at No. 32 Grimsby Grove, waking to strobing blue lights and the police hammering at her door. She was running down the passage and bursting into her father's empty room . . .

'Roo? Roo, you're safe. I've got you.'

The office swam back into focus. Joni was holding her tight.

'Let's get you back to Green Acres. We can watch the report later or not at all.'

'No, I'm fine.' Roo pulled away. 'I want to see it now.'

The salesman, who'd paused the video in consternation, pressed play again. A BBC anchor said crisply: 'Thieves have targeted the West Sussex estate of teenage showjumping sensation Rhianna Cooper, making off with her famous horse, Wonder Boy.

'In echoes of the tragic case of Shergar, the £10 million Derby winner who vanished in Northern Ireland in 1983, Wonder appears to have disappeared into thin air.

'By coincidence, Cooper's £250,000 chestnut champion had been sold just hours earlier to two strangers claiming to be fans . . .'

Roo felt as if she'd been parachuted into a nightmare. *Her* dream horse, *her* Wonder Boy, had been stolen the day before she was due to collect him.

'Is something wrong?' enquired the salesman. 'Do you know the Cooper family?'

Joni's phone pealed, sounding extra loud in the enclosed space.

'Excuse us,' she told the salesman. 'Thanks for Bluebird. We'll look forward to being reunited with her tomorrow.'

She answered the call while shepherding Roo across the car park. Roo caught snatches of the one-sided conversation:

'This is Joni Jackson. Yes, Officer . . . No, Officer . . . That's the nuttiest thing I ever heard in my life . . . Apologies, Officer. Yes, yes, I do understand, and I'm very, very sorry . . . We'll be there in ten, Officer . . .'

Tugging Roo after her, she ran to the Range Rover and dived in.

'What's going on?' cried Roo, fumbling for her seat belt. 'What did the police want?'

'They want to interview us down at the station. I got the impression that we're high on their list of suspects. Roo, they seem to think we stole Wonder Boy!'

17.

MURKY WATERS

'Are you sure this is a good idea?' worried Roo as Joni parked outside the village print shop. She was still shaken by the way they'd been treated at the police station. Still struggling to process the rapid turn of events.

Before he'd even met them, Detective Inspector Percival Pickle had catapulted Joni and Roo to the top of his list of suspects, which included jealous rivals, disappointed buyers, assorted tradesmen, and Starwood staff.

'Correct me if I'm wrong, Ms Jackson,' he'd begun, 'but as a woman of no fixed abode, with a long history of being broke and/or unemployed, you could scarcely afford a showjumper worth a quarter of a million. Even if it were possible, where would you have kept him? You're living on a campsite.'

'Yes, but—'

He'd steamrolled over Joni's attempts to explain.

'Ms Jackson, you'll save us both a lot of time and trouble if you simply admit that, on February first, you and your niece, posing as buyers, visited Starwood Farm for one reason, and one reason only, and that was to case the joint so that you could return to steal Wonder Boy later that same night.'

'That's a lie!!' Roo burst out, forgetting her aunt's instructions to let her do the talking. 'I adore Wonder. I'd rather cut off my own arm than harm one hair on his body.'

It took a phone call from Mr Doukis, their solicitor, who sent proof of the lottery win and, as Joni put it, 'read Pickle the riot act,' for the detective to apologise and release them.

By that time, Roo and Joni were starving. It had been a gruelling morning. After a brief stop to place an order at the village printers, they'd nipped to a local café for an avocado and halloumi wrap. Now they were back at the printers.

'Are you sure that this is a good idea?' Roo asked again.

'No, I'm not,' said her aunt. 'It could easily be the worst idea in the history of mysteries, but we have to do something. Agreed?'

'Agreed.'

'We can't simply do nothing while terrified Wonder is spirited further and further away by evil thieves who see him only as walking money.'

'But what about Detective Inspector Pickle?' asked Roo. 'After the way he treated us, I don't really trust him, but maybe we should give him a chance to crack the case.'

'Oh, please,' said Joni. 'There are plastic Cluedo game figures with more pizazz and imagination than "Detective Inspector" Pickle.'

'But won't he get annoyed if he thinks we're interfering? He promised he'd leave no stone unturned trying to find Wonder.'

'And good luck to him,' retorted her aunt. 'Let's hope he turns up something more impressive than an earwig. I'm afraid I lost faith in Percival Pickle when he said he'd be waiting to see if there was a ransom demand before deciding what further action to take. When I suggested that time was of the essence because Wonder's literal life was at stake, the heartless man gave me a lecture about his team having other priorities: *"Grisly murders and such."* That's why we have to make it our mission to find Wonder Boy ourselves.'

'How?' Roo had taken it for granted that a detective inspector – even one without pizazz or imagination – might put some effort into finding a stolen £250,000 horse. Now she realised that her aunt was right. At the very least, the police might need some help.

Joni checked her watch. 'The printers should have our order ready. Let's go in and collect it.'

Back in the Range Rover, she unwrapped a slim package. Inside were fifty business cards. Beneath an ink design of a galloping horse were the words:

Joni Jackson

INVESTIGATIVE JOURNALIST

'Are you an investigative journalist?' asked Roo, trying to imagine when in her globetrotting past Joni might have found time to become an undercover reporter.

Her aunt waved a hand airily. 'Anyone can be an investigative journalist. If you decide you want to be one, you can start today. What's to stop you?'

'But were you an investigative reporter in the past? As a job, I mean.'

'I was indeed. For the *Bromley News Shopper*. Yeah, yeah, it's not the *New York Times*, but that's not the point. The point is, I was good at it.'

She turned on the ignition. 'Roo, if we volunteer to get involved in this business, we'll be dipping our toes into extremely murky waters. It's not too late to stop now.'

'I don't want to stop,' said Roo.

Beneath the surface, she boiled with fury at whoever had dared to steal Wonder. If a tiny thorn could turn the sensitive horse into a sweating, rearing wreck, how much worse must he feel now? She vowed to herself that she would not rest until he was found.

'Like you said, if we go to Starwood, at least we'll be doing something,' she told Joni. 'We can find out how we can help . . . *If* we can help. You never know, we might just stumble across some clue Pickle has missed.'

'What are the odds?' her aunt said drily. 'Okay, Starwood it is.'

18.

LOCKED-STABLE MYSTERY

What a difference a day makes, thought Roo, as Starwood Farm's spiky gates once again slid open to allow them entry.

In under twenty-eight hours, she'd gone from being Wonder Boy's fan, to his almost-new owner, to a suspected accomplice in his kidnapping. And now, just possibly, she and Joni were going to help track down whoever had snatched him.

And who would Wonder belong to if Roo did save him? That was the £250,000 question.

'Best keep an open mind on that,' her aunt had advised. 'I know you'll be devastated if you lose him, having come so close to owning him, but Rhianna looked pretty devastated herself in that news footage. She may have realised that winning isn't everything and want to keep him after all.'

Roo didn't want to admit that the words 'finders keepers' kept running through her mind. If she and Joni risked all to locate Wonder, surely that should give Roo more chance of keeping him always, not less?

It was twilight when they walked into the yard. The sky was streaked with an eerie purple light. In contrast to their previous visit, the place was deserted. The horses were tucked up in their beds. Most staff had gone home.

'If you're looking for Rhianna, she's at a meeting in the Nerve Centre,' said a groom they unearthed polishing saddles.

He shuddered. 'Bad business, this. If a thieving gang can make Wonder vanish off the face of the map, no horse is safe.'

Joni knocked at the grey door with the gold star. When they entered, Dale Dering was lounging in his chair in the middle of the room, watching a man in a SECURITY SYSTEMS jacket scroll through CCTV footage.

Flanking the coach were Rhianna, her father, and Wonder's groom, Eddie. Rhianna's mum, Rosslyn, was on the sofa nearby.

A cartoon image of Coach Dering as a spider at the centre of a web popped into Roo's head. Once seen, it was difficult to unsee.

None of the adults looked pleased to see the visitors. Quite the opposite. Only Rhianna managed a strained smile. She ran to Roo.

Gone was the poised young professional of the previous day. Her face was puffy and blotchy, her jumper stained. 'What are you doing here? Haven't you heard the news – Wonder's been stolen.'

'It's the worst news ever,' said Roo. 'I'm so sorry. We came to see if we could help.'

'Oh, Roo, I'm so frightened for my baby,' said Rhianna with a sob. 'I'm petrified I'll never see him again.'

She flung her arms around her startled new friend.

'You will see him again. A hundred per cent definitely,' Roo found herself saying. Lying, possibly. 'We have to stay strong and believe he'll be found safe.'

Rhianna pulled herself together with effort. 'You're right. For Wonder's sake, we have to keep hoping. It's just such a maddening mystery. The police can't understand it.'

Her father said: 'Joni, if you want your deposit back, I'm afraid—'

'Forget the money.' Joni handed him her investigative journalist card. 'As Roo said, we came to ask if there's anything we can do to assist you and the police. I have some experience in these matters.'

'Is there any chance you could tell us what happened, Mr Cooper?' asked Roo.

Rhianna's dad looked less mournful and a great deal more friendly now that he didn't have to part with Joni's cash. He handed her business card to Dale, who glanced at it and gave a small nod.

'It was the night guard's shift,' Lloyd Cooper began. 'Between 8 p.m. and 8 a.m., he patrols the barns every thirty minutes. At 3.45 a.m., CCTV shows him patting Wonder as he passes his stall. Ten minutes later, when the camera pans around, Wonder's napping.'

He took out a handkerchief and blew his nose. 'But, at 4.05 a.m., Wonder's stall is empty. It's like a conjuring trick. Twenty minutes after the guard petted him, Wonder had evaporated.'

Roo stared at him. 'You mean, there are no images of Wonder being taken off Starwood?'

'Zip,' replied Rhianna. 'Not even a shadow or an ear. It wasn't until the guard's next patrol at 4.15 a.m. that he noticed Wonder was gone. The cops arrived, all guns blazing, about half an hour later.'

She dashed away another tear. 'At first, the police were super helpful. But once they discovered that there was no evidence of theft on our CCTV, they started to question whether Wonder had been stolen at all. They seemed to think that losing a horse was like losing a cat or dog. That we'd just mislaid him on the farm or in a basement or something.'

'It's not surprising they're baffled,' sympathised her dad. 'When the guard discovered Wonder was missing, the stall door was bolted, as if he'd been airlifted out of it by a spacecraft and flown off the farm.'

Roo said: 'It's like a locked-room murder mystery. Like one of those Sherlock Holmes stories where the victim's found in a locked room with no window or fireplace and the key's on the inside of the door – only this time, the victim's vanished from a locked stable.'

'A locked-stable mystery!' cried Rosslyn Cooper from the sofa. 'That's it exactly. How does one disappear a horse from an alarmed and guarded estate?'

'The thieves disappeared themselves too,' said her daughter. 'Even if it was an inside job – and I'm crossing every finger that it wasn't – the security cameras should have picked up anyone trying to sneak Wonder away.'

'Were those cameras all working last night?' asked Joni.

'Perfectly,' said Mr Cooper. 'Well, except for the one by the field gate, but that's been broken for a month. The police checked the CCTV of the farmer who owns the field. Nothing stirred between midnight and dawn except for a fox moving her cubs.'

Dale turned to the security man. 'Jiang, is there any chance that the CCTV system could have been tampered with, so it seemed that Wonder was in his stall when he'd already been stolen?'

'Not a chance, Coach. Every frame is timed and numbered.'

'Then we'll need to widen our search. Check the footage for Barn B. Start at around midday yesterday when that scrap metal merchant and the son with the bad attitude were hanging around. That teenager's a born criminal if ever I saw one.'

Beside her, Roo felt Joni go rigid.

'I'm old enough to remember when you thought my eleven-year-old niece and I were also born criminals, Mr Dering,' her aunt said pointedly. 'About three hours ago, to be precise. Detective Inspector Pickle told us it was you who'd reported us as likely suspects even though you sat in that same chair yesterday and witnessed us pay a £1,000 deposit for the horse.'

Rhianna's mum started off the sofa. 'Is this true, Dale?'

'I was only trying to cover all bases in our search for your daughter's horse, Rosslyn,' blustered the coach. 'Ms Jackson, apologies if Pickle was heavy-handed. It's just that you were – how shall I put this? Unusual buyers. The detective's explained everything and you'll have my full support when Wonder's found, which of course he will be.'

He flashed a reassuring smile at Rhianna.

Roo studied him with renewed dislike. She hadn't forgotten how he'd spoken to poor Vano and his son. He'd also set the police on her and Joni. He seemed a nasty piece of work.

'Coach, you might want to see this,' said Jiang. Everyone gathered around his screen.

Roo's stomach did a horrified flip.

Black-and-white footage showed Hoody Boy entering Barn B at 13.08 the previous day. Moments later, he took a small bottle from his pocket and let himself into River Spirit's stall.

'What did I tell you!' crowed the coach. 'I knew that teenager was shifty as soon as I laid eyes on him.'

'The sheer brazen nerve of the boy,' blasted Lloyd Cooper. 'What's he up to?'

Roo had asked herself the same question when she'd found Hoody Boy kneeling at the grey mare's feet, shaking a brown bottle. She'd convinced herself he'd meant no harm, but what if he had?

She began to panic. What if security cameras had captured her actions too?

'That boy's in that stall for twelve minutes,' said Eddie, watching the timer. 'What do you reckon's going on?' Since there was no security camera in River's stall, the answer remained a mystery.

'Two guesses,' Dale told him. 'Either he's been paid by one of Rhianna's rivals to dope River, or he's giving her a tranquilliser to make her easier to handle when he steals her later. Maybe he and his dad planned to take her when they stole Wonder, but got interrupted.'

Roo was paralysed by guilt. What if it was her fault that Wonder had been stolen? What if he was dead or gone forever and Roo was partly responsible because she'd caught a boy in the act of administering a strange substance to a horse and had covered up for him?

Before she could think how or what to confess, her own image appeared on the screen. Her face burned as she watched herself silently yelling for help before moving off to distract the groom.

Out of the corner of her eye, Roo caught her aunt's startled look and Rhianna's questioning one.

Roo stared fixedly at the floor, filled with shame.

'My, what a coincidence that Ruby just happened to be in Barn B at the same time as that hooded menace,' said Mr Cooper reproachfully. 'Ruby, did you witness that brat up to no good?'

'No, I did not,' answered Roo, which was true. Even with the aid of CCTV, it was impossible to tell what Hoody Boy had been up to in the stall.

'You were just metres away from River's stall! It's hard to credit that you saw and heard nothing,' accused the coach.

'For goodness' sake, listen to yourselves,' interrupted Rhianna's mum. 'Are you seriously suggesting that a girl who's been a fan of Wonder for years is in league with scrap metal merchants? Wasn't it you who originally hired Vano last December, Dale? I distinctly recall you saying he was very helpful.'

'He took away a muck spreader,' the coach retorted with a scowl. 'It's hardly rocket science. And last time he didn't bring along the son.'

'Has it occurred to anyone that Roo might have foiled a second crime?' demanded Joni. 'It's entirely possible that she saved River Spirit from harm by interrupting whatever it was the boy had planned? *If* he had anything planned. He could just have been admiring the horse, as Roo herself did only a few minutes later.'

'Excellent points,' said Rhianna.

Roo was grateful to her aunt for standing up for her. She didn't feel capable of defending herself.

'As to whether or not the boy drugged or injured River Spirit, surely it's easy enough to discover,' Joni went on. 'Did anyone ride or train the mare today? How was she?'

'Shelby rode her this afternoon,' answered the coach. 'Admittedly, she was raring to go and jumped like a star. If the kid did give her a sleeping potion, she must have slept it off.'

Lloyd Cooper had stopped listening and was peering at the screen. 'What's that, Jiang? Can you zoom in on it?'

Roo's stomach did another quadruple flip. The camera technician was homing in on the message Hoody Boy was crafting in the shavings outside River's stall. A streak of shadow obscured the first line, but the second was readable when the boy stepped away.

YOU'LL REGRET IT

'Well, there it is in black and white,' thundered Mr Cooper. 'We have the Roma boy on tape, threatening us. Obviously, he and his dad have some grudge against Starwood Farm. Look at him running away, furtively checking over his shoulder. That's it. I'm calling Pickle. I'd say we have our chief suspects.'

'And I'd say we've heard about as much as we can bear,' said Joni.

Roo fervently agreed. She turned to Rhianna. 'Good luck finding Wonder. Keep our deposit and use it to help with the search. Goodbye.'

19.

PRIVATE EYES

'Okay, spit it out, Roo,' said Joni as they walked back to their car. 'What haven't you told me?'

'I didn't not tell you on purpose,' protested Roo. 'We were busy looking for cottages and buying Bluebird and being grilled by Detective Inspector Pickle.'

'I understand, but tell me now. Leave nothing out.'

So Roo filled Joni in on the conversations she'd overheard in Barn A, and described her encounter with Hoody Boy and the mysterious brown bottle.

When she got to the part about the message, Joni said: 'You're certain that's what he wrote? "DON'T DO IT. YOU'LL REGRET IT."'

'Uh-huh. Except that now Wonder's been stolen, I'm worried he could have meant: "Don't buy the horse because we're about to steal it."'

Roo groaned. 'I did the wrong thing, didn't I? I should have reported him. It's just, well, after the way Coach Dering treated his dad, I didn't want to get them into trouble.'

'Your heart did the right thing,' her aunt said firmly. 'That's what matters. It's also important to keep in mind that everybody in this sorry business is innocent until they're proven guilty. Nothing enrages me more than what just went on in that room.'

'You mean, because they didn't just question what Vano's son was doing in River's stall?'

'Which would be fair,' said her aunt. 'Any horse owner would have a stroke if a stranger started creeping about in their pride and joy's stall, writing weird messages.'

'But Mr Cooper went further,' Roo went on. 'He mentioned the boy being Roma the same way Dale talked about Vano and his son as gypsies who couldn't be trusted. It's like they've already tried them and found them guilty.'

'That's why I'm so furious,' said Joni. 'For centuries, Roma communities have been the victims of relentless racism and persecution. If some lazy detective watches the Starwood CCTV footage and rushes to judgement, Vano and his son might find themselves being framed for a crime they didn't commit.'

'Then shouldn't we try to warn them?' asked Roo, feeling the same strong instinct to shield the teenager from those who'd judge him as she had in Barn B. 'And what do we do about Wonder? I don't want to give up on trying to find the real thieves.'

'We're not giving up, I can promise you that,' her aunt said with conviction. 'We're only just getting started. And, yes, we will try to find a way to warn Vano and his son.'

They'd reached the Coopers' Tuscan mansion, where Joni had parked. Night lights made magic of its dusky pink walls, manicured lawns, and the blue sliver of pool sparkling through the shadowed shrubs.

A week ago, Roo couldn't imagine anywhere she'd rather live. Now she recalled her father's words. *Ruby Roo, perfect plus perfect plus perfect doesn't always add up to happy or lucky . . .*

Their rented Range Rover gave an electronic squeak as Joni unlocked it. Before she and Roo could hop in, they heard rapid steps. Breathing hard and clutching a stitch, Rhianna's mum came running up to them.

'Ms Jackson, Ruby, thank goodness I caught you.'

She handed Joni a fistful of cash. 'This is all the money I could gather at short notice. It's not quite £2,000 but it's close. I want to hire you to investigate Wonder Boy's disappearance.'

Roo and Joni stared at her in astonishment.

Joni recovered first. 'But what about the police? Your husband seems to have complete confidence in Detective Inspector Pickle and his constables.'

'Ms Jackson—'

'Joni.'

'Joni, I think we all know that the combined energy of Pickle and his three stooges wouldn't light a twenty-watt bulb.'

Roo snorted with laughter but managed to turn it into a cough.

Rosslyn Cooper went on: 'My husband just called the detective about the CCTV footage. Pickle informed him that the soonest he can spare a man to interview Vano and his son – whom I believe to be blameless – is Friday.

'Personally, I have no faith that the police will find my daughter's horse before it's too late. By contrast, you and Roo have shown you care deeply about Wonder Boy. If you agree to take on his case, I believe you'll give it your all.'

'Yes, we will!' answered Roo and Joni together.

Rosslyn gave them a tired smile. 'Added to which, I don't want any gossip. I trust you'll be discreet?'

'You can count on it,' Joni assured her.

'Then can I speak frankly? Long before Wonder was stolen, there were issues of concern at our yard. Unexplained accidents. Equipment tampering. On their own, they didn't amount to much, but some of the incidents could have led to serious injury or worse. It's almost as if someone is trying to jeopardise Rhianna's Olympic hopes.'

'Are you suggesting sabotage?' asked Joni.

'Truthfully, I don't know. However, if you'll agree to search for Wonder, I want you to follow the trail wherever it leads.'

Roo tried to keep the shock from showing on her face. For years, she'd seen Starwood through rose-coloured spectacles. On the evidence of two brief visits to the yard, nothing and no one was quite the way she'd imagined. Not even Rhianna's strawberry-cheesecake-baking mum.

'What if the trail leads back here?' asked Roo, thinking of the uneasy feeling that had crept over her as she walked around Starwood; the sense that something wasn't right.

'*Wherever* it leads,' Rosslyn Cooper repeated.

'We'll do our best. More than that, I can't promise,' Joni cautioned her. She returned Rosslyn's cash with a smile. 'Keep your money. If we do find Wonder, that'll be reward enough.'

'That means more than I can say. Whatever the outcome, I'm indebted to you.'

Rosslyn pressed a scrap of paper into Joni's hand. 'Here's my private number. Keep me posted.'

A moment later, the front door clicked shut. Viewed from the outside, the Tuscan mansion was perfectly peaceful once more.

20.

COVER STORIES

With no time to lose, the new sleuths launched their investigation at the campsite that night. Wonder had been missing for fifteen hours. The clock was ticking.

'It's a pity that we have to wait until 4 p.m. tomorrow to get Bluebird,' remarked Roo over sweetcorn chowder at the Ranch House Café. 'Do you think we should beg the salesman to get her ready sooner?'

'I think that taking a morning to plot our next move is exactly what's needed,' said Joni. 'If we're to succeed in finding Wonder, preparation will be key. This is no ordinary crime. To abduct a highly strung horse from a secure estate, leaving no sign, takes cunning and planning. If we're to have any hope of catching the villains, we'll need to outsmart them.'

'*But how?*' asked Roo.

'Attention to detail,' replied her aunt, starting a list on her phone. 'We'll be no use to Wonder if we track him down only to realise that we forgot to charge our phones or should have brought a Swiss Army knife or crampons—'

Roo's eyes widened. '*Crampons?* Aren't those the things you use to climb cliffs?'

'I only meant that, as far as possible, we should leave nothing to chance.'

'Then we'll definitely need a headcollar, some pony nuts, and an equine first aid kit. And matches,' Roo added cheekily. 'We mustn't forget a king-sized box of waterproof matches.'

Joni laughed. 'Trust me, matches, a fire flint, thermal vests, multitools, and four-seasons sleeping bags are top of my wish list. The only thing more important is enrolling you in an online school.'

Roo's heart sank. 'Who cares about school when Wonder Boy's missing!'

'I do, and so will you when you realise how much catching up you have to do.'

Joni added a laptop to the list, along with a human first aid kit, hiking boots, groceries, and 'accessories' for their cover stories.

'*What* cover stories?' asked Roo.

'If we're to follow Wonder Boy's trail wherever it leads, we might have to play different parts, like actors, in order to get access to the people and clues that will lead us to the kidnapper's hideout,' explained Joni.

Roo tried to visualise that hideout. In films, stolen horses were invariably found in abandoned barns on remote farms. Would Wonder be in a broken-down barn too? How long would it take to find him?

'Good thing we bought Bluebird,' she told her aunt. 'Now we'll have our own mobile detective agency!'

Thinking about the camper made Roo reflect on the twists of fate that had led them this far.

It was sheer chance that she'd saved the rucksack containing her dad's coat, lighter, and lottery ticket from the Betty inferno. Chance that Roo's dream horse had come up for sale, chance that he'd been stolen, and chance that she and Joni had been hired to find him.

Were her parents watching over her?

Roo hoped so. It comforted her to believe that they were out there among the stars, lending her courage. Willing her on to find Wonder.

***

It had been a long, long day, but Roo and Joni still stayed up late, ordering supplies.

Joni kept having a fit about the cost of things, but Roo reminded her that, since they hadn't yet parted with the cash for Wonder, they had plenty.

As the bill mounted, Roo had a funny image of Mr Doukis, their solicitor, having kittens as he reviewed the credit card receipts for items as varied as a Monty Roberts Dually Halter, a lab coat, and manuka honey wound dressings.

The next morning, deliveries arrived thick and fast. Joni popped out to collect a few items from nearby stores too. By lunchtime, Roo was setting up a super-fast laptop at the Ranch House Café.

While her aunt made notes in a scrapbook on what they knew so far, Roo created a digital file: 'THE CASE OF THE MISSING SHOWJUMPER'.

She sat back, daunted by the sheer scale of the task ahead.

'Where do we begin?'

Joni was sipping a milkshake beside her. 'Like all good investigators, we begin at the beginning – with the five W's and an H.'

'What are those?'

'Questions that might lead us to an answer or, better still, to Wonder himself. Here, let me show you.'

Joni typed:

Who stole Wonder Boy?

What happened?

When was he snatched?

Where was he stolen from?

Why was he stolen?

How was it done?

'We know the when, what, and where,' said Roo, typing as she spoke. 'Wonder Boy was kidnapped between 3.55 a.m. and 4.05 a.m. on Tuesday, February second, from his stall at Starwood. We don't know the who, why, or how. To get to the truth, we need to start with number one. Who stole Wonder Boy?'

She considered the question.

'Rhianna and her mum are worried that it was an inside job. Rhianna's dad, Dale, and DI Pickle seem to have made up their minds: Vano and his son are their prime suspects. We believe they're innocent. Before we go hunting for the real thieves, we need to warn Vano and Hoody Boy that the police might pitch up to interview them on Friday.'

'I spoke to Rosslyn Cooper,' said Joni. 'She's going to find their address for us. She stressed again the importance of keeping our investigation confidential. She hasn't breathed a word to Rhianna, her husband, or Dale, and doesn't plan to. She doesn't want to worry them any further. She ended the call by saying: "Forgive my husband's ill-chosen words about the scrap merchant's son the other night. It's completely out of character."'

'That's weird – Dale used the exact same words about Wonder when he went berserk for no apparent reason,' said Roo. 'What's going on at Starwood that's making people and horses act out of character?'

'An excellent question,' replied her aunt. 'That's what we need to find out.'

***

On Wednesday afternoon, when Roo should have been taking delivery of her dream horse, she was instead moving into a Mediterranean-blue camper with a white trim.

The salesman had restored Bluebird to her full glory so lovingly and expertly that there were gasps of envy from their fellow campers when he drove her into Green Acres.

The silver wings on her front bumper shone in the sunshine.

Inside, every glass, pan, and surface gleamed, and the bed linen had been washed and ironed. There was even a vase of fresh daffodils in the kitchen.

Roo's heart swelled with pride as she stepped in. And when she climbed the ladder to her sleeping nook, Fearless Fire was waiting for her on the bedside shelf.

Was *he* the reason they'd been lucky enough to get Bluebird?

Everything about the camper felt friendly and homely. Just being in her colourful living area made Roo feel safe. But camper storage was tight, and they had to get creative to fit everything.

Joni had ordered a month's worth of groceries. Roo found herself breathing in as she squeezed black rice, noodles, miso, Keralan curry paste, teriyaki sauce, ketchup, strawberry jam, peanut butter, and tinned beans, tomatoes, and coconut milk into Bluebird's slender cupboards.

There were fresh and frozen bits too: blueberries, bananas, bread, veggies, tofu, kimchi, cheese, yoghurt, oat milk, and vegetarian sausages and burgers.

Finding space was a military exercise. By nightfall, Roo was shattered. Given a choice, she'd happily have retired to her new sleeping nook with a peanut butter sandwich and a mystery novel, but they had a real-life mystery to solve.

Shortly after 8 p.m., Rosslyn Cooper sent through Vano's address.

Roo did a Google search for New Forest Metal Merchants. 'It's an hour and forty minutes away.'

'Easy,' said Joni. 'We'll drive there first thing.'

Roo glanced up. 'What's to stop us leaving now? We have a portable hotel room.'

Joni grinned. She reached for Bluebird's keys. 'You're a girl after my own heart, Roo. Let's go. We'll spend the night at a secret spot I know, and surprise New Forest Metal Merchants with an early morning visit. In the unlikely event they *are* harbouring a chestnut showjumper, we'll catch them red-handed.'

'And if they're not?'

'We'll question them, as we would with any potential witness. Perhaps they noticed something suspicious on that day they visited Starwood, something that has so far escaped anyone's notice. If we help them, maybe they'll help us.'

21.

MORNING STAR

'Wakey wakey, rise and shine!'

Roo groaned. 'But it's the middle of the night. I can see a star.'

'That's Venus, the morning star,' said her aunt, reaching up to Roo's sleeping nook and tugging her toes. 'We're in the New Forest, remember? It's time for you to shower and put on your detective hat. I'd like to do a recce of New Forest Metal Merchants before the place opens.'

'But this bed is bliss.' Roo stretched, reluctant to leave her soft, warm cocoon. Then she remembered Wonder. Where was he waking up? A musty, cold barn? A rival showjumper's secret hideaway? Wherever he was, it would be somewhere where love didn't matter at all. Roo shuddered at the thought.

Joni didn't notice. 'The good news is, your bed will still be blissful when you return to it this evening. Now move. I'll start making breakfast.'

***

Twenty minutes later, Roo was sitting at Bluebird's wooden table eating banana pancakes from a cherry-red plate, exactly as she'd visualised herself doing. Drenched with maple syrup, they were every bit as delicious as she'd imagined.

Through the camper's rear window, sunrise was bronzing the

ancient leaves of the New Forest. Roo held her breath as a herd of fallow deer moved like spotted faeries through the misty glen.

Watching them, Roo resolved to rise early every day. If dawn was when nature was at her most magical, Roo would have no trouble getting up with the birds. She didn't want to miss a minute.

As she savoured the last bite of pancake, her whole body thrummed with anticipation. It was hard to take in that her new life was real.

She was a lottery-winning millionaire.

She was a robbery suspect turned private investigator, hired by her hero's mum to find her stolen dream horse.

She was in the New Forest, where wild ponies had roamed since the Ice Age, eating breakfast in a winged camper.

In some ways, that was the most mind-blowing detail of all.

After just one night in Bluebird, she understood why Joni always talked about Betty as if she'd been a cherished co-adventurer rather than a hunk of ageing metal. Already, the camper felt like a friend.

First, though, they had to take care of business.

Roo tried once more to think like a detective.

'We've come to the New Forest for two main reasons,' she said to her aunt: 'To investigate whether Hoody Boy and his dad had anything to do with Wonder's disappearance, and, if not, to find clues and information.'

'Right,' replied Joni. 'From what you heard, they were at Starwood for over an hour waiting to speak to Dale. Did they observe anything unusual or suspicious? Bear in mind that we still don't know what the boy and his little brown bottle were doing in River Spirit's stall. Until we do, let's proceed with caution.'

'Got it.'

Roo bent to lace up her Converses. In that instant, their mission – FINDING WONDER – became real.

At she stepped out into the misty morning, Roo had a sense of a page being turned in her life. What would the next chapter bring?

Excitement, mingled with apprehension, surged through her veins.

Ready or not, their adventure was beginning.

22.

CENTAUR

Staking out a scrap metal yard from behind a rusting minibus, toppled, like a dead beetle, on the edge of a dank and lonely wood, was spookier than any TV mystery Roo had ever seen. She flinched at every screech and snapped twig.

Behind a chain-link fence, a peeling sign warned: BEWARE OF THE DOGS. Teetering car parts, radiators, and rusting farm machinery clanked and squeaked beside a shuttered mobile office. Not a single bird sang.

Roo didn't need her aunt to tell her that this was the hidden New Forest, a secretive world far from Lyndhurst's trendy cafés, gift shops, and tarot readers selling tourists dreamcatchers and crystals.

'New Forest Metal Merchants should be open by now, but it looks boarded up to me,' said Joni. 'Let's try the cottage we saw on Google Maps. We'll take the path through the woods to avoid attracting attention.'

'What about the vicious dogs?' worried Roo, but her aunt was already moving off through the trees.

Roo put a hand in her pocket and held tight to Fearless Fire. Almost immediately, she found herself thinking not about the slavering hounds that might tear her limb from limb, but about the free-roaming ponies that had trodden these paths for over 500,000 years.

A swishing tail caught her attention. Beyond the treeline was a band of New Forest ponies. They'd stopped grazing to gaze in her direction. Roo stared at them in delight. Most were bay or chestnut in colouring, with sloping shoulders and strong quarters. There wasn't a glimmer of white on any of them.

From what she'd read, around five thousand ponies wandered the New Forest. Most were screened by trees or field shelters, or covered from ears to tail in winter rugs. Where better to 'disappear' a stolen showjumper?

The ponies had settled Roo's nerves. A rush of energy spurred her on. She caught up with Joni at the edge of the wood and they crossed a wooden bridge together. Beyond it was a picket fence and two thatched cottages.

A mailbox confirmed that the one on the right was Vano's. A life-sized metal sculpture of a galloping racehorse graced a lawn strewn with cherry blossoms.

When they reached it, Roo bent to read the horse's name on a copper plate: 'ECLIPSE: 1764–1789.' Beneath it was written: 'Eclipse First, The Rest Nowhere . . .'

'Dad and I watched a documentary on Eclipse,' she told Joni excitedly. 'He was the great-great-grandson of the Darley Arabian, one of the founder stallions of the Thoroughbred breed. About ninety-five per cent of racehorses have Eclipse in their pedigree.'

She ran a hand over the cool steel muscles of the sculpture. The glint in its shining eyes gave the impression that it might spring to life and make a bid for freedom at any moment.

'It's not for sale,' called a voice. A woman was leaning over the porch railings of the cottage next door. 'Not for any price, and, believe me, Elena's had offers that would make your eyes water.'

'It's stunning,' said Roo, following her aunt over to the fence.

The woman smiled. 'You love horses, I see. Some say Eclipse was the greatest of them all. Never beaten in any of his eighteen races. He only retired because there was no competition.'

She gestured towards the trees. 'Some New Forest ponies have his sire's blood in their veins. What was his name again, Rod – Eclipse's daddy?'

A man joined her on the porch. 'Marske.'

'That's it, Marske,' said the woman. 'Now, pets, if you're looking for Elena and Vano, they've done a midnight flit.'

Roo stared. 'What do you mean?'

'They've done a bunk. Came and went in the dead of Tuesday night without so much as a goodbye. Left their dogs with relations and a note in my mailbox saying they've gone to Spain to visit a sick relative.'

'The old "sick relative" excuse,' Joni whispered to Roo. 'We need to be careful. We may have misread this situation. People who do midnight flits abroad are often running away from trouble. I should know. I've done it myself.'

Roo had a sudden memory of Hoody Boy pressing his finger to his lips in River Spirit's stall. She'd so wanted to believe that he and his dad were innocent. What if they weren't?

'Any idea where in Spain they've gone?' Joni asked the woman.

'Not the foggiest. Possibly Andalusia. Elena's mother has a farm there. Where is it that they grow all the oranges?'

A hard knot formed in Roo's stomach. What if Wonder had already been smuggled to Europe? The thieves could have dyed his white blaze and cut his chestnut mane.

They might be planning to give him a new identity and launch him on the international showjumping circuit. He was still a champion, even if he wasn't an Olympic-level champion.

Still worth a quarter of a million.

Joni prompted: 'Is Elena's mum's farm near Valencia or Seville?'

'Seville, that's the one,' confirmed the woman. 'If it's the farm they've gone to, Vano will find it tough. He's a wizard with dogs, but nervous of horses. Some childhood accident or other. Elena's the opposite. Makes a living sculpting them. And hares. She does love a hare.'

'Did the note say when they'd be back?' Roo interjected before the woman could go off on another tangent.

'Only that they'd be grateful if Rod would keep an eye on their cottage. Obviously expecting to be gone a while. Well, you don't know with a sick person, do you, especially if they're elderly. Could be days, could be months.'

'Did their teenager go with them?' asked Joni.

'Skylar? Doubt it. Skylar will be with Magician. They're inseparable. Like one being, really. Like a – what's the word, Rod? Centurion?'

Roo was still taking in Hoody Boy's unexpected name – a name like a starry summer's night. And who was this magician?

'Centaur,' supplied the neighbour's husband. 'Half person, half horse.'

For Roo, that's when the penny dropped.

Joni said casually: 'Do you know where we might find Skylar?'

'Ooh, I can't help you there. Haven't seen Skylar or Magician in ages. Last I heard they were working for – what was it, Rod? Unicorn something or other.'

'It was Pegasus, sweetness. Pegasus Productions.'

MAGICIAN

23.

SKYLAR

Roo held her breath as Bluebird crawled one vehicle closer to the film set security gate. A guard with a clipboard was grilling each driver.

According to their website, Pegasus Productions trained stunt horses for movies. Magician, a black Friesian stallion, was their brightest star. Finding him had proved unexpectedly easy. The challenging part, Roo and Joni knew, would be talking their way on to the set of *The Last Messenger*, his latest project, currently being shot at a stately home in Somerset.

They still didn't know what Skylar did. Amid the runaway stagecoaches and rearing steeds on Pegasus's website, there'd been no mention of any human employees. But, Roo reasoned, if they could find Magician, Hoody Boy wouldn't be too far behind.

'This could be tricky,' said Joni as the car in front moved off. 'Do you have our props ready?'

'Think so.' Roo's voice was muffled by the bouquet of red roses she was clutching. 'One feed bucket, one laboratory coat, one equine first aid kit, and two dozen red roses. Anything else?'

'My business cards. They're in the glove compartment.'

Roo extracted them with difficulty. Joni selected the Massage Therapist, Veterinary Nurse, and Production Assistant cards and handed the rest to Roo to put away.

'Are these real or fake?' asked Roo, wondering if her

aunt was in the habit of getting business cards printed for non-existent roles.

'They're real,' said Joni, affronted. 'What can I say? I've had a lot of jobs. Oh dear, the guard looks as if he eats nails for breakfast. That's the third person he's turned away. Quick, Roo, hand me my lab coat. Have the equine first aid kit in full view and follow my lead.'

It was late afternoon on February fifth. They'd been in Somerset since lunchtime. While recceing the area around the stately home, they'd spotted a notice from the filmmakers apologising to local residents for any disruption that might be caused by that evening's night filming.

'That suits our purposes admirably,' Joni said. 'If we talk our way on to the set a couple of hours before the shoot begins, the actors and crew will be absorbed in their preparations. They'll be less likely to notice a couple of interlopers.'

'What's an interloper?'

'Someone who enters a place or social gathering without being asked and without permission.'

'Yep, that's us,' agreed Roo.

Joni lowered her window as the stony-faced guard approached.

'Nurse Jackson for Pegasus Productions,' she said briskly, passing him the Veterinary Nurse card. 'They have a horse down. Suspected colic. It's an emergency.'

The guard was unmoved. 'Don't know nothing about that. You're not on my list. No authorisation, no entry.'

Roo leaned forward. 'Do you have any idea how much agony a horse suffers if it's dying from a twisted gut?'

'Don't care,' said the guard. 'I have my orders. If a horse has a bellyache, tell 'em to give it cod-liver oil. Worked a treat for my granny. And next time, get proper authorisation.'

Joni matched his steely stare. 'Sir, the horse with suspected colic is a bigger star than any human on this production, including Adele Warner. He's taken years to train. If he dies, *The Last Messenger* will be shut down in days.'

She took out her mobile and began tapping in a number. 'I'm getting the director on the line just so he knows who's responsible if his production goes bust.'

The guard practically snatched the phone from her hand. 'Lady, stop! I never said I wouldn't let you through, only that you weren't on my list.'

He raised the barrier. 'There's a vacant space next to the catering trailer. Hope you save the horse. What did you say his name was?'

'I didn't,' was Joni's tart reply as she put her foot on the accelerator.

***

'You're good at blagging your way into things,' said Roo in a suspicious tone as her aunt parked Bluebird beside the catering trailer.

Every time she thought she was getting to know her aunt, something happened to make her think again. Joni seemed to have more secrets than the average MI5 spy.

'Do you think so?' Joni removed her white lab coat to reveal a black T-shirt and blazer. 'Ah, well, needs must. Give me the roses. You bring the bucket.'

'What's the bucket for?'

'People seldom question a person carrying a bucket or a bouquet of flowers. They figure they have a purpose.'

Roo climbed out of the camper and took in the bizarre sight of World War II nurses and soldiers, some bloodied or on crutches, eating hot dogs and chatting on their phones.

'There's the sign for the equestrian block,' said Roo. 'If we head for the horses, hopefully we'll find Skylar.'

Despite the seriousness of their mission, Roo was wide-eyed with amazement as they walked along a street built to resemble Paris in World War II, and past a field in the final stages of becoming a scorched and barren battlefield.

A cannon was being hauled into place by a beeping machine. Elsewhere, crew members tidied away wires, organised lights, and sprayed rust paint on to curls of barbed wire.

On towering scenery boards behind the battlefield, a painted storm was brewing.

Suddenly, a door in a rain cloud burst open. Adele Warner, *The Last Messenger*'s star actress, came flying out and stalked across the battlefield in stilettos, talking on her phone.

'Darling, they don't pay me enough for this,' she ranted as she swept past Roo and Joni. 'I want out of my contract. The director just called me a prima donna. Is it unreasonable to expect a dressing room that doesn't stink of horse manure? He thought he could make things better by spritzing it with Chanel No. 5.'

'Now there's a star in need of red roses,' was Joni's droll comment. 'Roo, you carry on to the equestrian block. I'll meet you there shortly. I'm going to have a little chat to Adele Warner. As Magician's co-star in *The Last Messenger*, Adele will be working closely with his handlers. We're presuming Skylar is one of them.

Adele might be able to give me an insight into the boy's character, good or bad.'

Joni hurried after the actress, thrusting out the bouquet. 'Pardon me, Ms Warner, it would be my great honour to give you these . . .'

'Oh, my word, you've made my day!' exclaimed the star, burying her beautiful face in the crimson blooms. 'You're a total love. What did you say your name was?'

Grinning to herself, Roo continued towards the equestrian block. She rounded the corner of the stately home and stopped dead. She set down the bucket.

A black horse so exquisite that it could have been a figment of her imagination was prancing beside Hoody Boy/Skylar in a practice arena.

Roo realised with a thrill that the teenager was the stallion's trainer, not a mere groom. The pair were rehearsing a scene, but it wasn't going to plan.

Skylar was trying to persuade the horse to gallop to a striped post at the end of the arena, and wait until he whistled for it before trotting back. The stallion seemed reluctant to leave his side. When he finally did, he quit halfway, and raced back to Skylar.

The young trainer never lost patience or used a whip. He simply slowed everything down and returned to basics. He and the horse trotted the length of the arena together. They had a little fun with a Swiss ball. They shared half an apple.

The magnificent creature wore no bridle or saddle. His rippled mane and tail flowed free. His feathered feet high-stepped proudly. When he cantered, pools of shine rolled across his black coat like sheet lightning.

Hoody Boy's black hoody and jeans looked less threatening in this environment. If anything, they seemed exactly right.

At long last, the stallion seemed to understand what was required of him. This time, when he returned, Skylar reached up to hug him, burying his face in the horse's thick, crinkly mane.

Roo was close enough to see the stallion's dark eyes squeeze shut in silent joy. Leaning together, the two seemed for a moment to become one.

In a world of lights, cameras, and action, Skylar was the horse's safe space.

'Can I help you?' asked a man pushing a wheelbarrow, jolting Roo from her trance. He smiled. 'Sorry, I didn't mean to startle you. They're quite something, aren't they? Hard to believe the kid's only sixteen.'

Roo said: 'I was hoping to talk to Skylar.'

'Hey, Skylar! There's someone to see you.'

Hoody Boy signalled to Magician. The stallion gave a disdainful snort and took himself off to a green horse lorry parked on the other side of the arena. There, he began tugging wisps of hay from a hanging net.

Skylar turned to stride towards Roo, pushing back the hood of his sweatshirt as he came.

Roo gaped.

Walking towards her was a tall teenage girl with short, tousled dark hair, and an impish face full of light and fun and mischief.

'Who's asking?' Skylar said with a grin.

24.

TRICK HORSE

'What are *you* doing here?' asked Skylar, recognising Roo at once and staring at her in surprise.

'You're a girl!' Roo burst out.

Skylar gave a derisory snort. 'Does it matter?'

'I just assumed . . .'

'People often do. *Assume*, that is. I'm part person, part horse . . . Couldn't care less about the rest.'

Roo grinned. 'Me neither. Anyway, it's way cooler to be a centaur. I've been thinking that since—' She almost let slip about the New Forest neighbour but caught herself in time. 'Uh, I'd like to be a centaur, too.'

Skylar's own smile faded. 'Why are you here? Do you know someone working on the film? I hope you didn't go telling tales on me at Starwood? The whole reason I risked making you a message was to thank you for not ratting me out. Did you even take my advice?'

'What advice? Are you talking about your message on the floor of Barn B? So it *was* for me?'

'Who else?' scoffed Skylar, as if only a dimwit could have misinterpreted the meaning behind her wood-shaving wordcraft.

She added more graciously: 'What you did that day took guts. I could tell you were scared, but you took a chance and trusted me.' She glanced at Magician. 'If you'd called security, I wouldn't have been able to help River Spirit, and I certainly wouldn't be here now.'

'It was nothing.' Roo was embarrassed. 'I overheard Dale Dering. I was in the tack room, and I saw how he treated you and your dad. I couldn't bear the thought of getting you into trouble.'

The memory of his vile remarks – *Keep an eye on those gypsies. I don't trust them an inch* – made Roo feel sick.

Skylar grimaced. 'I was fuming, but me and Dad are different that way. He doesn't rise to that stuff. When people hate on him or put him down for his job or his Roma heritage, he just shrugs it off. Says it shows him the measure of a person.

'But that's also why he was floored by the way the coach talked to him. The last time Dale Dering asked him to pick up scrap metal at Starwood, he could not have been more friendly or polite. Tipped Dad for doing a great job. Insisted on paying for his lunch and fuel. Told him he'd be in touch with more work.

'Dad couldn't get over the change in the man on Monday. "Jekyll and Hyde" was how he put it. Then, to add insult to injury, Dale goes and lies about ringing Dad in the first place.'

Roo was struck by the 'Jekyll and Hyde' description of the coach. What had changed between Vano's December and February visits to Starwood?

'Your father's sure it was Dale who rang him?'

Skylar was distracted. She watched anxiously as a worker in paint-splattered overalls paused beside the green lorry to pet Magician. The stallion dipped his head towards her.

It made Roo realise how vulnerable horses were. Rhianna herself had described Starwood as 'Grand Central Station' busy.

Literally anyone could have slipped Wonder Boy a tranquilliser that made him easy to handle later that night when he was stolen.

The woman moved on and Skylar relaxed.

'Where were we? Oh yeah, the phone call. To be honest, Dad couldn't say for certain it was the coach's voice on the line. Also, by the time I asked him about it, he'd had a shock, so he wasn't thinking straight.'

'What kind of shock?' asked Roo, who could hardly admit she already knew that Skylar's parents had done a midnight flit to Spain to be with a sick relative.

'My grandma in Spain broke her hip,' said Skylar. 'Dad and Mum were in Margate visiting cousins. They had to rush home to the New Forest, pack up, and catch a red-eye flight to Seville on Wednesday. My nana's still in hospital.'

She broke off. 'Oh, no. Not again.'

Two child extras dressed in hessian orphan costumes were offering treats to Magician.

'Don't feed him sweets!' yelled Skylar, breaking into a sprint. Roo ran after her.

When they reached the green lorry, the stallion was already munching up something tasty.

'Sorry, miss,' said the boy, not sounding sorry. He and his mate tore away laughing.

Skylar rounded on the guard who'd come to investigate. Roo was close enough to see her dark eyes flash.

'Tyrell, this is supposed to be a secure area. Any time I turn my back, random people start feeding the horses toffees and bits of burger bun. If Magician gets colic or drops dead after eating chocolate, this movie is over. He's in every second scene.'

Her words were uncomfortably close to those invented by Joni to get them past the main gate. Roo felt slightly guilty.

'Geez, Skylar, chill,' groused the guard, clearly irritated at being told off by a teenager. 'They're only kids.'

'Did you get their names?'

'Funnily enough, no, I did not. I was too busy looking out for psycho fans and pyromaniacs, like the one who shut down the set two days ago. Or has that slipped your mind already?'

'From what I've heard, all that happened is the sleeve of one costume was found smouldering,' said Skylar. 'I don't understand why they cancelled the shoot.'

'Because we still haven't discovered who left a glowing cigarette butt in the most flammable unit on site,' Tyrell told her crossly. 'If the wardrobe mistress hadn't come in on her day off, it might have been deadly serious.'

Roo couldn't believe her ears. *Psycho fans? Pyromaniacs? Sneaky extras endangering star horses?* She'd pictured film sets as glamorous affairs, full of pampered actors and professional crew. The *Last Messenger* set had more intrigue than a thriller.

As Skylar and Tyrell speculated about who might be responsible (A deranged fan? A fired cast member?), Roo took the opportunity to get acquainted with Magician.

His crinkly mane was as soft as bunny fluff. His ebony coat slipped like satin beneath Roo's palm when she stroked his powerful shoulder. Long black lashes shaded his kind, patient eyes.

The guard's radio crackled and popped. He lowered the volume.

Skylar was looking shamefaced. 'Sorry for overreacting, Tyrell. It's just that Magician's extra valuable now he's been voted Animal Actor of the Year.'

Tyrell was unimpressed. 'I'll do what I can to keep people away from him, Skylar, but I'm one guard for twelve horses, two dogs, and a coop of chickens. I'm not a robot with eyes in the back of my head.' He marched off.

Skylar checked her chunky diver's watch and glanced at Roo. 'I need to get Magician prepared for his scene. Uh, I still don't know your name.'

'Roo Thorn.'

In a parallel universe, Roo would have liked to be friends with Skylar and her magical stallion, but she wasn't here to make pals. She was a private investigator on an urgent quest. If Skylar and her dad were innocent – and, based on what she'd learned, Roo would have staked her life on it – she and Joni needed to hit the road to hunt for the real thieves.

Before she could beat a hasty retreat, Skylar said: 'You haven't answered my question, Roo Thorn. Did you take my advice and tell the Coopers that you didn't want their overpriced showjumper?'

'Yes and no,' hedged Roo.

'Can't be both. If you bought him, you're nuts. He's completely wrong for you.'

Roo was stung. 'No, he's not. You don't even know me. Anyway, it's none of your business. And now that he's been stolen, I'll probably never see him again.'

'*Stolen?*'

Skylar seemed stunned.

'Haven't you heard?' said Roo. 'It's all over the news.'

25.

PERSON OF INTEREST

A garish sunset was flaming over the charred battlefield when Skylar said: 'I haven't seen the news. I caught a train to Bristol on Tuesday and I've been working round the clock ever since.'

To Roo's surprise, Skylar's eyes were bright with strong emotion.

'I'm so sorry, Roo. I know how I'd feel if something happened to Magician. You must be ill with worry. I take it he's still missing?'

'He's been gone for four days. The police have got nowhere. There've been no ransom demands. No sightings. Wonder's just vanished off the face of the earth.'

'But the Coopers have about a thousand security cameras!'

'That's what's spooky. CCTV shows him dozing in his stall at 3.55 on Tuesday morning. Ten minutes later, the stall's empty. Rhianna's dad says it's like he was airlifted out of it by invisible aliens.'

'I think we can safely guarantee that Wonder was not airlifted into space by invisible aliens,' was Skylar's dry reply. 'He was ridden or driven off the farm by completely visible humans. It's like a special effects trick in a movie. It's a matter of figuring out how it was done.'

She started brushing Magician so vigorously that the stallion gave her a playful nip in reproach.

'The minute I walked into the yard at Starwood, I got a bad feeling about the place. Dad felt the same the last time he worked there. That's why he asked me to go with him. Everything about Starwood is so Instagram-perfect. I kept wondering if it was a facade just like that one.'

She gestured towards the storm-cloud scenery beside the battlefield.

'You'd never guess it, but there's a hive of activity behind that screen. Make-up artists are transforming actors into World War II characters. Special effects technicians are playing with lighting and gunpowder. Then there are the hangers-on – managers, agents, publicists, all sorts. Starwood's the same. Find out what's going on behind *their* screen and you'll have your thieves.'

Skylar's hand froze on the stallion's arched neck. She put down the dandy brush.

'Hold on, is that why you're here? You think that me and Dad might have had something to do with stealing Wonder?'

'Of course not,' protested Roo.

Skylar glared at her. 'I don't believe you.'

Roo blushed furiously. 'Okay, obviously, we didn't know for sure, but we were sure in our hearts that you were innocent. We came looking for you and your dad to warn you that that police might try to frame you. We also wanted to ask if you saw anyone acting suspiciously while you were at Starwood.'

'Can't say I did,' Skylar retorted mutinously. 'I didn't look in the mirror.'

'I'm very sorry,' said Roo. 'We're detectives. We had to keep an open mind till we spoke to you. Also, I did see you taking a small brown bottle into the stall of a horse that didn't belong to you. You just had a fit because strangers were getting too close to Magician and feeding him dodgy treats.'

Skylar grinned. 'Fair point. I'd have been suspicious of me too. I can explain—'

'You don't have to,' said Roo. 'Anyone watching you with Magician would know that you're incapable of harming a horse. Believe it or not, me and my aunt were only trying to help.'

'I don't need your help.'

Joni stepped out from behind the lorry. 'I think you might,' she said. 'I'm Joni Jackson, Roo's aunt. I'm not sure what she's told you, but we've been hired by Rhianna Cooper's mum to help find Wonder Boy. Skylar, Detective Inspector Pickle of the Sussex police has just arrived on set, so we don't have much time.'

She held out her phone. 'Take a look at this.'

The Argus had an 'exclusive' front page CCTV image of Skylar sneaking out of River Spirit's stall. Below it was a brief story . . .

HOODED FIGURE CLUE

Detectives on the trail of champion showjumper Wonder Boy, stolen on 2 February from the Sussex estate of teenage Olympic hopeful Rhianna Cooper, have released CCTV images of a 'person of interest' in their inquiry.

The alleged suspect appears to declare malicious intent by writing 'YOU'LL REGRET IT' in wood shavings on the barn floor.

A reward has been offered for information leading to an arrest. Contact DI Pickle of the Rural Crime Team on this number . . .

Skylar stared at the screen in horror. 'Malicious intent? I was doing the opposite. No, this can't be happening. Gerry, my boss, will go berserk. I'll be fired. He's forever telling me off for using my nana's healing potions on other people's sick animals.'

Magician's dark eyes never left his mistress's face. Sensing her distress, he nuzzled her. She stroked him gratefully and her shoulders squared with defiance.

'I've done nothing illegal. If the cops arrest me, I'll tell them the truth.'

'What is the truth?' asked Roo.

'That if Dale Dering couldn't tell River Spirit was lame, what he knows about horses wouldn't fit on a postage stamp. You could tell there was something wrong with that mare and you only watched her for a few minutes.'

'I thought that maybe, possibly, she was limping, but then I overheard Dale saying that the farrier had examined her and she was fine.'

'If you'd believed that I was hurting that horse, you'd have screamed blue murder,' declared Skylar. 'Instinctively, you knew I was helping. For your information, River Spirit had the early stages of pus in the foot, a hoof abscess. I used a plum blossom hammer to infuse the hoof with my nana's herbal mix.'

She added defensively: 'And before you ask, there was nothing in it that would contravene any regulations. Just manuka honey, calendula flower, tea tree oil, and silica salts.'

'And you just so happened to have your nana's herbal mix and a plum blossom hammer in your pocket?' Joni said with scepticism.

Skylar reddened. 'No, I fetched it from my father's truck after I noticed the mare limping. I was going to give it to her trainer, but I never got a chance. After the coach was rude, Dad wanted to leave that minute. I persuaded him to let me check on the mare. When I got to her stall, she was in so much pain, I couldn't just abandon her. I figured that nobody would ever be any the wiser. How was I supposed to know that Wonder Boy would be stolen on that exact night?'

The seriousness of her predicament struck her. 'What am I going to do? It'll be my word against Coach Dering's. Three guesses who the cops will believe.'

Roo suddenly remembered she'd videoed the mare. 'What if we could prove your story? The police would have to believe you then.'

Skylar and Joni leaned in as Roo played the clip on her small phone.

'The horse looks fit to me,' said her aunt.

Roo hit replay: 'No, Skylar's spot on. Watch River's right front foot.'

This time Joni noticed the limp immediately. 'Once you see it, it's impossible to unsee.'

Something similar had crossed Roo's mind when she pictured Dale as a spider at the centre of a web. Once seen, it was impossible to unsee. Was there really something sinister going on behind the scenes at Starwood Farm?

Roo was suddenly reminded of Rosslyn Cooper's fears about sabotage. *Follow the trail wherever it leads*, she'd urged them.

Where *would* it end? Roo was afraid to imagine.

A crew member jogged over to them: 'Skylar, the director says he'll be ready for Magician in thirty minutes.'

'Thanks, Hani.'

He tugged the stallion's forelock. 'Don't break a leg, Magician.'

As soon as he was gone, Skylar said: 'Maybe I should make a run for it?'

'Running will only make you look guilty,' Roo told her. 'If you'll trust us, we'll do everything we can to help you.'

'We certainly will,' promised Joni. 'Roo, with your permission, I'd like to show the video of River limping to DI Pickle. It'll prove that Skylar had a genuine reason for entering her stall and trying to treat her foot. I'll also inform him that I'm a private investigator tasked with looking into Wonder's case, though I won't tell him who hired me. That'll take the wind out of his sails.'

She smiled. 'Skylar, best of luck with your scene. Don't stress about Pickle. I'll handle him.'

'If he needs a witness, tell him that I saw Skylar trying to help River Spirit, and that the message on the barn floor was for me,' added Roo.

There was a catch in Skylar's voice. 'You'd do that when you hardly know me?'

'Any time,' Roo told her. She felt unaccountably sad that it was unlikely they'd ever meet again. As eventful as their film set visit had been, it hadn't turned up any new leads.

'I suppose I'd better start warming up Magician,' said Skylar.

She frowned as she put on his bridle. 'Wake him up, more like. Maybe we did too much rehearsing earlier. He seems half-asleep . . . Umm, Joni, Roo, if you fancy watching the shoot, you're welcome.'

'That would be so cool!' cried Roo. 'Please, can we stay, Joni?'

Her aunt smiled. 'Of course. I'd enjoy that too. But the moment Skylar and Magician are done with their scene, we'll need to leave. Okay, I'm going to try to knock some sense into Pickle. I'll meet you near the cannon at the battlefield.'

'Meet you by the cannon!'

After her aunt had gone, Roo said shyly, 'Can't wait to watch Magician, Skylar. Catch you later.'

She started to walk away.

'Roo, hold on,' called Skylar.

She came over with Magician. 'Sorry for what I said earlier about Wonder. He's a great horse. I only wrote "DON'T DO IT, YOU'LL REGRET IT" because I'd seen you ride him earlier.'

Roo was hurt. 'I know I'm not a very good rider – not compared to you or Rhianna. I haven't had a lesson in ages.'

'Whoa! I didn't mean your technique, which is sound. You ride beautifully, by the way. I mean that you have a connection with horses that's rare. For what it's worth, you're a natural. In time, you'll find a horse to match. Trust your instincts. A strong bond with a horse can save your life. Save theirs too.'

A shadow crossed her face. 'My nana taught me that. Everything I know about horses, I learned from her.'

She pulled up her hood and swung on to Magician's bare back. His black mane flew as they cantered into the twilight. From behind, they were a centaur once again.

26.

DISAPPEARING ACT

At the battlefield, Roo and Joni watched from behind a security cordon as the film crew buzzed about, making last-minute adjustments to lights or props.

'You should have seen Pickle deflate like a failed soufflé when I showed him your video clip,' Joni told Roo. 'By the end of our little chat, even Pickle realised he was playing a losing game. He'll need to ask Skylar a few questions, but she and her dad have been crossed off his suspect list.'

'I'm glad,' said Roo. 'With her gran in hospital, the last thing Skylar needs is the cops on her case.'

Watching Magician prance on his mark, Roo wasn't sure who she felt more nervous for – the stallion or Skylar.

After their warm-up, she'd accompanied them to the battlefield.

'Something's off, Roo. I can feel it in my gut,' Skylar had confided. 'So can Magician. What makes it worse is that, usually, when he performs tricks or action scenes, I'm either riding him or close by but just out of shot. Tonight, I have to send him on to the battlefield alone. When he reaches the other side, he has to wait there until I signal to him, then come trotting back by himself.'

'Why?' Roo was horrified. Sending the black stallion into battle alone, even if it was only a pretend battle, sounded unwise.

'Health and safety. According to the DOP – that's the director of photography – there'll be so much smoke that when Magician's on the other side of the field, we won't be able to see one another. I've had to train him to respond to this.'

She'd showed Roo a silent dog whistle.

'He's a quick learner, but we've had to rehearse it in a rush. Magician enjoys his job and, usually, he's cool under pressure, but he's still a horse. Horses are prey animals. If they're afraid, they run for their lives.'

Watching the stallion now, Joni exclaimed: 'What a horse! Like a creature from a myth.'

'Yes, he is,' said Roo a tad enviously, but not because she wished Magician was hers. He and Skylar were soulmates. What she longed for more than anything was to find the connection they had with a horse of her own.

Would that horse be Wonder Boy?

Roo no longer knew. A couple of hours with Skylar had made her think differently about a great many things . . .

Adele Warner swept by in a satin dress. She was beaming.

'How did you get on with her?' Roo whispered to Joni.

'Fabulously,' replied her aunt. 'I helped organise a new dressing room for her. The production manager agreed that the one they'd given her was not fit for pigs. It smelled as though something had died in it.'

'Quiet!' ordered an assistant.

'And . . . action!' the director sang out.

The cameras began to roll. The stallion took one look at the battlefield, shrouded in fog-machine mist, and swerved back to his young trainer's side.

'Cut, cut, cut,' shouted Bryce Temple, the director. 'Skylar, what's up with Magician?'

'Sorry, Bryce. It's a little overwhelming for him. Mind if we give him five minutes before we try again?'

Twice more they attempted the scene, each time with the same result.

To Roo, the stallion's movements seemed sluggish. He kept shaking his head as if he were trying to clear it.

A thought struck her. What if the sweets he'd eaten had given him colic?

Skylar was concerned too. Roo saw her pleading with the director and gesturing towards Magician, appealing for another break.

Her boss intervened. 'The horse is not himself,' Roo heard him say. 'This is not fair on Magician or Skylar . . . How 'bout we try this again tomorrow?'

The director dashed his baseball cap to the ground. He started ranting about 'millions down the drain . . .'

After more wrangling, the three compromised on: 'One last try.'

'If it's a no-go, we'll quit for the night,' agreed the director.

The crew took up their stations. Skylar's expression was shrouded by the hood, but her body language was tense. She led Magician into position.

'And . . . action!'

The cannon fired. The blast was so loud that it boomed in Roo's chest. Artillery rifles crackled. Smoke billowed across the battlefield, rising into the indigo night sky.

Whether through fear or because he understood what was needed, Magician bolted on to the battlefield. He leapt a trench and swerved around a fallen soldier before weaving his way between the coils of barbed wire.

His proud black head was held high.

As he began to gallop, the smoky darkness enveloped him. His flying tail was last to be erased. His hoofbeats faded to nothing.

Skylar was timing him on a stopwatch. When she judged that he'd reached the end of the field, she waited four minutes before blowing the silent whistle.

There was an ominous rumble of thunder, but no hoofbeats. No straining sinews or scarlet nostrils. No lightning-coated creature of myth.

Skylar blew the silent whistle with increasing desperation. There was consternation among the crew.

The fug of smoke began to dissipate. As it thinned, the wartime props revealed themselves one by one. So did the distant trees that marked the boundary of the estate.

Nothing stirred on the desolate battlefield.

Magician had vanished into the smoky air.

27.

CLUELESS

'Testing, testing. One, two, three, testing,' intoned the film company publicist, tapping the microphone.

From the depths of a threadbare armchair in the stately home, Roo waited for Detective Inspector Pickle to take the stage. It was midday on Saturday. Magician had been missing for sixteen hours. Since the black stallion had, in effect, been abducted on his watch, the Sussex policeman had found himself thrust into the spotlight.

Suddenly, he was the one being grilled – by reporters.

'Pickle's in a right pickle,' Joni remarked unsympathetically.

The media had swarmed in soon after daybreak, gripped by what some were calling the 'Vanishing Trick of the Decade'.

The fact that the story involved a glorious Friesian stallion and his cool teenage trainer only added to the mystique.

Posing as an investigative reporter, Joni had managed to get herself and Roo into the press conference. It was being held in a drawing room at the stately home where *The Last Messenger* was being filmed.

Curled up in the armchair, Roo felt hollow and cold, and not just because the stately homeowner didn't believe in heating. The expression on Skylar's face, when the movie fog lifted and she realised Magician was gone, would be seared on Roo's memory for all time.

In the space of three days, the only two horses with which Roo had been in physical contact had been stolen. Was she jinxed?

And where was Skylar now? Nobody had seen her since the search was called off soon after midnight. Was she still out searching for the stallion? Was someone taking care of her? Had she slept?

Numbly, Roo watched Detective Inspector Pickle being led to the podium. He leaned into the microphone with all the enthusiasm of a losing game-show contestant ordered to eat grubs.

His constable joined him, impassive as a lump of granite.

The *Times* correspondent launched the offensive.

'Detective Inspector Pickle, we understand the reason you were on set last night is because you were waiting to interview Skylar Heathcote about the theft of Rhianna Cooper's showjumper. Would you mind explaining how the sixteen-year-old trainer of the Animal Actor of the Year – a horse later kidnapped right in front of you – came to be one of the chief suspects in your Wonder Boy inquiry?'

A blogger jumped in: 'Yes, Detective Inspector, what evidence did you have to pin the theft of Wonder on Skylar and her dad? After all, there were so many more likely suspects – *adult* suspects. Actual known horse thieves.'

Rashly, the detective tried to shift the blame.

What a weasel, thought Roo, as Pickle snarked: 'If you're trying to imply that my team was biased against the Heathcotes because they're from the Roma community, you're barking up the wrong tree. Instead of casting aspersions, why don't you ask Skylar what she was doing creeping around a restricted area of Starwood on Monday looking guilty in a black hoody?'

'Was her hoody anything like this one?' enquired a reporter, pulling up the hood of his black sweatshirt. 'Am I now under suspicion for, ooh, I don't know, stealing Magician?'

Every other reporter wearing a hooded jacket or jumper followed suit, and those that didn't have hoods fashioned them out of scarves or put on beanies.

'Do I look guilty in this?' they asked one another, falling about laughing.

Pickle went purple with annoyance.

The publicist stepped smartly to the podium. She tapped a glass with a pen.

'Might I remind you that a sixteen-year-old is traumatised after seeing her best friend disappear in front of her eyes. For anyone not yet familiar with him, Magician is no ordinary horse. He's a sensitive, intelligent, supremely talented Friesian stallion, who has been abducted by goodness knows who and dragged away to goodness knows where. Every hour matters if he is to be found alive and unharmed.'

She had the attention of everyone in the room. Chastened, they sat sober and listening.

'Ma'am, could you please give us some background on Ms Heathcote?' asked an American podcaster.

Roo leaned forward. Like everyone else, she was fascinated by Skylar's background, but she tried to listen with a detective's ear. Something in Skylar's past might hold the key to what had happened to Magician.

'In a nutshell,' said the publicist, 'Skylar's Spanish mum, Elena, is an award-winning metal sculptor. Vano, her dad, is a metal merchant, who was born in Transylvania and is descended from a long line of revered Roma horsemen. Personally, he prefers dogs.

Skylar grew up among the wild ponies of the New Forest. Since babyhood, she's spent almost every summer on a farm near Seville, where her grandmother Sofia, a legendary trick rider and horse healer, trains Andalusians.'

'So trick riding and training horses is literally in her blood?'

'You could say that. A couple of years ago, Skylar was asked by Gerry Raven, a family friend who heads up Pegasus Productions, if she'd be willing to nurse back to health a damaged three-year-old colt. Magician had been bought as a promising youngster but, after an unfortunate experience with a bad-tempered stunt rider, had become an unmanageable tearaway. The pair bonded over a summer in the New Forest.'

Roo could picture the then fourteen-year-old Skylar in her parents' wildflower garden, patiently building connections with the tearaway Friesian colt. She saw them playing among the autumn leaves, or standing together in the heart of the peaceful forest, watching the deer go by.

'To thank Skylar, Gerry gifted her Magician,' said the publicist, 'on condition that a percentage of the horse's performance fees go to Pegasus. The rest, as they say, is history.'

'Any chance of interviewing Skylar?' asked a man from the *Daily Mail*.

'Zero,' replied the publicist.

The reporter said testily: 'Then can you ask Ms Heathcote why she left a threatening message in a barn at Starwood minutes after Coach Dering had ordered her and her dad off the property?'

'That,' said the publicist, 'was a misunderstanding.'

Roo almost felt sorry for Pickle as the journalists once again turned their fire on him.

She paid attention when they asked questions that were on her own mind too.

'If Magician was being filmed when he was stolen, why weren't the thieves caught on camera?'

'Are any of the actors or crew under suspicion?'

'Is it true that Rhianna Cooper's showjumper was also the victim of a vanishing trick?' demanded one. 'Quite the coincidence, don't you think? CCTV shows Wonder Boy in his stall one moment, then gone as if he's been magicked away by a conjuror. Care to comment, Detective Inspector?'

'We're dealing with robbery, plain and simple,' snapped Pickle. 'No conjurors involved. Forget the showjumper. We're here to talk about Magician. I've already deduced how he was stolen.'

'How?' cried Roo before she could stop herself. The reporters turned to stare at her.

'Yes, how exactly was Magician stolen?' asked Joni, earning a scowl from DI Pickle.

'For health and safety reasons, the horse crossed the battlefield alone. The scene was so smoky that, by the time anyone realised he was missing, he'd been out of sight for seven minutes. The thief must have been lying in wait.

'Skylar believes the horse had been given a sleeping potion earlier, so he'd have been easy to handle. The thief or thieves then smuggled him out of the south gate of the estate. It's seldom used, but the lock had been cut and my constable here found black tail hairs on the bars.'

'Magician's?' asked the *Times* correspondent.

'Forensics confirmed it this morning,' Pickle said importantly. 'The hoof prints match his too. There is no CCTV in that area, but we think the horse was taken through the woods to the road. The gang probably had a horsebox waiting. Local police are checking traffic cameras, isn't that right, Constable?'

The lump of granite came to life and nodded.

'Once we have a licence plate number, arrests will, I hope, soon follow,' continued DI Pickle. 'If the same person or gang stole Wonder Boy, all the better. Two birds knocked on the head with one stone. Case closed.'

He'd sounded almost gleeful, as if the arrests had already happened.

As if, Joni remarked afterwards, he had a clue.

28.

RED HERRING

Back in Bluebird, Roo and her aunt considered their next move.

'We need a base from which to conduct our inquiries,' said Joni. 'An investigation headquarters. How would you feel about Devon?'

Dazed and yawning, Roo was struggling to focus. She'd been up past midnight helping search for Skylar's stallion. Afterwards, she'd been unable to sleep.

Now it was lunchtime on Saturday. She and Joni were torn. It felt wrong to leave so soon after the press conference and with Magician still missing, and wrong to stay when they were supposed to be out hunting for Wonder. Neither of them wanted to leave without saying goodbye to Skylar.

As they deliberated, Skylar knocked at Bluebird's open door.

'Skylar! Come in—' Roo began, but Skylar was already bounding up the steps.

'Those dud detectives are chasing a red herring!' she burst out.

'I – uh – how do you know?' stammered Roo.

Emptying her pockets of crumpled pound notes, Skylar said fiercely: 'This is all the savings I have. You told me that Rhianna Cooper's mum had hired you both to find Wonder. I want to hire you to find Magician.'

Scooping up Skylar's cash, Joni returned it to her.

'Slow down. Breathe. Take a pew. Can I get you some chai?'

Mutely, Skylar slumped on the sofa. She looked pale and drained in yesterday's black clothes.

Joni handed her a steaming mug. 'What makes you so sure that Detective Inspector Pickle's chasing a false lead?'

Skylar flipped open her phone and zoomed in on a photo. 'The hoof prints the police found, they're Magician's but also not Magician's. The shoes are his for sure. His Pegasus number, 77, is stamped on the bottom right corner. But he's not the horse wearing them.'

Roo was intrigued. 'How can you tell?'

'Magician has a long, flowing stride. Even if he were unsteady on his feet after being doped, he's incapable of the short, choppy gait made by whichever pony left these tracks.'

Joni sat up. 'You're saying that a decoy has been used to send the police off on a wild goose chase?'

'Sounds far-fetched, but yes. I told the police, but they weren't interested.'

'How would the thieves have got hold of Magician's shoes?' puzzled Roo.

'Easy. The farrier comes to our Pegasus yard near Newbury a couple of times a month. We toss the used shoes in a bin. Anyone could have taken them.'

A thought occurred to Roo. 'Which farrier do you use?'

'Clancy Jones. He's great. He's been Pegasus Productions' smithy for years. But it's not just the fake hoof prints that bother me. If Magician was ridden or dragged through the gate in a hurry, his tail hairs would most likely have snagged on the gatepost or the fence beside it. The ones the constable discovered were draped over the bars. It's almost as if they were placed there on purpose.'

'Another red herring?' suggested Roo.

'Maybe the thieves wanted to distract the police with a trail of false clues around the south gate in order to buy themselves time to escape with Magician some other way,' said Joni.

'But which way?' cried Skylar. 'The estate only has two exits. If Magician didn't leave via the south or main gates, how did the thieves smuggle him out? It's impossible. It's like he was wrapped in an invisibility cloak.'

'Except he wasn't,' Roo reminded her. 'When I told you how Wonder vanished, you said there was nothing supernatural about it. He'd been led or driven off Starwood by completely visible humans. Same's true of Magician. It's a special effects trick. We just need to work out how it was done.'

'Yes, but now . . .' Skylar fought to control her emotions. 'N-now it's happened to my own horse, I don't know where to start. That's why I'm counting on you.'

'We'll move heaven and earth to help you find him,' said Roo with an appealing look at her aunt. Without Joni's agreement, her words meant nothing.

Thankfully, Joni was just as eager to assist.

'I'm with Roo,' she told Skylar. 'But the heist that the thieves pulled off last night tells me we should be under no illusions that we'll catch them quickly. We're up against criminals of exceptional daring and cunning.'

Roo realised even then that the pressure on them to succeed would be immense. Two horses' lives were at stake. Failure was not an option.

She opened the laptop. 'I'll start a new file for Magician.'

'My fear is that it's an inside job,' said Skylar. 'It's the only thing that makes sense. Whoever did this not only had to slip a sleeping draught to Magician on a secure and busy set, they also had to be in position for the exact seven minutes when Magician would be obscured by smoke. Only a handful of trusted cast and crew knew the timings for the battlefield shoot.'

'What if the schedule was hacked?' asked Joni. 'When I was chatting to Adele Warner yesterday, she complained that, along with a stinking trailer, she'd had to cope with her laptop being hacked earlier in the week. As the film's leading actress, surely she'd have had the battlefield timings?'

Roo stopped typing. 'But if the schedule was hacked, doesn't that mean the hacker could be anywhere in the world?'

'Yeah, it does,' was Skylar's flat reply. 'We can forget trying to trace them. We'd have more chance locating one unique sardine in an ocean.'

'Well, we shouldn't forget about the pyromaniac,' Roo told her.

Her aunt said sharply: 'What pyromaniac?'

'The film set was shut down for a day earlier in the week, because someone left a cigarette burning and nearly set fire to the wardrobe department.'

'Hmm,' said Joni. 'Once the thieves had their hands on the filming schedule, they might have deliberately started a blaze. They'd have needed to empty the set in order to get things into place for their "vanishing trick".'

Roo glanced over at Skylar. 'How well do you know the cast and crew working on the film?'

'My Pegasus crew are family to me,' said Skylar. 'When we're not on the road, we share a big house at our yard in Newbury. I'd vouch for any of them. Before we came here, me and Magician also spent two weeks rehearsing with Adele Warner, the lead actress. She's not a diva at all. She's funny and I like her. But I hardly know anyone else on the movie. Shooting on *The Last Messenger* only started ten days ago.'

'How about those kids who gave sweets to Magician?' asked Roo. 'Could those have been laced with a sleeping potion?'

Skylar shook her head. 'Turns out they were nephews of one of the actors. He's apologised for giving them sugar cubes for the horses. It must have been someone else.'

Joni said: 'Skylar, if we're to solve this mystery, we're going to need an insider – someone who can keep an ear to the ground and pass us information.'

'You could be our deputy!' suggested Roo, trying not to look too enthusiastic at the prospect. This wasn't a game, after all. 'Only if you want to!'

'I do,' said Skylar with a smile.

She slipped a black bracelet off her wrist and handed it to Roo. 'If I'm to be your deputy, I want you to have this. It's a friendship band braided from Magician's tail. If you wear it, you won't forget us.'

Skylar stood up. For the first time, she seemed to take in her surroundings. 'Wait a minute – are you nomads too? If it's not a rude question, where were you planning to keep Wonder – on the top bunk?'

'We were searching for a proper house with stables, but we fell in love with Bluebird,' Roo told her.

'It was her silver wings that did it,' explained Joni. 'When Roo's dad passed away in January, he left her a little money—'

'Actually, I found a winning lottery ticket in his old coat,' supplied Roo. The friendship bracelet had been a gesture of trust on Skylar's part. She wanted to repay that trust.

Skylar caught Joni's *gee thanks for telling a near-stranger that we've won the lottery* look. 'It's all right, Roo,' she said wryly. 'Your secret's safe with me. Go on. So, you chose a camper over a house. Good move.'

'Dad left me a letter telling me to grab life by the wings and fly. When I saw the wings on Bluebird's bonnet, it was like he was standing beside me, urging me on. It was only after we'd paid for her on Tuesday that we found out Wonder had been stolen.'

Skylar pushed her dark fringe out of her eyes.

'Let me get this straight. Roo, you lost your dad and won the lottery? I'm so sorry about your father. Congrats on the lottery. I understand now why you were buying your dream horse. After he was stolen, nobody would have blamed you for taking an extended holiday. Instead, you and your aunt agreed to investigate his case after first driving to the New Forest – yeah, the neighbour rang my mum last night after she heard the news about Magician to report two suspicious strangers, asking questions . . .'

'I was going to tell you,' said Roo. 'Somehow, there wasn't a good moment.'

Skylar didn't seem bothered. 'When Dad and I weren't there, you came all the way to Somerset just to warn me the police might try to frame me.'

She paused for breath. 'When Magician vanished too, you could have decided that we were more trouble than we were worth, yet you stayed to help search.'

'Of course,' said Roo.

Joni shrugged. 'What else would we do?'

A slow grin spread across Skylar's face.

'An hour ago, I was in the deepest despair. Now, the most unlikely investigators ever have taken on Magician's case, and are setting out to find him in an angel-winged camper. That gives me hope. And my nana always says that as long as you have hope, you have a light that keeps shining, no matter how dark the day or fierce the storm.'

She looked from Joni to Roo. 'Okay, team, where do we begin?'

'We need to establish alibis and run background checks on everyone who was on the film set last night,' said Joni. 'Perhaps you can help with some of those, Skylar. Roo and I will be doing the same with Starwood. We need to put anyone who had the motive and opportunity to steal Wonder Boy and Magician under a microscope.'

'On it,' said Skylar. 'I'll report back if I find anything.'

'Great,' said Joni. 'Roo, you and I will need a base. I have friends with an orchard by the sea in Devon. We could park Bluebird there if you like. What's on your mind? Do you have any questions?'

'Only the obvious one,' answered Roo. 'Are the thefts connected?'

DRIFTER

29.

SEA CHANGE

'Come on in, Roo,' called Joni, riding another turquoise swell on her bodyboard. 'The sea's fine.'

'No, it's not. It's freezing,' said Roo. 'Anyway, I like it up here.'

'Up here' was high on the back of a hairy piebald cob named General. Roo didn't add that she felt safe on him, or that having to take care of him and Shorty, his even woollier Shetland companion, took her mind off her troubles.

The sea helped too. She wasn't brave enough to swim in Devon in February, but when she rode General along the water's edge, the salty spray splashed her bare feet. The knife-sharp shock of it stopped her from thinking.

Twenty-six days had passed since audacious thieves had made off with Wonder Boy.

Twenty-three had gone by since Magician had vanished in a puff of smoke.

From time to time, Detective Inspector Pickle or a junior detective from the Avon and Somerset Police issued a statement to reporters. 'We're pursuing new lines of inquiry ... We remain hopeful of a breakthrough ...'

In reality, the police had got nowhere.

Within days of Magician's disappearance, Pickle's case had collapsed.

He'd correctly deduced that a horse lorry had parked beside

the woods next to the film set at around the time the stallion went missing. And traffic cameras had indeed captured its number plate.

Unfortunately for the great detective, the lorry had been stolen earlier that day from outside a Pony Club gymkhana. When it was found abandoned on a country lane, it had a confused and hungry Connemara pony inside it.

Like Magician's shoe prints, the lorry was another red herring.

Roo and Joni had been convinced that Magician was smuggled off set in an equipment truck. All they had to do was work out which one. Skylar had spent hours tracking down inventory lists and scanning gate camera footage.

But that theory went nowhere too. Only a couple of trucks large enough to carry a horse had left the estate on February fifth. Both had arrived on time at their final destinations, with all gear present and correct.

It was then that it dawned on Roo that the storybook rescue she had in her head – the one in which she and Joni would, within days, track Wonder and Magician to an isolated farm and be hailed as heroes for saving them – might be many weeks, and hundreds of miles, away from reality.

In the fortnight since, there'd been no sightings of either horse. No ransom demands. No anonymous tips. Just an eerie silence.

The not-knowing haunted Roo. Was Wonder being ridden in bits or spurs that drew blood in some ruthless, lawless competition yard? Was Magician being whipped and forced to perform tricks in an exotic circus?

An online search for UK horse thefts had revealed that at least two other horses, and possibly more, had been stolen in similar circumstances.

One was a top-flight polo pony, which had 'vanished, as if by magic' from the Beaufort Polo Club in Gloucestershire nearly three years earlier.

Two months later, a champion junior eventer had been whisked away from a rainswept horse trials north of Edinburgh.

'I only turned my back for a minute,' her weeping owner had told the *Scotsman*.

'What are we going to do?' despaired Roo when she and Joni chanced upon the story. 'We can't be everywhere all at once, saving every horse.'

'That's why we need to avoid getting sidetracked,' said her aunt. 'The sad fact is, hundreds of horses are stolen every year. We must keep a laser focus on our own case. If we unlock the mysteries of Wonder Boy and Magician and uncover where they've been taken, we might find some of the other horses too.'

***

Riding General across a wildflower meadow near Bantham Beach, Roo tried to block all thoughts of stolen horses from her head and remind herself how lucky she was.

Bluebird had spent most of February parked in the Devon orchard of Paulo and Meera, travelling buddies of Joni. The couple had twin boys and a large menagerie of rescue animals on their smallholding by the sea.

In return for helping out with the garden, horses, hens, pygmy goats, and rabbit, Joni and Roo had free parking for Bluebird

– their Investigation HQ – for as long as they needed it.

Looking after General and his Shetland companion had been the highlight of a difficult month for Roo. She had to stand on a stool to brush the piebald cob, but he and Shorty made her smile every day.

It made her happy to make them happy.

Less fun was the homeschooling. Hour upon hour of it. Her aunt insisted. Over the past year Roo had missed dozens of lessons. Catching up was hard.

On the flip side, her classroom had a sensational view. The sea filled Bluebird's rear window. Even on cloudy days, the sound of the surf and its ever-changing colours gladdened Roo's heart.

Back at the orchard, Roo fed the horses and turned them out into the field. Singing to herself, she ran up the steps of Bluebird.

The first thing she saw was her aunt's sketchbook, open on the table.

Not long after they'd arrived in Devon, Joni had begun sketching and 'messing about with paint' for what she said was the first time in years.

She was strangely shy about her work and only occasionally allowed Roo a glimpse of a pen-and-ink bird or watercolour sunset. Those had been good. This latest painting stopped Roo in her tracks.

Tears sprang into her eyes as she realised that her aunt, who sometimes had a faraway look in her eyes when Roo was attempting to tell her something important, *had* listened when Roo described a dream she'd had two nights earlier.

With loving detail, Joni had painted Roo flying along a beach on Wonder Boy, riding bareback, in cut-off denim shorts. The sunlight was glinting on Wonder's chestnut coat, and he and Roo looked happy and free.

Roo wished she could step into the picture. It was so atmospheric, heartfelt, and *real* that she could virtually hear Wonder's hoofbeats and the roar of the surf. She couldn't stop staring at it.

Why had no one told her that her aunt had this extra-ordinary gift?

Or had they? Thinking about it, she remembered her mum remarking that Joni could have been a celebrated artist if she'd only stayed at art school and had faith in herself.

Roo decided that if Joni couldn't believe in herself, Roo would do it for her.

Closing the sketchbook, she turned her attention to the case file on the laptop. Seeing her dream brought to life made her more determined than ever to find the missing horses.

For the past few weeks, she, Joni, and Skylar had concentrated on checking backgrounds and alibis – who was where when the horses were taken.

Skylar was working her way through the *Last Messenger* cast and crew, a tricky business because filming had stopped until Magician (or a replacement horse) was found, and everyone had scattered to the four winds.

Joni and Roo were focused on anyone who might have had the motive and opportunity to steal Wonder.

Rhianna's mum was secretly helping them to run background checks on Starwood office staff, gardeners, cleaners and assorted tradespeople, as well as the 'key players' in the investigation:

Dale Dering, Coach

Shelby Raine, Eventer

Eddie Gault, Wonder's groom

Russ Wheeler, Farrier

Paddy McGuire, Vet

Rhianna's three rivals for the Olympic team (Lindsay, Jasper & Dina)

From Rosslyn Cooper, they'd learned that when Wonder was snatched, the vet was performing emergency surgery on a Clydesdale, Shelby was at the cinema with Wonder's groom Eddie, and the farrier and his wife were celebrating their anniversary in Paris.

'The Wheelers dashed back from Paris as soon as they heard the terrible news. They've been so kind and supportive,' Mrs Cooper told Roo and Joni on the phone. 'Russ's wife, Violetta, has even offered a £1,000 reward for information leading to an arrest on her dog-grooming website.

'As for Rhianna's rivals, I should let you know that Dina has always been insanely jealous of Rhianna, and Jasper was expelled from his Very Expensive Public School for repeatedly cheating in exams. But hand on heart, I don't believe they had anything to do with Wonder's disappearance.'

'How about Dale Dering?' asked Joni. 'What's he been doing since Wonder was stolen?'

'Pacing, mainly,' replied Rosslyn Cooper with a hint of bitterness. 'He's like a tiger with a thorn in its paw. I think he blames himself.'

I'll bet, Roo thought darkly. *Probably has a guilty conscience.*

'Dale's been fantastic with Rhianna, but he's a bit of an odd fish,' Rosslyn continued. 'Lives a frugal, almost monk-like existence in a cottage in the grounds of Starwood. I can't imagine what he's done with all his money over the years. Probably hidden it under his mattress.'

Much to Roo's frustration, they'd discovered nothing incriminating on the coach. On February first, CCTV showed him entering his home at sundown and not leaving until the guard raised the alarm at 4.15 a.m.

Excluding a rival coach, who'd dismissed him as an 'arrogant upstart, headed for a fall', it had been hard to find anyone with a bad word to say about the man. He had a reputation for being tough but fair, with a knack for getting the best out of riders and horses.

Who are you, Coach Dering? mused Roo as she pulled up the photos she'd uploaded into his case file. In some, he was granite-jawed and grim. In others, he was laughing with Rhianna or giving a treat to a horse.

'What's your opinion?' Roo had asked her aunt just that morning. 'Is Dale nice Dr Jekyll or evil Mr Hyde?'

'My opinion doesn't matter. Like him or loathe him, security cameras confirm the man's story about his movements on the night Wonder was taken. He never left his cottage.'

Roo's finger hovered over the delete button now, but she couldn't quite bring herself to remove Dale's name from their suspect list.

She shut the laptop, feeling dejected. Day after day, they drew a blank.

Then she remembered the painting. The joyous beauty of it renewed her determination. Roo imagined herself racing along the beach on Wonder, happy and free. If she wished hard enough, it might become real.

30.

COWGIRL COUNTRY

Roo stopped stirring the pasta sauce and yelled: 'JONI, COME QUICK! Listen to this!' She turned up the volume on BBC Radio Devon.

'A teenager volunteer has been praised for his quick thinking after he questioned why a star Akhal-Teke was being loaded into a small, unmarked horsebox on the eve of the West Coast Endurance Challenge . . .'

'That's the race we read about – the 50-kilometre endurance ride across Dartmoor,' Roo said breathlessly. 'Akhal-Tekes are phenomenal endurance horses. They have metallic coats—'

'Shhh! I can't hear!' Joni put down her sketchpad and turned up the radio on Bluebird's counter.

'Police rescued the horse and apprehended the driver of the horsebox, Scooter Tulley, who was out on parole after serving two years in prison for horse theft. The suspect was wearing a stolen jacket branded with the logo of the rider's support team.

'Security for tomorrow's endurance challenge, which has a starting field of a hundred and forty-seven horses, has been tightened. Scooter Tulley is back behind bars after just twenty-one days of freedom . . .'

Roo felt as if she'd been woken from a long sleep. After weeks of getting nowhere, a real-live horse thief had been caught red-handed. Not by her and Joni, unluckily, but the important thing was, he was under lock and key.

'Scooter Tulley can't have stolen Wonder or Magician,' Roo remarked to Joni. 'He was in jail when they vanished.'

'Yes, but he could be part of a larger gang,' said her aunt. 'How would you feel about going to the race tomorrow, Roo? Dartmoor's only about an hour's drive away. We could watch for suspicious activity.'

Roo's spirits soared at the prospect of a detective adventure that might move their investigation forward. But how did a girl watch for thieves when the race crossed a vast, lonely moor?

'You follow the race on an American Quarter Horse!' replied Meera, their orchard-by-the-sea hostess, when they asked her for local advice. She'd been born and raised near Dartmoor and knew it like her own garden.

Roo was astonished. 'There are American Quarter Horses in Devon?'

'At least four of them,' responded Meera with a smile. 'My farmer friends, Prue and Derek Cutter, use them for rounding up cattle. They're ideal. Nimble, hardy, and swift. As I'm sure you're aware, they're the fastest horses on earth over a quarter of a mile – hence the name.

'By coincidence, I spoke to Prue Cutter earlier today. Her daughter is your age, Roo. She and her brother are planning to ride part of route of the race on their Quarter Horses tomorrow. How would you like to go with them?'

***

Roo leaned from the window as Bluebird flew into the blue morning.

The whipping wind numbed her cheeks, but she didn't mind. She wanted to be the first to spot the wild ponies that roamed the rugged, myth-soaked landscape of Dartmoor.

The ponies were not the only reason Roo had sprung out of bed as if her mattress were on fire. She couldn't wait to be a mounted detective, patrolling the race route, looking out for thieves.

She and Joni had split tasks. While Roo rode with the Cutter kids and kept an eye out for criminal activity on Dartmoor, Joni was going to spend the morning at the race start venue, near Moretonhampstead.

'Endurance races have strict checks,' Roo explained to Joni now. 'There'll be vets and farriers doing every kind of test for fitness. You'll have a better chance of spotting thieves than I will on the moors, but you never know.'

At the wheel of Bluebird, Joni was uncharacteristically quiet. It worried Roo. The previous evening, she'd overheard her aunt talking to Meera in the kitchen.

'I'm dreading tomorrow,' Joni had confided. 'It's always painful, every March third. Never gets any easier.'

'No,' her friend said with sympathy. 'It never does.'

Roo had been struck by the sadness in her aunt's voice. She'd wanted to know more, but it had felt wrong to eavesdrop.

Backtracking, she'd opened and shut the front door noisily. This time, she'd called out before strolling into the kitchen with the basket of leeks Meera had asked her to pull. By then, the women were discussing soup recipes.

After dinner, Roo had gone to put the goats and chickens to bed. She loved the naughty pygmy goats and the crooning of the hens as they got ready to roost.

The path to the orchard could be a little spooky when darkness fell. Roo had sprinted back to Bluebird. Bursting in, she'd found her aunt sitting on the floor holding a midnight-blue jewellery box.

Quick as a flash, Joni had locked it in a drawer and pocketed the key.

'What do you keep in there?' asked Roo, surprised.

Joni had turned away and started washing dishes. 'Just boring grown-up stuff. Passports, banking things, etc.'

'Oh.'

Roo had put on her pyjamas without another peep. But that didn't mean she wasn't curious about the midnight-blue box – the kind of box that held an engagement ring.

Now, as they drove in silence across the moors, Roo wondered if that small velvet box was in some way connected to March third, the day that never got any easier.

She wanted to ask her aunt why today's date mattered and was dreaded, but couldn't quite pluck up the courage. The closer she and Joni became, the more Roo feared losing another person she cared about. Why had her aunt been so secretive about the ring? Had an ex-suitor proposed marriage to her? Maybe she was worried about breaking the news to Roo.

'Joni, are you okay?' she asked hesitantly.

Her aunt slowed to take a bend. 'I'm fine – apart from a headache. I didn't sleep well. Neither did you. I heard you tossing and turning.'

Roo forced a smile. 'Too much excitement, I guess. I couldn't stop thinking about riding a Quarter Horse today.'

Joni didn't respond. She was concentrating again.

They ramped over a rise. Beyond it was a sunlit valley. Nestled in its folds was Bellwether Farm, a picture-postcard spread with a red-roofed farmhouse and silver-timbered barns. Sheep dotted the patchwork of fields surrounding it.

As they drove into the farmyard, a girl was playing fetch with a golden retriever. Bluebird's Mediterranean blue alone was enough to turn most people's heads, but the girl didn't stop what she was doing or look round.

It made Roo feel uncomfortable. Before Joni had even turned off the engine, she wanted to leave.

'Disappointing news, I'm afraid,' was Prue Cutter's greeting. 'Roo's horse has thrown a shoe, and the weather forecast is dire.'

'*Dire?*' Joni shielded her eyes from the sunshine. 'There's hardly a cloud in the sky!'

'Impossible to believe it'll turn, isn't it?' said Mrs Cutter. 'That's why Dartmoor's so treacherous. Tropical one minute, blizzards the next. I've just got off the phone with the organisers of the West Coast Endurance Challenge. The race is still going ahead, albeit with extra support points for competitors, but they're warning spectators not to attempt to watch the riders on the moors. Conditions this afternoon will be hazardous. Sadly, that means that it won't be possible for our kids to follow the race.'

Roo was so crushed, she could hardly breathe.

No Quarter Horse ride.

No endurance race watching.

No mounted detective work.

'That's okay, Prue,' said Joni, shooting Roo a sympathetic

look. 'We totally understand. Roo can come with me to Moretonhampstead to watch the start.'

But Mrs Cutter was shaking her head and smiling. 'Don't worry, Joni. We've come up with a Plan B.'

She called to the girl in the garden: 'Calliope, come say hi to our visitors. I've told them we have a Plan B.'

Calliope obeyed her mum, but only after making a show of fussing over the dog. As she walked, the fringes of her tan suede chaps swished like cats' tails over her denim riding tights and cowboy boots.

Up close, she had the air of a girl who'd recently thrown a major tantrum. Her heart-shaped face was puce-coloured, her lips drawn tight.

She smiled sweetly at Joni, while covertly regarding Roo as if she were somehow to blame for the weather forecast and cancelled race plans.

Her mother gestured towards the barn. 'My son is fetching the horses.'

Joni was confused. 'I thought the ride was off.'

'Following the race is not possible. However, six of our cows have wandered on to a neighbouring farm. Cormac and Calli are more than capable of rounding them up. It's an easy ride on a straight road. They'll be back by midday, long before any rain or mist moves in. Roo's welcome to go with them on my Quarter Horse. That way, she can ride and you won't have had a wasted journey.'

Roo didn't fancy going anywhere with Calli, who, for reasons unknown, was still looking daggers at her, but before she could conjure up an excuse, the decision was taken out of her hands.

'Here come Honey, Rebel, and Drifter!' announced Mrs Cutter.

A boy in a Stetson and cowboy shirt crossed the farmyard leading a palomino, a stocky black horse with a star, and a striking red roan.

He lined them up and left their reins trailing. They stood without moving as he shook hands with the visitors. Unlike his sister, he had a pleasant, amiable manner. Introductions over, he set about tightening cinches and checking ropes and straps on the Western saddles.

Roo was riveted by the red roan. Her shoulders and quarters bulged with muscle. Her coat colour reminded Roo of a photo her mum had loved of snow falling on the red desert of New Mexico.

'Drifter's our newest addition,' Mrs Cutter said with pride. 'She's only been with us a month, but we have high hopes. She's descended from some of the best bloodlines in American history.'

'And the fastest,' put in Cormac.

'And *you're* going to be riding her, Roo.'

Roo was taken aback. 'But she's your special new horse. Are you sure?'

'One hundred per cent. I heard how much you were looking forward to riding a Quarter Horse and don't want you to leave Devon without having tried it. Ever done any Western riding, Roo?'

'Never,' admitted Roo. Under the Cutters' gazes, she felt as clueless and inept as she had on that first morning at Starwood Farm.

'See, Mum, it would be better for me to ride Drifter and Roo to take my horse,' cajoled Calli. 'Honey's old and wise. Drifter's still getting used to the moors.'

Roo knew at once that she, Roo, had been the focus of whatever argument they'd had.

'I really don't mind which horse I ride,' she said. 'I'd be happy with any of them.'

Mrs Cutter sent her daughter a pained glance. 'Thanks, Roo, but Calli and I have already had this discussion. As our guest, I'd like *you* to ride Drifter.'

Joni looked as uncomfortable about this exchange as Roo felt.

'Prue, it's lovely of you to offer Roo your new horse, but Honey might be a safer choice if she's a steadier character. Drifter looks ... valuable.'

The farmer's wife laughed. 'She was a little pricey, but that makes no difference. We bought her as a working cattle horse, not to be wrapped in cotton wool. You needn't stress. She's as docile as a lamb and rides like a dream.

'As for Western riding, it's child's play. I've set aside some chaps for Roo. They'll keep her warm and help her sit more securely in the saddle. I'll also give her a lesson in neck-reining. In the event of an accident, split reins prevent the horse from breaking them or injuring itself.

'Not that there'll be any accidents,' Mrs Cutter added, as if willpower alone could ward off disaster. 'Split reins were mainly useful in the Wild West, where bandits and rattlesnakes lurked behind every other cactus. We don't have those on Dartmoor.'

'Cacti? Or rattlesnakes and bandits?' quipped Joni.

At the mention of bandits, a chill went through Roo. It was unnerving to think that, at that very moment, thieves might be skulking in ditches or behind stone walls like trolls, ready to ambush unwary endurance race competitors.

'Some of those Arab and Akhal-Teke horses are worth a fortune,' Skylar had told her. 'Out on the empty moor, they'd be easy pickings for greedy thieves.'

Roo wanted desperately to tell Joni that she'd changed her mind and would prefer to go with her, but she appeared to be on a train that was already in motion. She couldn't think how to get off.

Cormac called cheerfully: 'Mum, the horses are ready.'

'Excellent,' said his mother. 'Let's get you kitted out, Roo.'

31.

DANGEROUS DETOUR

The horses were fresh and eager. As they jogged up the path that led out of the valley, some of the joyous anticipation Roo had felt earlier returned.

She was going to ride across the moors on a red roan Quarter Horse.

She might glimpse the wild ponies.

The dire weather forecast might have scuppered her mounted detective work, but Roo hadn't given up on the hope of seeing a few endurance horses in the distance.

Drifter moved up the slope like a dancer, responsive to Roo's slightest touch. Her saddle was as comfy as an armchair, her gait smooth and easy.

Before they'd left the farmyard, Roo had been a nervous wreck. Despite Prue Cutter praising her as a naturally gifted rider, *what ifs* had crowded her mind.

What if she couldn't keep up with the Cutter kids? What if they were mean to her? What if she fell off and Drifter raced away and sank to her doom in a bog?

As she'd fidgeted in the unfamiliar saddle, Joni came to say goodbye.

'I wish I was going with you, Roo,' she said anxiously. 'Since that's not possible, I'd like you to take a friend.' She'd pressed Fearless Fire into Roo's palm. 'If he's with you, I know you'll be safe, whatever the weather.'

From that moment on, Roo had felt less alone. Now she had two friends: the little chestnut in her pocket and the kind-eyed red roan. She and Drifter had liked one another on sight.

The three riders reached the brow of the hill. Ahead lay the open moors. The Cutters reined in their horses.

Calli jumped off the palomino and stepped in front of Drifter. 'Change of plan, Roo. You're riding Honey.'

'But why?' cried Roo, though she could guess.

'For a start, you riding Drifter isn't fair or right. Mum promised that the first time anyone other than her rode her new horse it would be me, not a total stranger. Secondly, the moors are full of dangers. Escaped convicts. Man-eating pumas. If Drifter gets spooked and you end up in A & E, me and Cormac will get the blame.'

She put a hand on Drifter's bridle. 'You told Mum you'd be content with any of our horses. Honey's perfect for you. Go on. Hop off. We don't have much time.'

Roo looked to Cormac for support, but he was leaning on his saddle horn, staring into the middle distance.

She knew now who Calli reminded her of. At her old school, a popular girl had randomly decided to make Roo's life a misery. For weeks, Roo had cried herself to sleep, trying to work out what sin she'd committed to make the girl want to bully and mock her so remorselessly.

Finally, she realised she hadn't done anything wrong. Nor would she ever do anything right. The girl bullied her simply because she could.

Calli was waiting impatiently, a hand on her cowgirl hip.

Roo was about to dismount when she remembered her aunt's parting words. Why should Roo roll over like a Labrador puppy just because one spoiled, petulant girl told her to?

She settled back in the saddle. 'I'm sorry if your mum broke her promise, but that's between you and her. I'm fine where I am.'

Calli said coolly: 'Drifter's *our* horse and I want to ride her.'

Roo's temper flared. 'What you're asking isn't fair or right. This might be the only chance I ever get to ride a Quarter Horse and you want to spoil it. Your mum trusted me to take care of Drifter. That's what I'm going to do.'

'I couldn't care less which horse you take, Calli, just make up your mind,' interrupted Cormac. 'If the weather turns ugly, we don't want to be out on the moors.'

Releasing the roan's reins, Calli mounted the palomino.

'Oh well,' she said to no one in particular. 'It was worth a try.'

Whether it was because Roo had earned her respect or because, deep down, she knew she'd been unkind, Calli dropped the attitude.

She rode Honey alongside Drifter and gave Roo a few tips on technique. But the real change came after Roo asked the name of a speckled brown bird with a forked tail, flitting amid the bright yellow gorse.

'That's easy – it's a meadow pipit.' Calli's face lit up. 'Do you like birds? Dartmoor's heaven for birders. Skylarks, hen harriers, and curlews are my favourites. Ever heard a curlew's haunting cry?'

Out on the moors, the siblings were different. Cormac was less relaxed and his sister less precocious. Both were in tune with nature.

Cormac led the way, reins in one hand, following a worn

network of paths and tracks. As they rode, he showed Roo a dormouse burrow, deer droppings, and other traces of the creatures who lived among the bracken and wildflowers. A dozing polecat beat a hasty retreat from almost beneath Rebel's hooves.

Gradually, the girls found common ground chatting about horses and wildlife. Before long, Calli had appointed herself Roo's personal Dartmoor tour guide.

The satin coats of the Quarter Horses – Honey's gold, Drifter's russet-red and silver-mauve, and Rebel's granite-black – blended into the landscape so seamlessly anyone might have thought they'd been there since ancient times.

'If we find the cows soon, we might be able to see some of the race after all,' Calli told Roo. 'There's a great view from the top of our favourite tor.'

As appealing as that sounded, butterflies fluttered in Roo's stomach. Prue Cutter had been adamant that they head home the instant they'd rounded up the cows.

'Mum said no sightseeing,' Cormac chided his sister. Yet when they located the cattle quicker than expected and the sun continued to shine, he was the one most eager to take Roo to 'their' tor, a dramatic outcrop of 295-million-year-old granite boulders.

They left the horses at the bottom, reins trailing. The climb to the top was hot and hair-raising. The flat rock they perched on hung over the edge, giving Roo a touch of vertigo. She held tightly to Calli's arm until it passed.

But it was worth it for the roof-of-the-world view. The wild moors stretched as far as the eye could see in every direction. A symphony of birdsong and wind song rose and fell with each fresh gust.

For Roo, who'd spent much of the past two years confined to a dingy flat, or walking gritty urban streets, the sense of space and freedom was irresistible. She envied the Cutters, having Dartmoor as their playground.

As a red kite rode thermals overhead, Calli pointed out distant landmarks. 'Buckfast Abbey's that way. Dartmoor Prison's to the west.'

'Are there really escaped convicts?' asked Roo, scanning the contours below. She half expected to see men in prison boiler suits fleeing across the moors.

'Only the Mad Axeman,' bluffed Cormac. 'If you see him, run for your life. He's properly psycho.'

Calli rolled her eyes. 'Ignore my brother, Roo. The Mad Axeman escaped in the sixties and died soon afterwards. These days, the prison only has low-risk prisoners.'

'What about the man-eating pumas?' asked Roo. 'Are they low-risk too?'

Calli giggled. 'The Beasts of Dartmoor? Two escaped from a local zoo and were eventually recaptured, but their offspring still supposedly stalk the moors. There've been endless sightings of massive black cats with green eyes. Wolves and lynxes too. And our neighbour vows she once found a Wisht Hound paw print.'

'What's a wish hound?'

'Wisht, not wish. It means eerie, uncanny, or haunted in the local dialect. Wisht Hounds are red-eyed black hellhounds, like the ones in *The Hound of the Baskervilles*. Legend has it that their lair's in Wistman's Wood. You can just about see it to the east of that mushroom-shaped tor.'

'Calli refuses to go there because it's crawling with adders,' teased her brother.

'And Cormac's too scared to go because it's groaning with ghosts and ghouls,' retorted Calli.

'Am not,' Cormac protested hotly. 'I just don't get why anyone would want to visit a dwarf forest full of lichen, skeletons, and slime. It's creepy as anything. Two boys in my class started telling ghost stories there on Halloween. Next thing, a spirit floated out of a crack in the rocks. They've slept with the lights on ever since.'

Roo wished once more that she'd gone with Joni. 'Where are the wild ponies hiding?' she asked, eager to change the subject. 'I'm longing to see them.'

'They're everywhere,' said Calli in surprise.

'That's what my aunt told me, but I haven't seen a single one... Oh, hang on. What's that? Are those wild ponies?'

Fast-moving specks were crossing a purple patch of moor.

'That's the race!' cried Calli. 'Those must be the leaders. They'll pass quite near to us on their way to Princetown before circling back to Chagford.'

Roo hadn't realised how much their stalled investigation had weighed on her spirits. Here, at long last, was an opportunity to be a detective again. To make a difference. With her bird's-eye view, she'd be able to spot any thieves coming from a mile off.

Scanning the area keenly, she watched and waited. She'd expected a long-distance race to be slower, but the horses approached at a cracking pace.

Two greys swept by, followed by an Appaloosa, which seemed to be flagging. They passed so close that Roo, looking down, could see every streak of sweat on each horse's neck and rump, and the concentration on their riders' faces.

'Cormac, look over there!' Calli was so excited she almost toppled off the boulder. 'Do you think that might be Firefly and Desert Rose?

'They're the favourites,' she explained to Roo. 'It would be ace to see them go by. We wouldn't be able to tell Mum, of course, but we could tell our friends.'

Roo squinted into the sun. Two shimmering, red-gold horses were moving like a brush fire across the moor.

Cormac gave a sudden shout. 'Calli, look! We have to go.'

Behind them, grape-coloured clouds were bubbling into the sky. Parts of the moor had faded, like an old photo.

'Just five more minutes,' pleaded Calli. 'Firefly and Desert Rose are almost here—'

But her brother was already scrambling off the rock and offering Roo a hand.

'Calli, we need to gather the cows and get home NOW. It was a mistake to take a detour. Let's hope we're not too late.'

32.

WHITEOUT

Getting home was easier said than done.

The six cows had found a juicy patch of spring grass and they objected to leaving it. Roo got to see Honey and Rebel in action. They ducked, dived, and wheeled on a dime, shepherding the cows as effectively as Border collies.

The cows were finally on the road and trotting home when one made a break for it. Without any prompting from Roo, Drifter streaked in pursuit.

It was then that the Quarter Horse's inexperience on the moors showed. She was in full flight when a gully opened up before them.

Panic flooded Roo's body. It was an impossible leap. They'd never make it. Drifter would surely shatter a cannon bone and Roo would be stretchered off the moors.

But there was no time to stop. Roo felt the red roan's powerful quarters bunch. Every sinew strained as Drifter hurled herself as high and far as she could over the rocky stream bed. Roo hung on and tried not to look down.

Drifter cleared it by millimetres, albeit with some scrambling. She barely broke stride before getting straight back to work. Within minutes, she'd returned the cheeky cow to the others.

'Well ridden, Roo,' said Cormac, openly astonished.

Inside, Roo was silently thanking her big-hearted but sergeant-majorish London riding teacher, who'd demanded that

Roo trot and canter in circles, with two pennies between her knees and the saddle, for hours and hours.

'I'm not sure I'd have stayed on for that leap,' admitted Calli.

''Course you would,' Roo responded generously. 'Anyway, it was nothing compared to the skyscraper jump I went over on Wonder Boy.'

She felt a pang, remembering how sweet-natured the chestnut had been with her that day. How she'd sensed he was taking care of her.

Where in the world was poor Wonder now?

Calli was wide-eyed. 'Are you talking about some riding school pony with the same name as Rhianna Cooper's showjumper, or do you mean *actual* Wonder Boy who was stolen last month?'

Roo regretted mentioning Wonder. She wasn't about to tell Calli that she and Joni had tried to buy him before being hired by Rhianna's mother to find him. Their investigation was confidential.

'I mean Rhianna Cooper's Wonder Boy,' she admitted.

Calli said enviously: 'Are you friends with Rhianna?'

'I've met her a couple of times, but we're not close or anything,' was Roo's awkward response.

'No offence, but if you hardly know her, why would she let you ride her champion horse?'

Calli's hand flew to her mouth. 'Unless . . . Was it something to do with your dad? I heard he passed away in January. I'm so sorry.'

Roo fought back sudden tears. Calli's unthinking words were like salt in a raw wound. She missed her dad and mum every day.

After a pause, Calli pressed: 'Did one of those Make-A-Wish charities help you meet Wonder?'

'Sort of.'

It had been weeks since Roo had felt the pain that the girl's casual remarks inflicted. She clammed up. Not for anything would she relate one detail of her Wonder Boy encounter.

They rode on in silence.

'Funny about Wonder being stolen, isn't it?' remarked Calli, adding hastily: 'Not funny ha ha. Just a bit too convenient, don't you think?'

'What do you mean?' asked Roo, ready to defend Rhianna if necessary.

'So, Rhianna and her family live in a mansion and have all of these gold-plated horses. Yet a friend of Mum's, who knows Rhianna's mother, went to a restaurant with them. When the bill came, Mr Cooper's credit card was declined.'

Roo tried not to dwell on the many times that ATMs had spat out her own father's card.

'Stop gossiping and look at the tor!' shouted Cormac.

Roo swung in her saddle. The tor was gone, as if an illusionist had vanished it the way David Copperfield once magicked away the Statue of Liberty.

The change in the Cutters was night and day. They moved their horses alongside Roo and Drifter, flanking them so closely that their stirrups kept clinking.

Roo was touched by their concern. 'Thanks, guys, but I'm fine. It's only mist.'

'Have you any clue how many people have perished mistaking Dartmoor fog for mist?' scolded Calli. 'If it's a proper pea-souper, it's impossible to tell up from down. Stick close to us and we'll get you home safe.'

'Roo, if we get separated, find the road and follow it south,' instructed Cormac. 'It goes directly to our farm. If you go north by mistake, worst-case scenario, you'll end up at the Reids' farm. They'll take care of you till Mum can pick you up.'

'What about the cows?' asked Roo as the Cutters spurred their horses past them. The temperature had plunged, and she pulled the hood of her jacket up over her riding helmet.

'Forget the cows,' Cormac said shortly. 'Unless they stumble into a bog, they'll live. If we get lost on these moors, we might not.'

Roo thought he was being a touch melodramatic. According to Calli, they were barely fifteen minutes from home.

But as he spoke, a tentacle of mist swirled in out of nowhere. It encircled him like a lasso, before moving on to his sister and Roo.

More tentacles followed, rising from the bracken like swamp creatures. They swallowed the horses and sent exploratory tendrils upwards. A dense foggy dampness filled Roo's lungs, making her cough.

She had a flashback to the battlefield scene on the film set, with its machine-generated fog. Under controlled circumstances on a country estate, with Skylar watching and cameras filming every move, Magician had disappeared off the face of the earth.

How much greater was the risk in a real fog on these wild moors?

But she was anxious rather than afraid. The Cutter kids seemed unfazed by the fog. They were following a road and routine they'd known all their lives.

Too late, a squeal of tyres alerted them to disaster. An electric car zoomed out of the mist and almost hit them, skidding to a crooked stop.

Utterly unprepared, the riders were almost hurled from their terrified horses. Rebel reared. Honey bucked so high that Calli ended up halfway down her neck.

Drifter recovered quickest. Roo barely moved in the saddle. She felt quite proud that two Dartmoor newbies had coped best.

'I'M SOOO SORRY!' said the driver, projecting her voice through a crack in the window of her Mini Countryman while her companion restrained a hysterical Yorkshire terrier. 'Are you and your horses okay? It's impossible to see a thing out here.'

'You might want to try switching on your fog lights,' was Cormac's caustic advice as he struggled to control Rebel. 'Fog lights. F-O-O-G LIGHTS.'

The woman pressed her ear to the gap. 'Apologies, it's difficult to hear. Quiet, Trixie! Are you kids with the endurance race?'

'Do we look like we're with the race?' replied Calli through gritted teeth, adding more politely: 'No, we're not. The competitors will probably be held at support points until the fog lifts.'

'What a nuisance. We've been driving in circles for nothing. Any chance you could point us in the direction of Chagford? Our phones are out of charge.'

'MAKE A U-TURN AND TURN LEFT AT THE T-JUNCTION,' instructed Cormac, raising his voice above the dog's yammering.

'WHAT NOW? QUIET, TRIXIE! I NEED TO GO WHERE?'

She opened the window wider. The terrier shot through the gap like a furry missile, Yoda ears flying. It launched itself at Drifter at the exact moment that the driver, clambering out, pressed the car horn in error.

The horses scattered in three directions.

To Roo's horror, the naughty terrier came after Drifter, spooking her into the mist. Now it was Roo's turn to try to stay aboard as Drifter bucked and plunged.

A whistle pierced the gloom. The car purred away soon afterwards.

With the yapping dog gone, Roo had no trouble reining in Drifter. The mare was the best-schooled horse she'd ever ridden, and that included Wonder. Still, her small hands trembled on the reins. She took her time settling the horse before looking around.

The world had turned white.

Roo could no longer see the Cutters.

'Calli! Cormac!'

'ROO! Over here!'

Roo rode in the direction of their calls.

They kept shouting but, weirdly, their voices grew more and more muffled. Soon she couldn't hear them at all.

She was beginning to panic when she found the road. Drifter was insistent that they should go in the opposite direction, across the moors, but Roo soon set her straight.

'Cormac said if we stick to the road, we'll get to Bellwether Farm. Worst-case scenario, we'll find their friends' house.'

It entered her head that the Cutter boy had mentioned a T-junction. Surely that meant that while one road ran north to south, another ran east to west. What if they'd found that one by mistake? Where did it lead?

To Roo's alarm, Drifter began to plunge and yank at the bit as if something larger than a terrier lurked in the mist. Something like a puma.

'Easy, girl, what's upsetting you?' Roo steeled herself to look over her shoulder and nearly fainted.

A black SUV with blacked-out windows was creeping along behind them, its engine almost soundless.

Roo was scared but also relieved. At least she was no longer alone. Talking to a stranger on a misty moor was not ideal, but Roo felt safely out of reach, high up on Drifter.

If the driver was a local, she could ask directions. If the stranger turned out to be a weirdo, she and Drifter could take off across the moors. Fat chance they'd have of catching Roo's Quarter Horse. In this fog, she and Drifter wouldn't need to go far to be out of sight.

Whoever was at the wheel was invisible behind blackout windows. Roo was about to flag them down when she noticed that the car's number plate had been concealed with tape.

Roo could think of no good reason why any honest driver would want to conceal their number plate.

She urged Drifter into a rapid trot, overtaking the vehicle and leaving it in her wake. If the driver's intentions were honourable, they would keep their distance and leave her alone.

Before she could relax, the SUV zoomed past her and stopped again, its lights fuzzy in the fog.

Roo was disturbed. What was it doing?

Drifter skewed to a halt. Roo yearned to yell for Cormac and Calli, but instinct told her to stay silent. Icy fingers of dread crawled down her spine.

The mare stood unmoving, her eyes on stalks.

Unsure what to do next, Roo sat deeper in the saddle and tried subtly to get Drifter to trot on. Her heart clattered in her chest.

The back of the SUV hissed open. Roo cried out in fright.

Two immense dark-grey wolfhounds, eyes shining red in the glow of the brake lights, were poised to pounce.

At some unheard command, they jumped out. Crouching low, they began herding Drifter along the tarmac like sheepdogs.

Before Roo could blink, the Quarter Horse was facing the other way.

She stifled a scream. A horsebox was parked on the road, mist swirling like dragon's breath around its crimson lights. The lowered ramp was a hungry maw, trying to lure them in.

The wolfhounds drove the roan towards it, snapping at her heels.

Roo felt almost incredulous as it hit her that the thieves she'd sought for a month had somehow come to her.

Was this how it had happened for Magician? Were she and Drifter to be abducted in real time? Or was it just the horse the gang wanted? Would she be dumped in the middle of nowhere?

The foggy moors were full of invisible dangers: bogs, ditches, and beasts. But the horsebox was a clear and present danger. It had only one intention: to gobble them up.

Girl and horse were on the same page as to which terror was more terrible.

As Drifter exploded into a Quarter Horse gallop, Roo flung herself forward and held on tight. A split second later, she was riding for her life.

33.

HAUNTED WOOD

Roo's dad had been obsessed with horse racing, and she'd spent many weekends watching it with him. 'Sofa jockeys,' he'd called them. But nothing had prepared Roo for the brutal reality of hurtling blindly across a moor on an out-of-control Quarter Horse, chased by killer dogs.

A single misstep would be the end of them.

Roo concentrated on staying still and staying on. Her eyes streamed. She longed to wipe them but didn't dare distract Drifter or touch the reins.

The dogs were lean, mean running machines but, for the first quarter of a mile, Drifter's speed left them in the dust. Their blood-curdling baying faded. Soon Roo could hear nothing but the red roan's breath coming in gasps.

Then Drifter began to slow. She was spent.

Sensing weakness, the wolfhounds reappeared. They gained on the horse with every stride.

Lights careered in the distance. The SUV was ramping across the moors. The dogs wore thick tracking collars. If the Quarter Horse faltered, she and Roo would be hunted down like deer.

In vain, Roo searched the blurry shapes and shadows for some sign of help or refuge. A cave? A crumbling bothy? An endurance race refreshment station or support team on the lookout for lost riders?

But there was nothing and no one.

It was then, when Roo was at her most desperate, that she heard her aunt's voice as clearly as if Joni was riding beside her.

If he's with you, I know you'll be safe, whatever the weather.

'Fearless Fire,' cried Roo, *'do something!'*

Out of the mist swerved a Dartmoor stallion, his coarse black mane whipping in the wind. He galloped alongside Drifter, his muscles bunching and releasing like pistons beneath his shaggy bay hide.

A wolfhound went for him, fangs bared. The wild pony wheeled with a shriek of rage. Two kicks, two yelps. The dogs lay still in the heather.

As Drifter galloped on, Roo's ears filled with the thunder of hooves. The stallion had summoned his entire herd.

The mares formed a protective shield around Roo and Drifter, running with them as if they were part of their wild family. The stallion led the charge.

Nobody, thought Roo, *will ever believe this.*

A calm sensation stole over her. She felt cloaked in wild magic, lighter than air. Drifter drew strength from it too. She picked up speed again. Her breath came more easily.

Just as Roo was starting to recover, a grotesque forest of shrunken oaks loomed out of the fog. It was one horror too many for Drifter, who slammed on the brakes. Roo shot over her head.

She landed on her feet, teetered, and crumpled dizzily to the ground. By the time her head cleared, her pony protectors had melted into the mist. She and Drifter were on their own.

Roo struggled to comprehend what had just happened. Why had the wild herd saved them from the dogs and hunters only to deliver them to Wistman's Wood, den of adders and ghouls, and lair of the Wisht Hounds?

There was no time to feel sorry for herself. Sweeping searchlights were combing the moors. The hunters were coming.

Roo ran for the shelter of the twisted trees, dragging Drifter under low branches, draped with horsehair lichen. She and the roan squeezed between mossy boulders, and slipped and stumbled over tangled and slimy roots.

When the roan refused to move another step, Roo sat at her feet, holding the reins in one hand and Fearless Fire in the other.

Car doors slammed. Men's voices snarled. Boots clomped across the granite rocks, sounding like soldiers on a route march. Nearby, a dry branch cracked.

Roo shut her eyes and squeezed closer to Drifter, quaking with terror. If the hunters didn't get her, the ghouls or adders surely would.

An enraged shout cut through the fog. 'Wrong ponies, you clueless dolts. What happened to the horse and rider you were chasing? Surely even you can tell the difference between the endurance champion in the photo and these stumpy feral beasts. Now I have two dogs down and nothing to show for it. The boss is going to murder me.'

The doors slammed again. An engine revved and roared. Tyres scrabbled on the stones. Silence fell.

Roo opened her eyes. She was surrounded by wild ponies. They'd been there all along, guarding her and Drifter.

Her head swam as she grappled with what she'd overheard. She and the Quarter Horse had been hounded almost to death by vicious, bungling thieves. They could have fallen into a bog or broken legs or neck in holes, and it was all a case of mistaken identity. It was mind-boggling.

Which endurance champion were they really after?

With the men gone, the Dartmoor ponies crowded closer, A curious foal snuffled Roo. As the stallion kept vigil, the peaceful energy and heat emanating from the thick coats of his herd warmed Roo's heart and bones.

Drifter's knees buckled. She collapsed in a nest of moss, huffing with exhaustion. Roo used her silky neck as a pillow.

In another moment, they were both asleep.

34.
DESPERATE MEASURES

Roo woke in a shaft of otherworldly light. A silver moth twirled in it.

The ponies had gone, but she was no longer afraid. They'd led her to Wistman's Wood because it was their safe place. Forever afterwards, she'd see the forest through their eyes, not as the haunt of hellhounds but as a place of enchanted oaks, fluffy foals, and pony angels.

The memory of running with the wild Dartmoors, of being under their protection, would stay with Roo for the rest of her life.

She stood up. Drifter, her pillow, got to her feet too, shaking off scraps of moss and fern. Roo wasn't sure how long they'd been there, but she did know that Joni and the Cutters would be worried.

Wrapping her arms around Drifter, she pressed her cheek to the red roan's warm shoulder, overwhelmed with love and gratitude. The roan had given her all to carry Roo to safety. How could Roo ever thank her enough?

Trust your instincts, Skylar had advised. *A strong bond with a horse can save your life. Save theirs too.* Drifter seemed to feel the same way. She kept nudging Roo with her muzzle, breathing her in.

Out on the open moor, the fog had given way to bolts of blue and patchy sunshine. Roo and Drifter took a long drink from the sparkly West Dart River and got their bearings. Using a tree stump for a mounting block, Roo swung into the Western saddle like an old hand. Her pre-ride nerves had gone.

She felt different. Lighter. Stronger. Braver.

Part of the reason she'd got into difficulty in the first place was because she'd ignored Drifter when the roan had tried to communicate that they were on the wrong track. This time, Roo let her have her head. Drifter turned confidently for home.

They traversed the moors at a lope. The Quarter Horse's stride was so comfortable that Roo could have napped in the saddle. It helped, too, that they could finally see where they were going.

They found the north–south road first and Calli and Cormac soon afterwards.

Honey and Rebel neighed a greeting to Drifter.

'Roo, I've never been so relieved to see anyone in my life!' cried Calli. 'You've been missing for nearly two hours. We tried looking for you but had to give up and take shelter. You must have been so frightened! Where were you?'

Belatedly, Calli noticed that Roo's jacket was covered in green slime and moss.

'Omigod, you fell off! Are you hurt? I *told* you to let me ride Drifter. Did she run away with you?'

Roo was fizzing with adrenaline. She couldn't wait to tell Joni what had happened. She was even overjoyed to see the Cutters.

'Drifter didn't hurt me. She *saved* me,' she said to Calli.

On the twenty-minute ride back to Bellwether Farm, she told the Cutters about the black SUV with the taped-over number plates, the horsebox with the dragon's mouth, and about being pursued across the moors by wolfhounds with red eyes.

She described Drifter's breathtaking speed and the Dartmoor

stallion's courage. She told them how the wild herd had led them to Wistman's Wood and kept them safe from a murderous gang.

With every sentence, the siblings' disbelief grew. Cormac's mouth dropped open. Calli stared at Roo as if she'd lost her mind in the fog.

'*Two giant wolfhounds?* We saw the dog that went after Drifter with our own eyes. It was ONE Yorkie the size of a mouse. It came whimpering back to the car as soon as its owner called it.'

'Why would anyone steal Drifter, anyway?' demanded Cormac. 'She's pretty and has a great pedigree, but she's only a cattle horse.'

Only a cattle horse that saved my life, thought Roo.

'Your wild pony story sounds far-fetched too,' accused Calli. 'This morning, you were complaining that you hadn't seen one. But apparently, an entire wild herd came to your rescue like some Dartmoor pony cavalry.'

Cormac sighed with disappointment. 'And you expect us to believe that all of these adventures happened in the couple of hours since we last saw you?'

***

'They didn't believe me,' Roo told Skylar and Joni.

It was late afternoon and she and Joni were sitting side by side in Bluebird, sipping chai and watching the goats play under the apple trees in the orchard by the sea. The camper's rear window was thrown open to the spring air and they were chatting to Skylar – on video.

As the sun painted rainbows in puddles left by a downpour, Roo described every detail of her escape across the moors.

'I don't blame them,' she said of the siblings' reaction. 'If I'd been them, I'd have thought my story was fantastical too.'

'*We* believe you,' said Skylar and Joni together.

'*You do?*' Roo felt a rush of affection for her friends. 'Even though my story sounds like *The Hound of the Baskervilles* meets the *Silver Brumby* series?'

'Especially because it sounds like *The Hound of the Baskervilles* meets the *Silver Brumby* series,' said her aunt. 'That's life, isn't it? Frequently stranger than fiction. I'm just thankful that you were riding the fastest horse in Devon. I'll be eternally grateful to Drifter and the wild ponies for returning you to me in one piece.'

'And Fearless Fire.'

'Fearless Fire too.'

'You're ten times braver than I am, Roo Thorn,' said Skylar. 'Well done for staying on and staying strong. I wonder which horse the thieves were really after.'

'A horse that looks like Drifter,' Roo replied simply.

Joni pursed her lips: 'This mistaken identity business could be the key that unlocks our case. Those rogues would not have taken such extreme measures unless the horse they were after was worth a huge sum. That narrows things down.'

She passed her phone to Roo. 'Take a look at the pics I snapped at the start venue. See if you think any of these horses may have been the intended target.'

Roo scrolled through and paused at a photo of a perlino Akhal-Teke.

'Desert Rose, the Akhal-Teke, is a long shot, but Firefly could easily be mistaken for Drifter. There might be others. I'll go through the list of entries.'

'So what's our plan?' asked Joni. 'What should we do next?'

To Roo's embarrassment, tears filled her eyes. 'I feel so guilty. I can't believe I was so close to the hunters and can't describe one thing about them. Not their hair colour. Not even their height or build or make of vehicle.'

Her aunt gave her a consoling hug. 'Roo, you were riding for your life in a fog. Don't worry, we'll catch those monsters if we have to pursue them to the ends of the earth.'

'Yes, we will,' said Skylar. 'Thanks to your courage, Roo, we've filled in a massive piece of the puzzle today. Finally, I can see a pattern.'

'*What pattern?*' asked Roo, but then she realised it was glaringly obvious. The 'vanished' horses had all been supreme performance horses and best of breed. A showjumper, a Friesian who could do dressage and tricks, an eventer, and a polo pony. The thieves had also tried and failed to get a champion endurance horse.

'It's as if the thieves are collecting playing cards, using living horses,' she said thoughtfully.

'If they'd succeeded in stealing an endurance horse, all they'd have needed is a racehorse and they'd have a complete set,' added Skylar. 'Of course they might already have one. They could have stolen it last year, or even recently, and we might not have heard about it. What are they planning to do with all these elite athletes? That's what we need to figure out. Are they changing their appearance, then reselling them abroad? Is Magician going to be used for breeding or some other purpose we haven't ever thought of?'

She yawned. 'Speaking of racehorses, I'd better go. Between film jobs, I help out at Queen's Reach, a racing yard near Newbury

I have to be on the gallops by 4 a.m.'

Roo's regard for her friend went up another notch. 'Queen's Reach? That place is legendary! You ride there? Why didn't you say something before?'

Skylar retreated into her hoody. She didn't like a fuss. 'Like I said, I only help occasionally – when they're short of riders.'

She smothered another yawn. 'Exercising racehorses is fun and an adrenaline rush, but the early mornings are killing me. Hope the thieves don't pop up at Queen's Reach. I'll be too tired to fight them off. Speak tomorrow . . .

'Oh, wait, I almost forgot. Last week, I overheard the farmer who supplies Pegasus Productions with hay moaning to my boss about bad payers. Turns out, Rhianna Cooper's father is one of them.'

'But the Coopers are millionaires!' said Roo.

Skylar snorted. 'Don't believe everything you read. Anyway, this farmer sold Rhianna's dad a ton of his best hay last October. Mr Cooper was supposed to pay cash on delivery, but it took months to get a penny out of him. Even then, he only paid half. He complained the bales were mouldy when they weren't. Either the Coopers are loaded because they don't pay their bills, or bankrupt but pretending they're not.'

Roo felt a bit sick. Rhianna had been really kind to her. It felt wrong to be gossiping behind her back.

But then she remembered Calli's story about Lloyd Cooper not being able to pay the bill at the restaurant. It suddenly seemed important that she share it with Skylar and her aunt.

'After she told me the story, Calli made an odd remark. She said that Wonder Boy vanishing was a "bit too convenient".'

Skylar raised an eyebrow. 'Maybe she's heard the rumours.'

'What rumours?'

'The horse circuit is buzzing with talk that Wonder wasn't stolen at all. That it was a staged robbery to scam money out of his insurance company.'

'Hmm. Unlikely but not impossible,' said Joni. 'We need to investigate Lloyd Cooper's finances, Roo. Remember how he tried to pressure us into paying instantly for Wonder – before we'd even had a veterinary inspection done? Desperate people sometimes resort to desperate measures.'

GHOST FLIGHT

35.

QUEEN'S REACH

Roo fumbled for her phone in the dark. 'H'llo.'

'ROO, WAKE UP! THIS IS AN EMERGENCY!'

'Skylar, it's 3 a.m. What's the emergency?' Roo pressed a button and her sleeping nook blind slid open. The sky was as black as a raven's wing.

'There's been a break-in at Queen's Reach. Thieves just attempted to steal a £1 million filly called Dynamic.'

Roo bolted upright, sleep forgotten. 'Well, why didn't you just say so?'

Five minutes later, Roo was logging into Skype on the laptop. Skylar appeared on-screen in a rock band T-shirt, her dark hair sticking up on end.

'Shoot, Skylar,' said Joni, plonking two mugs of chai down on Bluebird's table. 'Tell us everything.'

'Two hours ago, a guard at Queen's Reach heard a noise in the Fillies' Barn and went to check it out. Dynamic's stall was empty. Before he could raise the alarm, a gardener was woken by Dynamic herself. She was in the greenhouse, helping herself to carrots. The thieves had scarpered.'

'Thank goodness they failed,' said Roo.

'Maybe they wanted to fail,' Skylar told her.

Roo stared. 'Why would they want to fail?'

'If this wasn't a genuine attempt to steal Dynamic but only a practice run for a bigger payday.'

'You've lost me,' said Joni.

Skylar gave a tired smile. 'I'll explain. Queen's Reach is the home of Ghost Flight, the fastest filly since Black Caviar and Zenyatta. My question is, why didn't the thieves target her, or one of the other great horses at the yard? The roll call of champions at QR is the envy of everyone in racing.'

'Maybe they decided that stealing Ghost Flight or another champion wasn't worth the risk,' suggested Joni. 'If Dynamic's worth a million, they'd still have made a fortune if they'd got away with her.'

'See, that's where it gets interesting,' said Skylar. 'Dynamic cost a million, but she's not *worth* a million. There's a big difference. In racing circles, her nickname's Lethargic. Any time she can refuse a jump or throw her rider and start chomping grass, she does. I have a hunch that the thieves staged a pretend robbery as a dress rehearsal for the main event.'

Roo was on the edge of her seat. 'What's the main event?'

'Stealing Ghost or another champion at a later date.'

Roo's pulse quickened. It was late April. Bluebird had spent so long parked in the orchard by the sea that grass was hugging her wheels.

For five frustrating weeks, the investigators had waited for the thieves to make a move. If they were right about the gang collecting at least one brilliant athlete from each discipline, a racehorse would be the next target.

Nothing had happened to prove that theory until now.

'Do you really think these could be the same thieves who snatched Wonder and Magician?' asked Roo.

'I'm sure of it,' said Skylar. 'If the gang have a perfect racehorse in their sights, there'd be few greater prizes than Ghost Flight. She's worth five times as much as Dynamic.'

'*Five times?*' cried Roo. 'FIVE *MILLION* POUNDS?'

'Yes. And each time Ghost wins, she's worth more.'

'Joni, what if we went undercover at Queen's Reach?' Roo asked her aunt. The idea of laying a trap for Wonder's kidnappers sent adrenaline pumping through her veins. 'Skylar could use her connections to get us in. That way, if thieves strike again, we'd be right there to catch them in the act.'

'If only it was that easy,' said Skylar. 'Security was tight at QR before this break-in. It'll be like Fort Knox now. And there's no way of knowing when or if the gang will come back. Could be days. Could be never.'

'Skylar, you called us for a reason,' Joni reminded her. 'Instinct tells you that the thieves will return for a bigger prize. We trust you on that. But I think Roo's idea is a good one too. What if I tried to get a job at Queen's Reach? Something that would allow me and Roo to live on site and get to know the staff, visitors, and horses. If we were there every day, we might spot weak links in security.'

'Joni can turn her hand to anything,' volunteered Roo. 'Gardening, massage, veterinary nursing . . . And I could muck out or help around the yard.'

Skylar looked at Joni. 'Anything?'

'Anything at all.'

Roo and Joni were eating a hot-cross-bun breakfast when Skylar sent through a link to the *Racing Post*.

WANTED: ARTIST IN RESIDENCE

To capture the spirit and speed of Queen's Reach's illustrious champions in oil and watercolour. Please email portfolio to kathryn@queensreach.com.

Roo let out a squeak of delight. 'Artist in residence? Joni, you'd be an amazing racehorse painter. If you send in your paintings of Wonder and Magician, they'll hire you in a second!'

'No,' Joni declared emphatically. 'N. O. No.'

'But you told Skylar you'd do anything,' Roo reminded her, feeling deflated. She couldn't understand why her aunt was so lacking in confidence about her gorgeous pictures, especially when she'd been to art college. What had happened to rob her of her self-belief?

'Anything but that,' said Joni.

***

In the end, Roo and Skylar decided to take matters into their own hands and secretly send photos of Joni's horse paintings to Kathryn Irving, racing manager at Queen's Reach. Kathryn was on the phone to a surprised Joni, delightedly offering her the job of artist in residence, within the hour.

Joni made a big show of being miffed at the two of them for going behind her back, but she couldn't stay mad at them for long.

'For the sake of Magician, Wonder, and, potentially, Ghost Flight, you've done a good thing,' she admitted to Roo. 'We'll be living at Queen's Reach for at least a month. Hopefully, we'll be able to prevent any robberies. Also, I know your heart was in the right place. "Joni Jackson – artist in residence!" I keep pinching myself. It's been decades since I felt like a proper artist.'

She and Roo packed up Bluebird that morning, waved goodbye to General, Shorty, and their other friends at the orchard-by-the-sea in Devon, and drove north to Newbury. By sundown, they were sharing patatas bravas and other Spanish tapas treats with Skylar at the Goat on the Roof restaurant, near Queen's Reach.

It was the first time Roo had seen Skylar in person since Magician was snatched three months earlier and she couldn't decide whether to jump for joy or shrink with shame because Skylar's beloved stallion was still missing.

Skylar solved the dilemma by hugging her and Joni in turn, holding them tightly as if she'd never let go. But there was no disguising the toll that losing Magician had taken on her.

In real life, the spark that made Skylar Skylar was gone. The purple shadows around her eyes spoke of a hundred sleepless nights. Her pale blue shirt hung loosely from her boyish frame.

'I'm happy that I'll get to see you at Queen's Reach,' she'd told them over dinner, 'and, of course, I desperately want answers in our case. At the same time, I'm hoping that my hunch about the robbery is dead wrong. I'd hate for anyone else to go through what I've been through. I miss Magician every second of every hour and I'm sure Rhianna feels the same about Wonder Boy.'

Roo wasn't so sure. She'd watched a clip of the young showjumper winning a big championship on Fleetfoot Amberwell at the weekend. If Rhianna was still heartbroken about Wonder, it didn't show.

It didn't matter. Roo cared about finding Wonder and reuniting Skylar and Magician more than anything.

For all the laughter and smiles at dinner, the three investigators knew that the closer they got to the thieves, the greater the risk.

In Roo's nightmares, danger stalked her like a wolf. One false move and she'd be devoured.

36.

HOUSE OF CARDS

'I don't envy you, having to get Ghost Flight down on canvas,' the gate guard remarked to Joni when they arrived on May fifth. 'She's no oil painting, if you'll pardon the pun. Then again, neither was Eclipse. Hulking great brute of a creature with a massive head, according to the history books.'

Roo wanted to shriek: *Don't put my aunt off! Have you any idea how difficult it was to talk her into being an artist in residence!*

But Joni just smiled. 'Well, looks aren't everything. It's Ghost's essence I'm here to capture.'

'If it's her essence you're after, that only shows when she runs,' the guard said with authority. 'Some mornings, I get here early for my shift just so I can walk up to the gallops and watch her train. She's merely breezing along there, mind. Barely going at half her racing pace. And yet . . .'

A strange expression flickered across his face, as if he'd witnessed something supernatural but was hesitant to admit it.

'You'll see. Sends chills through you, it does.'

He cleared his throat. 'I'll need to inspect your camper. We had an attempted break-in recently and we've beefed up security.'

'We heard,' Joni said with interest. 'Was it you who chased off the thieves?'

'No, it was our new guard, Brandon. He'd only been with us a week, so quite a feather in his cap.'

There was a hint of sour grapes in his tone. He said nothing more until he'd examined Bluebird inside and out.

'Nice wheels. You'll be with us for a while, I'm told. Hope you brought your glasses as well as your easel.'

'Glasses?'

'For the solar eclipse. Six days from now. You'll need 'em if you're looking at the sun.'

The guard raised the barrier. 'On you go. Stay safe now.'

***

As Bluebird rolled forward, the guard's words sent a tremor through Roo. The thieves who'd snatched Wonder and Magician were showmen. There was something theatrical about the scene of each of their crimes – the locked stable, the film set battlefield, the high-stakes kidnap attempt on a misty moor . . .

What could be more dramatic than snatching Ghost Flight during a solar eclipse?

Joni drove slowly up an avenue of chestnuts and braked to read a signpost.

'Fillies' Barn, Stallions' Barn, equine pool, vet boxes, gallops, all-weather track, riders' house, gym . . . main house. That's the one we want.'

On a distant hill, horses sped along the sunlit gallops.

Roo could hardly believe that her home for the foreseeable future was a world-famous racing yard. Or that her journey here had begun at another famous yard. Was Queen's Reach, like Starwood, mired in secrets?

Roo found herself thinking back to Rhianna Cooper's home,

as she'd first seen it in February. Despite her dad's advice about perfection not adding up to happy or lucky, all Roo had been able to think about as Rhianna showed her around was how perfect everything was.

Now Roo knew the truth. Starwood Farm was a house of cards. It could collapse at any time.

Joni had persuaded a tax expert friend to do some digging into Mr Cooper's finances. First thing that morning, he'd emailed to say that Lloyd Cooper's hay and restaurant credit problems were isolated incidents.

'So, the Coopers are fine?' Roo had asked when Joni told her about the message. 'No cash-flow problems?'

'That's one way of putting it,' said her aunt.

'What do you mean?'

'The only reason there are no cash-flow problems at Starwood is because all bills for the farm and the Cooper family are paid in full and on time by a mysterious person called Barney Rotten.'

'Why mysterious?'

'He's a ghost,' replied Joni. 'Online, at least, Mr Rotten barely exists. My friend could discover almost nothing about him except that he's chief executive of EQ Enterprises Ltd, a financial services company with just one employee: Barney Rotten himself. That makes me nervous. As my friend put it, Mr Cooper is spending for England, but the entire time, his debt to Barney Rotten is mounting.'

'I don't understand,' said Roo, though she thought she did. Everything in their case kept circling back to Starwood.

'Put simply, your own dad only owed fifty pounds to the bank,' explained Joni. 'Knowing Jim, he'd have repaid that as soon as he could. Lloyd Cooper's debts are in a whole different league. He owes nearly a million pounds to a single creditor: Barney Rotten. Hardly surprising that Rhianna's dad was so eager to sell Wonder Boy to us. He needed cash, fast.'

'A million pounds in debt?' Roo was incredulous. 'How did he spend so much money?'

Then she remembered Rhianna laughingly saying: *We have so many painters, broadband fixers, farriers, grooms, and vets coming and going that it's hard to keep track of everyone. Dad's going mad with the expense. I keep telling him that it'll all be worth it when we win gold at the next Olympic Games.*

But what if they didn't win gold? What if Rhianna or Fleetfoot Amberwell suffered a career-ending injury, or even a minor setback that caused them to miss a whole season of events?

'Basically, it appears that Lloyd's gambling that his daughter will become a superstar with multi-million-pound sponsorship deals and he'll have no difficulty repaying the loan,' said Joni. 'While it's sweet that he has such faith in his daughter, he's taking a huge risk. If EQ Enterprises suddenly demand their money back, the Coopers' life will come crashing down. That means we can't rule out fraud.'

'No!' cried Roo.

'Yes,' said her aunt. 'Rhianna's dad seems a decent, caring husband and father, but his back's against a wall. If Wonder was insured for more than he was worth – say, for half a million rather than the £250,000 we were going to pay – Lloyd might have been tempted to get rid of the horse and claim the money.'

Roo felt quite shattered. She'd spent so long picturing the Coopers as a family whose greatest daily challenge was the pool cleaner not showing up that she found it hard to conceive of Rhianna's dad as a calculating criminal.

Yet, as a detective, she had to consider it.

'The key to untangling the secrets of Starwood lies with Barney Rotten,' said Joni. 'He might be a kindly soul or perhaps even a distant cousin, helping Rhianna's dad out, or he might be a blackmailing loan shark. I've asked my tax expert friend – an ex-suitor, as it happens – to investigate further.'

'Not *another* suitor?' asked Roo, amused.

Joni gave her a look. 'Don't be judgemental, Roo. Ninety-nine per cent of my suitors haven't even made it through the soup course on our first date but, along the way, I've made some good friends.'

She smiled but her eyes were sad. 'The only suitor who counts is the one I loved. And before you ask, that's my final word on the subject.'

Roo opened her mouth to speak before deciding against it. But she pictured again the midnight-blue box.

***

A sleek and shiny colt bounced past Bluebird's window, returning Roo to reality. His fit young rider managed him with ease.

Joni waited until the pair turned the corner before steering the camper between the rows of red-brick barns and turning right towards the main house.

She parked Bluebird in the shade of an oak tree. Switching off the engine, she sat for a moment, drumming her fingers on the steering wheel.

'Roo, what we're about to attempt here – going undercover,

nosing around, asking tricky questions – is fraught with risk. If the thugs you encountered on Dartmoor are planning a high-stakes robbery at Queen's Reach, they'll stop at nothing. For all we know, they could already be here, working undercover like us. We need to be alert to the slightest threat.'

She smiled. 'At the same time, we're allowed to enjoy ourselves. We'll be rubbing shoulders with racing royalty – and that's just the Thoroughbreds.'

Roo laughed, but she had a terrible sense of foreboding. Before they'd even met Ghost, the countdown had begun. Six days until the solar eclipse? She and Joni would have to hit the ground running.

37.
THE SPEED GENE

'If you're anything like me, you'll be disappointed the first time you see Ghost,' said Kathryn Irving, leading Roo and Joni past Thoroughbreds enjoying spa treatments in swimming pools and doing circuits on horse walkers.

'She was only a yearling when we bought her and she looked like a thousand other youngsters, only worse. Gangly and awkward, with a large head and knobbly knees. I said to my husband, Finn, and son, Keyne: "But why *her*?"

'We'd seen so many gorgeous yearlings that day. I just couldn't understand why they wanted this dirty-grey filly with the lopsided gait. Keyne said: "It's just a feeling." And Finn went: "Sometimes that's all you have to go on." Six months later, Ghost ran her first race and left the whole field in the dust.'

At Queen's Reach, racing was a family affair. Kathryn's husband, Finn, was Ghost's trainer, and the couple's eighteen-year-old son, Keyne, was the filly's jockey.

Roo and Joni had been welcomed into the Irvings' light and airy kitchen with smiles and cinnamon rolls. The family's lovely old house hummed with life.

Roo found the Irvings' positivity infectious. Though she was there on serious business, the sunshine, the racehorses, and the promise that she might, just might, be allowed to ride along the gallops with Skylar filled her with hope.

When Joni let slip that she was nervous about not being a good enough artist to do justice to Ghost Flight, Kathryn quickly set her at ease.

'Joni, the paintings Skylar showed me are exquisite. You're immensely gifted. However, anyone will tell you that Ghost's at her best when she runs. She's resting after her latest triumph, so you'll have a few days to observe her. We'll resume her training on Friday, the morning of the eclipse. Racing is when she comes alive.'

She smiled. 'Meantime, just settle in and get to know our yard, our riders, and our wonderful horses. Sketch and paint to your heart's content. Now, if you've had your fill of pastries, I'll show you around.'

***

First stop was the indoor school, where athletic young riders were riding their fourth mount of the morning. Every horse did a five- or six-furlough trotting warm-up before heading out to the gallops.

As each rider went by, Finn called out their training plan for the day. There were a hundred and thirty horses at Queen's Reach and he treated every one the same, whether they were owned by royalty or factory workers who'd clubbed together to buy a horse because they liked its name.

Thirty of those horses lived in the Fillies' Barn, but Roo had no difficulty identifying Ghost Flight.

The champion racehorse was being hosed down by a girl groom. Her wet coat had the shimmer of rare pearls. Her legs were strong and true. Her head was fine-boned and elegant. In short, she was perfection.

'How can you say that Ghost Flight's ugly or boring?' cried Roo. 'She's *stunning*.'

Kathryn laughed. 'That's not Ghost! That's her sister, Dynamic. Looks are why her billionaire owner paid a million for her. That's Ghost over there.'

Roo loved horses too much to ever be disappointed by them but, as she followed Joni into the superstar filly's stall, she was mystified.

In the flesh, Ghost was more carthorse than racehorse. It was hard to believe that she was capable of putting on a turn of speed.

'How in the world did Finn and Keyne know that she was a potential champion?' Joni asked Roo. 'She has the most peculiar barrel chest.'

'Her "peculiar barrel chest" was what caught our attention,' said Finn, joining them in the stall. 'It made us wonder if she had an extra-large heart like Secretariat and Phar Lap, two of the greatest racehorses ever. Turns out she does. We also knew that she and her sister had classy pedigrees. Their grandsire was the great Galileo and their dam – that's their mum – was a Derby winner.'

'If they have the same pedigree, what made you choose Ghost?' asked Roo.

'Besides the fact that she was nearly a million pounds cheaper?' The trainer laughed. 'Detective work.'

Roo was fascinated. *'Detective work?'*

'Sales are not the easiest places to buy horses. They're loud, stressful environments for highly strung baby Thoroughbreds. The auctioneer is drumming up bids on the loudspeaker, and people are shouting down their phones, buying horses for owners across the world.

'Dynamic was the star of the auction that year. There was a frenzy of bidding for her. Nobody wanted Ghost because she had a clumsy, lilting stride. One buyer joked that she ran like the mythical haggis, as if two of her legs were shorter than the others.'

With every word, Roo warmed to Ghost more. She hoped that if she were in Finn and Keyne's shoes, she'd have chosen the clumsy, 'ugly' filly that no one else wanted, too.

'Keyne and I had a gut feeling about her,' Finn went on. 'We questioned her groom. Turned out, Ghost had been kicked in the shoulder as a foal and never fully recovered. We were convinced that, with therapy and patience, we could heal her. Now she smashes records every time she goes out.'

He rubbed the filly's ears. 'Everyone in racing is searching for the X factor.'

'What's the X factor?' asked Roo, trying to look at Ghost through X-ray eyes and wishing that she had Finn's gift for seeing the rare qualities inside a horse.

'Honestly? We don't know,' admitted Finn. 'Some think it's the speed gene. Some buyers hire specialist companies to DNA-test embryos to tell them whether a foal might grow up to be a sprinter or a stayer. Stayers are horses which do better over long distances.'

'You mean it's possible to detect actual go-faster genes?' asked Joni.

'Yes, but criminals are getting in on the act. The biggest threat to horse racing of the future is gene doping. Unlike drugs, it's undetectable.'

'What's gene doping?' asked Roo.

'Tampering with genes to artificially enhance performance,' explained Finn. 'Rogue scientists are already experimenting with it – editing out genetic weaknesses in embryos and adding, say, a speed gene to a stayer, or an endurance gene to a sprinter. If they succeed, theoretically they could breed superstar racehorses by the dozen.'

'What about superstar showjumpers or dressage horses?' asked Roo, thinking about Wonder and Magician. 'Could you breed those by the dozen?'

Finn looked at her in surprise. 'In future, that might possible, but you'd always be missing a few ingredients. If creating champions was that simple, Dynamic would break as many records as her sister. The fact is, she's never finished higher than third. She can't be bothered. You can't breed courage, charisma, or willpower into a horse. Those qualities come from within.'

'But what made you think that Ghost could have them?' Joni persisted. 'She seems so docile and . . . ordinary.'

Finn turned round. 'Think so? When I buy a horse, I'm not concerned with whether they're small or weak or strong. I look for their soul. The window to a horse's soul is its eye. Ghost has a nice big eye. An honest eye. A *genuine* eye.'

Keyne appeared at the stall door. 'Dad, can we chat about Say-No-More's schedule? Oh, sorry, I didn't realise you were busy. Hi, everyone. Morning, Ghost girl. See you on Friday.'

At the sound of her teenage jockey's voice, the filly's head shot up. A memory flickered across her eyes, as if the adrenaline rush of their latest triumph surged once again through her veins. Roo caught her breath. The fire that drove Ghost blazed in them.

Then it was gone, and she was more carthorse than racehorse again.

Joni had seen the fire too. She seemed a little shaken.

'Ah, now I understand,' she told Finn.

Roo waited until she and her aunt were walking back to Bluebird to say: '*Gene tampering? Gene editing?* Could that be why Wonder, Magician, and the others were stolen – for their perfect genes?'

'I think,' Joni said, 'we need to examine this case in a whole new light.'

38.

RACE DAY

Every morning since arriving at Queen's Reach, Roo had risen at sunrise to watch the young riders take the horses out to the gallops. She enjoyed walking through the barns as they were shaking out rugs and tacking up.

Today, May tenth, it was finally Roo's turn to ride. She felt quite proud and grown-up as she walked among the shiny, sinewy Thoroughbreds, who were champing at their bits and snorting and stamping as the girths were tightened on their featherweight racing saddles.

But she found herself looking at them differently, thinking about Finn's words about gene doping. If the thieves were targeting certain horses for their rare and unique genetics, there was no way of telling which racehorse they'd go after. They might want Ghost or one of the great stallions for their speed genes, or they might target a champion 'stayer' for its ability to endure.

For that reason, Roo was jumpier than a cat on hot bricks. If the thieves were planning to use the theatre of the solar eclipse as cover for a robbery, they could be moving into position at this very minute, posing as groundskeepers, grooms, or even riders.

'When the moon passes between the sun and earth, day will turn to night for seven and a half minutes,' Joni had explained. 'Imagine if the gang got away with "disappearing" one of racing's fastest horses during a total eclipse. It would make international headlines. Our job is to try to prevent that.'

Roo found Skylar in the weighing room, where the jockeys kept their colourful racing silks. Its walls were lined with cabinets of silver trophies and black-and-white photographs of famous victories.

The room positively crackled with atmosphere. Sometimes, Roo just stood there, inhaling the heady fragrance of leather, polish, and past glories. She wished that her dad, who'd been passionate about racing, and her mum, who'd loved horses just as much as Roo did, could share in it too.

Skylar helped her into a back protector, racing helmet, and goggles. 'Perfect fit,' she said with a grin. 'Don't worry, Roo. We'll be back in plenty of time to be ready for the eclipse. It's due at 11.15 a.m., right after Ghost's first training session.'

To Roo, no solar eclipse could match the prospect of riding the gallops herself. It didn't matter that the ex-sprinter she'd been loaned was a creaky twenty-six-year-old called Benjy. His refusal to rush as she set off, accompanied by Skylar on an energetic bay, only made Roo appreciate him more.

She'd had a taste of the speed gene on her wild ride across Dartmoor on Drifter. A sedate canter suited her just fine.

Benjy was one of QR's 'teacher' horses. It was his job to show naughty or fearful youngsters how to behave on and around the track.

This morning, he was 'teaching' a couple of two-year-olds, one of which Skylar was riding. Benjy's relaxed body language showed the newbies that their home track was the place to safely stretch their legs, not bolt over the horizon like maniacs.

Racing was strictly for the racecourse.

Roo crouched over Benjy's withers like a jockey. Though his stride was steady, not speedy, it was a thrill to 'race' along the gallops. In her mind's eye, roaring crowds lined the track, cheering Roo and Benjy on to victory.

She grinned as she swept past her aunt. Joni was sketching behind the white railings while keeping her eyes peeled for suspicious activity. She gave Roo a thumbs-up as she went by. It was code for: so far, so good.

39.

DEVIL'S BARGAIN

After Roo and Skylar had hosed down their horses back at the Fillies' Barn, they returned to the gallops to wait for Ghost's training session.

Joni was sketching horses at the start of the gallops, close to the yew hedge that marked the boundary of Queen's Reach.

From time to time, there was a commotion beyond the hedge. A frozen fish truck had broken down. It was blocking the lane as it waited for a repairman.

Skylar bent towards Roo. 'The chaos on the lane is upsetting some of the young horses. Finn has told Keyne to wait until after the eclipse before running Ghost. He doesn't want a sudden blast of horn or a motorbike frightening her.'

A crowd was beginning to gather on the gallops. Skylar spotted a friend and went to say hello. Roo sat on a bench, watching out for anyone who looked as if they were 'up to no good', as her aunt had instructed.

Snatches of conversation came and went on the breeze.

'The great Eclipse was born in a solar eclipse on April Fool's Day in 1764,' a wizened ex-jockey was telling two apprentices. 'Talk about destiny being written in the stars.'

'In a hundred years, that's how they'll be talking about Ghost,' said one of the teenage riders. 'Five million, she's worth, and she's not even four.'

Roo turned her head as a well-dressed man in a shirt and tie hurried past to the next bench. He gave an audible sigh as he sank down beside the manager of the Stallions' Barn.

'Sorry I'm late, Scott. Tailback on the lane.'

'No worries, Connor. You haven't missed anything. Finn's going to wait until after the eclipse to start Ghost.'

From what Roo could gather, Connor, the man in the shirt and tie, was a successful racehorse owner.

'Ghost has no idea how fortunate she is,' he told the barn manager. 'Finn is a decent trainer who puts the horses first, unlike some I've seen. Mine try their best for him because they're happy and healthy. Too many in this business treat young horses like machines.'

'Tell me about it,' said Scott. 'I've seen first-hand the damage that can be done when a gifted youngster is pushed too hard too soon – and not just in racing.'

'Care to share the story?'

Surreptitiously, Roo wriggled nearer. She was intrigued.

'It happened many years ago, but sure,' said Scott. 'I was eighteen and working in my dream first job – grooming showjumpers, dressage champions, and eventers at a competition yard.

'The star of the yard was an ambitious young trainer. Like me, he came from a rough, foster-care background. I'd hoped we might be friends, but he barely spoke to me. He was going places and nothing was going to stop him.'

'Any good?'

'Not as good as he thought he was, but he got results. He had the golden touch. Every horse he took on became a champion One day, the son of a wealthy businessman arrived at the yard with a talented showjumper. He wanted this young trainer to work with the horse. Wouldn't hear of anyone else touching it.'

Roo looked over at Skylar. She was deep in conversation with her friend. Joni was still some distance away, meandering along the railings, pausing to sketch.

Roo tuned back in to the conversation on the next bench.

'Was the young man's confidence in the trainer rewarded?' asked Connor.

'To begin with, yes,' replied Scott. 'This horse got on to a winning streak. Trophies and medals piled up. Then the whispering started. Some claimed that the trainer and the young owner were using brutal training tricks. Double bits that drew blood. Painkillers to dull lameness. Rapping the horse's legs with a pole as it went over a jump to teach it to tuck its feet up. Dried hedgehog skins—'

'Hedgehog skins!'

'In days gone by, cruel trainers would hide them in leg bandages or boots, or tie them to poles, as a painful reminder to the horse to clear a jump by a good margin.'

Roo went cold. She remembered the strange thorn in Wonder's brushing boots, the one that made him rear in terror.

'What a monstrous duo,' Connor said in disgust. 'I hope they were banned for life. What happened to the horse?'

'They wrecked it. It was my job to groom it. It went from being a high-spirited but good-natured horse to being petrified of its own shadow. It hated to be touched. In a fury, I confronted the trainer. Naturally, he denied it. It was his word against mine and I was fired. I needed that job, and I was devastated.

'The night I left, I was fetching my jacket from the boot room when I heard the two men arguing. Despite his denials to me, the trainer was well aware that he'd ruined this horse. He seemed riddled with guilt and regret. He told the rich kid that if he had a chance to start from scratch with the tragic beast, he'd do things differently. Be kinder. More patient. He said that it was unfortunate that, in life, that there were no "do-overs".'

'No second chances, you mean?' asked Connor.

'Precisely. The kid laughed and said if one was wealthy enough, there was always a second chance. Sometimes even a third, fourth, or fifth "do-over". If you broke something – whether it was a car or a horse – you simply bought another.

'The trainer was incensed. He said it didn't work that way if one was poor. His career would be over if word ever got out that he'd destroyed this amazing creature.

'The kid told him not to worry. His wealthy, influential father would help hush things up. They'd pay a farmer in some remote country hamlet to give the horse a quiet forever home. If anything ever came out about why the creature had broken down, the rich kid promised that he'd take the blame.

'In addition, a hefty donation to the owner and staff of our yard would erase the entire episode from their minds. The trainer would leave with glowing references, his reputation unstained.

'The trainer went silent for so long that I became afraid I'd cough and be caught eavesdropping. My throat had a fiendish tickle. Eventually, he asked: "Why would you do that for me?"

'The rich kid said: "Because then you'll owe me."

'There was a nervous laugh. The trainer went: "If you mean money, I don't have any."

'"Nah," said the kid. "You'll repay me with a favour to be decided at a date in the future."

'I could almost hear the other guy sweating. "What sort of favour?" he asked, but the kid just laughed it off. "Don't worry," he said. "It might be years before I call it in. Decades even. But count on this: the debt will be repaid. You'd be a fool to believe I'll forget it."'

'Good grief, Scott,' exclaimed Connor. 'You're describing a devil's bargain. Outside of fiction, I've never heard the like. What happened? Did this young devil ever call in the favour?"'

'I've no idea. Shortly after I lost my job, Finn offered me a place as an apprentice jockey here at Queen's Reach. Being in this happy place was such a contrast to my previous experience that I blocked those ruthless men from my head. From what I heard, the trainer seemed to have learned his lesson and found work at a respectable yard. The rich kid quit showjumping altogether and went off to the US to study at Harvard University.

'Two and a half years ago, this kid – now in his thirties – resurfaced on the UK horse scene. After dropping out of Harvard to embark on a series of failed business ventures, he'd decided to change tack. You'll never guess what he does for a living now.'

'Enlighten me.'

Roo was eager to be enlightened herself, but Scott's words were drowned out by a loudspeaker announcement about the eclipse.

By the time it was over, Connor was saying: 'What became of the trainer?'

'He became a coach to the stars,' reported Scott. 'Mended his ways and is now a virtual horse whisperer. But every time I read about another of his clients reaching the heights, I wonder if he's been up to his old tricks.'

'What's his name?' asked Connor.

Roo knew the answer before Scott replied in a low voice: 'Dale Dering.'

'Rhianna Cooper's coach?' Connor was dumbfounded. 'I read a piece on him recently in *Horse & Hound*. I wonder if his nemesis ever called in that favour.'

Numb with shock, Roo sat unmoving as Connor and Scott ended their conversation. They turned to greet Kathryn Irving, who was escorting two men in oil-stained jumpers to a spot near the railings.

'I'll have someone bring you sandwiches and a flask of coffee,' she told the newcomers. 'We'll get you some eclipse glasses too. Enjoy the show.'

The new guard caught up to Kathryn as she passed Roo again. 'Mrs Irving, d'you think it's wise to have strangers on the premises . . .'

She paused. 'Brandon, at Queen's Reach, we believe in welcoming strangers. Roo and Joni were strangers. Now they're friends.' She smiled in the direction of Roo. 'Those young guys have had a dreadful morning trying to get their truck fixed and being shouted at by their boss and every driver who squeezes by on the lane. If you're concerned that they might be horse thieves, it's your job to watch them.'

The horse thieves had gone clean out of Roo's mind. All she could think about was Dale Dering and his cruel past. She no longer cared that he had an alibi for the night that Wonder was snatched. He ran things at Starwood. He could have paid Jiang to fix the CCTV for all anyone knew.

What pact had he made with the sinister young man? What was he capable of?

Most importantly, what did it mean for their case?

Skylar came rushing back and hooked her arm through Roo's. 'Quick, put your special glasses on. It's eclipse time.'

40.

TROJAN HORSE

Hours later, Roo still tingled when she relived Ghost Flight's run.

Keyne had planned to ease Ghost into her training run with a relaxed gallop, but seconds before light returned to the gallops, a mechanical hare had zoomed out from under the hedge. It almost struck her.

Roo was at the railings with Joni and Skylar when the frightened racehorse streaked out of the darkness like a beautiful phantom.

In flight, she was the colour of mercury.

'I could hardly breathe, she was going so fast,' Keyne told them afterwards, his sinewy jockey's frame trembling from the thrill of it. He ran a hand down Ghost's grey neck. 'I swear there was lightning in her hooves.'

Roo couldn't help smiling. Ghost looked so pleased with herself.

Finn was livid. Not with his son, who could never have contained the filly once she bolted, but at whoever had sent the remote-controlled hare – the kind used in greyhound racing.

The guards tracked the hare only as far as the lane, a few metres away. There, its metal paw prints were erased by the tyre tracks of dozens of passing vehicles.

'I wish I could stay and be another pair of eyes,' Skylar told Roo that evening as they waited for her car to Pegasus Productions. She was on her way to meet Art Levine, the producer of *The Last Messenger*.

'He left a voicemail message saying he has a new job for me – something about training his wife's Arabian for her birthday trick-riding display,' said Skylar. 'Sounds fun, but I'd rather be here watching out for you and Joni. The robot rabbit that almost crashed into Ghost was no joke. Keyne could have been killed. Ghost could have broken a leg. What if the thieves were using it to create a diversion?'

She looked around. 'What if they're already here, inside the gates, biding their time, like warriors inside a Trojan Horse?'

The face of the new guard, lecturing Kathryn Irving about the importance of NOT welcoming strangers, came into Roo's head.

Something about Brandon made her skin crawl. She didn't buy the story about him single-handedly saving Dynamic from thieves in his very first week. He wasn't the heroic type. Too weak and smarmy. What if *he* was the gang's inside man – the warrior inside a Queen's Reach Trojan Horse?

He wouldn't be the first thief to warn others to watch out for thieves in an attempt to shift the focus from himself.

Skylar was watching her intently. 'Don't take any chances, Roo. Promise me.'

'We'll be fine,' said Roo. 'Finn's putting an extra guard on patrol and Keyne kidded that he knows Ghost's back to normal because she's eating like a horse. The robot rabbit was probably set off by some stupid prankster.'

'I'm sure you're right,' said Skylar, not sounding sure. But the Pegasus driver was pulling up beside them and there was nothing more she could do.

***

After dinner, the racing yard was briefly deserted. The young riders who lived in the on-site boarding house were usually napping or refuelling before hitting the gym, the pool table, or the TV room. The Irving family did the same.

Walking alone through the echoing buildings, Roo felt unnerved. To get to Bluebird quicker, she took a shortcut between the long barns.

Footsteps sounded behind her. When she turned, there was no one there. Roo's heartbeat spiked madly. She had the overwhelming sense that someone was watching her. Someone who meant her harm.

Breaking into a run, she made it to Bluebird in record time, almost colliding with Brandon, the guard, who was coming down the steps of the camper. He smirked at Roo before sauntering away.

Inside, Joni was seething. 'I returned to Bluebird to find Brandon sitting on our sofa. He claimed he decided to investigate because the door was ajar. I don't understand it. I'm positive I locked it.

'I was so furious that I took the opportunity to ask whether he was acquainted with the men from the fish truck. I saw him laughing with them as they were handing out free crates of cod and prawns.'

So it was an act, thought Roo, *Brandon pretending to warn Kathryn against the stranger danger of the fish men. He must be the gang's inside man.*

'How did he react?'

'Not well,' said her aunt. 'His bland, goofy demeanour transmogrified into something altogether more menacing. He told me I was being ridiculous. How could he know two random fish salesmen who just happened to break down in the lane? He claimed he'd warned Kathryn Irving about the danger of strangers. "Strangers like you, Joni Jackson," he added nastily.'

'What a beast!' cried Roo.

'Indeed,' said her aunt. 'And that wasn't all. He said: "Don't think I haven't noticed you and your niece poking your noses into everyone's business. You want to be careful. People who stick their hands into hornets' nests are liable to get stung."'

Roo was horrified. 'How dare he threaten you!'

'He denied it was a threat. His gormless grin returned, and he said: "Just passing on some friendly advice. Have a nice day."'

Roo decided not to mention her own fears that she'd been followed. She gave her aunt a hug.

'Oh, a pipsqueak like Brandon doesn't bother me,' said Joni. 'If we weren't undercover, I'd rip him to shreds. Only verbally, of course, although a roundhouse karate kick would be more effective.'

'Have you done much martial arts training?' asked Roo. Self-defence was one area of her aunt's CV they hadn't yet tackled.

Before Joni could answer, an email popped up on the open laptop. Joni scanned it and clapped a hand to her mouth.

Roo was alarmed. 'Is it bad news?'

'It's from my tax expert friend. The one I tasked with trying to trace the invisible man to whom Rhianna's father is so heavily in debt.'

'What did he say?'

Roo was getting worried. Joni looked shell-shocked.

'Barney Rotten changed his name, aged seventeen, perhaps

suspecting that few people would want to hire a trainer named Rotten.'

'What kind of trainer?'

'A horse trainer. Nowadays, he's better known as . . . Dale Dering.'

Roo felt as if a meteor had struck her brain.

She said slowly: 'You're saying that Rhianna's dad owes a million pounds to the man who coaches his daughter and trains her horses?'

'What's more concerning,' said her aunt, 'is that until the loan is repaid, Coach Dering holds the title deeds to Starwood Farm and the ownership papers for Fleetfoot Amberwell.'

'Wonder's replacement?'

'Yes. It's what's known as collateral. If Lloyd Cooper pays back the cash, everything will be returned to him. Until that day, Dale holds the Coopers' fate in the palm of his hand. If he and Lloyd fall out . . .'

She shut the laptop with a snap. 'Well, let's hope they don't.'

Roo was reeling. 'So, basically, Dale has two options: He can either save Rhianna's family or destroy them.'

She thought again about the devil's bargain and the ruthless young man who'd proposed it. Where was he now? Was Dale at his mercy? Could his own life also be saved or ruined on a whim?

'Roo, I'll be honest. I'm worried,' said her aunt. 'Brandon's threat today was a wake-up call. I'd never forgive myself if something happened to you . . .'

'Nothing's going to happen,' protested Roo. Surely her aunt wasn't suggesting they throw in the towel. They'd come too far to give up now. 'Brandon was just being an idiot.'

'And what if he was deadly serious? Honey, I know you're desperate to find Wonder and Magician. But every instinct is screaming at me to get out. There are dark forces at work in this business – forces we can't yet see or understand.'

A sudden pounding nearly frightened them out of their skins.

Roo got to the door first. She scowled at the guard on Bluebird's step. 'What do *you* want?'

To her astonishment, Brandon's face crumpled like a child's.

'It's Ghost Flight, miss! She's gone. Will you and your aunt join the search? We need all the help we can get.'

41.

THE ART OF DETECTION

THE GHOSTING OF GHOST HAS ECHOES OF TRAGIC SHERGAR

String of Horse Heists Has Detectives Scratching Their Heads

Roo pushed aside the *Racing Post* in disgust. 'Why do journalists always do that?'

'Do what?' her aunt asked absently. Leaning over her canvas, she dabbed at Ghost's ear with a fine paintbrush.

Bluebird had been transformed into an artist's studio. Linseed oil scented the air. Tubes of paint and rolls of canvas cluttered every available surface. Roo loved it. When her aunt was at her easel, the sadness that Roo sometimes saw in her melted away. Despite all that had happened since Ghost Flight had vanished five days earlier, Joni was in her element.

Setting down her brush, Joni wiped her hands on a rag. 'Go on, Roo. You were saying something about the "Ghosting of Ghost" article.'

'Why do headline writers always make it seem as if something supernatural has happened when it hasn't? Also, we're not sitting scratching our heads. We've chased the thieves all over the country and we're getting closer. One of these days, we'll be in the right place at the wrong time—'

'Or the wrong place at the right time,' put in her aunt.

'And we'll catch the thieves...' finished Roo. 'If Scotland Yard hasn't caught them first.'

Because Ghost was no mere showjumper or trick horse – she was a £5 million racing legend – Scotland Yard had sent their best and brightest detectives to Queen's Reach within two hours of her disappearance.

Roo had watched from the steps of Bluebird as forensic specialists poured out of a van in papery white suits. Flashbulbs popped. Yellow crime-scene tape fluttered in the breeze.

Two gimlet-eyed detectives with smart haircuts had screeched into the yard in a BMW. They'd set up an interview room in the Irvings' house. By 8 a.m. the next day they were taking turns to grill anyone who'd set foot on Queen's Reach in the past month.

Skylar was among the first to be interviewed. Given what had happened with Detective Inspector Pickle back in February, Roo was relieved for her friend's sake that it went well. A pleasant, professional detective had interviewed her. She'd been particularly interested in Skylar's thoughts on Magician's disappearance, and wondered if Skylar thought there were similarities with Ghost.

Roo was absolutely dying for her turn in the 'hot seat'. She couldn't wait to swap theories with the detectives and perhaps share her case files. But it was late afternoon by the time she and Joni were summoned, and she didn't get a chance.

The interview began badly and went downhill.

'I see from my notes that you were a suspect in the theft of Wonder, Ms Jackson,' the detective said conversationally.

'Briefly, yes, but—'

'You were also present during the theft of Magician?'

'Yes, but—'

'And here you are again, just metres from the robbery of another valuable horse.' The detective folded his arms. 'Call me suspicious, but that's an awful lot of coincidences.'

'We can explain,' said Joni. 'As a matter of fact, I'm an investigative journalist. My niece and I have been helping Skylar Heathcote—'

'Ah, Ms Heathcote. Another person who was briefly a suspect in the Wonder Boy case.'

Just as Roo was thinking, with disbelief, that this man was another Detective Inspector Pickle, Kathryn Irving burst into the room. She'd been doing laundry next door and had heard every word.

'Stop! I won't have it! Not under my own roof. Detective, I know you're only trying to find Ghost Flight, but it can't be at the expense of our friends and family. Joni Jackson is our artist in residence. She and Roo are here at *my* invitation. I won't have you accusing them of . . . of what exactly? It's hardly their fault that Brandon, our guard, was too lazy to do his job and inspect every stall in the Fillies' Barn last night. It's not their fault that he peered half-heartedly through the barn door, mistook a hologram of Ghost for the real horse, and went whistling on his way. Roo and Joni didn't hide Ghost in the builders' storeroom, dye her black, and smuggle her into the field opposite.'

'Yes, but—' huffed the detective.

'I know that for a fact,' Kathryn went on, 'because I passed their camper several times during the traumatic events of last night. Any time Joni wasn't helping us search, she was at her easel, painting our beautiful filly. What Joni's doing – keeping Ghost

Flight's flame burning on canvas – is one of the only things giving Finn, Keyne, and me hope at the moment.'

Roo, who was watching Joni's expression, saw something inside her light up.

After Kathryn Irving had gone, the detective was stiff but courteous. He even listened patiently as Roo explained that the fish men, Scotland Yard's chief suspects, couldn't have stolen Ghost because it was too obvious and because of their jumpers.

'She means the gansey jumpers they were wearing,' explained Joni. 'They're made of oiled wool to shield fishermen from sea spray and the elements.'

'I remembered they had those special knitted patterns that show what village they're from in case they get lost at sea,' Roo told the detective. 'That means they were real fishermen, not thieves.'

He laughed indulgently. 'Are you aware that ganseys are in fashion at the moment? You can get those jumpers in any high street store.'

Roo shrank into her seat, feeling small.

Joni glared at the detective. 'What Roo's *trying* to say is that we believe the thieves who snatched Ghost are the same criminals who took Wonder and Magician. This theft has the gang's modus operandi stamped all over it. In our opinion, it's doubtful the fishermen were involved.'

Roo knew the gangs' playbook off by heart. She'd written it up in Ghost Flight's case file.

Pre-Robbery Smokescreen: On April 28, thieves use attempt to steal Dynamic as cover to install a hologram projector in the Fillies' Barn. They also identify a future hiding place for Ghost – a storage unit being used by builders, 110 metres from the filly's stall.

Red Herrings: On May 10, solar eclipse day, guards at Queen's Reach have their attention diverted by a) a mechanical hare causing chaos on the gallops, and b) a broken-down fish truck.

Vanishing Trick: Ghost is kept in the builders' storage unit until it's safe to move her to the field. Last sighting of her is at 1.43. A wildlife camera catches her rump going by, now dyed black. From there, she disappears into the night.

Getaway Vehicle: ????

Since the fish truck, miraculously repaired, had driven away shortly before Ghost was taken, detectives had named the 'fishy' fish men as 'persons of interest' in their inquiry.

Nearly a week on, Roo found it impossible to fathom how the great detectives of Scotland Yard had frittered away three whole days before confirming what Roo and Joni had suspected from the start. The fish men had been framed. Two weeks before, a bearded, 'softly spoken' stranger in a Glasgow pub had offered them a pile of cash each to spend a day pretending to have engine trouble in the lane outside Queen's Reach.

They'd taken the money without asking questions, not knowing that they'd be the 'suspicious strangers' the police would focus on after the robbery.

When they'd later returned from a North Sea fishing trip to find themselves briefly under arrest for unwittingly aiding Ghost's thieves, they were mortified – especially since Kathryn Irving had been so kind to them.

Five days after Ghost was stolen, Scotland Yard detectives were back to square one.

'It's good to know that we're not the only ones who keep going back to square one,' remarked Roo. 'Although, technically, we're now on square two. We've learned something new from this robbery.'

'What's that?' said her aunt, who was at her easel again. She hadn't allowed Roo even the tiniest glimpse of the painting. Any time she wasn't working on it, she kept it covered.

'We've always assumed that Wonder and Magician were whisked away instantly by the thieves,' Roo told her. 'That didn't happen with Ghost. The thieves stuck her in a builders' storeroom just metres from her stall and only moved her hours afterwards when the fuss had died down.

'Maybe that happened with Wonder and Magician too. Maybe they were tranquillised and kept on Starwood or the film set in a shed or truck or something? The police were looking for a standing, lively horse. A sleeping, lying-down horse is easier to hide. Magician could have been hidden behind scenery boards or film props or something. Wonder could have been hidden under carpets or paint sheets and driven away in a decorators' lorry or something.'

The clatter of hooves took her to Bluebird's open door. A line of sweaty horses was returning from the gallops. Roo missed seeing Skylar, who'd taken a train to the Scottish Highlands to begin training Antonia Levine's Arabian for the birthday trick-riding display.

At her easel, Joni laid down her brush. She glanced anxiously at Roo.

'It's finished! Roo, tell me what you think. I need your honest opinion. Don't hold back.'

Roo rushed to look at the painting. She was expecting it to be good, but it was much more than that. With love and dazzling skill, her aunt had captured Ghost Flight's otherworldly beauty at the moment the filly streaked from total eclipse darkness into the light.

'It's a masterpiece,' breathed Roo, and she meant it.

The Irving family agreed – the painting *was* a masterpiece.

So powerful was the portrait that Kathryn Irving asked Joni's permission to send a photo to the media.

'If anything can nudge the conscience of a regretful thief, or inspire a witness to come forward with information that might help detectives find her, it's your unforgettable painting,' she told Joni. 'You've captured the spirit that lives in Ghost when she runs.'

Before the day was out, a fresh lead came to Joni and Roo, out of nowhere, like a gift.

SHAMAL

42.

CASTLE IN THE SKY

'Are you *sure* we're on the right road?' asked Roo with trepidation as Bluebird rounded a hairpin bend and kept climbing. The deeper they drove into the mountains, the more the dark pines leaned in.

Joni gritted her teeth as a rock bashed the camper's low undercarriage. 'Skylar did recommend that we hire an SUV before venturing into the wilds of the Scottish Highlands, but I told her that was quite impossible. We need Bluebird the way a tortoise needs a shell, or a robin needs a nest . . .'

'Or a joey needs a kangaroo's pouch,' finished Roo with a giggle. 'Bluebird's our shell, nest, and pouch rolled into one. Best of all, she's portable. If we were stuck in one place, we wouldn't be headed to a celebrity party at a Scottish castle. Skylar says the locals call it the "Castle in the Sky".'

Under normal circumstances, Joni would rather have eaten bugs than drive halfway across the country for a celebrity party. The only reason they were risking Bluebird's health on a remote mountain road was because Skylar had stumbled on a vital new lead.

As pines and granite peaks filled the camper windscreen, Roo felt the way her father must have done as he headed out to buy his weekly lottery ticket. Hopeful yet not hopeful. Braced for disappointment. After so many near-misses, it was tough to believe their luck would ever change.

And yet something about this trip did feel different, *had* felt different from the moment Skylar called six days earlier and said in a hushed tone: 'Roo, you're not going to believe this. Antonia's Arabian is a red roan.'

'There are quite a few red roans in the world, Skylar!' Roo said with a laugh. 'Millions probably.'

'Yes, but they weren't all competing in the West Coast Endurance Challenge on March third,' said Skylar. 'It was Shamal's first race after she arrived in the UK from Sharjah. She's a gold-medal-winning champion, worth a king's ransom. Exactly the sort of elite performance horse our thieves might target.'

The blood began to sing in Roo's ears. 'But that's impossible. I went through the race results ten times. I'd have remembered Shamal's name and her colour.'

'Of course you would – had she finished. Shamal never did. Six kilometres into the race, she shied at a rabbit and pulled a tendon. A veterinary support team had a nightmare trying to rescue her and Antonia from Dartmoor in the fog.'

Skylar was breathless with excitement. 'Roo, I've checked the timings. Shamal had her accident shortly before you were chased across the moors by the hunters and dogs. Those thugs must have been lying in wait for her, not realising that she'd already been trailered off the course.'

Roo couldn't get over the quirk of fate that had carried Shamal and Antonia to safety while she and Drifter were hunted like deer. All the same, she wouldn't have traded places with them. The wild ponies had saved her and the Quarter Horse, and Shamal had been safe at the castle ever since – until now.

'I believe there's a high chance that the thieves will strike again on May twenty-third, the evening of Antonia's party,' said Skylar. 'We need to try to stop them.'

'Which thieves?' Joni had asked, overhearing as she returned to Bluebird with groceries. 'Whose party?'

Skylar had explained, but Joni took a lot of convincing.

'The Dartmoor race was two months ago. If the gang had wanted Shamal so desperately, they'd have tried again by now. Why wait until a crowded birthday party with a ton of witnesses?'

'They stole Magician in front of a ton of witnesses – and rolling cameras,' Roo reminded her aunt.

'The Castle in the Sky is like an eagle's eyrie – one with high-tech security,' said Skylar. 'Under normal circumstances, breaking in would be close to impossible. There's nothing for miles around. Any stranger or disturbance would be noticed. But on the night of the party, there'll be dozens of strangers coming and going. If you're a thief, it would be the ideal time to strike . . .'

She grinned. 'Did I mention it's a fancy dress party? You, Roo, should go as Nancy Drew.'

'And I could go as my namesake, Joni Mitchell, the legendary folk singer,' smiled Joni, unbending. 'I have the cutest green velvet bell-bottoms. But how would we get an invite?'

'You won't need one. Antonia is so concerned I'll get lonely at the castle she's practically begged me to invite my friends. If I'm wrong about the thieves making a second attempt to steal Shamal, the three of us can just hang out. You'd have your own room at the castle in case you needed it, and free use of the tennis courts, archery range, pool, equestrian centre, spa . . .'

Joni beamed. 'A spa? What do you think, Roo? If the thieves come after Shamal, we'll be ready. If not, we can unwind and recharge.'

'I forgot to mention that I need a good groom to get Shamal show-ready for my trick-riding display,' said Skylar with a smile. 'What do you think, Roo? Would you do it?'

'Yes!' cried Roo. 'Yes, yes, yes!'

Skylar laughed. 'My nana has a saying: *"Para cada pregunta la naturaleza tiene una respuesta."* In English, it means, "For every question, nature has an answer." Up here in the mountains, we might find that the key to the mystery has been staring us in the face all along.'

***

Bluebird veered uncomfortably close to a precipice on the mountain road, spitting shale into the void below.

Roo was relieved when the sign for the castle appeared soon afterwards. An arrow pointed left into the wilderness.

As Bluebird puffed up the steep, forest-lined drive, a headache gnawed at Roo's temples. Once again, her sleep had been plagued by dreams she couldn't remember. She had a bad feeling about the weekend ahead.

At the same time, would anyone really attempt to stage a horse theft up here? No chance of a quick getaway. And Skylar had assured her that security at the party would be intense.

Joni leaned on the accelerator and the camper rounded the final, steep bend. There, hewn into the mountainside and outlined against dove-grey clouds, was the Castle in the Sky.

'It's not a real castle,' Skylar had explained, 'but Antonia says it's better. There's underfloor heating and a total ban on tiger-skin rugs.'

A guard in a scarlet uniform with gold epaulettes waved Bluebird through the security gate. A valet directed Joni to a parking space on the edge of a cliff.

As Roo climbed out, a touch of vertigo made her wobble. The mountain air was as cold as sorbet. The view was out of this world. As far as she could see, there was nothing but forests, streams, and a loch the blue of Antarctic ice.

A shrill scream made her jump. Alice in Wonderland, giggling madly, flew past her. Spiderman and a boy-sized gorilla were in hot pursuit.

A footman approached. 'Joni Jackson and Roo Thorn? Welcome to the Castle in the Sky. If you'd like to freshen up, I can show you to your room. We'll be serving a cream tea in the drawing room at 3 p.m.'

Following him up the path, Roo tried to think positively. All she had to do was professionally groom a desert-born Arabian for a trick-riding spectacular at a film producer's clifftop castle, while keeping an eye out for ruthless horse thieves.

What could possibly go wrong?

43.

MASQUERADE

'Wow, Skylar! You look sensational!'

Roo couldn't stop staring. Lean, fit, and bronzed in her grandmother's cream satin waistcoat and bow tie, sequinned black riding tights and polished long boots, her friend looked every inch a circus star as she strode across the yard at the Castle in the Sky's equestrian centre.

Skylar grinned. 'Wow, Roo, so does Shamal. Great job on her grooming.'

Roo flushed with pride. 'Hard to improve on perfection!'

It was true. Shamal moved as if the fierce desert wind for which she was named still lived in her. She didn't so much walk as float. The legacy of her spirited ancestors showed in every line of her exquisite dished face.

The rose-copper sheen of her coat was all natural, but Roo had been working hard, burnishing it with a body brush, shine spray, and a sheepskin grooming glove.

After combing out Shamal's rippled mane and tail and oiling her hooves, she'd put on the Arabian's ceremonial bridle. It was decorated, Bedouin-style, in colourful silks and beads.

It was forty-eight hours since they'd arrived at the castle. Roo loved her sleeping nook in Bluebird, but it had been enormous fun to spend two nights in a four-poster bed and take a not-so-secret tunnel each evening to the dining hall.

Antonia Levine was a vegetarian like Roo and Joni. Roo had laughed so hard when she saw that, in the great tradition of castle dining halls, the Levines' was lined with stags' heads – only these were cheerful vegan ones, made of felt.

For two days, she and Joni really had got to unwind and recharge. They'd tried the Jacuzzi, the steam room, the archery, and enjoyed an unforgettable cream tea and many sumptuous vegetarian meals.

But as ever, Roo's favourite thing were the horses – six strong Highland ponies, a gentle giant Clydesdale, and, of course, Shamal.

Watching Skylar work with the Arabian had taught Roo so much about the importance of patience and connection with horses. The mare was intelligent, bursting with energy, and eager to please, but it was Skylar's understanding of how horses think that made it possible for them to achieve in days what would normally take months.

The real test would come in just over an hour when the trick-riding display began. Up at the castle, the party was already in full swing. As far as Roo was concerned, from now until Antonia's birthday celebrations were over, she had one and only one job: protecting Shamal.

The castle stable yard had become the unofficial rehearsal space for any performer who needed it. An acrobat was doing a handstand on a hay bale. Three jugglers were tossing skittles near the feed room.

Skylar started doing stretches. With a wink at Roo and only the shortest of run-ups, she did a handspring, a couple of backflips, and a cartwheel across the yard.

A posse of passing guests joined the acrobat in cheering wildly. The jugglers bowed and clapped.

As Roo turned to smile at them, she noticed a black SUV with blackout windows idling at the gate of the equestrian centre. Its boot popped open.

Involuntarily, Roo shrank back, terror gripping her heart. In an instant, her mind was back on Dartmoor, watching the red-eyed wolfhounds spring out.

But there was nothing in the boot except an exuberant cocker spaniel. Four giggling mini dinosaurs spilled out of the car doors. A T. rex father herded kids and their dog up the path.

Roo breathed again.

Skylar swung into the Arabian's saddle. 'I hope Shamal holds her nerve. Magician adored the drama and attention. Shamal's more highly strung. I'm not sure how she'll cope with flashing lights and blaring music.'

At the thought of her precious stallion, anguish flitted across Skylar's face, but she was too much of a professional to let it linger.

'Break a leg, Skylar,' called one of the jugglers.

'Good luck,' seconded Roo. Her stomach churned with nerves.

Skylar smiled down at her. 'Roo, try not to worry too much. No one's going to steal Shamal during the trick-riding display. Too many witnesses. The danger hour will come afterwards. That's when we'll need to be on our guard. In the meantime, just chill. Enjoy the show.'

Up at the castle, a band began to play. The performers set off through the twinkling gardens. Roo followed. It was her job to watch the guests around the arena while the guests watched the show. She was to message her aunt instantly if she saw anyone getting too close to the arena or trying to feed Shamal treats.

Joni was going to spend the evening roaming the castle and grounds with a sketchbook. Under the guise of capturing costumes and special moments from the party in pen and ink, she'd be looking out for impostors.

'Watch for things that don't add up,' she advised Roo. 'Inconsistencies. A person in a glamorous dress wearing trainers underneath. Someone spending more time speaking on their phone than enjoying the party. People who behave suspiciously as Skylar's performance comes to an end. Call me if you notice anything at all. The smallest clue might be important.'

***

The towering turreted walls glowed gold against the evening sky as Roo climbed the terrace steps.

Stationing herself behind a wisteria-covered trellis, she studied the scene. Waiters bearing silver platters served Scottish delicacies to costumed guests at long tables. Crystal glasses sparkled in the candlelight.

It was surreal to watch rival superheroes chatting over poached salmon and vegan haggis. Spies, Mafia gangsters, and Wild West outlaws were also popular themes. How was Roo supposed to tell the real villains from the costumed ones?

Cruella de Vil swept past the trellis in a spotted fur cloak, leading a boisterous Dalmatian. The dog sniffed out Roo's hiding place in seconds. Cruella shot out a crimson-gloved hand and gripped Roo's shoulder.

Roo let out a squeak of fright.

'Are you spying on people? Is that what you're up to?'

'I'm Nancy Drew,' protested Roo, holding up her magnifying glass. 'I'm solving a mystery.'

'Are you now? Curiosity killed the cat, you know.'

Roo was ready to call security by the time the woman took off her dark glasses and smiled broadly. Behind her disguise, she had a dimpled, likeable face.

'Just teasing. Sorry if I scared you!'

She patted the Dalmatian. 'Come on, Rollie. Let's go get you some biscuits. Bye, Nancy Drew. Hope you solve your mystery.'

No sooner had she gone than Roo had the feeling of being watched. She looked up. A small figure was gazing from a tower window. It was Antonia's five-year-old daughter, Bonnie. She'd been at the children's party earlier but had gone, protesting, to her bedroom when the grown-up party began.

Roo waved, but Bonnie was already turning away to talk to her au pair.

Her hiding place rumbled, Roo returned to the patio below. The lawn had been carpeted in sawdust for the trick-riding display. Security guards patrolled the perimeter.

With so many faces obscured by masks, Roo decided her best chance of identifying thieves was to use her ears. She'd listen for the man who'd called the other thieves 'clueless dolts' when she was hiding with Drifter in Wistman's Wood. She still heard his harsh tone in her nightmares.

Roo was attempting to eavesdrop on the conversation of a man who sounded uncannily like him when a stern person in a castle uniform asked her to stop.

Roo gave up. She was sneaking a meringue off the dessert table when the show began.

Perched on an ivy-covered balustrade, Roo was enthralled as jugglers, dancers, and singers brought the arena to life. A trapeze artist performed jaw-dropping stunts.

At last, it was the turn of Skylar and Shamal. The Arabian had no previous circus experience, but her beauty and charisma, coupled with Skylar's skilful showmanship, more than made up for it.

Thanks to her nana's early training, Skylar was a gifted gymnast. Her handsprings, backflips, and flying dismounts wowed the crowd.

She and Shamal ended by bowing deeply to one another before lying down, side by side. By then, many of the diners, Roo included, had been moved to tears. Antonia led the standing ovation.

Afterwards, Roo was dying to congratulate Skylar, but hung back. The performers were having their photos taken with Antonia and a throng of admirers.

As Roo waited in the lilac-scented shadows, a fluff-ball ran full pelt into her left boot.

'Beau! Beau, come back here!'

A small girl in a meerkat costume dashed from the shadows. She knelt down and held the puppy close, smothering him with kisses.

It was Antonia's daughter.

'Hi, Bonnie! What a cute puppy. Is he yours?'

The girl nodded proudly. 'He's a Samoyed. He died and came back to life.'

Roo smiled. 'You mean, the vet resuscitated him?'

'No, he died in summer, then came alive again on Christmas morning. Only he wasn't old any more, he was a puppy.'

The girl's au pair ran up the path.

'Bonnie, you and Beau are giving me grey hairs. You must stop tearing off like that.'

She smiled at Roo. 'Thanks for rescuing them.'

'You're welcome,' said Roo. 'Uh, Bonnie was just telling me how her puppy rose from the dead.'

The au pair gave a nervous laugh. 'I wish I could say she was making it up, but it's sort of true.'

'How does a dog sort of rise from the dead?'

The au pair glanced around, and lowered her voice. 'Last summer, the Levines' eight-year-old Samoyed, also named Beau, went missing on a forest walk. He was never found.

'Fast forward six months to Christmas Eve. The castle doorbell rang. When the footman answered it, he found a Samoyed puppy in a basket on the snowy steps – like a Christmas miracle.'

'Who left it there?' asked Roo.

'We don't know. There were footprints in the snow, tapering off into the trees, but no one in sight. The castle gates were open because we were expecting visitors, so anyone could have come in, but, as you can see, we're in the middle of nowhere. It's not like anyone might be casually passing.'

'Maybe Bonnie's parents bought the puppy as a surprise for her,' said Roo.

'That's what I thought, but they were as confounded as the rest of us. Weirder still, the two dogs are uncannily alike. The original Beau had three tiny black spots behind his right ear and a heart-shaped birthmark on his tummy. Beau II, as we call him, has the identical markings.'

Roo had a sudden memory of standing in Ghost Flight's stall, listening to Finn talk about the rogue scientists 'playing God' with genes. How they were experimenting with editing out genetic weaknesses in foal embryos and adding other bits in.

If they succeed, theoretically they could breed superstar racehorses by the dozen, the trainer had told her.

Roo stared at the Samoyed. Could expensive pedigree dogs be bred by the dozen in Petri dishes too? But, no, that couldn't be the case with Beau because he was more like a copy of the Levines' original dog. Perhaps Beau's breeder had heard of the family's loss and given them a puppy from their latest litter as a secret gift.

Bonnie was giggling as she tried to fix a lead to the wriggling puppy's collar. The au pair whispered to Roo: 'This new dog is Beau, but not Beau, if you catch my drift. It's kind of creepy, to be honest. Reminds me of that sheep . . .'

'What sheep?'

Roo's mind was racing. She was thinking about Wonder and Magician. About why they might have been stolen. She needed to talk to Joni and Skylar.

'Kyra, can you help me with Beau?' asked the little girl.

As the au pair bent to assist with the puppy, Roo caught sight of the time. 'I have to run – I'm needed at the stables.'

44.
INFINITE MYSTERY

An hour later, Roo was sitting alone in her castle bedroom, feeling empty.

The following morning, she and Joni would leave the Scottish Highlands, having failed in their mission. They hadn't unmasked any thieves. Nor had they found the missing horses. The harsh truth was, they were no closer to finding Wonder than they had been three and a half months earlier.

Everything had been for nothing.

Due to the castle's remote location, the party had ended at 10.30 p.m. – early by grown-up party standards. Most guests had been taken by coach to a nearby hotel. Those who remained were close friends of the Levine family.

Apart from the caterers, castle staff, and clean-up crew, the grounds were almost empty.

'On the one hand, I'm relieved that my hunch about Shamal being stolen during the party was wrong,' Skylar had told Roo. 'I'll watch her till midnight just in case, but, with the guests gone, any stranger trying to get away with her now would be spotted in minutes. Sorry to have dragged you and your aunt all the way to the Scottish Highlands on a wild goose chase. If it's any consolation, I've loved having you here. Thanks for working so hard to make Shamal beautiful. You're a great groom.'

Before Roo could tell her about the uncanny encounter with

little Bonnie and her Samoyed puppy, a castle footman had brought a message for Skylar from Art and Antonia. The couple wanted to see her at the castle.

Skylar was frustrated but too polite to say so. Leaving the guard to keep a close watch over Shamal until she returned, she and Roo had been whisked up the hill in the footman's golf cart.

The luxurious castle room was empty when Roo let herself in. Joni had left her a 'Back soon!' note in indigo paint. Roo didn't mind. She wanted to be alone with her thoughts.

Like Skylar, she was relieved that Shamal was safe, but she was distraught that they were no closer to catching the thieves. Every day, the trail got colder. Very soon – possibly even tomorrow – her aunt would say enough was enough. They'd have to give up on the Case of the Vanishing Horses, settle down, and focus on finding a good school for Roo. Joni had said as much when Roo and Skylar were trying to persuade her to come to Scotland.

But it wasn't all about Roo's education. Her aunt needed a job or a purpose too. Roo was painfully aware that they couldn't spend forever searching for lost horses.

Roo's gaze went to the laptop, open on the coffee table. Her aunt had a stubborn streak, just as Roo herself did, but she was open to persuasion.

If Roo could convince her that they were so, so close to solving the mystery, Joni might agree to give their investigation one more day. Anything could happen in a day. Wonder Boy being stolen the day before Roo was due to collect him had kick-started their entire adventure.

One more piece of the jigsaw puzzle – the right piece – might end it.

Roo took an ice-cold can of sparkling apple from the minibar and carried the laptop to her four-poster bed.

She began scrolling through her case notes. Leads, false starts, and red herrings went off in all directions, like balls of wool ravaged by kittens.

Just looking at it made her feel overwhelmed.

Opening Wonder Boy's file, Roo read through it twice. What wasn't she seeing?

The list of possible suspects with the motive and opportunity to steal Wonder had stayed the same for months. As each person's alibi was confirmed, Roo had crossed out their names – with one exception.

She hadn't proved Coach Dering guilty, but she refused to believe that he was entirely innocent either.

Now she added a new suspect to the bottom of the list.

Dale Dering, Coach

~~Shelby Raine, Eventer~~

~~Eddie Gault, Wonder's Groom~~

~~Russ Wheeler, Farrier~~

~~Paddy McGuire, Vet~~

~~Rhianna's three rivals for the Olympic team (Lindsay, Jasper & Dina)~~

The Puppet Master: ???

The 'Puppet Master' was the nickname Roo had given to the spoiled young man who'd made the devil's bargain with Dale.

From what she'd heard, he'd appeared to enjoy pulling strings and playing games with the lives of men and horses.

If Scott, the storyteller, was to be believed, the Puppet Master had had no regrets about destroying his wonderful showjumper. He'd even laughed about it.

He'd told the young Dale that if one was rich and powerful, there was always a second, third, or fifth chance. Another 'do-over'. If he broke something – whether it was a horse or a car – his wealthy dad would simply buy him another.

Fifteen years had passed since then. Where was the Puppet Master now?

To Roo, there were two possibilities. 1) Life had taught him a few lessons and he'd become a better, kinder person. 2) He was worse. More devious. Even crueller.

What if the Puppet Master had turned up at Starwood one day and demanded the 'to be decided' favour he was owed by Dale Dering? What prize would he have asked for? Money, or something more precious?

One thing was certain. If the Puppet Master was blackmailing Rhianna Cooper's coach, he was connected to Starwood Farm. And if he was connected to Starwood, he was connected to the Case of the Vanishing Horses.

Like Lloyd Cooper's £1 million debt, he was a bomb ticking right under Starwood Farm.

Ever since she'd overheard Scott's tale, Roo had felt guilty about concealing what she and Joni knew about Dale and Mr Cooper from Rhianna.

She kept picturing Rhianna going about her daily routine, schooling horses and working out in her state-of-the-art gym, oblivious to the secrets and lies that lay beneath the surface of her own home.

'Can't we at least tell her mum what we've discovered?' Roo had begged Joni. 'Mrs Cooper did ask us to follow Wonder's trail wherever it led, even if it circled back to Starwood.'

But her aunt was adamant that they couldn't do a thing without proof.

In Roo's opinion, the email from Joni's tax expert friend detailing how Rhianna's dad owed a fortune to Dale Dering was proof. But, apparently, the tax expert had uncovered Lloyd Cooper's secret using 'unconventional methods', so it wasn't evidence that counted.

Gossip overheard on the gallops didn't count as proof either.

'Entertaining as it is, Scott's tale has the ring of a fireside ghost story told on a dark and stormy night,' Joni had told her. 'We still don't know which bits, if any, are true. Nor is there any way of confirming them. The showjumping yard where this dreadful pact was made went out of business a decade ago. I've left a voicemail message for a riding instructor who was teaching there when Dale was a young trainer. Until we know more, we say nothing.'

***

Roo hopped up to get another sparkling apple juice from the minibar. Where on earth was Joni?

Cracking open the can, she read through her notes on the conversation at Queen's Reach.

Two and a half years ago, he resurfaced on the UK horse scene . . . Scott had said, adding sarcastically: *You'll never guess what he does for a living now . . .*

What *did* the Puppet Master do now? He couldn't be a rider or a trainer, or Scott would have just said so.

And if he had a history of failed businesses, he probably wasn't a businessman.

If he was a college dropout, he was unlikely to be a vet, equine physiotherapist, or anything else that required years of study.

Roo had had the impression that whatever the rich young man did these days, it was the last thing Scott might have expected of him.

Could he have taken up a trade he once considered beneath him? Was he a groundskeeper or an office worker? Could he be . . . ?

Lightning sizzled in Roo's brain.

I don't like him as much as the farrier we had before, Rhianna had told her on that first morning at Starwood, *but Russ is the best and that's what counts.*

Could the Puppet Master be a farrier?

Russ Wheeler and his wife had a cast-iron alibi for the night Wonder was stolen. They'd been in Paris celebrating their anniversary. It was such a great alibi that Roo and Joni hadn't even thought to check it. After all, Rhianna's mum had confirmed it.

According to Rosslyn, the Wheelers had come rushing back from Paris after hearing the news about Wonder. They'd been kindness personified ever since. Violetta had even offered a £1,000 reward for information leading to an arrest on her Happy Petz dog-grooming website.

Roo decided to pay happypetz.com a visit.

A wall of cuteness came at her. Poodles and Pomeranians in

ribbons. Heart-melting labradoodles and collies. Proud German shepherds.

Judging by the photo on her 'ABOUT ME' page, Dr Violetta Wheeler took as much care of her own lustrous locks as she did of the pooches'.

She was a Doctor of Science, not of medicine, but, after falling for Russ at the campus theatre club at Harvard, she'd hung up her lab coat and opened a British branch of Happy Petz, her California family's pet-grooming parlour.

Roo scrolled through the menu of spa treatments for dogs. Apart from being wildly expensive, it all seemed above board.

Yawning, she zoomed around the site. There was a page of dog agility tricks, a shop for brushes and shampoos, and a link to something called Petz Unlimited.

Roo clicked on it. Up popped a MEMBERS ONLY page illustrated with a silver infinity symbol. Without a password, Roo was unable to glimpse what lay hidden behind it.

Next, she checked Russ's Facebook page. Joni had connected with the farrier when they were about to buy Wonder. Three and a half months had passed since then.

Remembering how nervous, shy, and bubbling over with excitement she'd felt as she passed through Starwood's gate for the first time made Roo feel strange. It was like something that had happened to someone else in another lifetime.

On Facebook, she found what she was looking for. Russ Wheeler had put up a photo of himself and Violetta raising a glass of champagne in front of the Eiffel Tower on February 2, just hours after Wonder had been stolen.

Roo felt crushed with disappointment. The couple really did

have a cast-iron alibi. For a moment, she'd believed she'd solved the mystery on her own.

She was about to log off when she noticed a hazy patch of lavender in the background of the Paris photo. It was blurred, but there was little doubt that it was a flower display.

Joni was always saying she loved Bluebird's colour because it reminded her of lazy summers in Provence when the lavender fields were in bloom.

If lavender bloomed in summer, then the photo Russ had posted could not have been taken on a winter's day. The weather was a giveaway too. Roo Googled it. On February second, it had been freezing and pouring with rain in Paris, not mild and bright as it was in the picture.

A sudden knocking made Roo jump clean off the four-poster.

She opened the door on the chain.

A smiling young waitress offered her a hot chocolate on a silver tray.

'Your aunt ordered this for you. She wanted me to let you know that she'll be another hour or so. Antonia's asked her to do pen portraits of some of the guests. You're not to wait up for her.'

Hot chocolate in hand, Roo was about to return to her four-poster bed when Joni's phone, charging on the coffee table, chirruped with an incoming message.

Rosslyn Cooper's name popped up. Roo clicked on the text in case it was important.

Joni, sorry to bother you so late. This a.m. my husband and Dale had some silly row. In the middle of it, Dale suddenly froze and said, 'The fox saw it all' – whatever that means! Lloyd thought he'd been taken ill. Then Dale jumped in his car and drove away. Nobody has heard from him since. Please let me know if he contacts you. I'm concerned the strain of everything has pushed him over the edge. All best, Rosslyn x

Roo's mind was a whirl of confused thoughts. *What fox?*

She looked again at the laptop. She was bursting to tell someone about her discovery. If her aunt was going to be busy for another hour, Roo had time to run down to the yard to talk to Skylar. By now, Skylar would be watching over Shamal again.

Nobody saw Roo as she slipped out of a side door and jogged through the moonlit gardens. Once Skylar heard that Russ Wheeler had no alibi for the night of Wonder's disappearance, she'd see at once that the farrier was the most obvious suspect in the theft of Magician too.

If Russ had found out that the black stallion's shoes had his Pegasus number, 77, stamped on the bottom right corner, he'd have had the skills to make a copy of them himself.

He'd also have had the ability to attach the new shoes to the hooves of the decoy horse stolen from the Pony Club gymkhana shortly before Magician vanished.

The castle stable yard was deserted. As Roo pushed open the gate, a ghostly shadow pounced on a brick wall. She almost turned tail and fled. Then the shadow pounced again. Roo breathed a sigh of relief. The culprit was a creaky Scots pine.

Shamal craned over her stall door. She whickered with pleasure when she saw a friend. Roo felt better. No matter how mixed up or miserable things got in her world, horses had always been her safe place.

The Highland ponies and Clydesdale also woke up and tried to get Roo's attention. She forgot her nerves and walked along the lines of stables, petting each of them in turn.

Where were Skylar and the guard?

Just as she was starting to worry, the guard returned. Roo hurried to meet him. He seemed surprised that Skylar wasn't back yet.

'Don't panic – Shamal's been alone for six minutes, max. Some critter keeps triggering a boundary fence alarm. I have to go and reset it on the main system. I don't mind keeping an eye on the Arab till your friend shows up, but I can't guarantee I won't need to nip away again.'

'I'm happy to stay with Shamal till Skylar gets back,' Roo told him. 'That way, if you do need to reset the alarm, Shamal won't be on her own.'

The guard looked dubious. 'Okay, but isn't this way past your bedtime? I don't understand why Skylar thinks the Arab might be stolen. *How?* We're on a mountaintop miles from anywhere. No one's going to steal Shamal unless they've got a helicopter, and even the sleepiest guard's going to notice that.'

45.

TRAPPED!

As soon as Roo let herself into Shamal's stall, something felt wrong.

It wasn't just that the Arab mare was noticeably more subdued than she'd been mere minutes earlier, it was that the air felt disturbed. It even smelled different. Along with the comforting perfume of horse, there was a trace of something chemical.

'How's she doing?' asked the guard, leaning over the door. He'd been checking on the other horses.

'Something's off,' said Roo. She felt feverish with fear. 'Shamal seems listless. This is how Skylar's stallion behaved before he was stolen. Is it possible that someone could have got in to dope her while you were resetting the alarm?'

'Dope her? I don't see how. I was only gone for two shakes of a lamb's tail. She's tuckered out after her trick display, that's all.'

As if to prove him right, Shamal came to life. Her head lifted and she took a step towards them.

'What did I tell you?' said the guard.

Roo wasn't convinced. To her, Shamal seemed slightly cross-eyed, as if she was finding it hard to focus.

'We can't take any chances. Please, please can you phone Antonia? We need to let her know that there's a possibility her horse has been given a sleeping potion. You might want to call for backup too.'

The guard looked at her as if she'd grown two heads. 'Call Antonia? Are you out of your mind? I'm not going to ruin her birthday for nothing. As for backup, there are only four other guards, and they're busy taking care of our VIP guests. Relax. Take a deep breath. The horse is fine.'

His phone buzzed and he rolled his eyes. 'Fourth time tonight. I need to reset the alarm again.'

'Don't leave me!' cried Roo. 'If Shamal's been drugged, she's about to be stolen.'

The guard tugged open a vent at the back of the stall and indicated the security booth across the car park.

'Miss, I need to go and enter a code on the system. I'll be back in a jiffy. Any hint of trouble and I'll come running. If Shamal's still poorly when I return, I'll call Mr Levine.'

Roo watched through the vent as he crossed the car park, waving to the bathroom attendant, who was hitching a Land Rover to the mobile unit. There was something familiar about the man, but Roo couldn't think why. The guard disappeared into his booth.

Roo returned to Shamal's side. She wished she had her phone and could message Joni to ask her advice. Thinking about her aunt reminded her of Rosslyn Cooper's peculiar message about Dale losing the plot.

The fox saw it all …

A chill as cold as helium filled Roo's veins. She remembered now where she'd last seen the bathroom attendant. He'd been glaring up at her from the steps of the mobile bathroom behind Barn A at Starwood Farm.

Sorry, love, the loo's out of order. Don't want anyone else blocking it up. That's why I'm taping up the door. Wretched unit sprang a leak and we're waiting for a replacement part.

When Wonder Boy vanished, she and Joni had missed one crucial clue. The field CCTV had shown a fox moving her cubs in the early hours of February second. The vixen had a den close to where the mobile bathroom had been parked. If she was distressed due to some disturbance – thieves loading Wonder, say – she'd have whisked her cubs to safety.

Dale Dering must have arrived at the same conclusion. Could that mean that Roo had been wrong about him? Where was he now?

A five-alarm fire was going off in Roo's head.

She put an eye to the vent, desperate for the guard's return. She'd heard that wildlife vets used tranquilliser darts to subdue rhino or lions from a distance. Could the thieves have thrown a dart through the vent to dope Shamal?

On the far side of the car park, the woman in white overalls was carrying a mop and bucket into a storeroom.

People seldom question a person carrying a bucket or a bouquet of flowers, Joni had told Roo on the film set. *They figure they have a purpose.*

In that instant, Roo understood how the thieves had got away with so much for so long.

To avoid arousing suspicion, the vehicles used to abduct the horses – the mobile bathroom at Starwood and the film set dressing room – had started out as fully functional units. Roo remembered that there'd also been a mobile loo parked beside the gallops at Queen's Reach on eclipse day.

Shortly before each robbery, those units must have been

converted into horse transporters. The clever part of the plan was that those transporters had stayed where they were until the fuss had died down – maybe even the next day.

While Rhianna was sobbing on the steps of her Tuscan mansion, and Skylar was searching the Somerset estate, Wonder and Magician had probably been sound asleep just metres from where they'd been taken.

At some point, the horse transporters would have been driven quietly away, barely noticed. What guard or police officer would bother searching a stinking toilet, or a dressing room that smelled like something had died in it, especially when they believed the stolen horses to be long gone?

Peering out at the near-empty car park, Roo felt ill with fear. Where was the guard?

She was in a dilemma. Should she sprint across car park to the security booth, or was it safer to stay with Shamal until the guard or Skylar returned?

The bathroom attendant was carrying two mugs into the storeroom where the woman had gone. The door closed behind them.

Roo decide to risk racing to fetch the guard. The police had to be called, and Shamal needed a vet. Her eyelids drooped and she seemed unsteady on her feet.

With a last, worried glance at the mare, Roo slipped out of the stall. Keeping to the shadows and walls, she ran to the car park gate.

To her immense relief, the guard emerged from the security booth at that precise moment. Before Roo could signal to him the woman in overalls called out. He veered off in her direction.

Through the gap between the Land Rover and the mobile unit, Roo saw the portly man leave the storeroom. He was heading in her direction. If she ran back to the yard, he'd spot her.

Panicking, Roo flew up the bathroom steps, ducking under an out-of-order sign. If these really were the thieves, her life might depend on what she did next.

She'd hide until the coast was clear, then she'd make a break for it. If the loo attendant did see her and challenge her, she'd pretend she'd only popped in to get a tissue.

Once inside the unit, she began to have doubts about her toilet horsebox theory. It was an ordinary bathroom. Three stalls. Two basins. A cheap mirror that revealed Roo's wan and scared face in grim fluorescent detail.

The floor was laid with the non-slip rubber matting often used in horseboxes, but that was common in hospitals and kitchens too.

It was only when Roo opened the cupboard beneath the basin that she found anything out of the ordinary. Between the spare loo rolls and cleaning products was a bag of stink bombs.

Remembering the reeking bathroom at Starwood, Roo decided the stink bombs were evidence enough that this one was being operated by horse thieves.

She peered out of a narrow window. Disturbingly, there was no sign of the guard. The woman in overalls was strolling across the car park, peeling off silicone gloves. The Land Rover lights caught her expression. It chilled Roo to the bone.

Roo decided that her tissue excuse would be no defence if she was caught by these sinister people. She'd have to make a run for it. She was reaching for the door handle when she heard the woman call: 'Better lock up in case an unwelcome visitor ignores the sign.'

The man grunted a response. Boots clanked on the steps.

Too frightened to cry out, Roo darted into a stall.

A key turned. Bolts shot into place.

A generator started up. Diesel fumes wafted in, adding to the chemical odour of the blue water in the toilet bowls.

All at once, the cubicle walls snapped back, hugging the loos. Roo had to jump out of the way to avoid being crushed.

A horse-sized compartment had opened up. Out in the main section, Roo had seconds to act. Scooping the bags of toilet rolls, stink bombs, and a small shelf out of the cupboard, she tossed them into the bin. Then she squeezed into the tight space and tugged the door shut. The cupboard had a sickly stench that made her gag, but at least she could see through the slats.

The back wall was being lowered to form a ramp. Dragged by the woman, Shamal came stumbling into the trailer. Her legs trembled with effort. After securing her lead rope to a metal brace, the woman hopped out.

'If you need to wake her, give her a shot of adrenaline,' she told her accomplice. 'I've left a loaded syringe in the tote bag. This horse will be even more of a handful than the last one, so only use it in an emergency. Just jab the needle in her neck muscle.'

'Will do. Cheers, Starr. Now, let's get going.'

He pressed a button to raise the ramp.

The whole operation had taken less than five minutes.

Roo was alone with Shamal in the near-dark box. She was afraid, but still hopeful. Any moment now, the guard, Skylar, or her aunt would discover that both Roo and Shamal were missing. They'd put two and two together, just as Roo had done.

If this theft followed the pattern of the others and the mobile unit stayed where it was until morning, Roo would yell her head off until she was rescued.

That hope was shattered when the Land Rover engine fired up. As the unit began to move, Roo clambered out of the cupboard and risked yelling for help.

There was no one to hear her. The driver had his windows closed, and his partner in crime was already lifting her mountain bike through a hole in the perimeter fence. From there, Starr freewheeled down a track to a waiting van and was gone in sixty seconds.

Bound and sedated under the desk in his booth, the security guard snored on.

The Land Rover hauled its priceless cargo to the castle gates. The driver signed out.

'Don't know how you stand that chemical pong,' Roo heard the guard say.

The driver chuckled. 'Ach, you get used to it. Pays the bills. I confess I'm looking forward to the end of my shift and a wee dram of whisky.'

'Good man. On you go.'

The mobile unit jerked forward. Roo tried to scream, but no sound came out. Through the slats of the cupboard, she watched Shamal slump to the floor as the driver negotiated a sharp bend on the steep driveway.

When he paused before the main road, Roo heard the whoo-whoo of a spotted eagle-owl. It felt like an omen of something terrible to come.

An instant later, they were accelerating into the night.

46.

SAVING SHAMAL

Within ten minutes of leaving the castle, Roo had decided that being kidnapped in a mobile bathroom fell into the Downright Unpleasant category of adventures.

One moment, she'd been proudly preparing a desert-born Arabian for a trick-riding spectacular at a film producer's castle. Next, she was cramped in a toilet cupboard, being asphyxiated by the fumes of Meadow Dream loo spray.

Meadow Dream should be renamed Rotting Fruit Nightmare, thought Roo with disgust as she clambered out of the cupboard, joints aching. She had to thump her own calf to try to restore the blood flow.

The driver chose that second to swerve to avoid something on the road. Roo reeled across the makeshift horsebox, bashing her shoulder.

Seat belts not being an option, it felt safest to kneel beside Shamal. The Arabian was lying on the floor, unconscious.

Once again, Roo was alone with her fears. She tried to block the worst of them from her brain. She'd be no good to Shamal if she melted down, imagining the unimaginable. For both of their sakes, she had to use the time between now and when the driver next stopped to refuel or take a break to come up with an escape plan.

Shamal twitched in her sleep. She seemed so fragile and

vulnerable. Whatever hideous fate awaited her, she didn't deserve it. Neither did Roo. If she could save Shamal, maybe Shamal would save her.

As she ran a gentle hand along the Arab mare's satin neck, a slow fire began to burn in Roo. How dare the thieves infect such an exquisite creature with their vile sleeping toxin? What did they plan to do with her? Where were they taking her? A remote farm? A gangsters' hideout? Another country?

If the Wheelers really were behind these thefts, maybe Shamal would simply be driven directly to Kent or Sussex or wherever it was the farrier and his wife lived.

Escaping in familiar countryside would make her getaway infinitely easier. Roo had a vision of herself and Shamal fleeing across meadows and leaping stone walls with Russ and Violetta in hot pursuit.

Would Shamal wake up in time to carry Roo to safety?

The Velcro straps on one of the mare's brushing boots had come undone. As Roo refastened them, she remembered Wonder going berserk when Roo touched his brushing boots. How she'd later found the long, sharp thorn threaded through one.

Her stomach flipped.

The one person at Starwood Farm whose innocence nobody had ever questioned was Rhianna.

Grown-ups often assumed that kids were too wrapped up in their own lives to notice when their parents were struggling with money or anything else.

Rhianna adored her dad. If she'd somehow discovered that Lloyd was drowning in debt, and that her showjumping career was the cause of it, she might have been prepared to go to any length

– including hurting the horse she loved – to bring in extra money.

Soon after the rearing episode, Rhianna had been in tears. *Showjumping is a business*, she'd told Roo. *Love is not enough.*

Whatever the motives of the horse thieves, they too were doing it for money. Robbing-a-bank kind of money. Nobody would risk stealing five-million-pound racehorses or one-million-pound Arabians from mountaintop castles unless the rewards were gigantic. And if the Puppet Master was one of those thieves, he wouldn't care who or what he broke along the way.

A shiver went through Roo. She put her arms around the sleeping horse.

'What do we have that could be useful to us?' she asked Shamal. *'What aren't we seeing?'*

The tote bag swung on its hook. Lifting it down, Roo peeked inside. The loaded syringe set her nerves jangling again. She set it aside carefully.

Next, she dug the stink bombs out of the bin. She was tucking them into her jacket pocket when she found Fearless Fire. Roo was so glad to see him, she kissed him on his tiny white blaze. Her spirits leapt.

She was no longer alone. She had a team.

It was true that one team member was sleeping and the other was a toy, but just knowing they were with her lent Roo courage.

Fearless Fire was her talisman; her lucky charm.

As for Shamal, the blood of her Arabian ancestors flowed through her veins. If she could survive endurance races across deserts in boiling heat and sandstorms, she could survive anything. If she were awake and in possession of her usual powers, no thief would stand a chance against her.

The Land Rover engine changed pitch. The driver turned and braked. There was the sound of an electric gate rolling open.

Roo's heart rate spiked. She'd expected to be travelling for hours or even days, not twenty-five minutes. A whiff of forest gusted in through a vent as they bumped along an uneven track.

There was no time to plan. No time to think. Unclipping Shamal's lead rope, Roo reached for the syringe.

47.

SEEING DOUBLE

Squashed in the cupboard, Roo didn't witness Shamal's getaway, but she heard it. The splintering of wood beneath flying hooves was followed by a yelp of pain and lots of cursing.

'The filthy creature has broken my collarbone!' whined the driver. 'Wait till I get my hands on it. I'll turn it into dog meat myself. Help me, Curtis!'

'Man up, mate. She hardly touched you. Now I have to go after the savage beast.'

'Forget the mare. She'll survive in the forest till morning. She can't escape unless she leaps the river—'

'The burn, you mean? That's what we call it here in Scotland.'

'Same difference. I doubt that even the showjumper could get across – not without risking life and limb on the rocks. The current alone would finish him.'

Roo's ears pricked up. A showjumper? Could they be talking about Wonder?

The men moved off. Roo strained to hear them.

'I can't understand what went wrong,' one was saying. 'Starr gave that minx enough knock-out drops to stun an elephant. And how did Shamal undo her lead rope?'

Curtis snorted. "That's Arab horses for you – smarter than your average brain surgeon. She's a rocket scientist compared to you, mate! *That's* what went wrong. Better hope the boss doesn't find out or our heads will be on the chopping block. "No more mistakes," she warned us. She wanted this last operation to be perfect.'

'Perfect, perfect, perfect. That's all we ever hear,' groused the driver. 'I'm sick to death of it. After she found that the producer's supposedly flawless Samoyed mutt was chock-full of hidden flaws, she was so enraged that I'd suggested it, I thought I'd end up at the bottom of the waterfall wearing concrete boots . . . What's up? What's wrong?'

'Did you hear that noise? A sort of thud.'

In the bathroom cupboard, Roo had shifted to ease the cramp in her calf. The Rotting Fruit Nightmare was making her throat itch. Any minute now, she'd have a coughing fit.

'Probably a deer. Forest's full of 'em. Let's go. I could use a whisky and some kip. We'll catch Shamal at first light.'

'How's your collarbone?'

'Nothing a painkiller won't fix.'

***

Free of the stinking cupboard, Roo allowed herself the luxury of a coughing fit.

Curtis and his pal had gone, leaving the horsebox ramp lowered. Roo peeped out nervously. Being Shamal's protector had made her feel brave. Alone, she felt small and scared.

The night air was heavy with threat. Roo tried to get her bearings. The track from the gate cut through a dense forest of pines. Shamal had vanished into its depths.

In front of Roo was an impressive but unfinished timber

welcome centre. *Golden Eagle Horse Safaris* was scrawled across its glass front in gold lettering. Pots of paint, decorators' sheets, sawdust, and an untidy heap of planks cluttered the porch.

Through the window, there was more evidence that the welcome centre had yet to welcome anyone. There were two desks, a filing cabinet, and a security light, but no computers, books, or other signs of life. Wires trailed everywhere.

The ordinariness of everything almost made Roo worry that there'd been some colossal misunderstanding. That if she simply rang the bell of the sparkly house she could see through the trees, clean-cut, smiley Russ Wheeler or his glamour-puss wife would appear at the door with a Pomeranian under one arm.

They'd be shocked to see Roo, of course, but she'd explain how she'd popped into the mobile bathroom to get a tissue and it had unexpectedly begun moving.

They'd all have a laugh and chat about the coincidence of them knowing one another from Starwood Farm. They'd make her a cup of cocoa and call Joni. It would turn out that they were borrowing Shamal from the Levines for a month or two for their horse safari business, only their horsebox was broken so they'd had to use the portable loo . . .

As Roo moved cautiously around the back of the welcome centre, she wondered if there was another explanation she hadn't considered.

Could this be a film set – perhaps even for a movie produced by Art Levine? Maybe Shamal was here because she was the star of his new film. Art hadn't told Skylar because it was going to be a surprise . . .

But Roo's racing heart told her that this was no Hollywood

movie. The ordinariness of everything only showed the extent of the thieves' cunning. A fake horse safari business was the ideal cover for horses coming and going at all hours in a remote corner of the Scottish Highlands.

She had to find a phone, or a horse on which to escape. If morning came and she was still stuck here, the odds of her breaking free of the thieves' evil web would shrink dramatically.

Behind the welcome centre, Roo was relieved to see a smart new sign to the stable block. As she kept to the shadows of a neat path lit by catseyes, she wondered again why the horses had been stolen. Surely not for use as high-end trekking ponies?

Despite her predicament, Roo smiled at the thought of Ghost Flight, reinvented as a tourist ride, taking fright at a deer and streaking over the mountains, with some petrified beginner clinging on for dear life.

There was no evidence of security guards, cameras, or dogs, but Roo was sure there'd be all three. She moved along the path as if she was crossing a field of landmines. When she finally reached a green barn, her hands shook so badly it was a struggle to open the bolt.

Inside, there were ten near-dark stalls. As her eyes adjusted to the light, she made out a bay horse in the first stall. He appeared to be a Dutch warmblood, but his temperament was nothing like Wonder Boy's. As Roo put out a hand to touch him, he lunged at her with bared teeth, almost taking off her arm.

She sprang away in fright, tears stinging her eyes. Over the years, she'd had her share of nips from naughty ponies, but none had ever gone for her with such venom and hatred.

It shook her that it had happened now, when she needed horses most.

At the next stall, she did a double take. The second horse was uncannily like the first, only younger. This one wasn't aggressive, but there was a strange blankness in his eyes. He stared past her as if she wasn't there.

Roo shuddered. She had to find a horse to ride, and it wasn't going to be either of these.

It was when she saw the third horse that all the hairs stood up on her neck. This yearling looked to be the identical twin of the yearling in the second stall, except that it was blind in one eye and had one withered ear.

Three matching polo pony foals with robot gazes followed, watched over by a brood mare who looked nothing like them.

Roo felt as if she'd stumbled into a horror film. Her entire soul rebelled against what she was witnessing.

She didn't have the strength to approach the last set of stalls. She could tell from where she stood that while one Welsh mountain pony foal was a dead ringer for the mare in the next stall, its twin looked stunted and sick.

So that's what the Levines' au pair had meant when she said that the Samoyed puppy, Beau II, reminded her of the sheep. She was referring to Dolly, the world's first cloned animal.

Were these horses clones, as Bonnie's puppy had appeared to be? If so, something had gone hideously wrong during the copying process. These were tragic, mangled copies of the perfectly imperfect original.

Tears streamed down Roo's face as she stumbled from the barn. Every one of the horses looked haunted and alien. Were they being created to order for wealthy buyers? Was that why Wonder, Magician, Ghost, and Shamal had been stolen – to be clones? Would copies of them soon stalk the earth like twisted ghosts?

Terror rippled through Roo. The monsters who'd created those horses in Petri dishes were capable of anything. She had to call for help or get away.

When the driver had complained that his boss was so enraged when she discovered that the film producer's dog was flawed that he feared he'd end up at the bottom of the waterfall, Roo had hoped he was exaggerating. But what if he wasn't? What if his boss truly was a psychopath?

Roo found it impossible to imagine glamorous Violetta Wheeler being part of this Frankenstein operation. It was a world away from the blow-dried labradoodles of the Happy Petz grooming parlour. Could she have been wrong about the Wheelers? But if not them, who?

Running low, she continued to the next building – a futuristic silver barn with few windows. Above its locked double doors was an infinity symbol.

Roo stopped dead, remembering the infinity symbol on the Members Only Petz Unlimited page. 'Unlimited' and 'infinity' meant much the same thing. Endless or unending. An unending line of identical performance champions. Was that what the thieves were trying to manufacture here?

For Roo, it was then that the last piece of the jigsaw slotted into place.

A castle groom had told her that a farrier who lived nearby came once a month to tend to Shamal and the other horses' hooves. She hadn't thought to ask the farrier's name, because it hadn't seemed important.

Now she realised that if Russ Wheeler was the Levines' neighbour, farrier, and, perhaps, friend, he'd have known that Shamal was competing in the endurance race on Dartmoor in March. He'd have had a good idea how much she was worth.

He would also have known about Magician, because the stallion was starring in Art's latest film. The Wheelers might even have been given a day pass to the set.

There was no obvious link between Russ and Queen's Reach, but, with so many racehorses to shoe, farriers came and went from the yard almost daily. He could easily have been on QR's farrier roster.

He'd have been a familiar face to the gate guards. Over weeks or months, he might have spotted weak links in security.

He might have learned from yard chatter that Brandon, the new guard, was lazy and guessed that he might mistake a hologram of Ghost for the real thing. It was probable that he'd have known about the builders' storage unit behind the Fillies' Barn, and the field across the way.

Emboldened by their successes with Wonder and Magician, the Wheelers might have stolen Ghost Flight just because they knew they could get away with her. *Make a copy of her.* If Ghost's cells were cultivated in a lab, and multiplied into lots of mini Ghosts, any healthy foals would bring in millions.

Was that what Violetta's grooming parlour side line, Petz Unlimited, did for its members – create clones of their dogs and horses?

Roo couldn't decide which was the least-worst option

– stumbling around the dark and spooky forest in search of Shamal, who might carry her to safety, or risking discovery by trying to locate a phone.

The main door of the futuristic building was locked. She was about to turn away when she noticed a window ajar.

Standing on a flowerpot, Roo was able to see into a small office. There was a telephone on an office desk. Roo levered open the window and wriggled through the gap.

She was lifting the phone when she heard a horse snort.

Roo put down the receiver and rushed to the door. She was in a sophisticated steel barn, dimly lit by night lights and blinking machines. One half of it was a cutting-edge laboratory. Shining counters and benches were topped with microscopes and testing machines. A wall of glass separated it from a sterile concrete floor edged with rubber matting and four horse stalls.

The first stall was empty – perhaps waiting for Shamal. Roo's chest cramped when she saw Ghost Flight, scared and sad, in the second stall. Wonder Boy was in the third. The fourth was separated from the others and down a short corridor. It was fortified like a padded cell. Roo bent to look through the inspection slot.

Inside was Magician, his magic quite gone.

Tears filled Roo's eyes. She couldn't begin to imagine what they'd been through. Her heart contracted when Wonder retreated, quaking, to the back of his stall. When she spoke his name, he whickered, remembering her, but he stayed where he was, his breath shallow and stressed.

There was a padlock on Ghost Flight's stall, but Wonder's door was only bolted. Roo let herself in. He trembled with fear, but she stood quietly until he calmed.

When he finally came to her and let her stroke him, Roo could have sobbed. He was hollow-eyed and timid, his fiery coat dull and dusty.

Suddenly, his head shot up. The lab's steel double doors glided open. Fluorescent lights blazed, blinding Roo. She shot behind Wonder, but it was too late.

'Well, well, well, if it isn't Wonder Boy's biggest fan,' drawled Violetta Wheeler. 'I've been watching you on our security cameras. Months ago, my husband told me that you and your aunt were like dogs with a bone. That you wouldn't quit until you'd found the showjumper. I didn't believe that a couple of amateur sleuths could come close to discovering us, but somehow here you are.'

Roo came out from behind Wonder, but she kept a hand on his neck in the hope that they could somehow defend one another.

'What have you done to them?' Roo demanded, fury lending her courage. 'Wonder, Ghost, and Magician, they're all traumatised. And the horses in the barn – your sick experiments – they're in hell. Can't you see how much they're suffering?'

'Admittedly, we made a few mistakes early on,' purred Violetta. 'Who knew that horses would be so much trickier to clone than dogs. But we got it right eventually. And once we saw how profitable the great performance horses could be, we turned our attention to those. Everybody loves a winner.'

'But those horses are living beings with feelings just like you,' cried Roo. 'Well, maybe not like you, but like anyone who has a heart. Why did you do it? For money?'

'Not just money,' said Violetta. 'For the thrill of getting away with it. When we pulled off the Magician theft, spiriting him into the dressing-room trailer from the foggy battlefield while movie cameras rolled, the rush was like nothing else.

'But I won't lie – the cash is attractive. People will pay anything to get their hands on the exact copy of a favourite pet that died. But the real money comes from recreating one-in-a-million racehorses or showjumpers, or perfect breeding specimens. Everyone wants a slice of perfect – even you. You tried to buy Wonder, didn't you?'

'But not because he was perfect,' said Roo, and realised, to her shame, that it wasn't true. She'd loved Wonder before she ever met him because he was a gorgeous talented champion and seemed kind. But she'd wanted to own him – wanted him for herself – because he was perfect.

'Your aunt told my husband that Wonder Boy was your dream horse,' Violetta said coldly. 'You were planning to pay a quarter of a million for him. If another girl had the cash and wanted to buy him, why shouldn't she have her wish when science can easily make a copy of him? Why should special creatures like Ghost Flight or Magician be the preserve of the lucky few?'

Russ Wheeler came running into the lab. 'Violetta, we have a major problem. Shamal's headed for the waterfall.'

'Darling, we have *two* major problems,' said his wife. 'Nancy Drew here has shown up. She somehow stowed away in Shamal's trailer.'

'You wicked, spying girl,' yelled Russ, rushing at Wonder's stall. Roo cowered behind the horse. The chestnut wheeled and smashed at the door with his hooves, squealing at the man with pure hatred.

'Leave the brat for now, my love,' said Violetta. 'She wanted her dream horse. Now she's got him. Let's see how much she likes it.

No one will hear her scream in here. Lock the office, so she can't escape the way she came in. We'll deal with her later. For now, catching the Arabian is more important.'

'I might also put a stop to the chestnut later – permanently,' snarled Ross. 'He's becoming as much of a nightmare as the black stallion.'

The outer doors slid shut and they were gone.

48.

TICKING BOMB

Roo sank into the shavings and put her head in her hands. There was no hope.

Whatever happened now, it was going to be bad. It wasn't like the Wheelers could just let her go with a warning. 'Breathe a word and your life won't be worth living!' By a tragic twist of fate, Roo was now a ticking bomb under *their* lives.

So long as she remained on the earth, knowing what she knew, the couple would be in limbo. They could neither return to the world of doggie day spas and posh equestrian yards, nor could they enjoy the luxury lifestyle their stolen millions might buy them.

Even if they threatened her, there'd always be the danger that Roo might let slip something to someone, who'd expose their crimes and blow up their world.

They had no choice but to erase Roo from existence. Delete her.

Russ had all but said that he was planning to 'delete' Wonder Boy. It might have been an idle threat, but Roo doubted it. The Wheelers were experts at vanishing horses. No doubt they'd be equally expert at disappearing problem children too. Plenty of woods around in which to hide a body.

The chestnut seemed to sense what was coming. He'd retreated once more to the back of his stall.

At that precise moment, Roo would have given anything for one of Joni's hugs. They made her feel safe. Made her feel loved.

Recently, Joni had begun adding an 'I love you' to the Bluebird bedtime ritual. 'Night, night, Roo, I love you,' she'd say in such a warm, lovely way that Roo often fell asleep smiling.

Yet Roo had never said it back. Not even once. It had felt disloyal to her mum and dad's memory. She'd got it into her head that any love she gave her aunt would somehow lessen her love for her parents. Now, Roo was riddled with regret. Love didn't run out, like water spilled from a cup. Love was infinite – in the best way. The more you gave, the more you got. Her mum had taught her that.

Her mother, more than anyone, would want Roo to tell Joni, her sister, that she was loved. If Roo stayed alive, she intended to do that.

The lab was cold. Roo put her hands in her jacket pockets to try to warm them. That's when it hit her that she wasn't entirely without hope. She had her talisman, three stink bombs, and three equine athletes on her side.

Looked at in that way, she had a whole bag of superpowers up her sleeve.

Now all she needed was a plan.

***

Even criminal masterminds make mistakes, reflected Roo as she used a hoof cutter and rasp to lever off the bolts securing the padlock to Ghost Flight's door.

The reason the Wheelers had got away with their high-stakes horse robberies for so long was that, with the exception of the Dartmoor drama, each theft had been planned and executed perfectly.

But all it took was one careless error. Russ had been so busy ranting and raving at Roo that he forgot he'd left a bag of farrier tools in plain view. Roo had made good use of them.

'They looked at me and all they saw was a frightened little girl,' she told Wonder. 'They didn't think about what was underneath. But when we get out of here, which we will, you and me will be a centaur, and centaurs are a force to be reckoned with.'

The chestnut had settled down again. He watched Roo with interest as she tossed a towel over a security camera. Ghost was looking over her door too. Only Magician was silent in his padded prison cell.

For all her big talk, Roo was shaking like a leaf. Skylar had taught her that the best way to keep horses calm in stressful situations was to pretend to be calm, even if you were actually scared to death. So far, Roo wasn't having much success.

Keep your movements slow and steady and regulate your breathing using the 4-7-8 technique, Skylar had advised. *It's an ancient method, but it's so effective that even special forces soldiers use it. Breathe in through your nose for the count of four. Hold for the count of seven. Exhale through your mouth for the count of eight. Do that four times and you'll feel the difference. So will your horse.*

Before Roo could put it into practice, she heard noises in the office. Behind the locked door, someone was moving. Panicking, Roo scuttled behind a rack of horse rugs.

She'd had a Plan B. If the Wheelers returned before she'd finished freeing the horses, she'd throw a stink bomb at them, and try to flee on foot into the forest. If she couldn't find Shamal, she'd swim the burn if she had to.

But now that someone had returned unexpectedly, Roo found she was incapable of moving. She felt like a person in a dream, unable to make her legs work as the bogeyman approached.

Keys jingled in the office.

The handle twisted ominously. The door squeaked open.

Skylar tiptoed into the lab.

Roo sprang out from behind the rugs with a shriek of joy, nearly giving Skylar a cardiac arrest. When she'd recovered, the girls clung to one another in silent gratitude.

'What are you doing here?' asked Roo. 'How did you find me? It's a miracle.'

Skylar looked worried. 'We're not out of the woods yet.'

Her expression darkened as she took in Wonder and Ghost. 'Where's Magician?'

Wordlessly, Roo led her to Magician's airless, windowless cell.

When Skylar saw her stallion's prison, she wrenched furiously at his door. It was no use. It was as secure as a bank vault.

Most frightening of all was how Magician just stayed where he was, head down, even when Skylar spoke to him. Like the spirit had gone out of him.

In Skylar's shoes, Roo would have broken down in tears. Rage made Skylar stronger. Her back straightened. Her shoulder muscles tensed beneath her hoody. When she spoke, her voice was steady.

'Roo, Magician's been drugged. He can barely move. I can't leave him. He's completely helpless. You're going to have to go for help on your own while I distract the thieves. Russ Wheeler's behind this, isn't he? Wait till I get my hands on him. He'll wish he'd never heard of Magician.'

'There's no way that I'm leaving you to face those monsters on your own,' cried Roo. 'Russ and his wife are lunatics. Shamal got away and they've gone hunting for her, but they'll be back any minute now.'

'Doubt it,' said Skylar. 'I saw Shamal tearing off in one direction and the Wheelers driving off in the other. They passed so close to me, they'd have spotted me if they weren't in the middle of a blazing row. They've probably given up on Shamal till daylight.'

'Maybe, but they'll see us on CCTV. Once Violetta knows you're here, we're dead. She's dangerous.'

Skylar's face was grim. 'I believe you, but she's not going to be able to spy on us. I've disabled the security feed for this barn. Nothing technical – I just pulled the plug out. There's a risk they'll want to check what's gone wrong, but with any luck they won't notice for a few hours.'

Roo exhaled. It was a relief to think that she and Skylar might have some breathing space. 'How did you find me?' she asked again.

'Finding you was the easy part. The guard had messaged me to say you'd volunteered to help with Shamal and was that okay? When I got to the yard fifteen minutes later to find you and Shamal gone and the guard missing, I knew you'd been kidnapped.

'I was about to have a meltdown when I noticed stable shavings on the ground right where the portable loo had been parked. Everything fell into place. I could see how the other horses had been vanished. I didn't want to waste time going all the way to the castle to get help, so I ran to the tack room to get the office key. That's when I saw Russ Wheeler's business card on the noticeboard.'

Listening to Skylar, Roo could feel her friend's fear as the drama unfolded. In that instant, Skylar remembered the castle groom pointing out the back gate of the next-door estate when they were out on a hack and saying that that's where Shamal's farrier lived when he was in Scotland, but that he and his wife spent most of the year travelling.

'At the time, I didn't ask the man's name because it didn't seem important,' said Skylar. 'As soon as I made the connection with the Wheelers, all I could think about was rescuing you before they hurt you. I left a couple of notes for your aunt and the Levines. Hopefully, someone's found them by now and called the police. Then I borrowed one of the Highland ponies and came over the mountain. Hamish is so sure-footed, he could climb a cliff blindfolded.'

Roo suddenly remembered the landline in the office. She started towards it. 'There's a phone—'

'It's been disconnected,' said Skylar. 'We're on our own.'

'How did you get through the security fence? Can we get out the way you came in?'

'No chance,' Skylar told her. 'The gate's alarmed and the fence has razor wire on top.'

Roo was confused. 'Then how did you get in?'

Skylar grinned. 'I'm an acrobat. I shinned up a tree and swung over. Easy-peasy . . . After that, it was a twenty-minute jog. One look at the tragic horses in the barn and I came here.' She glanced around. 'Any idea how we open that steel door?'

'I don't think we can,' said Roo. 'It's padlocked on the outside.'

'Then we'll need to wait till they open it and take them by surprise. I'll distract them. You shoot past them on Wonder. For that to work, you need to have him warmed up and ready to go. Behind the green barn, there's a track to the main gate. There's a couple of keys in the office that might open it. If not, you'll need leave Wonder behind and do what I did. Climb a tree and—'

Roo felt as if an elephant was standing on her chest. The pressure of everything, the life-and-death-ness of it all, was overwhelming. 'NO!' she said. 'N. O.'

'Roo, it's the only way.'

'Skylar, I understand why you won't leave Magician. I'd be the same. But I'm not leaving you either. We have each other's backs. You said so. When Shamal was doped, I gave her a shot of adrenaline to reverse it. Maybe we can find another bottle. Where would they keep it? In a fridge?'

For the first time since she'd arrived, Skylar looked hopeful. 'Adrenaline can't be stored in sub-zero temperatures. It'll be somewhere dark and cool. If you start searching, I'll try to unlock Magician's cage.'

49.
LEAP OF FAITH

Later, the thing that would stay imprinted on Roo's memory was falling asleep on Wonder Boy's back, her face buried in his chestnut mane. It was Skylar's suggestion. They had to be ready to go from 0–35 km in sixty seconds.

To Roo's immense relief, Skylar had revived Magician with the aid of the adrenaline Roo found in Violetta's handbag.

The black stallion, Wonder, and Ghost Flight were primed and ready to run. It wasn't easy warming them all up in a confined spice, but Skylar and Roo had massaged the muscles of all three horses, and walked them around the barn until they were ready to drop themselves.

As they worked, Roo filled Skylar in on the Wheelers and their false Paris alibi. She also told Skylar about Rosslyn's cryptic text about Dale Dering and the fox.

'There's a chance we might have been mistaken about the coach. Maybe he's on our side. If he likes foxes, he can't be all bad.'

'He's not on my side,' retorted Skylar. 'He didn't trust me and Dad an inch and I don't trust him either.'

For the next few hours, Skylar kept vigil, waking Roo at intervals so she could walk Wonder Boy in circles. They'd found the horses' bridles, but no saddles. As Roo tried to prepare herself mentally for whatever was to come, Roo did the same for Wonder. It seemed to be working. Stride by stride, she could feel the chestnut's spirit and energy flowing back.

When the birds began the dawn chorus, Skylar vaulted on to Magician and pulled her hood up over her head. She positioned herself close to the steel door. Wonder Boy and Ghost were next in line, standing side by side.

Roo threaded her fingers through Wonder's red mane, jittery with tension and tiredness. The horses began to fuss and fret too.

The thieves came on silent feet. Roo and Skylar had a split second's warning when the horses' ears flickered like radars. As the lock clicked and the steel doors slid apart, Roo tugged up her polo neck to cover her nose. Then she popped a stink bomb.

Revolting fumes filled the air. Ghost took flight and streaked towards the light, overtaking Magician in two bounds.

Violetta's expression was priceless.

'STOP THEM!' she screamed at Russ and Curtis.

Unwisely, Curtis leapt in front of the racehorse with waving arms. She mowed him down as if he were of no more consequence than a beetle.

Russ slammed a fist against the door switch, but quickly succumbed to the fumes. He reeled around like a zombie, coughing and spluttering.

Magician swerved around him but couldn't avoid Violetta when she lunged at him. She screamed as she went down in a flurry of hooves, her arm snapping like a twig. Skylar was almost thrown as the black stallion struggled to free himself and evade Russ's grasp.

The steel door was closing when Wonder surged to life and charged after his friends. As he bolted out into the crisp, cold morning, Russ Wheeler blundered dizzily into his path. Wonder popped over him as if he were a practice jump, clipping the farrier's shoulder with a careless shoe as he went.

When she stole a glance back, there was carnage. The thieves were retching, wailing, and bleeding. The horsebox driver was being sick in a flower bed.

Any fears that Roo and Skylar might have had about confinement destroying the horses' fitness were quickly banished. The three galloped with a decided glee.

Led by Ghost, they bounded over a low hedge, flew past the green barn, and shot up a forest trail carpeted in pine needles and wood chips.

Roo clung to Wonder like a limpet, terrified she'd fall and cause them all to be recaptured.

To start with, Ghost was out in front, her silver tail flowing behind her. Wonder and Magician had to scramble to keep up. But when Shamal came cantering from the trees to join them, Ghost slowed to greet her.

Seeing the Arab mare safe and well gave Roo a much-needed boost. It was just as well. An engine growled in the distance. The thieves were on the move, and they'd be madder than a nest of hornets.

'Hang in there, Roo – we'll get out of this,' said Skylar, urging the black stallion into the lead again. 'If things get hairy, stay close to me and Magician.'

Roo's body was electric with adrenaline, but she couldn't stop thinking about the locked gate and waterfall up ahead. Without help, they were on borrowed time. If the thieves came after them on motorbikes or with dogs, they'd be finished.

Through the tops of the trees, golden jet trails criss-crossed the dawn sky, but the forest floor was as black as night. In places, the trail narrowed and became so steep and rocky, they had to pick their way along the path.

Roo wished they'd been able to free the other foals and horses, but they could only do that if they first saved themselves.

At the edge of the forest, Skylar halted Magician. She and Roo listened hard. As far as they could tell, the Land Rover was on its way to the main gate, on the other side of the vast wood.

Skylar went first, nudging Magician out into the open. Roo watched for her signal before following on Wonder. This time, Shamal took the lead. She knew the way home. The horses cantered up the mountain track like a wild herd.

Despite Skylar's efforts to slow them with voice commands, the four skidded to a stop at the gate. Beyond the razor-wired fence lay the Castle in the Sky estate. The only thing standing between them and freedom was a thick padlock.

To their left, some five hundred metres distant and lit by a pale pink dawn, was a bridal veil of a waterfall. It dropped behind a screen of thick greenery with a musical roar. Roo presumed that the uncrossable burn that the thieves had spoken of was somewhere beyond it.

There was no way out.

'What now?' Roo asked desperately.

'We pray that one of these works,' said Skylar. She swung off Magician and began trying to open the padlock with the bunch of keys she'd found in the office.

Ghost and Shamal milled around anxiously. Wonder was bouncing all over the place, threatening to unseat

Roo. Exhaustion and fear had caught up with her. She was weak with it.

The other horses were agitated too. They were wild-eyed and dark with sweat. When Skylar dropped the keys, startling the jumpy horses, all hell broke loose.

Russ Wheeler blasted out of the trees on a quad bike. He'd been lying in wait. For reasons unknown, he was wearing combat fatigues. The blood from his injured shoulder was smeared all over his cheeks. He looked like a demented soldier as he drove at them, yelling threats.

Ghost was gone in a blur, shooting down the track that led to the waterfall. Shamal and Wonder galloped after her. Roo didn't get a say in the matter. She clung on for dear life as the quad bike roared in pursuit.

Roo felt as if she was back on Dartmoor, trying to outrun the hunters, only there she'd had the whole moor to escape on. If Russ chased them as far as the burn, she and the horses would be trapped.

Russ seemed oblivious to the peril that lay ahead. Intent on recapturing his £5 million prize, he overtook Shamal and Wonder and raced maniacally over the bumpy track.

As they raced around the bend, Roo gulped. A hundred metres ahead, the road ended in a gulley lined by ferns. On the far side of the burn was the Castle in the Sky estate. If she and the horses could get there, they'd be safe, but they couldn't.

It wasn't just that the force of the waterfall created a current as strong as a riptide, or that sharks' tooth rocks poked above the foaming water. If the weakened horses skidded in the mud or misjudged the distance, a fall would result in a broken leg or worse.

'Wonder, STOP!' yelled Roo, tugging helplessly at the reins. She felt sick with dread. Ahead of her, Ghost baulked at the looming burn.

It was then that Russ Wheeler made a fatal mistake. In his eagerness to turn her before she got to the water, he forgot to focus on his driving. His tyre burst on a sharp rock. The noise sounded like a bomb exploding.

Ghost Flight didn't pause for breath. She was travelling at full speed when she reached the edge of the burn. Her ears pricked and she arced into the air as if she were jumping a fence at the Cheltenham Gold Cup.

In those few seconds, Roo died a thousand deaths fearing for her, but the filly landed safely on the other side. She tore away, out of sight.

Roo was so transfixed by this spectacle, and by the realisation that the Land Rover was on its way to add to their troubles, that it took her a moment to notice that Russ had somehow grabbed hold of Shamal's headcollar.

He swung himself on to the horse's back. Roo recalled with a shock that he'd once been a professional rider.

The farrier had a stick in one hand. He brought it down with full force on Shamal's rump. The mare leapt forward in terror as he drove her at full speed towards the burn.

Roo had pulled up Wonder. She watched helplessly as the pair careered towards the deadly gulley. Russ appeared obsessed with pursuing Ghost at all costs. Shamal was plainly terrified. He beat her again as she hesitated.

Skylar came galloping through the trees on Magician. 'SHAMAL, TAKE A BOW!' she yelled.

Incredibly, the Arab mare did just that. She stopped dead on the rocky river edge, jettisoning Russ into space. He soared out over the burn like an eagle, but gravity got him eventually. Roo didn't see him land, but she heard him. If his screech was anything to go by, it didn't end well.

Just when Roo thought things couldn't get any worse, the Land Rover roared into view. Violetta's arm was in a makeshift sling, but she leaned from the window, screaming in fury. Roo caught a glimpse of Curtis's contorted, vengeful face at the wheel.

That's when she knew that they were out of options. The thieves would stop at nothing to prevent the horses from escaping.

To her horror, Skylar turned Magician and galloped him alongside the Land Rover. Lobbing a stink bomb through Violetta's open window, she pulled the black stallion clear as the vehicle slowed, weaving crazily.

'Go, Roo, go!' cried Skylar.

The chestnut was already in motion, flying towards the water. Fury lent Roo strength. *We're centaurs*, she thought, and her veins filled with steel and fire. *They can't touch us.*

She gave Wonder his head and she gave him her trust. She believed in him so that he could believe in himself.

He blasted along the gravel track, measuring each stride as if he knew he was jumping for his life. Roo could feel him balancing himself, calculating the distance.

Behind them, Magician and Shamal's hoofbeats were a drum roll on the hard ground.

Wonder Boy's muscles bunched. He tucked up his white socks. Spray stung Roo's face as he powered into the air. Defying gravity, he flew and flew and flew.

When he touched down on the opposite bank, Roo was almost catapulted over his head, but he steadied until she regained her seat.

He was snorting and prancing and immensely pleased with himself. He was a superbeing and he knew it.

Roo's heart was in her mouth until she knew that Skylar had made it too. The black stallion came trotting proudly through the heather, long mane flying. Skylar was pale but grinning.

An ear-splitting crashing and splashing terrified the birds from the trees. Curtis had miscalculated the effectiveness of the Land Rover's brakes on a slippery slope. Too late, he and Violetta discovered that crime doesn't pay, and cars don't float.

Roo and Skylar didn't look back. They cantered their horses around a stand of pines, stopping when they saw that Ghost and Shamal were waiting for them. Only when they knew the horses were safe did they allow themselves to relax.

'Roo, there are Olympic riders who'd never have been brave enough to pull off that jump – not without a saddle,' Skylar said in awe. 'I wouldn't have had the courage to attempt it if you hadn't done it first, and done it so magnificently. Magician and I sort of scrambled over. You and Wonder did it in style.'

Roo glowed. 'I told you Wonder was a wonder horse.'

'You're a wonder, too, Roo Thorn. I'd say you've officially joined the centaur club. Centaurs rule!'

They were high-fiving and laughing when Bluebird came ramping over the rise.

'About time the cavalry showed up,' said Skylar. 'Wait, who's that in the passenger seat beside Joni?'

Her smile vanished. 'Please tell me I'm seeing things. That your aunt hasn't brought Coach Dering.'

'Why don't you give him a chance – hear what he has to say?' suggested Roo. 'Joni says it's important to listen to others, even when you don't really want to. Everyone has their story.'

Skylar scowled. 'Okay, but it better be a good one.'

That was as far as she got before a police helicopter zoomed over the mountain, scaring the horses. Sirens sounded in the distance.

Joni jumped out of Bluebird and came tearing up to Wonder Boy. She was just in time to catch Roo, who slid to the ground, weak with relief.

Wrapped in her aunt's arms, Roo smiled at the sight of Skylar and Dale working together to soothe the other three horses.

Roo could tell from their body language that the coach was apologising, admiring Magician, and tenderly checking a scratch on Shamal's fetlock. Skylar responded stiffly at first, but gradually something shifted between them. Roo saw the light return to Skylar's face. Once, she even grinned.

Joni smiled as she stroked Wonder Boy's foam-flecked red coat. 'Roo, there are no words for how proud I am of you. You literally climbed mountains and crossed raging rivers, but you did it. You kept your promise. You saved Wonder.'

Roo rubbed Wonder's silky ears. 'Then he turned around and saved me right back.'

50.
HERO'S WELCOME

From the comfort of a squashy beanbag near the drawing-room fire, Roo watched as Dale Dering bit into a strawberry jam and clotted cream scone.

He was perched on the edge of a velvet wingback chair and seemed tensed for flight, as though he might bolt, like a horse, at any moment.

Roo could tell he was self-conscious about his scuffed Western boots because he was making an effort to keep them still on the Persian carpet. From time to time, nerves got the better of him. Scraps of dried stable-yard mud were dotted around his feet like breadcrumbs.

The fact that she, Joni, and Skylar were sharing cakes at the castle with Rhianna's fearsome coach made Roo's head spin. It was like taking tea with a barely housebroken tiger.

Just three hours had passed since Roo and Skylar, followed by Joni and Dale in Bluebird, had ridden up the driveway to a hero's welcome.

Wonder, Magician, Ghost, and Shamal had been given a breakfast fit for royalty and bedded down in the castle's best stables. The vet had examined them. He'd declared the horses surprisingly fit and unaffected by their ordeal.

By 9 a.m., Scotland Yard had been in touch with the Irving and Cooper families to tell them that Ghost and Wonder had been found. Finn Irving was already on a plane to Inverness Airport, desperate to see his precious filly.

Rosslyn Cooper had messaged Joni to say that she and Rhianna were overjoyed that Wonder Boy was safe, but that they were dealing with a family crisis. It would be a couple of days before they could get to Scotland to fetch him.

Reading between the lines, Roo guessed that Rhianna's dad had finally owned up to his disastrous finances. His wife and daughter would be waking up to the realisation that, far from being millionaires, they were broke and in debt to Rhianna's now ex-coach.

Dale Dering had resigned from his post at Starwood.

As if that weren't bad enough, the Coopers would be digesting the news that Wonder Boy's farrier and his wife had been charged with horse theft, kidnap, money laundering, breaking and entering, and more . . .

Earlier, the Wheelers and their dastardly accomplices had been taken away by ambulance, handcuffed to stretchers. They were as cross as snakes at being outwitted by a couple of kids.

But we're not just kids, Roo found herself thinking after the police officer who interviewed her relayed this nugget of information. *We're centaurs, and centaurs are a force to be reckoned with.*

'According to the Scotland Yard detectives, Violetta doesn't believe she's done anything wrong,' Joni had told Roo. 'She claims that she and Russ weren't *stealing* the horses, only *borrowing* them. As soon as they'd harvested their cells and had "perfect" offspring, they were planning to drop off the original horses somewhere close to their homes.'

Recalling Russ's dark threats about Wonder, Roo found that difficult to believe. The couple had expressed no remorse at all that their experiments had caused suffering to the 'imperfect' foals and yearlings in their barn.

One foal was so ill, it had been rushed directly to a veterinary hospital for an operation. The other sick youngsters would be treated and rehomed or placed in sanctuaries.

Roo had vowed to pay for a lifetime of care for at least two of them. Her aunt was in full agreement. Dale Dering had promised to do the same for two more.

'Who knew that Rhianna's coach would turn out to be one of the good guys,' Roo had remarked wonderingly to Joni as they spruced themselves up for tea at the castle.

'I wouldn't go that far,' was her aunt's caustic reply. 'Dale's no saint. What he did in February – telling bird-brained Detective Inspector Pickle that Vano and the "boy" we later learned was Skylar might be guilty of stealing Wonder, without a shred of proof – could have ruined their lives. It was fortunate that they're a close family surrounded by good friends and colleagues who believe in them.

'To Dale's credit, once he realised what a catastrophic blunder he'd made, he did all any of us can do when we wound someone or mess up.'

'Admit that we were wrong and do the next right thing?'

'Especially do the next right thing,' said her aunt.

***

Now that the burden he'd carried for over fifteen years had been lifted, Dale Dering was a different man. Not cold and supercilious, as Roo had judged him, but surprisingly thoughtful, and all too aware of his own failings. Roo was beginning to understand why Rhianna had always referred to him as her 'rock'.

'The video you took of River Spirit clearly in pain shook me to the core of my being,' he told Roo over tea. 'Without it, I confess I probably wouldn't be here.'

Haltingly, and with frequent pauses, he explained that the shame of what had transpired at the showjumping yard where he'd started his career had never left him.

'I couldn't change what had happened, nor my part in it, but I vowed that in the future, I'd do everything in my power to be a force for good in the lives of the people and horses who crossed my path.

'But when Detective Inspector Pickle sent me your video, Roo, showing a horse under my care being lunged while lame, I realised that I'd become so bitter, resentful, and caught up in my own problems, I'd failed River Spirit. Humiliatingly, the teenager I'd accused of being involved in the theft of Wonder Boy—'

He cast a glance at Skylar. 'Sorry again, Skylar.'

'Enough sorrys,' she said. 'Just tell us the story.'

He cleared his throat. 'When I realised that you, Skylar, had risked arrest to help a horse whose well-being I was supposed to be responsible for, it was plain that the past I'd tried so hard to bury was back with a vengeance. A decade and a half after I'd made the pact that has haunted me every hour since, Russ Wheeler was once again poisoning my life.'

'I'm confused,' said Roo. 'Russ is a horrible human, but it wasn't his fault that River Spirit was lame.'

'No, it wasn't,' agreed Dale. 'But he'd examined her that morning and assured me she was sound. Believe it or not, he was an excellent farrier. Either he missed the hoof abscess, which Skylar later noticed, or he did it deliberately to harm the horse and sabotage Starwood Farm.'

Looking back at her sunny first day at Starwood through Dale Dering's eyes was, Roo thought, a lesson in why you should never judge a person until they'd walked a mile in their shoes.

While she had been strolling around the yard with Rhianna, fangirling and marvelling at how marvellous everything was, Rhianna's coach was being battered by one crisis after another.

His morning had begun with a deadline.

Russ Wheeler had given Dale until 10 a.m. on February first to agree to his blackmail demands or see his and Rhianna's life and reputation destroyed.

The farrier had first shown up at Starwood the previous summer. To begin with, Dale had been terrified that Russ would try to blackmail him with a 'to be decided' favour he couldn't possibly repay but, in the beginning, Russ had seemed a changed man. He'd asked only that Dale consider hiring him to shoe some of the horses at Starwood.

By chance, the yard's regular farrier was soon to retire. Dale paid him to quit early and gave Russ the contract. He'd heard good reports about Russ's work on the competition circuit. With that, he considered his debt to the man to be repaid.

'I was gravely mistaken,' Dale told Roo, Skylar, and Joni over tea. 'The Wheelers took one look at Starwood Farm and decided they wanted it for themselves. By some devious method, Russ had learned that Rhianna's dad owed me a lot of money. He began pressuring me to call in the loan and take over the farm. Once my name was on Starwood's deeds, I could then sell it at a low price to the Wheelers. Russ said that only when the farm was theirs would he consider his long-ago favour to be repaid.'

'What did you do?' asked Roo, her pulse racing just listening to the tale.

'I told him it was impossible,' Dale told her. 'To me, the Coopers were the family I'd never had. I'd never have betrayed them.

'It was then the Russ who had held such power over me as a young man – the Russ who could be charismatic and charming one minute, cruel and sinister the next – revealed his dark side again. The longer I refused to call in Lloyd's debt, the more dangerous he became.

'Last November, he gave me an ultimatum. I had three months to do his bidding or be exposed as the man who'd ruined his showjumper fifteen years ago. He threatened to go to the press and tell them that Rhianna and I had been using cruel tricks to make Wonder Boy win.

'He knew that even if we were later found innocent, which we would be, our reputations would be forever tainted. Rhianna's future would be ruined. The Coopers would lose everything. So would I, because Lloyd would then have no chance of repaying the money he owed me.'

Roo had a flashback of Russ Wheeler leaning from his van to chat to Joni and Lloyd about his romantic Paris trip with Violetta. With his spruce haircut and genial manner, he'd seemed boyishly likeable and trustworthy.

Not like a blackmailer.

Not like a man establishing a false alibi so he could get away with stealing Wonder.

Not like an arch-villain, plotting to con the Coopers out of Starwood.

Joni said incredulously: 'Dale, are you saying that the moment of reckoning – when you had to tell Russ whether or not you'd help him force the Coopers off Starwood Farm – took place one hour before Roo and I arrived to see Wonder?'

Dale grimaced. 'Strange coincidence, but, yes.'

'What happened?' cried Roo, trying to imagine how she'd have felt in Dale's place. 'What did you do?'

'I didn't know what to do. I was a wreck. I hadn't slept, I was so worried about the consequences of refusing to go along with Russ's evil plan. To my astonishment, Russ came tripping into my office full of cheer and chat about his upcoming trip to Paris. When I could stand it no longer, I told him that I couldn't agree to his blackmail demands. Incredibly, he said he'd come to realise he'd been unfair. That I'd done more than enough by employing him as a farrier. "Consider the debt forgiven," he told me.'

'Just like that?' said Skylar.

'Just like that.' Dale shivered. 'Rather than being relieved, I smelled a rat. I was sure that he had another cunning trick up his sleeve. But there was no time to dwell on it. The gate bell rang right then. Joni and Roo had arrived.'

In the castle drawing room, the waitress was back with more warm scones on a silver platter.

As Roo helped herself to a blackberry jam one with an extra-large pillow of cream, she recalled how nervy and hopping with anticipation she'd been as Starwood's spiky gates rolled open. She knew she'd never forget the glamour and eye-popping colour of the sun-drenched yard, or how elated she'd felt at being given a personal tour by Rhianna.

Nor would she forget Wonder rearing, crazed with pain, when she touched his foreleg. Now at least she had an explanation for Dale's grumpy reaction. He was still smarting from his meeting with Russ.

'Did you suspect that . . . someone . . . might have put a thorn in Wonder's brushing boots?' she asked him, choosing her words carefully.

She saw the shock register on his face as he realised that she must have physically seen the thorn to know about it.

'Not at first,' he admitted. 'Wonder is so chilled usually that I was taken aback by his behaviour, but I've learned that even the gentlest horse can be unpredictable. Then I caught Rhianna's expression. She looked stricken. I suggested she replace the boots and left the barn right away. I dreaded having my worst fears confirmed.'

'Were they confirmed?' asked Joni.

'Sadly, yes,' answered Dale. 'When Roo was jumping Wonder, Lloyd asked if he could speak to me privately. Apparently, the previous evening, Rhianna had changed her mind about selling Wonder. She'd begged her dad to cancel the sale, not knowing that he secretly owed me nearly £1 million.'

Dale frowned at the memory. 'Lloyd is a good man underneath. All he wanted was to give his wife and daughter everything they'd ever dreamed of. In order to do that, he had to tell lie upon lie. Not only did he hide his money problems

– brought about by unwise business decisions – from his family, he boasted that business was booming. As a result, his wife kept buying ever more luxuries and Rhianna lived like a princess. But I drew the line at paying the decorators working on their mansion. With a huge bill due, Lloyd panicked. He told Rhianna that selling Wonder was a matter of "life and death".'

Roo was silent, recalling the many times she'd wished she could swap lives with Rhianna.

Frightened into drastic action, Rhianna had confessed to her dad that she'd threaded a hawthorn thorn through Wonder's brushing boots in the hope of ensuring that he jumped high enough to impress any buyer. She'd thought she'd positioned the thorn so that Wonder would only feel the tiniest pinprick. Enough to remind him to pick his feet up. She was gutted when it really hurt him.

That's the real reason Rhianna was crying, thought Roo. That's why she talked about showjumping being a business and love not being enough.

A knife of anguish turned in her chest. She got no satisfaction out of being proved right. She resolved to give Wonder an extra big hug when she next saw him.

'When Lloyd told me what Rhianna had done, I was speechless with rage – not at Rhianna, but at her dad,' said Dale. 'She'd never have been driven to such a desperate act had she not blamed herself and her showjumping career for his financial troubles. It reminded me of how every bad thing started at my old showjumping yard. One wrong decision led to another wrong decision, and it snowballed.'

Roo remembered running up to Dale in Barn A to ask him where Rhianna was. He'd swung around with a thundercloud stare. Now she knew why.

'I was still fuming when I marched into the barn to check on a couple of horses,' admitted Dale. 'That was unforgiveable. It's never okay to be angry around animals – or humans, for that matter. I immediately bit the head off poor Shelby for trying to tell me about River Spirit's sore foot.'

'That's where we came in,' said Skylar. 'Me and Dad.'

Roo could still smell the saddle soap and leather in the tack room that day, as she'd crouched in the shadows, watching the scene between Dale, Vano, and 'Hoody Boy' play out.

'When Dad first visited Starwood, he and Dale got on famously,' Skylar was saying. 'What neither of them knew was that Russ Wheeler had been on the lookout for a scapegoat – someone who might be blamed for stealing Wonder Boy. Sickeningly, an innocent Roma scrap metal merchant struck him as the ideal fall guy. Two months later, he called my father, pretending to be Dale, and asked him to come to Starwood to collect some scrap metal.'

When an emotional Skylar got to that part of the story, Roo realised that, to be an ally, it wasn't enough to stand silently by on the sidelines. Being an ally meant standing up and speaking out against racism and injustice because not everyone had a voice or was able to speak out for themselves.

'Like an idiot, I fell for Russ's ploy, hook, line, and sinker,' admitted Dale. 'The previous week, he'd told me that there'd been a spate of tack-room robberies at a couple of the yards he visited. He claimed that suspicion had fallen on the scrap metal merchant I'd used in the winter. He asked me if I noticed anything missing after his visit. I hadn't but I said I'd keep it in mind.'

'It was a set-up,' explained Skylar. 'Russ gambled that if Dad and I turned up out of the blue, seemingly without an appointment, Dale would think it was a trick to get into Starwood.'

'I'm ashamed to say his plan worked,' said Dale. 'Weighed down with worry, I lashed out at you both in the worst possible way, not knowing that Russ's story was a terrible lie.'

That lie was the beginning of Russ's undoing, thought Roo.

It was also when Dale did the next right thing. He emailed Skylar's dad and apologised profusely for his language and behaviour. He told Vano that if there was ever anything he could do to make it up to him or Skylar, he'd do it without question.

'Unluckily, the email went into Dad's junk folder and he never saw it,' said Skylar, picking up the story. 'Luckily, Mum found it last week when she was looking for a lost invoice. She wrote back and thanked him. That meant that Dale had her number when he needed to find me yesterday. It also meant that Mum was happy to help him.'

Roo knew how the tale unfolded because Joni had relayed some of it to her earlier. When Dale learned that the person arrested for the tack-room robberies was a delivery driver and that Vano had never once visited the yards where it happened, he began to question why Russ would tell such a wicked untruth.

Even then, he didn't suspect the farrier because as far as he knew Russ had more than enough money to buy all the fancy horses he could wish for. Added to which, Russ had lost all interest in riding or competing.

'It was only after a chance conversation with a client who mentioned that Happy Petz had a side line in dog cloning that I began to connect the dots,' Dale told Roo and Joni. 'Like you, I then spent months going round in circles, trying to find proof.'

'That's where the fox comes in?' asked Roo.

He smiled. 'Yesterday morning Lloyd and I were behind Barn A having a silly argument over two new wheelbarrows. In the middle of the row, I suddenly thought: *The fox sees everything. What did she see the night Wonder disappeared?*'

'The field CCTV!' Roo said excitedly. 'It showed the vixen moving her cubs.'

He nodded. 'For as long as I've lived at Starwood, I've fed the foxes scraps most nights. Their den is well-concealed under the bushes near Barn A. They're accustomed to lorries and horses coming and going. It suddenly occurred to me that something alarming must have happened close to the vixen's den shortly before she moved her cubs.

'That's when I remembered the mobile bathroom was parked just metres from Wonder's stall when he was stolen. I also recalled that Russ had studied engineering at Harvard and could easily have converted it into a horsebox.'

Roo knew the rest of the story off by heart.

Realising that he was going to need help if he was to prove the Wheelers' involvement, he'd tried to track down Joni and Roo. Rosslyn Cooper had recently let slip that they were investigating Wonder's disappearance. He also tried to contact Skylar to ask if she knew of any link between Russ and Magician.

Joni didn't return his call. Skylar's mum, Elena, did. When she told him that Skylar was working with a million-pound Arabian at a castle in Scotland, and that Joni and Roo were there too, he guessed that Russ was poised to strike again.

Jumping in his SUV, he drove without stopping to the Castle in the Sky. When he arrived after midnight, the place was in chaos. Shamal had been stolen and Roo and Skylar were missing. Joni was in floods of tears.

'I felt so helpless,' said Joni. 'We knew from Skylar's note and from the Levines that Russ and Violetta had an estate next door and that they were probably holding you and the horses captive. When Dale arrived and he and I compared notes on what we knew, we both wanted to race to rescue you instantly.'

'I can't believe that Scotland Yard threatened you with arrest if you came to help us,' said Roo.

'They were worried we'd endanger you further,' Dale told her. 'At the same time, they couldn't set foot on the estate without a search warrant. To get one, they needed more proof.'

To Roo, it was poetic and fitting that Joni's painting of Ghost Flight provided the final, final piece of the jigsaw.

After seeing the picture on the 10 p.m. news the previous night, an ex-employee of Happy Petz was moved to call Scotland Yard.

'It made me cry,' she told BBC breakfast news after they reported that Ghost Flight and eighteen other horses had been rescued from a Scottish estate. 'I'd been scared to tell the police what I knew, but when I saw the painting, I knew I had to try to help. I couldn't have lived with myself if the light in that special filly was stamped out by darkness and greed.'

Joni smiled at Roo and Skylar. 'As soon as Dale and I heard that the police finally had their search warrant and were on their way to the Wheelers' estate, we decided to lend a hand. Only by the time we reached you, you'd rescued yourselves.'

'If it wasn't for your painting, the cops might not have got the proof they needed to arrest Russ and Violetta and save the horses,' Skylar pointed out. 'And If Dale hadn't been on the spot to calm Ghost when the helicopter came over the mountain and frightened the life out of her, she might still be running. It was a team effort.'

'A team effort,' agreed Roo, after which the four had an awkward, but rather wonderful, bear hug, resulting in even more cake crumbs and bits of stable mud on the Persian carpet.

Roo was fairly sure that Antonia wouldn't mind.

'If there's one thing better than horses and happy endings,' she'd told Roo and Skylar when she was reunited with her beautiful Arabian, 'it's both at the same time.'

51.

REUNION

'Just so you know, we are on the right road!' said Joni with a smile, steering Bluebird around a TRACK CLOSED FOR EMERGENCY REPAIRS barrier and driving on.

'I trust you,' Roo answered lightly, hoping her aunt wouldn't notice that she was sitting on her hands to keep them from shaking.

After surviving Wonder Boy's death-defying leap across the burn three days earlier, Roo had been sure that nothing would ever faze her again, but from the moment her alarm had shocked her awake at 3.30 a.m. in their Edinburgh campsite, she'd been a quivering bundle of nerves.

When the road forked, Joni took the track signposted PRIVATE BEACH. Bluebird's headlights bounced up a black-shadowed slope and swung on to the open clifftop.

Roo caught her breath.

The sea and sky were silver. It was hard to tell where one ended and the other began.

Joni switched off the engine and double-checked the handbrake. She turned to Roo. 'You can do this, honey. I know you can.'

'Hope so,' said Roo. 'I'm looking forward to it. It's just—'

'You're not sure what to expect or how you'll feel?' guessed her aunt.

Roo shook her head. She didn't trust herself to speak. By

lunchtime, her dream horse would be on his way home. The question was, *which* home? Starwood or the Castle in the Sky. Antonia had told Roo that, if she got to keep Wonder Boy, he'd have free board and lodgings at the castle for as long as it took Roo and Joni to find a home of their own.

Joni passed Roo a fleece, gilet, and gloves to put on over her riding tights and boots. It was almost summer in Scotland, but the air had a real bite to it. 'How do you think you'll feel when you're reunited with the horses?'

Roo didn't hesitate. 'Over-the-moon happy and full of joy.'

'Well, then,' said her aunt. 'Start with them.'

***

On Leumadair (Gaellic for dolphin) Beach, they sat on the sand, close to the frilly waves, wrapped in rugs, and drinking chai from a flask. Breakfast was fat, buttery croissants still warm from the campsite bakery.

They sat on the sand, close to the frilly waves, wrapped in rugs, and drinking chai from a flask. Breakfast was fat, buttery croissants still warm from the campsite bakery.

A blush of apricot brightened the dawn sky. At length, a blood-orange sun climbed ponderously out of the sea. The clouds and cliffs turned gold.

Joni's phone lit up and she scanned the new message.

'The vet wanted to do a last-minute inspection, so they're running late,' she reported. 'They'll be here soon.'

'But not Dale?' asked Roo.

'Not Dale. Under the circumstances, he thought it might be

best for everyone if he went without saying goodbye. His flight takes off from Edinburgh Airport in a couple of hours. He'll be in Seville by lunchtime.'

Roo still couldn't get over the topsy-turviness of the past three days. No one was who they'd first seemed four months ago when she and Joni set out to find Wonder.

If she'd been told on the night of Antonia's party that, within the week, Rhianna Cooper's famous coach would have quit his high-powered, highly paid job as director of operations at Starwood Farm and be on his way to Spain to help out on Skylar's grandmother's horse farm, and that she, Roo, would be partially responsible, she'd have said there was more chance of Shorty the Shetland winning the Derby.

Yet that's exactly what Dale Dering was doing.

'Nana's still getting over her hip operation,' Skylar had explained. 'There were complications and she's still unable to ride. She needed someone reliable around the place – someone who understood horses and wasn't afraid of hard work. Dale seemed a good fit.'

Roo looked out to sea. Gilt-edged clouds were billowing above the waves. She sat up in wonder. 'Joni, this is the beach in my dream, the one in your painting. How did you know that we'd end up here, in this exact place?'

'I didn't,' said her aunt with a smile. 'You dreamed it and I was inspired by what you saw. Between us, we made it come true.'

Behind them, the headlights of the lorry swung into the clifftop car park. A second car followed it in. Roo leapt to her feet, fizzing with excitement. The horses had arrived.

Magician emerged from the lorry first, high-stepping beside Skylar, his crinkly black mane whipped by the sea wind.

Next came Shamal. The castle groom handed her lead rope to Roo, but it was the Arab mare who led Roo to the beach, dancing down the steep path at speed, her red tail held aloft.

As she ran to keep up, Roo felt a rush of affection for her. Their brief but harrowing journey in the horse transporter, when it was just her and Shamal facing an unknown enemy and uncertain fate, had bonded them for life.

In a perfect world, Ghost Flight would have joined them too, but the champion filly had been whisked straight home to Queen's Reach.

'Ghost will be nursed, pampered, and rested for as long as it takes,' Kathryn had told Joni. 'When she does race again, we'll send you VIP passes. It's the least we can do to thank you. Never forget, there'll always be space for Bluebird at Queen's Reach.'

Wonder was last to leave the lorry. Roo's heart skipped a beat when she saw him at the top of the cliff, the morning sun catching his chestnut coat. He came hesitantly down the path and stopped when he reached the beach, nostrils flaring in the briny air.

Staring goggle-eyed at the sea, he pawed at the sand.

Rhianna Cooper, immaculate in a white competition shirt and white breeches, grey show jacket, and shiny black long boots, tugged at his reins. 'Come on, boy. It's only water.'

Wonder dug in his heels.

Then he noticed Roo. Forgetting his fears, he rushed towards her, whinnying, almost wrenching the reins from Rhianna's hands.

Roo was so over-the-moon pleased to see him that she gave him a big cuddle and kissed him on his soft white muzzle.

The expression on Rhianna's face when she turned made her feel guilty. She felt something else too – something she'd never imagined she'd feel towards Rhianna. Pity. Brick by brick, Rhianna's glossy world was crumbling.

'Sorry,' Roo said quickly. 'We went through a lot, me and Wonder. I'm just glad he's okay.'

Rhianna smiled. 'Don't be sorry. You saved his life. No wonder he worships you. I'm also grateful. It's just . . . I have mixed feelings about what's happened and the future and, well, everything.'

'Me too,' said Roo with a rueful smile.

She glanced over at Skylar and Joni. They were talking to Antonia Levine and the woman from *The Times*. She was going to photograph Shamal, Magician, and Wonder Boy with their owners for a news story on the rescue of the horses.

Skylar hadn't wanted to be in any photos, but Antonia had appealed to her to do it for Magician. 'Great publicity for *The Last Messenger*!'

Skylar had grudgingly consented on the condition that Roo and Joni came along to the beach for moral support. Roo and Joni had happily agreed, provided that their involvement in the rescue was kept secret. Joni didn't want her past or Roo's plastered across the tabloids or social media. Skylar felt the same way.

It didn't bother the three that Scotland Yard would get the glory. The picture that appeared in *The Times* would be accompanied by the police version of events – the one in which clever detectives had tracked the cunning Wheelers to their lair in the Scottish Highlands and saved fifteen horses.

'Might be a while,' said Roo to Rhianna as the photographer set up her tripod and pointed to various parts of the beach. 'Would you like some chai?'

'What's chai?'

'Black tea with cashew milk, honey, and spices. My aunt thinks chai fixes everything. It doesn't, but it helps.'

Rhianna's eyes shone with tears. 'Will it help the Olympic selectors change their minds?' she burst out. 'Oh, haven't you heard? I didn't make the team.'

Roo didn't know how to respond. 'It's their loss,' she said at last.

'I'm heartbroken, to be honest, but it's probably for the best,' said Rhianna. 'So much is changing at Starwood, I'd have found it difficult to focus.' She wiped her eyes. 'Maybe I will have some of that chai.'

Roo poured her a mug from the flask in Joni's backpack. They sat on the sand. Wonder leaned over them like a gentle sentinel.

Rhianna looked away. 'Mum told me that you and your aunt know a fair bit about what's happened at Starwood. More than I do, probably. We've had to do a lot of talking as a family.'

Roo shifted uncomfortably. 'You don't have to—'

'I need you to understand that it wasn't all Dad's fault,' Rhianna pressed on. 'I took everything I had for granted. Took Wonder Boy for granted too. We were together for so long that I guess he became like a favourite pair of slippers. Nice and comfortable but not exciting. I always wanted the newest, shiniest toys, and Fleetfoot Amberwell was just another one. He and I never really connected. Not the way me and Wonder did. We won some stuff, but the magic wasn't there.'

Roo knew what was coming next. There was a pit of dread in her stomach.

Rhianna took a deep breath. 'Roo, I'm keeping Wonder Boy.'

For a minute, the only sound was the waves.

After months of wishing, searching, and hoping, Roo was expecting to feel devastated if Rhianna announced she'd changed her mind about selling him. Instead, she was relieved. Perhaps part of her had always known that her dream horse would remain just that – a dream. Still, it had been fun imagining it.

Besides, the last four months had changed her. She didn't feel right spending a quarter of a million of her lottery winnings on one horse when she could spend a fraction of that and help rescue dozens.

Rhianna said worriedly, 'I feel terrible, especially after you risked your life to rescue him.'

'Don't,' said Roo with a genuine smile. 'I'm glad for you. You and Wonder go together like—'

'Chocolate and cake?'

Roo grinned. 'Like music. Like notes in a symphony.'

Rhianna's face lit up. 'Do you really think so? That's the loveliest thing anyone's ever said to me. Don't worry, Roo. I've made mistakes with Wonder, but I've learned from them. I promise that this time I'll do it right – treasure Wonder the way he's meant to be treasured.'

The castle groom came over.

'The photographer's keen to make the most of the light, Rhianna. Are you and Wonder good to go?'

Rhianna jumped up. 'Yes, we are.'

As they walked towards the others, Rhianna's gaze went from

Antonia, who was wearing a flowing silk dress that matched the bright silks on Shamal's bridle, to Skylar, who was in her black sweatshirt and jeans. Her face was almost invisible beneath the hood.

'I thought Skylar might want to change her outfit – you know, to appear more professional for the shoot.' Rhianna sounded disappointed. 'The photographer said there's a high chance we'll end up on the front page of *The Times*.'

Roo smiled. 'Skylar looks the way she always looks – like herself. She looks great.'

Rhianna persisted: 'She's a bit odd, Skylar. No offence, but you can hardly tell she's a girl. Watching the CCTV footage that day at Starwood, I was positive she was a boy.'

'Does it matter?' demanded Roo, flying to Skylar's defence. 'She's brave, loyal, and kind, and she helped save Wonder and the other horses. Isn't that enough?'

'Of course it's enough and of course it doesn't matter what she wears,' Rhianna said hastily. 'I didn't mean anything by it. I was just saying . . .'

'I know that,' Roo said more gently. 'But sometimes "Just saying . . ." hurts and harms people.'

Rhianna's expression changed as it dawned on her that it was true. Thoughtless words or actions could cut deep. She'd experienced that herself.

'You're right,' she said with a slightly embarrassed smile. 'Note to self. Engage brain before speaking.'

As they rejoined the others, Roo felt quietly proud. Being an ally was a little like being an investigative journalist. There was nothing to stop you starting today.

52.

WILD GENE

The photographer took about a thousand photos of Wonder Boy, Magician, and Shamal with their humans.

When it was finally over, Antonia Levine asked Roo if she'd hold Shamal's reins while she had a quick word with Skylar and Magician. The pair were returning to the set of *The Last Messenger* the following morning.

Roo took the opportunity to give Shamal a parting cuddle.

'This is not goodbye, because I believe our paths will cross again,' she told the mare. 'Until then, *ma'a salama*. If your Arabic's a bit rusty, my aunt says that means: "Go in safety. Go in peace."'

Roo was dreading saying goodbye to Wonder. She knew in her heart that he and Rhianna belonged together, but that didn't change how she felt about him. Like Drifter, Wonder had given his all to save her life. For that reason and a million others, she'd love him forever.

Rhianna led him over. She was smiling.

'Roo, before we go, you're welcome to go for a canter on Wonder Boy. In fact, I'd be honoured if you'd ride him. We both owe you so much.'

Roo was ecstatic. It felt like a reprieve – a few more precious minutes with the horse she adored. 'Just me and Wonder?'

'Just you and Wonder,' said Rhianna, laughing. 'Feel free to do whatever you like. Take him for a paddle in the waves or a canter on the sand. Try a little dressage. He's amazing at flying changes and circles and serpentines . . .'

'Anything?' asked Roo.

'Anything you dream of.'

'Mind if I ride him bareback?'

Rhianna smiled. 'Be my guest. I'll unsaddle him for you.'

By the time she'd run a dandy brush over Wonder, Roo had shed her gilet, fleece, boots, and riding tights. Underneath, she wore cut-off shorts and a long-sleeved blue top.

'Ready, Roo?' asked Rhianna.

'I am,' said Roo.

As she took Wonder's reins, she had a clear memory of doing the same at Starwood Farm. Back then, she'd wanted to be a famous showjumper like Rhianna. That was the last thing she wanted now. She wasn't sure what she did want to be when she was older, but it wasn't that. Perhaps she'd become a wildlife vet or photographer. Something that involved nature and freedom.

Roo bent her right knee obediently. Cupping her hands, Rhianna boosted Roo on to Wonder's smooth chestnut back.

That's when Roo decided that she wanted to give Wonder a parting gift. The gift of freedom.

She smiled at Rhianna. 'Please would you take his bridle off?'

Rhianna laughed. 'You're kidding, right? No. There's a reason I ride him in a double noseband or a martingale. When his blood is up, he's extremely strong.'

Skylar said: 'Rhianna, for what it's worth, Roo knows what she's doing. She's proved it over and over. You can trust her. She and Wonder have an understanding.'

Rhianna looked at Joni. 'And you're okay with this?'

Joni shrugged. 'It's your call. Wonder is *your* horse. All I can say is, they're friends, Roo and Wonder Boy. Friends take care of one another.'

Rhianna removed Wonder's bridle without another word.

Wonder shook his head and snorted loudly, as if testing the air. Then he wheeled, almost depositing Roo on the beach.

Just as she was thinking she'd made a huge mistake, he trotted down to the sea as daintily as any show pony. He waded into the glittering depths having decided that he did like waves after all.

Roo glanced over her shoulder. Rhianna, Joni, and Skylar had stayed where they were, near the cliff, watching. She urged Wonder a little deeper.

The water lifted him off his feet and he began to swim, blowing bubbles, ears pricked. They were weightless, rolling with the incoming breakers. It was the most magical sensation Roo had ever experienced – like riding a dolphin.

The current carried them towards the beach. Wonder was still knee-deep in water when he began to canter, powering through the waves, whipping up foam. The water was freezing, but it made Roo feel alive.

As soon as Wonder's hooves touched the sand, he slowed to a walk. His head dropped, as if he were sad that the fun was over. Roo felt the same way. She decided she wasn't ready to let him go just yet.

Waving to her friends on the beach, she turned him in the opposite direction. He was dying to feel the wind in his mane, she could tell.

The sky was filled with golden clouds, billowing up against the blue.

At the slightest squeeze from Roo, Wonder moved easily into his collected, showjumper canter. It was smooth and balanced, but Roo could feel him holding himself back.

She realised then that he didn't know how to be any other way. Trained since he was a foal to suppress his wild instincts, he'd forgotten how to kick up his heels and let go. Fleeing from the Wheelers, he'd been driven by fear. Without that, all he could think about was trying to please his rider.

Roo leaned over his withers. She forgot to be self-conscious because Rhianna Cooper watching her. Forgot to behave or be careful or be in control. Forgot everything except channelling the energy of the wild ponies who'd raced with her on Dartmoor.

'Run, Wonder! Run like the wind,' she urged. In her mind, she heard the thunder of their hooves. Beneath her, she felt something shift in the chestnut champion. His wild gene kicked in.

Wonder Boy exploded along the beach. His fiery mane stung her face as he galloped for the sheer joy of it, stretching out with such power and grace that soon Roo could no longer feel him touch the ground.

They were flying.

Wonder Boy was the horse in the painting, happy and finally free, and Roo was living her dream.

***

'Well, Roo, I guess this is it,' said Joni as they strolled back to Bluebird after the horse lorry had left and Roo had said an emotional goodbye to Skylar. 'We've solved the mystery of the vanishing horses. I suppose we should head south again. Start searching for a place to call home.'

'Why can't we go north?' asked Roo. 'What happens if we drive out of Edinburgh and keep going? Where does that road lead?'

'To the Highlands and islands,' Joni told her. 'If we put Bluebird on the ferry, there's Shetland, Orkney, and the islands of the Outer Hebrides. Only fifteen of those are inhabited.'

'Then can we be nomads for a little while longer?' asked Roo. 'I'm not ready for our adventure to end.'

WANDER GIRL

53.

ALCHEMY

Two weeks later, Roo and Joni caught a ferry to South Uist in the Outer Hebrides. It was June twelfth, Roo's twelfth birthday, and she had only one wish: to see the wild Eriskay ponies.

From the harbour, they took the A-road to the ponies' favourite shore, stopping only to pick up cake and other birthday treats from the pretty port town.

At South Glendale, Joni parked Bluebird on a track leading down to a crystalline beach. As she climbed out, Roo inhaled.

The air smelled like freedom.

Casting off their shoes, the pair walked barefoot between the dunes to the sea. A boy and girl in summer wetsuits were coming the other way, bodyboards tucked under arms studded with diamond droplets.

'Morning, miss,' they said politely to Joni.

'Hey,' they greeted Roo, smiles white against their nut-brown faces.

'Hey,' she responded with a grin, and had the oddest feeling that she'd see them again and they'd become friends.

On the Isle of Skye, Joni had persuaded Roo to swim in the fairy pools. The water was bone-chillingly freezing, but the rush of heat afterwards was exhilarating. Someday soon, she planned to learn to surf.

Today, though, was all about the Eriskay ponies.

They found the herd in the next cove, grazing on a slope among the wildflowers, succulents, and seaweed.

'Happy twelfth birthday, Roo!' Joni said with a smile. 'Enjoy your wish come true. Spend as long as you want hanging out with the ponies. I'm going to sit on this rock and sketch.'

Roo took her time approaching the Eriskays. Peeking out from behind their mums' flanks were two doe-eyed, dark chocolate foals. As they got older, they'd lose their baby fluff and turn a creamy grey like the rest of the herd.

They'd never grow taller than twelve hands high, but they'd be immensely strong and hardy like their forebears, shrugging off the most brutal of island winters. It blew Roo's mind that it was possible to loan or even own a pony descended from one of the world's most ancient breeds.

As she drew nearer, a speckled mare separated from the herd and came towards her. Ears pricked, she walked with a curious confidence, as if recognising an old friend. Roo's spirits soared, but she stayed still, letting the pony find her own way.

Time stopped. Roo and the mare stood gazing out across the turquoise bay, the breeze tugging at the pony's forelock. Her woolly coat was sticky with salt. She smelled of the sea, as though she were part dolphin.

Before she and Joni left the cove, Roo glanced back. The pony was still watching her.

***

They picnicked on the powdery white beach, beneath a lightning-blue sky.

To Roo, every moment felt extra precious because she could so easily not have been there. And so, although the last thing she wanted to think about was the Wheelers and their laboratory, somehow they came into her head. The senseless greed of everything remained a mystery to her.

'I don't understand how the Wheelers thought they'd get away with it,' she remarked to Joni. 'They seemed to think they were untouchable.'

'It's called hubris, hon.'

'What's hubris?'

'Violetta was so convinced of the genius of her plan to make millions mass-producing superstar horses that she forgot about the X factor. What makes Ghost and Wonder who they are, or you and me who we are, can never be reproduced in a lab, because who we are is alchemy.'

'Alchemy?'

'The sum of our experiences. A mother's caress, the words of an inspiring teacher, the love of a beloved animal, or the never-forgotten cruelty of a bully. It's the freedom of racing a horse bareback along a wild shore, or this – right here, right now – a picnic on a sunny beach in the Outer Hebrides . . .

'Your mum and I had the same parents and the same stable but slightly dull upbringing, but we were opposites. She was shaped by her experiences as a nurse, mum, and wife. I was shaped in different ways. By lonely motel rooms and Goan sunsets. By mountain hikes and Australian and American road trips. By the kindness of strangers.'

'Maybe you have a wild gene too,' said Roo.

Joni laughed. 'I think that's a gene you and I share.'

Roo said emotionally. 'Joni, when I was sure I was going to die, all I could think about was the things I wish I'd said. You're the best aunt in the universe. I love you so much.'

'I love you more,' Joni assured her, smiling through tears. 'But, Roo, for the avoidance of future doubt, I need to tell you a story.'

She unzipped a pocket in her daypack and took out the midnight-blue box. It did contain a ring, but it wasn't a diamond one. It was a tiny woven reed.

'This was given to me on my twentieth birthday by Stefan, the love of my life. We were penniless art students, but we were deeply in love. When he asked me to marry him, he made me this in lieu of the engagement ring he promised to buy me just as soon as he could afford it.

'Our dream was to have a big family. "Four kids, at least," I'd say. "How about eight – almost a football team?" he'd tease. From memory, we settled on six.

'We were halfway through our second year at art school when he was diagnosed with a brain tumour. He died three months later. We'd been so wrapped up in one another, so delirious with happiness, that few people knew of our relationship. With the exception of your mum, I told hardly anyone of my loss. I dropped out of college, gave up painting, and fell to pieces. My life went off the rails. The agony of grief was unbearable.'

Wordlessly, Roo hugged her aunt. She'd lived through the agony of grief twice and understood how alone and empty Joni must have felt. It explained so much.

'I'm so sorry about Stefan.'

Her aunt squeezed her hand. 'Don't be. I find March third, the day of his passing, tough to get through, but otherwise I don't dwell on it. However, I never did meet another love of my life, which meant I never got to have the children I so longed for. For many years, I couldn't hold down a job or a relationship. I found solace only in travel and nature.

'After your mum died, I hoped I might be of help to you and your dad, but he made it clear that he considered me too unreliable to take care of a child. That day that he and I argued, I drove away with his words ringing in my ears.'

'He didn't mean it,' Roo assured her. 'He was just sad and angry about losing my mum. He never got over it.'

'All the same, I vowed to change. I made it my mission to get a real job and a real home and settle down with a long-term partner. I was determined to prove that one day I'd make a great mum. Along the way I forgot that, in order to be good for anyone else, we have to first be true to ourselves.'

She put an arm around Roo and pulled her close.

'So, you see, Roo, being with you, spending time with you, will always be the best, most beautiful thing that ever happened to me. Roo, you're *my* lottery.'

Out in the bay, a silver dolphin surfaced, flicking up a spray rainbow as it arched over the waves. It was as if it was meant to be.

54.
LOST & FOUND

'This has been the best birthday ever,' said Roo after finishing the last yummy bite of cake. She lolled back on her beach towel. 'Thanks, Joni. For everything.'

Her aunt smiled. 'You're very welcome, honey. It's been a pleasure.'

Roo turned to gaze at an empty house they'd passed on the way to the beach. It was as weather-beaten as the Eriskay ponies, but it held a commanding position overlooking the bay.

'Imagine if we lived there,' she said dreamily 'We'd wake every morning to waves and wild ponies. Any time we wanted, we could go snorkelling with seals or kayaking with dolphins.'

Joni laughed. 'It's not always like the Bahamas in these islands, Roo. Some months, one-hundred-mile-an-hour gales are so common that the locals consider them a breeze. In the winter, it's mostly dark.'

'But in the summer, it's mostly sunny,' persisted Roo. 'And in the dark months, you told me there's always the promise of the Northern Lights.'

She sat up. 'Oh, please, Joni, just think about it. Remember what Dad wrote in his letter? *When you're young, time seems as infinite as the stars, stretching out like an endless summer . . .*" He told me he took time for granted. We have to make the most of it now, while we're young.'

Her aunt's smile was wry. 'I'm not that young. Not any more.'

'You're young at heart,' Roo said firmly. 'That's all that matters.'

Overhead, seabirds twisted like origami on the wind, the light catching the sharp angles of their wings.

'We should probably go.' Joni started packing up the picnic things.

Roo's shoulders sagged. 'Do we have to?' Reluctantly, she rolled up her towel.

'We do if we're going to make the ferry. Honey, I've loved every minute of our island-hopping adventure, but even the best adventures come to an end eventually. It's time we settled down. How would you feel about moving to Kent, the garden of England? Great schools. Nice neighbourhoods.'

'But imagine living on an island? I could be happy here. Couldn't you? You could paint. Open an art gallery.'

'Roo, it's a nice thought, but in a few months' time you'll be starting high school. As your guardian, I have a responsibility to consider your future.'

'Don't they have good schools in the Outer Hebrides?'

'Yes, but—'

Joni stopped. Roo had begun a frantic search of her pockets and rucksack. 'What's wrong? What have you lost?'

'Fearless Fire.'

Roo felt quite panicky. He was only a silly toy, but he'd been her talisman for so long that she couldn't bear the thought of him being discarded like trash by a beach cleaner or tourist.

Or, worse still, being swept out to sea to spend an eternity drifting on the bottom of the sea, adding to the planet's plastic pollution.

On land, he wasn't a problem, he was a friend.

'Let's retrace our steps,' said her aunt, seeing how upset Roo was. 'We won't leave until we find him.'

'But w-what about the ferry?'

'Would it really be so awful if we had to spend another night in this peaceful place?'

They searched the length of the beach but found no sign of the little chestnut horse. They were close to giving up and on their way back to Bluebird when Joni spotted him near the derelict house.

Roo ran to pick him up. As she lifted him, she noticed a toppled For Sale sign. Grass and weeds had grown over the sun-bleached board. Rising above the green tangle was a cluster of magenta flowers with purple-spotted leaves.

Roo touched a flower reverently. 'What is this?'

'A machair – a Hebridean spotted orchid.' Joni bent to inhale its rich perfume. 'These islands are famous for them.'

Roo's heart felt strange, as if a whale song was playing in it. 'Orchids were my mum's favourite flower.'

Joni glanced at the house. 'No harm in peeking through a window, is there?'

Standing on tiptoes, she attempted to see inside, but soon gave up. The glass was encrusted with dried salt and gull goop.

Next, she tried the rain-warped front door. As Joni suspected, it wasn't locked. A firm shove and a couple of kicks opened it.

Nervously, Roo followed her in.

'Isn't this called breaking and entering?'

Her aunt waved a hand. 'The door was unlocked, so we're not breaking anything, and if the decaying For Sale sign is anything to go by, it's been on the market for a long time. The owner might be quite pleased to have a viewing, even if it's not an official one.'

A yellowing gas bill in the hallway was addressed to a Mr Nate Fairweather of Bluster House, South Uist, Outer Hebrides.

'Mr Fairweather must have taken a fair bit of ribbing for his name, living here,' observed Joni. 'Probably fled to sunnier climes. Fancy calling this amazing place Bluster House.'

The house needed work. A lot of it.

The kitchen needed ripping out. The bathrooms had been invaded by alien mould. The living room was an art exhibit of cobwebs and mouse tracks. There was a broken window and the remains of a bird's nest in the dining room.

But, beneath the grime, there were real oak floorboards and hurricane-proof walls. The sea filled almost every window.

At the top of the creaking stairs, they found a second bathroom and four bedrooms.

'Which would you like, Roo?' Joni asked jokingly. 'I'll have the one with the bay window if I may.'

Roo had already decided on her room. It was the smallest, but it had a corner view of the sea. She could imagine herself reading, drawing, or doing homework on a squashy old sofa by the window.

Kissing Fearless Fire on his chestnut forelock, she set him down on the windowsill. If it was meant to be, it would be, just like Bluebird.

The window on the upstairs landing looked out over wildflower meadows and a distant loch. Roo leaned on the sill, watching a family of cyclists ride past. A sudden thought occurred to her. When she and Joni had walked to the beach earlier, they'd been on the opposite side of the gravel track. There was no wind. How had Fearless Fire ended up outside the gates of Bluster House?

A tingle went through her.

Joni joined her on the landing. 'Well, what do you think?'

'I think,' Roo said, 'that we should call her "Joy Cottage", after my mum. That would make Dad happy too.'

Joni hugged her tight. 'Joy Cottage has my vote. By the way, the field opposite is for rent. It might make a good home for a couple of rescue horses. Crucially, there's space in the driveway for Bluebird. That way, if we woke up in the morning and didn't like the view – at the height of winter, say – we could change it.'

'I've thought of a name for that pony I met on the beach,' said Roo. 'If she were mine, I'd call her Wander Girl.'

Joni smiled. 'Wander Girl? It suits her. I can picture you cantering her bareback along the beach, just as you did with Wonder Boy. You look as if you belong together.'

**

Downstairs in the living room, Joni said: 'We're getting a little ahead of ourselves. We don't even know if the house is still for sale.'

She rang the estate agent. 'Joy Cottage' was available and her owner was prepared to reduce the price for a quick sale.

'It's still a lot of money,' Joni told Roo. 'Most importantly, it's your money. Don't feel you have to rush into a decision. We can take our time. Think it through.'

'It just feels right,' said Roo. 'Feels as if it's meant to be. Call the estate agent back. Let's seal the deal.'

When Joni hung up, she was shaking. She and Roo danced around the room, as ecstatic as they'd been after saving the horses.

With uncanny timing, Skylar rang right then to wish Roo a happy birthday. Roo put her on speakerphone.

'Skylar, we've found a new home! One with walls.'

There was a smile in Skylar's voice. 'How can any home be better than Bluebird?'

'Not better. Just different. She'll need a bit of fixing up—'

'A lot,' corrected her aunt. 'A gigantic amount of fixing up.'

'But when she's done,' Roo went on, 'we'll be able to lie in bed and look out at the ocean, the way we do in Bluebird. And Bluebird will be parked in the driveway in case we ever need a change of scene.'

Skylar laughed. 'Where is this paradise?'

'The Outer Hebrides,' said Roo. 'On a sunny day, it's the best place on earth. We'll have tons of room too. Will you come visit when we've finished patching her up?'

'Try keeping me away.'

'Bring your mum and dad,' put in Joni. 'We'd love to spend time with you all. Stay as long as you like.'

'Now that Nana's well again, we could help you restore the place,' said Skylar. 'Mum's pretty handy with a paintbrush, and Dad's a wizard when it comes to carpentry or electrical stuff. I'm best outdoors, digging veggie beds or putting up paddock fences. Let us know when you want us to visit and we'll bring you your gifts in person.'

'That's kind, but we don't need any gifts,' said Joni. 'You've done more than enough.'

'You won't be saying that once you've tasted Nana's secret vegetarian paella recipe. Mum's going to teach you how to make it the traditional way. She also has something for you, Roo. It's to thank you for your courage and friendship and, most of all, for saving Magician.'

'But I already have your bracelet,' protested Roo. 'That's all the thanks I need.'

'When Mum makes up her mind, resistance is futile,' said Skylar, laughing. 'She's gifting you her statue of Eclipse, only she's amending the inscription from *"Eclipse First, The Rest Nowhere,"* to *"Eclipse First, The Rest Equal."*

'Because a horse doesn't have to be Eclipse to be perfect.'

***

After they'd said goodbye, Roo perched on the edge of the stone fireplace. Already, she could imagine her and Joni toasting marshmallows on a winter's night, dreaming up exotic travels.

They'd get a dog. A rescue, of course. Wherever possible, he'd travel with them and share Roo's sleeping nook in Bluebird.

There'd be planned adventures, and unplanned ones, because adventures, she'd learned the hard way, didn't always come gift-wrapped. They were a surprise. Sometimes unpleasant. Sometimes miraculous.

Like this one.

They'd live every minute, because if there was one thing the past six months had taught Roo, it was that there'd be dark days, blissful, hopeful days, and days when it was sunny outside but raining in her heart.

But no matter which type of day it was, here, on Roo's island idyll, there'd be always be space and sea and horses and love.

And love, to Roo, was more than enough.

AUTHOR'S NOTE

Almost my earliest memory is being completely in love with horses.

From the moment I learned to read, and ride, I longed for a horse of my own – preferably a black stallion, silver brumby, or super-powered showjumper, or, after I discovered *For Love of a Horse* by Patricia Leitch, a chestnut Arab mare.

To begin with, we lived in a small house on a city street in what is now Harare, Zimbabwe, and a horse of any kind was impossible, but when I was eight, my dad got a job as a farm manager. After much begging and pleading, he finally bought me the only pony we could afford – a short, plump, elderly bay, who was blind in one eye and partially blind in the other. Charm was never going to make the Olympic team, or, for that matter, win a ribbon at the local gymkhana, but I loved her just the same.

By the time I was eleven, Charm was ready for retirement. My dad had promised that I could have the first foal born to his mare, Cassandra and I spent many impatient months waiting for its arrival. When she finally gave birth, one stormy afternoon, I was the only one there. I put my raincoat over her tiny colt – the son of a champion racehorse – and named him Morning Star.

Days later, Star almost died from Jaundice Foal Syndrome. He was moments from death when a quick-thinking vet and a blood transfusion from Charm, brought him back from the brink. It was then that I learned that the 'perfect' horse comes in many shapes and sizes. My ageing pony would never have won any gold medals or beauty contests, but she did something better. Something priceless. She saved Morning Star's life. He lived for the next twenty-two years. I've named one of the chapters in this book after him, in tribute to him.

That scrawny, wobbly colt grew into the black stallion of my dreams. When I was a teenager, he was my best friend. I spent every available hour hanging out with him, teaching him, learning from him, riding him or swimming him – as Roo does with Wonder – in the dam on our farm, Rainbow's End. There are no words for how much I loved him and how much he influenced how I think, feel, and relate to all animals today. In short, he changed my life.

Back then, I was forever being told that being horse-mad was 'just a phase' and I'd soon lose interest in both horses and children's books. As you can tell, I never did! Over the years, I've been fortunate enough to spend time with eventers at the Badminton Horse Trails, Arabians in Sharjah, racehorses at Kingsclere in Newbury and wild mustangs in Wyoming while writing my One Dollar Horse series, YA horse thriller, *The Glory*, and *Finding Wonder*. It's only ever made me more fascinated by horses and passionate about their wellbeing.

Any children's author will tell you that one of the most fun parts of writing books is doing research. There is no way that *Finding Wonder* could have been written without the kindness and expert counsel of five amazing people, each of whom generously gave their time to help and advise me.

I'm hugely grateful to Sacha Hamilton at whose livery yard I'm an occasional but very happy groom; Simon Knapp, clinical director of Berkshire Equine and one of the most gifted, experienced and caring horse vets in the world; Anna Lisa Balding, the generally amazing general manager at Park Lane Stables, Kingsclere, on which Queen's Reach is based; Luke Lillingston, a leading international bloodstock agent and owner of Mount Coote Stud and Professor Emmeline Hill, who discovered the Speed Gene and is a lecturer in equine science at University College Dublin.

Finding Wonder is as much about the importance of family as it is about horses, which to me includes friends, both human and furry. Heartfelt thanks to Jules and my support cats, Max, Skye, Freya and Brontë, to my parents, sister, Lisa, and niece, Alex, to my friends Emelia Sithole-Matarise, Reyhana Masters, Jean McLean, Jane Chablani, Abagail Gardiner and, of course, the utterly wonderful Pinklings!

Above all, thanks to my brilliant, and brilliantly patient, editor, Alice Swan, to my amazing agent, Catherine Clarke, to Levi Pinfold, who illustrated *Finding Wonder*'s STUNNING cover, to Marie-Alice Harel, who created the atmospheric and completely beautiful interior illustrations and to the phenomenal team at Faber, especially Leah Thaxton, Ama Badu, Bethany Carter, Sarah Connell, Simi Toor, Emma Eldridge, Natasha Brown, Camilla Braceschi, Lizzie Bishop, Louise Brice, Hannah Styles, Krys Kujawinska, Hazel Thompson and Sara Talbot and all her colleagues.

My hope is that *Finding Wonder* inspires young and old readers and riders to help abandoned, vulnerable, mistreated or unwanted horses. Few people do that better than Jenny Seagrove, Abi Smart and the wonderful team at Mane Chance Animal Sanctuary, of which I'm immensely proud to be a patron. Learn more about their incredible work and how you might get involved at www.manechancesanctuary.org.